D0915883

A Purple Thread for Sky

A Purple Thread for Sky

A Novel of Intertwined Lives

CAROL BRUNEAU

CARROLL & GRAF PUBLISHERS, INC.
NEW YORK

First Carroll & Graf edition 2001

Carroll & Graf Publishers, Inc.
A Division of Avalon Publishing Group
19 West 21st Street
New York, NY 10010-6805

Library of Congress Cataloging-in-Publication Data is available.
ISBN: 0-7867-0860-3

Manufactured in the United States of America

For my Aunt Elizabeth,
who has always believed.

The web of our life is of a mingled yarn, good and ill together....
—William Shakespeare, *All's Well That Ends Well*

I

Wares

The wind bloweth where it will, Grampa Silas used to say. And though you can hear it, you might as well have mud between your ears trying to figure out where it comes from or where it goes. Just like the traffic this morning up and down the road out front — it reminds me of the wind, this wicked wind stirring up a gum-wrapper confetti with each gust. What you can see for the paperwhites in the window, jars of them meant for Christmas. Already they're leggy as sprouted onions. And the smell! like used Depends mixed with scorched wire.

Ruby's idea, forcing bulbs. An expression that makes you think of *911*, some kind of emergency, and setting off fire bells. Forcing bulbs for Christmas. Forcing them for Jesus. You can almost picture that line in the *World Weekly News*, underneath the real-life one in last week's issue: "Astronauts hear God's voice in space." Amen. Grampa would've approved. He'd have answered.

Getting back to things more earthly, I should go out and pick up the litter. But doing so would cut into my knitting; and that wind is colder than a bugger's hand at midnight, excuse my French; colder than the quarters from Uncle's pockets when he kept his coat in the porch. The breeze would drive grit into your eyeballs like splinters; I have trouble enough already reading prices.

And though Lord knows where that wind is headed, presently it's like a bobcat stuck in mid-pounce, scaring the blue jays from the birches out back. Even with the blare of Ruby's TV show, I can hear the squawking, that cry like a clothesline pulley in need of grease. You ask me, that wind won't die quickly enough — never mind which direction it's from: north, south, east, west. As with the cars, I wish it would slow down. It reminds me of folks in a race. Somebody's got to be first, Grampa used to say, in that stuffed-pigeon manner of his that put some people off.

Oh, Grampa was full of sayings. "What can I do you for to-day?" — that was his favourite. Who knows how many customers, shoppers and tire-kickers alike, heard that one over the years, his idea of a joke. A catchy pitch. And how many times have I said it? I can't stand to think.

Beats the hell, though, out of "How may I help you?" — Ruby's line, like she'd gladly get down on all fours and lick dust off your shoes — and fat chance! But I guess whatever works; why, just the other day I heard her say that, never mind all the fellow wanted was a pack of smokes. It was last week — or maybe last month, that's right; now that I think of it, it was around her birthday.

Her ninetieth, can you believe it? My old Aunt Ruby, standing behind the cash in her pale moss dress, a string of pearls, a powdery pinkness to her cheeks — looking for all the world like a full-blown hydrangea. "How may I help you?" she asked, and the customer, some scrawny young man in a ball cap, said, "What?"

"Be with you in a sec" is my line. Don't make me get up, especially if I'm sitting down. Wait'll I finish this row, I always feel like saying. Don't interrupt my knitting. My reading. Both at once, I might add, not meaning to brag. But I regularly do both, knit and read; always got something on the go — a mitt, a sock. My *World Weekly News* propped against the register, needles going like mad. It keeps me sane.

It doesn't take long to get the rhythm — one pair of mitts today, for charity. 'Tis the season, and I've got time on my hands. Oh, I can knock off a pair in a day, so long as Ruby's not too demanding — or the *News* too racy, if you catch my drift. Customers aren't the issue.

Now would you look at that — *Four Horsemen of the Apocalypse Photographed in Arizona.* Lord love a duck, there's something good to knit to. A shadowy picture of some fellows on horseback, look like they're wearing bags on their heads. Knit one, purl two.

But my aunt, now, that's the kind of story grabs her. Anything religious gets her going — pooh-pooh this, pooh-pooh that. A throwback, maybe, to her adolescence, all those years under Grampa's roof, his churchy ways.

"Don't go believing in things you hear but can't see," she told me once when I was small, a long, long time ago. Denied it later, of course, but by then I suppose the damage was done. Not that I'm a disbeliever. But look what religion did to Gran — Grampa's views must've driven her off the deep end, I'd expect. Politics and religion: I say what you see isn't always what you get. Like these crazy tales; four horsemen, indeed.

And guess who'll have my *News* spread out later, studying it like gospel? And when I come in, quick — quicker than her old father used to shut the till — turn the page, point out some ad for wart or fat removal.

"Well, well, ain't that something," I like to say, to get her goat. This kind of trash she wouldn't have sold, one time; wouldn't have allowed it in the store.

"Don't say 'ain't'"; she's always been quick to correct me, my Aunt Ruby. "Don't say ain't or your mother will faint," she used to rag; I would've been around eight. But she always left off the part at the end, "Your father will fall in a bucket of——"

Paint! Now there's something this place could use a coat or two of, inside and out. A sight, it is. The ceiling used to be so pretty: stamped tin, dots and swirls like the frosting on a McCain's frozen cake. But about the same shade now, pissy yellow, as those flowers in the window. "What *is* that?" this fellow wanted to know last week, meaning the smell. He was a stranger, nobody I'd seen around before.

Then there's the floor, a sag like the trough of a wave. Makes you seasick going up and down the aisles, dusting shelves. And creak? Why, with a mob in here the sound's like a three-storey barn in a gale-force wind. Not that we get that too often — a mob, I mean.

Unless you count these kids, a whole horde of them from up the school. They congregate here each recess. You have to laugh, how they dress these days: big baggy jeans, show their cracks when they bend over, the tops of their underpants — "the crack problem", I call it. Lord knows who dresses them. Not their parents, you can be sure. Well. If I had kids, you can bet your life they wouldn't go around like that, the saucy pups; good thing I don't.

"Break it, you buy it," I'm all the time telling them.

"Linger and play, you'll have to pay" — I think that's Ruby's line, or something to that effect. She used it now and then when she was in charge, before handing things over to me.

Oh, you can call me Lindy, most do. Lucinda L. Hammond, proprietor, that's my real John Henry, never mind the sign out front saying "Clarke's" — that is, if all the rain lately hasn't washed it off.

Ruby had a fellow come in one time wanting credit; when she told him to put down his John Henry, that's exactly what he wrote. Stupid, you know. That was Ruby's reaction; disdain, I think is the word. Me, I found it funny — sad, though, almost as sad as if he'd signed an X on her old IOU.

Takes all kinds, you don't have to tell me. Not after forty-odd years behind this same counter. Oh, I've seen folks who'd give you the shirt off their back before they'd stiff you a dime; others who'd rob you blind in the time it takes to open a roll of pennies. The honest ones I tell not to worry, pay the tax next time you're in. But then you get the unreliables. Not to sound like the Bible, but there's something about an act of kindness, no matter how piddly, that separates the grain from the chaff.

Still, Christ knows the stock I've lost being so easy. Handing out the benefit of the doubt like free samples. Not like Ruby or Grampa Silas, when they were running things. The old fellow, oh boy, he'd make you pay for the drip off the molasses. 'Course, everything changed the years Ruby's husband took over. "The customer's always right," he used to say. Which is lovely, my darling, till you foot the bill for all those smashed ketchup bottles and bars — a whole box of Oh Henry! bar's yesterday when some tyke, couldn't've been older than three, came in and toppled the rack. The mother had her nose in the freezer chest, checking out "best befores" on the fish sticks. Claimed she couldn't have seen it coming, as much as to blame me for making that candy so tempting.

Heck, I said, and threw half the bars in with her High Liner, just because. "Merry Christmas," she squeaked back — that was all. I ought to have known her, the place being a village; she did look kind of familiar. The bars were too banged up to sell. What was I to do — ask for a rebate? (I've already tried.) All the same, she could've said thanks.

Less stuff to count later, I just told myself. Inventory? Most of it you could see through the steamed-up window (if I ever get around to cleaning it; must remember to save the *News* — newsprint and vinegar, Ruby's trick). If, from the road, you care to look past those dying flowers, the fringy gold banner I strung up yesterday: "Happy Holidays." Past me in the background, my nice green sweater no more, I'll bet, than a thumbprint through that dirty glass.

Pop, chips, cigarettes. Road salt, lottery tickets, hockey cards, milk. A few shelves of tinned goods: soup, peas. Old Dutch. Papers: the *Herald, Auto Trader,* the *News* of course. No smut, which is easier now we've quit carrying magazines. I draw the line at the *News*: nothing barer than a collarbone, and you'd need a cartographer to figure out their personals: "SWM sks NS-SWW, strt sx."

Clarke's is a family business. Apples, bananas, some frozen foods. A few specialty items — you can't avoid it, this time of year. Candy canes, Santa magnets, red tinsel balls and, this Christmas, Chia Pets, those little clay animals sprouting grass fur. The key, you'd think, to success, giving people what they want.

Convenience, that's an asset too. "Nice hilltop location," the 7-Up man remarked — why, just last week. We sell anything you need to get through a winter without trekking to Caledonia. I'd like to know what makes people so stunned as to think it's normal jumping in the car, driving twenty miles and back each time they need arse-wipe.

I don't get it. But let me tell you something, the damned truth. If not for the video games — those shagging noise-boxes down at the back — Clarke's would've folded ages ago, Ruby and me turfed out on our ears. More than a century's worth of business down the toilet.

"Hammond's", the sign out front should say — and would if I had a bit more gumption, were thirty years younger, and Ruby, all these years, had been less a force to be reckoned with.

Teenagers, that's our clientele. The parents now, they think nothing of hightailing it forty miles for a pack of smokes, a video for the night. Figure they'll get a better deal elsewhere, grass being greener and all. Leave the offspring here with me while they gallivant to town. Like I don't have enough to mind without every stroppy, hormonally challenged kid from here to Westchester in my hair too.

But the racket! Not to mention the hassle of those machines.

"Miss, I lost a loonie! Miss, got eight quarters for a toonie? Miss, this game just ate my money — five bucks the old man gave me for bread!"

Zap-zap! Beep-beep gazoooooom! The noise is like gunshots at first, then the Chipmunks playing Zamfir. Enough to drive a person round the bend — no wonder Ruby's happier wrapped in her quilt out back, watching the tube.

If it weren't for the profit, I'd unload those machines so fast heads would spin. Like that girl in *The Exorcist* — remember her? We've got the video, see, over there drawing dust between the D's and F's. Tried getting Ruby to watch it, even made up a batch of Jiffy pop. She used to like a good horror show, once. But she doesn't take much of an interest these days in movies, at least not ones in colour.

Excuse me, just a sec.

"What, dear? Cheezies, a pack of Player's? That'll be five-forty-nine plus ta...."

Now, if I did get rid of the machines, and those videos too — well, we'd go under faster than a swimmer in lead boots. 'Course, then I'd have more time for Ruby, not that she'd appreciate it, necessarily. Me either, for that matter.

"Look, why don't you kids go and play on the road? Just kidding. But aren't you s'posed to be in school? Any minute the principal could waltz in and find you playing hooky. I'd skedaddle, if I was you. Who was it wanted that can of Pepsi? You there, with whatever it is sticking out of your pocket! That's right, dear, you owe me one twenty-five."

Don't get me wrong — we need the business. But it's music to my ears, the bell dingling, that herd scuffling out the door. "Diesel dyke," one has the nerve to mumble. Smart-assed cuss, I'd clip his ears under that ball cap if I could.

Ah, the silence. Ten forty-six, a Monday morning, at long last those machines gone dead, screens black as swamp ice. Makes me want to pull the plugs for good, hang the *Back in ten* sign and go out to the kitchen for a pot of coffee. But for now a cup or two will have to do. I'll get the wash hung, then see what Ruby's up to — haven't heard a peep, come to think of it; could be she's asleep. Sometimes she drifts off watching *Dini Petty*, the latest *News* on her lap. Last week I caught her red-handed, reading about Sharon Stone and some "boy-toy," the headline said. Poor old Ruby, mouth open, snoring away, teacup akimbo in her lap, that chewed-looking old quilt sliding off. But I had to laugh; that's the kind of article I enjoy, the kind that'll put a fly in your knitting. Make you put a thumb on backwards, you don't watch out.

"Now if you'll excuse me, I have socks to make." The times I wish I could say that and get away with it, lock up for good.

That's the trouble. Whole days pass when it feels like being all dolled up with no place to go, waiting. Mare at the starting gate, the bets called off. I can't describe the days I've lost count watching cars going back and forth, back and forth — from town, I'll bet. And if I closed up, likely nobody would notice. Except maybe the highway crew putting in the new road, those fellows and their boss, I'm pretty sure he's their boss, looking for snacks and cigarettes.

"Hot coffee" — I could try that — "free cup with each Vachon cake." Worth considering, maybe.

Clarke's General Merchandising Limited. Mrs. Ruby Clarke, chief executive officer. Annual profits: seven grand and counting. "Welcome to the nineties" — we'd do better selling vacuums to cavemen, which is what I keep telling myself and Ruby too. It wasn't always this way, that's what she'd say. If she were listening now, and felt inclined to answer.

She's a character, all right; though she'd kill me for saying so, being not by any stretch an old person who's cute. I thought of throwing a party for her ninetieth — what a concept — just to see the look on her face. Enough candles to summon the Arcadia District volunteer fire brigade! A nice white cake ordered in; balloons. Oh, the look on her face: the waste. I could just see her at the head of a table, guests all around, even drinking a toast. Except who would I have invited? There's nobody around any more you'd want at a party; the nice folks, the ones who used to frequent the store, are all gone. And even then, there was never anyone you'd call a good friend. The Pykes — Edna, the busybody, her mortician husband? No, I can't see that at all, the Pykes sitting eating cake, especially knowing where his hands had been. Who else could we invite? The old doctor, who retired last year? The riff-raff from across the bridge? They'd live in hollow trees if they could. Or the teenagers, now there's a thought.

Plus a party would've meant I had to clean first, scrub the place from stem to stern. You reach that point where you don't know where to start; where, I'd like to know, does all that dirt come from? It's not as if Ruby and I are dirty people. Dust and rot, that seems to be the way of it, especially after a wet fall like this one we've had. Dampness and rot — on bad days it feels like the whole building's a pile of rotting wood.

But I've got other things to keep me busy.

Out at the clothesline, the laundry freezes like chicken skin; Aunt Ruby's undies are about that shade. I can see my breath, see the steam wisping off wet nylon. Stiff as sprockets, my fingers mess with the pegs. Ruby's drawers, silky-thin and droopy as flour bags. Her slip, a little gold safety pin holding one strap on. Her dress, its skimpy bow at the neck, a faded green paisley that reminds me of tadpoles. And her bedding — damp, the second time in as many days. The first time she never mentioned it. This morning she said something spilled, the drink she takes to swallow her pill, an aspirin a day to ward off stroke. "Apple juice?" I looked at her sidelong; she can be so hoity-toity. As long as we've been together, she's chided me for drinking in bed. Almost as bad as smoking, she said once. Her husband used to be one for that, I gather, my Uncle Leonard. Now there was a businessman. But that's another story.

And I've got to get the rest of this wash out before it clouds over and gets too damp. And then of course there's the store; God knows at noontime those men off the road — yes, and their foreman, Wilf, that's his name — will be wondering what this is, a place of business or an abandoned whistle stop, lights on but nobody home. Like the rest of this burg, actually, a hole in the woods. Which reminds me, Je-sus, how cold it's gotten all of a sudden: tree-splitting cold. A week and a half to Christmas, still no snow but raw enough to freeze a witch's tit. And I don't mean that little black Wanda riding broomstick by the cash out front, left from Hallowe'en. Still haven't got around to taking her down, what with seasons sneaking up so fast; before I know it, it'll be eggs for Easter.

And sometime, before the next millennium, I should check in on Ruby. Is that her snoring, I wonder, or some noise on TV? Who knows? Lately she's been up to something — hiding something — mischief? Not quite; this is Ruby we're talking about, straighter than the day is long, saner than a judge. It's just that lately there's something...different, something — I don't know — amiss. Whatever it is, I worry; it's something I wouldn't so much as dare bring up.

But you know what I found last week, under the radio on top of the fridge? The queerest thing — a map, drawn on the back of a flyer; it would've been different, showing directions to some *place*. But it was a map of the store, our flat — the kitchen, the bathroom, the parlour; our bedrooms, Ruby's marked with an X. Laid out with a ruler neat as you please, could've been a carpenter's plan. But it was hers all right, sketched in pen, the fine black one she uses to write cheques.

Coming in from outside, I stand in the kitchen thawing my hands. There's a door that opens into the store, right behind the cash. It's handy; from here you can keep an eye on things.

"Aunt Ruby?"

No answer. Out like a light, I bet; poor thing, she's always had trouble sleeping nights. Well, she *is* ninety, and the older you get, they say, the less shut-eye you need — to make the most, maybe, of what time you have left. Trouble is, when she gets drowsy in the daytime you can't quite trust her with the till.

Oh, she likes keeping a finger in the pie. Until lately I could count on her to spell me if I had errands to run or, God forbid, a "social occasion". The veins in her legs are bad, but she could sit, play a hand of solitaire behind the counter if things got too dull. Ruby always liked handling cash; in fact, it wasn't till three years ago she signed everything over to me, the books, the balancing, kit and caboodle. And none too soon; not long after, I caught her making change, handing some kid a ten when all he'd given her was a five.

"Aunt Ruby?"

Never mind our ages and the scary thought that in two measly years I'll be a "senior", I'm as careful now as I was when I was eight to call her "aunt" as in "rhymes with taunt". "I'm not an insect, Lucinda," she's still quick to remind me. "Ants live in hills, dear. Those nasty creatures that get into cupboards. A little honey and borax, though, that fixes them."

Lordy, Lordy, a remedy for everything. And fussy? It's the same with my moniker, Lindy, as if there's another soul alive calls me Lucinda. "That's not a real name, not for a girl." I can still hear her telling off my ma; I couldn't have been more than four years old. The two of them were having a set-to of some sort in the kitchen and I was in the sun porch, listening.

"Aunt Ruby? You there?"

Well, shit. She's not in the parlour. The TV blinks back at me like an eye. Her musty old quilt — one Gran made — is on the rug with the *News*. Her blue slippers are under the davenport. Her cup of tea stone cold on the tray.

"*Ruby?*"

She's not in the store, either.

Nothing for it but go jump in the truck — I don't rightly know what else to do. I'm just climbing in when I remember and have to go back and lock up. Calm down, girl, I tell myself; it's not like she's a little kid, it's a free country; and anyway, she can't be far. Just gone for a walk, is all; must've slipped out front while I was hanging clothes.

It's so damp, this pinky-grey chill to the sky, the grass pea-green. Thank Christ, though; if it were icy, then I'd have cause to worry. The sly old doll, slick as Wile E. Coyote and twice as independent.

Must be in the genes.

Come on, Betsy, I mumble to the truck. Don't fail me; crank 'er over, that's it. Trusty old pickup. Shiza, did I forget to leave the phone off the hook, the phone in the store? But the lights are on; it's okay.

Ruby — where the heck have you gotten to? I ask out loud, eyes peeled as I head down the hill. The long, long hill past the school, towards the river. You can see the old slag heap through the woods, trees bare as a picked carcass, that raw wind shaking the branches. Awful cold to go walking. Damn cold. This old truck, she's done yeoman service, but the heater's shot. Can't expect her to run forever, I guess, to start and keep you warm too.

The windows fog so I roll mine down a crack, take a big breath in. There's a smoky snap to the air, big grey clouds above the hills back of Westchester. Feels like hunting season, still. Across the bridge, along the hillside way over by the church, you can see the road crew standing around. I can't tell if the foreman's among them; they look like a bunch of hunters in their orange vests.

Not a soul in sight, though, this side of the river. The smoky smell gets stronger — I'm telling you, once the leaves fall here you could asphyxiate yourself on the air, all those woodstoves, chimneys going like crazy. The only sign of life most places; the few big old shabby houses still standing — nice, once. Though to tell the truth, I only half recall them back when I was a kid: big white-shingled places always in need of paint. Then they got the Insul-brick, next the vinyl siding. Now, if something could be done about the rusty cars outside....

Ruby? her name bleeps out. What's that moving through the trees? Through the gravestones up and over on Sore Finger Hill? A flash of red — someone sighting bunnies in the cemetery? I don't think so. Slowing down to get a good look, creeping over to the shoulder, I spy a red hat, can just make out a blue coat. Okay, I recognize her stooping over a stone; it has to be, it is, thank God.

Now if Betsy can make it the rest of the way, up the steep dirt track.... Heck, you need a Blazer to get in here, bushes scratching metal like fingernails on a chalkboard. Okay, I tell myself, take it slow. Roll down the window. Ride the clutch, pump the gas to give a little roar, get her attention.

"Ruby?" I yell — why bother with formalities? "What on earth are you doing? It's freezing out. Come on now, hop in. Before you catch your death of...."

She straightens up, giving me this stony stare. As if to say, Not in the graveyard, Lucinda; show respect, dear.

For the love of God, doesn't she make me jump out.

Then I see what she's been up to — laying flowers on a grave, not her mother's but another with a small pitted stone, a few yards away. I recognize the posies, some fancy fake poinsettias from the store. Not plastic, but the kind you have to touch to tell they're imitation. The headstone I've never noticed before — well likely I have, just paid no mind — why would I? It's not as though I come here often, stubbly old place; not exactly my notion of where to go for a party.

"Mum's firstborn," she says, patting the back of her woolly hat like she's in church — that is, if she'd darken the door of one. There's a little smile on her lips, as if any second she might burst out laughing — or crying; like she's half with me, anyways, half not.

"Oh sure, now I remember." I take her arm. "Come on, Aunt Ruby, let's get in the truck. You'll catch pneumonia out here." Though she's dressed warmly enough: her good black gloves; neat black overshoes, the fur around the tops glossy as the day she bought them five years ago.

Aunt Ruby doesn't get out as much as she used to, or as often, probably, as she'd like; it's a fact, there just aren't that many places to go.

"Please, Lucinda." She strains away — well pardon me, I think. The haughtiness, as if to ask: What do you think you're doing?

"Can't you wait until I'm finished visiting? Adam would've been my oldest brother," she continues, matter-of-fact, almost pouty. "Then there were others. Miscarriages. Two, I think, perhaps three, yes three, I believe it was. When your mother and I came along it was quite the miracle, you can imagine."

Wrenching away from me, she lopes to another grave, rubs her gloved fingers over the stone of sugary white marble. A child's. It gives me the willies to look; above the inscription there's a smooth carved hand holding a bunch of flowers. Looks like it's reaching out of nowhere, clutching lilies of the field.

"Mum's sister, her younger sister. She would've been *my* aunt, dear; Fanny, her name was. Oh, she died when they were just children. Fever. The diphtheria, I suppose."

Whatever — the mention of sickness seems suddenly to wear her out. She doesn't resist me tugging her back to the truck.

I open the door, help her up — no problem. I hardly have to remind her to do the seatbelt; maybe after her jaunt she's finally feeling the cold, is as anxious as I am to skedaddle. I'll give her this: for all her quirks and lack of a high life, she's as nimble as someone a third her age, when she wants to be.

People that don't know us assume we're sisters. Or something worse, unrelated. "Lezbe friends," one little twerp had the gall to quip once, leaving the store. "Lezbe not," I shot back, who knows if he heard.

'Course that's just people's dirty minds. Hyperactive imaginations; boredom: *So, what about them two old broads up at Clarke's?* I guess if they had something better to do they wouldn't waste time speculating, now would they?

When we get back, those same kids are milling around outside like hungry cattle. There's that saucy one, the fellow in the black ball cap. I don't like the looks of him; he's got eyes like screws, a smug, sneery grin. Wears an earring, too; it glints when his jaw moves cracking gum.

"'Back in ten'?" one of them has the nerve to shout while Ruby and I are getting out of the truck. I take her arm to help her up the back steps, not that she really needs it.

"My slip," she remarks. "You hung it upside-down; it'll leave peg-marks on the hem." But that's about all she says (could it be she's winded?), even while getting settled inside.

"Let me see what they want," I tell her, "then I'll fix you some lunch." She tugs off her overshoes and nods — in a distracted way, as if my voice bleats from the TV. Or she just plain wants me out of her hair, wants to be left alone. I'm gathering up her boots, her coat, when suddenly she coughs and brightens. It's like someone's twisted a loose bulb on a string of tree lights.

"Lucinda, dear. Do you suppose we could have one of those cakes, one of those lovely frozen things? They're so very nice with tea."

"Of course, Aunt Ruby. Anything else you'd like?"

Out front, the kids pay for one can of pop and one bag of chips — six of them. The fellow with the earring lingers by the counter, reading the cigarette names behind me: Du Maurier, Rothmans, Export A. His lips move, Adam's apple bobbing up and down, but no sound comes out. "Comin', Ronnie?" his buddies yell. He doesn't buy anything, doesn't blink when I roll my eyes and say, "Have a nice day." There's just that blank stare that makes you want to wave and shout, Hello, hello, anybody there behind those flat blue eyes?

Criminal mind, I'll bet; the type of kid winds up in Springhill sooner or later. Gives me the creeps, he does, but what can you do?

"Fuckin' old lezzy," he leers and gives his pal a chummy shove out the door.

I pick up my knitting, right where I left off. Good to have something in your hands, days like this; it keeps you steady.

You wouldn't know squat if it bit you on the arse, you miserable brat. This loops round and round my head like the bright red Sayelle over my needles. My fingers fly — who needs a machine? Strong as a teenager's, my hands, and just as quick.

I could string up a kid like that, oh yes. No problem. Wring his miserable neck.

The yarn shreds going over the needle points; some stitches divide in two. Darn it all. Maybe they're not so able after all, my hands. Or maybe it's just the cold, from being outside.

Frig them all anyway, I hear myself mutter. And then remember Ruby waiting for her pie. Cake, pie, whatever: Sara Lee. Depends what's left in the freezer, my luck only chocolate. The one thing she hates, chocolate.

II

Sleepwalking

What the heck...? What time...? For the love of God! I fumble for the lamp, nearly knock it over. It's a doll with an orange Phentex skirt for the shade. Ugly as sin but it was a gift, a prize I won, actually, in the Legion raffle. I nearly send it flying, anyways. My heart kicks. What the—?

You're hearing things, I tell myself, only Ruby going to the bathroom. Well, that's good. She had me concerned, those little accidents of hers. A rough patch, a fluke; too much tea before bedtime maybe. One of those things. But she's okay, sure, she's——

What was *that*, now?

I'm sitting up in bed, in this cockeyed halo of light. There's somebody creeping around out there — Ruby? The sound's coming from the kitchen, no, upstairs. Mice skittering across the floor? Serves us right for leaving it empty up there.

Four in the morning, the Little Ben beside my lamp clunks and churns.

Any sense and we'd have tenants, rent out the upstairs apartment. Oh, it's a lovely flat, except for the stairs; Ruby minds them something fierce, though she'd never admit it. Which is why — I mustn't be so lily-livered, of course it's only mice! — why we keep this place below. It's cramped but closer to the store. Like the one upstairs, a perfectly good apartment, Ruby says. A bit makeshift, if you look at the pipes where the loo went in what once was Grampa's office. Then again, who's looking?

There's a soft click, like the fridge door shutting. Definitely not rodents. My heart squirms halfway up my throat. That click again, soft but abrupt — like the last, winning number on a combination lock, *bingo*. Grampa's safe — shit! Next to the range in the kitchen. With fingers stiff as clothespins I flick off the light. Listen....

Nothing, just the freezer motor kicking in out front, a hum like a nest full of hornets.

"Ruby? Ruby," my voice hisses, "that you?"

The hell she'll hear, too, me frozen to my bed.

The bathroom light clicks on; I hear the chain clink against the bulb. A shuffling, a sigh — thank Christ! Then something else, I swear, something coming from the store.

"Aunt Ruby?" I whisper, a tad bolder.

After a while her shape fills the doorway, grey against grey. One hand fiddles with the ties on her fuzzy housecoat, the other clutching something, a Kleenex. Her face is a shadow, only her feet gleam yellow in the puddle of light from the bathroom. Her flat, bony feet, ankles pushed out on account of the bunions.

"My God, Ruby, you gave me a fright! I thought there was somebody...."

"For heaven's sake." She puts her finger to her lips and sniffs, correct as if turning down a kid demanding smokes. "Well. It's only me, of course — who else would be up prowling this time of night, making sure everything's okay? You can't be too careful, Lucinda. I was just checking the ice chest, dear. Those problems with it last week — we wouldn't want another leak, now would we, another dreadful mess on the floor...?" The sternness trails off like heat through a window.

"Right." I shrug, sinking back into the pillow, the muzzy flannelette sheets. Except now I'm wide awake, a tingle in my throat. Hasn't it been twenty years — twenty-five? — since we quit selling ice, since a fellow from Ferrona carted off that old chest in his truck? Twenty-five, maybe more; why, Ruby herself told him he could have it for the cost of hauling it away.

"Go back to bed, Aunt Ruby, you need your sleep. We'll call the doctor tomorrow, you know, that new one, get him to order a pill. Come on now, I need my rest too — I've got a pile of stuff to do in the morning."

Then I remember the things still out on the line — frig them, I figure, they won't go anywhere. But do you think after that I catch ten more winks? Lucky if it's five.

When the alarm goes off at six, I get up. What's the use anyways, lying there with your eyes open? Too much room for thought. All's quiet, at least. So I go and bathe and put on my clothes. Stretchy maroon slacks, the nice green pullover with the Christmas design I ordered from that place in Maine. It's supposed to be handknit, but I'm not sure. Shows a fireplace, a white cat curled up, stockings hung. A novelty item, Ruby hmphed — "Waste of money, something you only wear two weeks a year, tops" — no doubt thinking I could've knit it myself.

It's kind of cute; I like the seasonal touch. Besides, as we all know, Christmas starts and ends when you want. In Arcadia, Colchester County, there's Christmas, then snow, then mud; a month or two of swimming-hole weather, then school and moose season. And before a mother can say "gumboot" it's back to you-know-what, all over again. That's how it was when I was a girl; my, how things don't change.

For a bit of gaiety I put on some red and green kneesocks under my Reeboks. Ruby's right — they would look better on someone younger — but heck, with no snow you've got to do something to spike the spirit.

The outfit would look nicer on someone with more of a waist. Still, what I see in the mirror's not too bad. The Nice'n Easy helps; the shade is "mahogany fire". The name makes me cringe, and the first time I used it all I could think of was a certain customer with dyed hair — not her roots showing so much as the residue on her scalp, like the purplish crumbs from ketchup-flavoured chips. Cancer-causing, no doubt. However, the stuff does the trick and in the right light I could pass for fifty — so long as I stay indoors and keep on top of the grey.

But all this sitting and standing, see. Except when it comes time to clean. I'd happily pay someone — you should see the mess, for instance, that road crew tracks in, their boss included. Not a lick of care, as if the store's public property. Nobody wipes their feet. Those teenagers are the worst, look you in the eye demanding the winning lotto ticket, see-through sweet as a clear-toy candy, never mind the big muddy bootprints below. Yes, I'd pay someone all right. But Ruby'd sooner fly to the moon than part with good money for something you can do yourself.

Easy for you, I feel like winging back at her sometimes. All you've got to do these days is watch *Oprah* and roll dimes, for godsake. I've got a business to run.

But I always stop myself, wondering where I'd be if not for Ruby, the goodness of her heart. We've been partners forty-five years, can you credit that? Forty-five years we've worked elbow to elbow, shin to shin. And you know she didn't have to take me on in the first place. She did it out of her own kindness. Such as it is. Before that, anyone could tell you, she was doing fine, just fine, thank you. So I remind myself, those times when it feels like I'm holding the poopy end of the stick.

"It's a family enterprise, Lucinda. My father intended it so." That's what she said when I was eighteen, fresh out of school. Still says, when she's being cantankerous. "Now Lucinda, I'm counting on you, you're all I've got."

She's been at this seventy years, imagine. That's not counting the years before the old man let her take charge. Signed everything over, her father did, when Ruby married Leonard. Now there's a character, a real card; when they made that fellow they threw away the mould. So I hope, anyways.

God, I'm full of pep — odd what a lack of sleep can do. They're playing "Jingle Bell Rock" on the radio; wish I could keep it turned up all day, to hear out in the store. But it interferes with Ruby's programs; she'd crank up the tube till neither of us could hear ourselves think.

The parlour could use a good dusting, I see; is it my fault the place looks neglected? How's one supposed to keep house and store both? Don't know what would've happened if I'd had kids. Not that my own ma ever did both; no, she was out of the mix. No business sense whatsoever, no sense period, my mother — Ruby's sister, Dora.

Tut, tut. No wonder Grampa ceded everything to Ruby, the brains of the family.

The dust is like fur on the TV, the bookcase, the tops of the old man's books. The pages smell like a falling-down house, the sourdough smell of old wallpaper. *The Red Badge of Courage*. He was quite the reader, Silas. I was eleven when he died; funny, but about all I remember is this crotchety old man upstairs in bed, Ruby and me below. This would've been three, maybe four years after she lost Leonard; and the year after her father passed on, so did her mother, my granny Effie.

A bunch of blurry faces now; odd how the dead lose their features. Still, I try watching for them sometimes in Ruby's face, what bits I recall: Gran's blue wide-set eyes, old Silas's mouth weaned on a pickle. But nothing doing; Ruby's her own gal, always was. Do you know, when she calls sometimes from another room the picture that fills my head is of her as she used to be: forty, maybe forty-five years old, ramrod posture; this no-horsing-around, no-goofing-off smile; thick dark hair with a touch of grey springing from the part. On the tall side, not quite stout but far from slender: substantial, a lady of substance, that was her. Not a bit like her mum, who always seemed pale and kind of wispy, or her father either, stooped and leggy as a mantis, with that weak-tea-coloured hair of his.

Funny, though. I might not be so good with faces, but I can still hear them talking, oh yes, their voices; guess I've got a thing for sounds.

What's this now, half hidden under the davenport? I nearly mistake it for a cushion shoved under there with the dust bunnies. For godsake, that grungy old album, the Lewis family's; the whole tribe of them in there, all dead. I haven't gone through it in years; Ruby must've dug it out and forgotten — not like her, though, to leave something like that lying around. A while back she had quite the notion, wanting me to write and see if the historical society in town might be interested. Bunch of little old blue-rinsed ladies, I figured at the time, why would they want it? Dirty old book, velvet crumbling off the back; had a fancy ivory clasp once, seems to me.

I used to flip through it when Ma was off gallivanting or whatever she did, while Ruby and Leonard were minding me. Or supposed to be minding me, since they'd be in the store while I sat out back sucking humbugs, swinging my legs under the table in time with the radio, looking at the pictures. Half the folks I didn't recognize.

The thing's rotten enough to attract bugs, moulds too, those mites in the air people are allergic to these days. When I was young, it was hornets and wasps. Men too, ha-ha. More likely it was them allergic to me, or so it would seem now. Not that I wanted it that way; not that I haven't had my chances — or my regrets. Take for instance the afternoon that road foreman came in and I happened to notice the curly grey hairs poking through the collar of his shirt — oh, I have regrets; a few, okay? Despite what they say: "It's never too late." You've got to roll your eyes when those TV experts claim older women have a certain appeal. Well sure, I say, want to tell that to some of the geezers around here? 'Cause that's about it nowadays in this neck of the woods: nothing but geezers, except maybe for that foreman, Wilf — and those young fellows he's got helping him.

Enough to make you light up in despair and inhale, a single gal like me. Though I haven't smoked since I was eighteen, mind; haven't so much as touched tobacco. After her husband died, Ruby wouldn't allow it in the store. Smoking, I mean. Oh, she sold the stuff — how else you figure we got along before video games? But once you paid, buster, you had to take your smokes outside. "Can't abide the smell," she told me one time. "Reminds me too much of Leonard and his habits."

The charms of older women, indeed. How about one who can change a set of spark plugs, strike a deal with a Pepsi salesman, cook a mean ham and scalloped potatoes *and* run up a pair of mitts — all the same day? If I were advertising, that's what I'd put. But then would come the WANTED part; that's where I'd balk. The charms of older men, ten words or less.

"Handsome non-smoking retiree, maintenance-free home, bags of money." I doubt they'd print something like that, even in the *News*. Especially if they guessed my age.

Galling thing is, there's no limit to what I can do. But then it takes a certain type to gauge someone else's talents. A person like Ruby, yes, sound judgement right down to her X's and Y's. But a fellow like Wilf? Who could say? Lord Almighty, I don't even know the man's last name.

"Aunt Ruby?" something makes me call. "You up yet? I'm in here, in the parlour. Come look...."

She waltzes in wearing slippers, quiet as can be.

"See what I found? Grampa's old album — you must've been having a gander, were you? Haven't looked through this in a cow's age."

"It's been up there all along on the shelf." She sniffs, and for some reason her eyes look hot.

"You must've had it down last night, then."

She gives me this queer scandalized look, fishing under her hairnet. Wisps of her yellow-white hair stick out; flattened to her scalp, it's the colour of those flowers out front which, I keep reminding myself, have begun to smell like a bedpan — what I do recall from years ago of Grampa upstairs. That sickroom smell, like baking powder and vinegar mixed with something else musky and dank.

There's a pause; Ruby's eyes shoot daggers. "Well, yes, I suppose I must've," she blurts. "It's awful, you know, when a person can't sleep." Fumbling, she rolls her hands like the blades of a push mower; for the slimmest second I'm reminded of a little kid. *This old man, he played one, he played knick-knack....*

"It's just that — Lucinda?" As quick as they started, her hands stop. She bites the inside of her cheek. Takes her sweet time, eyeing me. *On his thumb, with a knick-kna*——"It sounds silly, I know, but I can't seem to help it," she finally says, her hands now fists tucked under her chin, "but you see, dear, I do get lonesome. To be expected, I guess, at this age...."

What do you say? I suppose she hears me sigh.

I lead her to the davenport, shake out that ratty old quilt of Gran's and wrap it around her, then flop down too, the album in my lap. I could sure use a coffee; feel an ache starting in one knee.

"You've got to start sleeping better, that's all. No sense fretting over it. See what that doc can do — there must be something, Aunt Ruby, some little pill or something to fix your problem. I bet he could fix you up right quick."

She shifts a bit, leaning her weight against me as I start flicking through the crumbly pages; they leave specks like dandruff all over my slacks. I feel her trembling a little through the quilt; a few of the patches look like the back cover, a brindled velvet that makes you think of a bulldog's coat.

"What's wrong, Aunt Ruby?" I clap the album shut, its binding so loose the stack of pages wobbles like a Slinky. "You got up too soon, that's all, I'm sure that's it. No need getting up this early — you go on back to bed while I fix us some toast." I start to slide the album away but she reaches out and grabs it. The thing weighs a ton.

The look on her face says, To *whom* are you giving advice?

"The heck with that doctor, anyway." She sniffs, heaving the album onto her lap, squaring it. Her lips purse like the twisted top of a paper bag as she opens it, turning the yellow lacquered cover as if handling the Dead Sea scrolls. The album must've been pretty, new — when bustles, whalebone and those huge wicker birdcages were the rage.

It thwunks open to a picture wreathed with thorny-looking twigs and bluejays, their sky-coloured wings dirt-streaked and faded, blotched with mildew. A tintype of mourners gathered around a fenced grave. Ruby's hand darts out, quick, before I can reach and turn the page, her palm brushing the sides of the photo as if parting curtains. I get a hazy feeling of having studied the picture once years ago at her kitchen table. But the faces in it mean bugger-all.

"Before my time." I suck in my cheeks and wait while Ruby lingers. I give her a little poke. About that toast, I feel like saying, Good God, can't you see I've got things to do? But what the hay.

"In memory of Robert Putnam," — you can just make out the words on the stone — "killed by explosion at blast furnace; April 21, 1907. Age 35 years. Erected by employees of the Arcadia Mines Iron Co." The mourners' faces look worn out, grey behind the white stone, the fresh white pickets. There are seven of them. Six are men. Only way you can tell the seventh is female is by the stark black bonnet, the hairless face; the rest have bushy beards and big waxed moustaches. Nobody looks to be crying; instead they have this raked-over look of anger spent. The lady fit to smite somebody, rip out his heart — if she could muster the energy to lift a knife.

Bent at the knuckle like a teller's, Ruby's finger slides over the woman's face, as if to rub up some colour.

The fellow's mother, my guess.

"Sad, sad thing," Ruby mutters, shaking her head. Her hand jumping to turn the page, pull the quilt closer. Drawing in this mournful sigh as if she belongs there in the picture, she fixes me with her moneylender's glare and announces:

"You realize, of course, I was present at that funeral. You just can't see me. But oh yes, I was around all right."

I give her a look — say what? — but she has clammed up. Lurching forward, she reaches for a piece of junk mail — an envelope lying on the TV, one of those things announcing, "Congratulations loser, you're a winner; send this in, win a million bucks" — and uses it for a bookmark. She slaps the album shut and with a grunt heaves it under the seat cushion beside her.

Sitting bolt-straight, sober as a preacher's wife, she turns to me, blinking. "So, Lucinda. Are you planning to make the coffee or shall I?"

Nothing for it then but get up and limp to the kitchen — I must've pulled something yesterday, hang it, reaching to tidy the cigarettes.

I plug in the toaster, drop in the bread, white with added fibre. How they pack in extra roughage is a mystery to me, but Ruby insists on having it; and if it says so on the bag, I'm not about to argue.

When the toast pops, I spread on some marge, a teaspoon of raspberry jam, and take it in to her. Damned if she hasn't drifted off sitting up — sound asleep as a dreaming baby, hands folded in her lap, knees squeezed together. Her mouth gapes wide enough to show her fillings, a wheezy snore whistles in and out. All her own teeth, perfectly straight, a pearly grey now, and she has to be careful what she eats.

But she always did have lovely teeth, my aunt; always watched her sweets, which could be why she's still with us, God love her. Testy as a bull at times and about as feisty, even if some days a touch of the arthritis slows her down. Damp days especially, and cold ones, which is why the coming of winter's such a pain.

I set the plate down on top of the TV. Ruby hasn't moved an inch, the quilt slipping off one shoulder. Just watching her makes me feel sleepy, my eyelids sticky as Krazy Glue. If it were Sunday I could open later; a nap would be just the thing. But I reach down and yank up the quilt — God knows the last time it was washed — uncovering that couch cushion buckled like a slab of sidewalk in a quake. Careful, oh so careful so as not to wake her, I bend and draw out the album, tiptoe to the kitchen with it.

The peace and quiet's like a swab of zinc oxide on a scrape, which is how my brains feel, grazed. Only sound is the wind whistling out back, twisting Ruby's old slip round and round the clothesline, one big knot; she'll have a kitten if she sees I've left it. But first I get the coffee going. This fancy doodad coffee-maker — Ruby's idea, but not a bad thing on a morning like this. Gurgle, choke; it sounds like a dog wolfing its breakfast, but never mind. While it does its job, I go and rescue Ruby's things.

As I'm slipping on my coat, the album catches my eye again, fat as a 'cordine (if Ruby heard me she'd moan, "Lucinda, please, the word is 'accordion'"), a smirch upon the kitchen table. I've never liked old things, they make me itch. But it's something to ponder over coffee, while Ruby's dozing.

Ever hear that joke, how seniors party? They sit around a parlour, polite company; chins wag at first, gradually droop to their chests. One person drops off, another and another, until the whole room's snoring. Then finally the first wakes up and nudges the next, so on and so on, like a set of dominoes. "Time to go home yet?" asks the first, still dozy. "Guess so," answers the next. "But aren't we already there?" says the one after that. "Well if that's true," the last one goes, all hot and bothered, "which way to my room?"

That's the punchline — some joke. It was Wilf, the foreman, told me that, one day in the store. The rest of the crew were out in their trucks; he seemed to have time to burn.

"Have you heard the one about the 'oldtimers' disease'?" was how he got started, Lord only knows why.

Very funny, I thought, you should talk.

"This what the Department of Highways pays you for?" I asked afterwards. Joshing him, you know. The truth was, I enjoyed his joke even if it wasn't funny. Well, not so much the joke itself as the way he told it. He seemed a bit shy, like somebody testing the water, not like he was being nasty or poking fun at anyone in particular.

"How come you're not retired yet?" I came right out and asked. 'Cause he looks about ready to. He's on the short side, stocky, barrel-chested; might've been a looker in his younger days. Hair's silver as a fox now and that belly he lugs around must be a burden. If I were bolder or less kind, I'd ask, "When did you say you were due?" Fooling around, of course.

But you have to wonder, where's his wife? Any self-respecting woman would put a man that size on a diet; I'm one to talk though, all this sitting. And being boss, I suppose he spends a good deal of time holed up in his truck giving orders — in a nice way though, I'd like to imagine. From what I've seen, the one or two times I've noticed, he's got an easy, good-natured manner about him, this Wilf. (Damned if I know his last name; if I'd heard it, you'd think I would remember.)

For a man his age — and by the looks of him, the way he talks, I reckon we've been around the track roughly the same number of times — for a man his age, he seems to have life in him yet. Like me, maybe, in this respect.

He's from up Caledonia way, I think he said once. Has a couple of acres outside town, a mobile home — that much he's told me. Has never mentioned a wife or kids, come to think of it, though if he had a family, they'd be out of his hair by now, wouldn't they? He could be a widower, I wouldn't know. See, I'm not that forward. It's not something you ask a customer, even a regular, and I wouldn't want to appear nosey.

But that Alzheimer's joke — the whole time telling it, he wore a slow quiet grin, peeling the cellophane off his Rothmans. A solemn grin, watchful, waiting to see how I'd react. Like he was set to jump in and add a new line if I didn't laugh straight off. But when I did, he nodded, this little glint in his eyes. God, I make him sound like Santa Claus, a rough-cut one. Though now that I mention it, there is a resemblance. A sawed-off Santa with stubble on his ruddy cheeks and an ever-so-slight crick to his nose, not to mention a few tiny broken veins.

Okay, okay. So I've looked at the guy. And yes, you can tell here's a man likes his beer. Which I wouldn't've mentioned except, well, maybe I notice what others might not. Given the hours I have for perusal, you understand. To observe and reflect on the state of man, the specimens that come in the store. Specimens all right, especially when you consider those teenagers.

"I'd put the boots to them if I were you. Kick their arses out of here, Lindy. Kids like that do nobody any good. If it were my business—"

That was the time he called me by name. "How'd you know?" I almost asked. But then, in these parts, the least little thing is public property, and what's a John Henry anyway? He could've heard it anywhere. But it gave me pause, I've got to admit. Something inside me almost corrected him: Well, really, it's Lucinda. But it made me look twice at him going out the door. The flat wide rear of his workpants, the way he tugged on his gloves, stomping outside in his Kodiaks, pantlegs tucked in — neat though, not floppy or bunched up like the young fellows with their bootlaces dragging. Clean sheepskin gloves, too, come to think of it, not those roughneck suede mitts some men wear. Nice hands underneath: big thick fingers, callused but clean, not what you'd expect on the hands of a contractor.

Ruby noticed him too that day. "Who's that?" she wanted to know, sneaking up behind me in the doorway. She had gloves on herself, green gardening ones. It was a nippy day just before Hallowe'en and she was going out to rake leaves.

I waited for some snide remark — figured she'd heard his joke and wouldn't be too impressed. But maybe, with the TV so loud, she'd missed it.

"Hmmm," she said, fixing her cuffs, "haven't seen him before. Must be part of that crew, is he? The ones from God knows where, digging up the countryside."

They'd just started work, see, the new bypass over Folly Mountain, aimed to cut through our valley. From the start I've been all for it, figuring we've got nothing to lose. But some, like Ruby, have taken it as an insult: the government or whoever riding roughshod, diggers and dump trucks churning everything inside out. As if it hasn't been already, by those old works that were here when she was small, and her parents before her. They used to call the place Arcadia Mines, as if a hundred years ago some Rip Van Winkle prospector died and went to heaven here in these hills. But after a fire wiped everything out, "Mines" got dropped. 'Course by then the mines were spent. So for years now it's been just plain Arcadia — which has a bit of a ring, like a few other places round and about: Paradise, Eureka, Garden of Eden. Arcadia it is — if you blink in time to miss all the car parts and trailers with tires on the roofs, the axles rusting in people's yards.

"The new road might put us on the map again," I suggested to Ruby over the rumble of those trucks pulling away, pointing out the line in the *Herald* saying so. She peeled off one of her gloves and picked up the *News* instead; licked her finger and ran it under the headline: HOW TO SURVIVE THE END OF THE WORLD.

Her reply? "A bloody mudbath in spring, you wait."

"But for safety — you can't argue with that," I said. "Get people around that bad stretch on the old road, accidents every time it snows." I was only passing on what I'd read.

"They just want to disturb things," she started in, pulling her glove back on. "Sure, they could've picked another route. I hope they lose their equipment down an old mineshaft." Huffy as all get out, she was, worked up. When she gets that way, there's no ignoring it.

"Well, Aunt Ruby" — I couldn't help sounding snippy — "that's progress for you."

The second this popped out, it dawned on me like a toothache what she was worried about.

"That's what they say," she answered; next came a crusty pause. "Well. My father would not have allowed it." And she gave me this look — would sooner have turned a screw in my heart than stuck in a needle — as if to say, Don't be so stupid, Lucinda.

The cemetery, of course.

Silas? Grampa? I almost blurted, Your old dad would've bent backwards jumping at the opportunity! But I caught myself, thank God.

"You watch," she charged on, not missing a beat. "They'll get it half dug and run out of cash. I've seen that before."

"Well, not this time, Aunt Ruby." I couldn't help myself. "You have to figure it's taxpayers' dough."

In a proper snit, she fluttered her hands about her head, like someone in vaudeville waving two hats.

"If they go near the Hill," she said, "I don't know what I'll do."

"I've seen the route — look, right here in the *Herald*. The *Herald*, Ruby." I even tried a bit of humour. "There's a nice dose of God, the Queen and highway safety."

But there was no point; her mind was set.

"If they do, you'll just have to stop them, Lucinda." Case closed.

I pictured myself arse-over-teakettle in some loader bucket, kicking the air with my sneakers. On television, like the crackpots you see chained to logs in the path of a grapple-skidder.

"I don't think so, Ruby," I said — under my breath, though by this time she'd already gone out back, was rummaging around the porch for the rake. "It's there somewheres," I started to shout, then decided to keep my tongue where it belongs, in my head.

But the nerve of her, the goddamn nerve, I thought. And all because she'd heard me talking to that fellow.

Wilf. Kind of a slow-moving, country name that rolls around your throat like a yodel. Like Wilf Carter, except not so rugged — gosh, the last thing you'd picture is this one strumming a guitar and warbling about blue Rockies — and he's hardly fit for the boneyard, not this man, not yet. Good name though, for an older, good-natured fellow. Wish I could say handsome, but I have to be frank. Handsome he isn't — well, not in your *World News* way.

"Ruby? Ruby?" After a minute or two something prompted me to yell. Last thing I needed was her stomping out mad. Leaving half the yard raked, those patches of crabgrass that pass for a lawn.

I should've gone out and reassured her, reeled off in my best knit-one-purl-one voice: "They won't touch the cemetery, honey. I've seen the plans." But I couldn't, somehow, and for once I didn't. Let her stew in her own juice, I decided. Then paid in spades the rest of the afternoon, feeling guilty.

III

Ashes

I've finished hauling those clothes off the line when I hear the mail. More flyers, a little padded envelope with a cassette and a five-dollar coupon inside. The tape is called "Trust Me, I'm a Doctor — How to Live Longer and Increase Your Life Expectancy", and there's someone's name with the letters DVM after it — doctor of veterinary medicine? Great, I think. Just what I need.

I fix my first cup of caffeine, nice and thick with the milk warm from the cupboard, and there's the spin of gravel out front, somebody pulling in. One of these years I'll get it paved so I can tell people baldfaced-honest, Look, I never heard your car and anyways, sorry, we're closed for inventory.

Oh my. I gather up my cup and on a whim the album as well, and go to open up. Through the streaky window I see a couple of road men, but no Wilf. When I unlock the door, they come stomping inside clapping their hands together, their breath puffing out in cartoon clouds.

"So where's the boss today?" I ask offhandedly. When one of them shrugs I feel myself blush. Is this any way for a woman my age to behave? Shameless as a schoolgirl with a crush on the teacher. Well, almost.

"While the cat's away the mice'll play, is that it?" I try covering up, dropping a can of pop into a paper bag. I take my time folding over the top, then remember to throw in a straw. The fellow pulls out the drink, biffs the bag and snaps the tab, throwing back his head to guzzle. He shuts his eyes; I watch them roving around under the lids.

"A guy gets thirsty, I s'pose," I say in a chirpy voice, to make conversation. But without glancing back he saunters out, his buddy behind him. There's a smack of cold air as the door swings wide.

I bend to crank up the space heater at my feet, then lean back in my chair, the bad knee braced against the counter. No way for a lady to sit — Lordy, I can just hear Ruby, as if I were eighteen. But right now I can't help myself, the coffee's not doing the trick and drowsiness climbs me like a spider, inch by inch. If not for the throb in my knee I'd drop off — must've done a number on it, twisted it somehow, maybe helping Ruby into the truck at the cemetery. The poor old bird, sometimes you wonder what gets into her head.

I've wedged the album on top of the phone book in the little shelf below the cash.

My coffee's gone cold.

I try swatting dust off the breath mints which it seems nobody buys. Those perfect smiles on the ads, beautiful boys and girls kissing, sporty types usually, or men and women wearing suits — no wrinkles or buckteeth there, you can bet on that. No beer guts or grey roots, or old ladies in furry boots. Is it any wonder some things don't sell?

Another day, another dollar.

Sometimes I could scream out loud, turn the till and every can, bottle and bag into the trash. Sweep one last feather-duster-full of dirt off the shelves, then stuff my purse with bingo dobbers and walk. That would be about the size of it, too, my prospects — the hope of winning at bingo. Ten cards on jackpot night at the Legion in Ferrona. Buy myself a Keith's Light or two and get lost driving home.

And what about Ruby?

I go to reach for my knitting, needles jabbed into the ball of wool, half a mitt dangling like a sad little flag, its finished mate pinned underneath. It's the matching one that's a pain to do; strike me dead for saying so, but how much easier if each charity case had just one hand! I don't mean it, of course I don't. But instead of getting at that second mitt, I wiggle out the album, open it to Ruby's marker; "Join our Millionaire's Club", it says.

Putnam, Robert Putnam. A common enough name around here; I might've gone to school with Putnams but can't really say, it's been so long. A company accident, a local tragedy. The company was no more than a mote in some old fellow's eye by the time I came along. Hard to imagine now, when all that's left is the slag heap like an old wasps' nest behind the maples, only visible with the leaves down, the grey plus some timbers sticking out of the hillside like bad teeth.

Oh, there are pictures. Grampa used to have an engraving in the store, a framed bird's-eye view of the valley like a huge chugging engine. Rows and rows of mills and warehouses, belching stacks, freight sheds, yards and train tracks criss-crossed like the zippers on a biker's jacket. There were blocks and blocks of houses, too, grand and small, the town itself gridded like an Eggo. Furnace Street, Broadway, Main and Pleasant, First and Church. When Ruby was a girl there was a skipping rhyme; she recited it just the other day, for Pete's sake, peeling apples for a crisp.

> From Chapel Bridge to Foundry Hill,
> You can do your banking, make a will.
> There's lots to see in this big town,
> All I can say is, come on down.

Old Silas would have you memorize the hot spots, pointing at the picture. "Look, look, right there — what's wrong with your eyes, girl? There it is, there's the store." 'Course, you needed a magnifying glass to pick it out, your head cocked back, his bony fingers digging into your shoulder. But if you looked long and hard you'd find it, perched on the hilltop some distance from the smoke and commotion. Hard to say what prompted his father, Malcolm, to build so far from the river, the centre of town — calculated risk or pig-brained stupidity. A lucky choice, though, as luck would have it: Providence looking out for somebody, some moment of silly obtuseness paying off in the end. Location location, as those real estate types say. Anything the Lewises might have missed out on at first, they made back tenfold when the town and most of the competition went up in smoke. Stores, banks, hotels, homes were lost in the fire, not to mention what drove the place, the blast furnaces and foundries; blooming, rolling and pipe mills. Not a thing left by the time I came along.

Ruby says a spark from someone's chimney caused it, a teeny-tiny ember wafting up and lighting the roof, leaping to the next house and the next, sending up streets like lineups of people passing fever. Almost before they knew it, I guess, the whole place was on fire, even the fields behind town, blades of grass like torches blazing up Foundry Hill till what was left resembled a waffle all right, one left on the griddle. A smoking rubble of bricks and bedsprings blacker than your arse at midnight, which was how my uncle — Ruby's Leonard — described it, the very words he used telling somebody once, a stranger who'd come in the store looking for directions. Somehow they got onto the fire, though Leonard couldn't't've known much first-hand, being new to the place when he married Ruby seven or eight years after it happened.

As I see it, I grew up in a ghost town. The only houses left were this side of the river; everything over in the flatiron section, the big clapboard houses, the fancy hotel with the wraparound veranda that Ruby remembers, most everything in Grampa's engraving was no more than a blip in an oldtimer's memory. A tick-tack-toe of dirt lanes is all that's left now, so overgrown the signs are practically hidden. Those neat green signs — give you the willies, those signs, marking streets with nothing on them but ragweed and alders. A nesting place for mice and toads, as familiar-looking to me as my own belly, smooth, white and flat once upon a time. You look at something long enough and it's as if it's always been there, rolls, moles, warts and all. After a while you hardly notice any more. Like the flesh around my middle, which I wouldn't miss one bit; but then who's to see?

The only thing new in that part of town is the loosestrife taking over, that gorgeous purple stuff you're not supposed to plant. We used to carry the seeds.

But I digress, as they say in those old books of Grampa's.

The album, the album.

You'd think someone would've taken a picture of the fire, or afterwards. But no. From what I gather, Gran and her girls, my ma and Ruby, escaped with their lives and not much else. They were home at the time finishing breakfast, preparing for church. Silas must've been at work — I don't remember him ever talking about the fire when I was a kid; or maybe by then, being bedridden, he just plain didn't talk.

Their house was near the centre of town, across from the Baptist church — the section that went up like a haystack with a match thrown in. They lost their place and everything in it, except the album, now I think of it, and the quilt, the one in the parlour so in need of a wash. If anything else was saved, I have no recollection. They got out in the nick of time with nothing but the clothes on their backs, Gran said.

God, that frowsy, malingering feeling keeps coming over me; I should do *something*.... But the damn album's like a magnet.

For goodness' sake, here's a picture of old Silas himself, pale, popping eyes, that queer stately stare. They must've taken forever back then to snap a picture — no wonder the subjects look so peaked, their faces against their crow-feather black clothes. Like birds parked on a hot wire.

There must be one of Gran too — Euphemia, or Effie as she preferred to be called; I'm sure there was, once. But do you think I can find the danged thing? I can almost see it: her wistful expression, her small nose; those luminous eyes turned from the camera; the dull fringe of curls on her forehead. She couldn't have been more than twenty years old in the picture I'm thinking of, another I'd linger over at Ruby's table. Aunt Ruby used to hover, making sure I didn't bend the pages. The front of her dress would smell like cough drops, tea and perfume — Evening in Paris perhaps, though that might've been later. I remember Gran's photo because of the trouble I had connecting it with her, the sickly crouched woman at the beck and call of the old man upstairs. The two of them fit together, see, like a hand and a mitt, one no use without the other — useless as tits on a bull. Pardon the expression but that's how my own father would've put it, what I remember of him.

Anyways, Gran's picture is nowhere to be found; at the very

back of the album is the spot where it should be, bordered with vines, white-veined ivy twisted around the hole. Maybe it's something I've dreamed up, this image of her — I suppose it could have been a portrait of someone else, since to a kid even the young look old; there's no connecting a smooth teenaged face to a wrinkled crone's. For a joke I should slip in a snap of myself, one I have somewhere of me behind our house on Station Road. It shows me scowling, playing in the dirt by the back step; I was four years old, a big white bow in my hair and a shadow on my face from whoever was aiming the Brownie. The glint from his watch is reflected in my eye — I say "his" because likely the person taking the picture was my father. Somebody's knees are sprouting out of my head, skinny female knees behind me on the step — my mother's. Her long fingers are dangling over them, her short painted nails that look dipped in tar in the deep dull black of the photo. You can't see her shoes — God, the shoes she used to wear, heels that would take out your eyes. Her feet are hidden by my flouncy dress; it was white, the same material as the bow, and smocked with short puffy sleeves. The wind has blown a hank of hair in my mouth and flattened the dress to my chest. I look about to cry.

A family photo. I should dig it out, it's around somewhere; I found it at the bottom of a heap of papers one spring, cleaning. Now if it were up to Ruby, she'd display it at the public archives. "See this antique?" she'd say. "My niece" — as if another living soul could give a hoot.

Jeez, yes. For a joke I should dig it out and keep it in the store — right on the counter maybe. Just casually set his change down beside it, the next time that certain customer comes in for smokes.

Anybody I should know? he'd ask.

At least I like to imagine he would.

Wilf.

But enough of this foolishness — *fooleeshness*, as Uncle Leonard used to say. Folks, some folks, used to get a charge out of the way he talked, how he mispronounced words. Like some hillbilly from beyond the beyond, big handsome fellow with all that money — oh, people used to shake their heads. My ma included, though more than likely she was jealous. I was too young to take much notice. But now when those teenagers come in and say "I seen" instead of "saw", and Ruby sucks her teeth and freezes up, I know what she's thinking. Like a whiff of tobacco, it raises Leonard's ghost. But you wouldn't dare say anything, oh, you've got to watch yourself around her, it's a fact. Not that she's always waiting to jump down your throat. But her look tells you she's got certain expectations: you can begin staying loyal by keeping quiet. You know what I'm saying.

What a time-waster, this old book, full of people you wouldn't know from Adam. One day Edna Pyke came in, found me poring over the *News.* "You like reading, Lindy?" she said. "Well, you should check out such-and-such; now there's a potboiler — if you don't mind all the skin and some of the language."

Edna, Edna, I was sorely tempted to answer back but didn't, Some people think I get nothing done now — what would happen if I took up reading books? Mother of God!

I give the Chiclets a going-over with my duster.

To think I've been doing this job forty-five years.

But there is one thing that's going to bug me the rest of the morning. That graveside scene; why would anyone bother fencing in the plot? Like a playpen or rabbit hutch — as if buddy inside had plans to rise up and beat it out of there. I don't think so.

The things that passeth understanding. And then Ruby taking a notion she was there when the picture was snapped. Well my darling, you wouldn't dare suggest she's mistaken. "Excuse me, Ruby — take a gander. That accident happened when you weren't much more than a shine in your old man's eye."

Enough nonsense. Back under the Yellow Pages, under a stack of accounts received, goes this foolish tome. If Ruby comes looking, I'll know where it is. Maybe she's right, it belongs in a museum, some backwater exhibit of hatpins and razors labelled by the owners in shaky script. Memorabilia, that's the word.

Personally I'm more interested in the future. There's an article this week in the *News* about a boy kidnapped by Martians; another, I see, giving thirty ways to lose weight, ten pounds in two days.

Every second there's a sucker born. Okay, so I read this stuff — sue me. It beats listening to the wind blowing through gaps in the shingles.

A fresh hot cup of coffee, that's what I need, and while I'm at it I should check on Ruby. Then I've got to get back at that knitting; the box at bingo was looking pretty empty last week. I'd better get a move on. How many days till Christmas? Seems every time you turn around someone's looking for donations. But the mitts I don't mind, like I said before.

Oh my. Oh God.

Someone's pulled in. It's Wilf. Have I brushed my teeth? Remembered my lipstick? I have a godawful time keeping it so it doesn't cake or fade or spread like ink in the cracks. And don't tell me that's yolk on my sweater! I catch a quick, sly glimpse of myself in the chrome strip on the counter. Which reminds me, I'd better dig out the Windex.

"How's it goin'?" He speaks in a fake Hank Snow drawl, sauntering over, blowing into his hands. The thumb on his right one looks jaundiced, the skin around his nail cracked from the cold.

"Some kid got your gloves?" I aim to say, but instead blurt, "What kind of dimwit goes out bare-handed on a day like this?"

He stops and gawps at me, his head cocked like he couldn't've heard right. Taken aback, as Aunt Ruby would say. *You stunned arse, Lindy, what have you done?* goes the voice in my head; *for godsake, zip your lip.*

He scratches his jaw with the signet ring on his right fist. Rocking back and forth on his big steel toes, he stuffs both hands into the pockets of his green vest. It's quilted, like a hunter's, and underneath he has on a blue flannel shirt. He looks squeezed into it — how many chops for supper last night? I wonder. Then for no good reason he leans forward, his elbows propped on the counter, his chin thrust out, perusing my *News* upside-down.

"Whatcha reading now, Miss Lucinda?" His big hands smoothing the page, righting it, he squints at the fuzzy shot of a flying saucer, a vague little being climbing in on all fours. It could be a child or a mid-sized dog. Wilf shakes his head, laughing out loud.

"What'll they dream up next, you figure?" He stamps his feet, sidling closer. I can see his legs through the smudged glass, dungarees, the knees faded yellow.

"You don't believe any of this stuff, do you Lindy? People that do, you know, folks out there that take it seriously...well, I'm telling you, you'd have to be a fruitloop; soft. Yep. Certifiable. Crazier than a sackful of screws."

"No crazier than someone going around with no gloves." It comes out sounding uppity, even a tad ornery, and I feel the heat starting in my neck. It happens when I'm cornered, when not a single word seems the right one to say.

Wilf sucks in his cheeks, still leaning over, and gives me the oddest look. For a second I feel squirmy as a fly on a pin.

But then, go for it, I think. What the bejeezus. Ask him.

"I'm surprised any woman would let her husband go out like that, no gloves. This raw weather, a man works outside all day."

"Is that so? Well, I suppose you'd know a thing or two, wouldn't you Lindy?" He lifts his eyes till they're about level with mine. Through the glass display I see the front of his jeans, the bulge where the snap does up. The man could stand to lose a few pounds all right, but then who couldn't?

He flips to the front page.

MIRACLE GRAPEFRUIT CURE FOR OBESITY. WATCH FLAB FALL OFF!!!

Under the slap of powder, my cheeks burn.

"Sounds like just the thing." He raises an eyebrow, rubs one sideburn. "I should give that a try sometime, what do you think?"

Who can tell if he's teasing or being straight as a nail? I give up. Brazen as can be — nothing to lose now, I figure — I let fly:

"Yup, you'll have to get your wife onto that, send her for the Indian Rivers."

'Course the second it's out I regret it, feel the blood singing in my ears, the same funny buzzing as when you sip a rye too fast. Now you've done it, I think; serves you right for being so frigging forward! Not just forward but nosy, damned nosy and stupid to boot. Heaven knows what he's thinking: "So much for this dive, this dingbat"? "People sticking their noses where they don't belong — help me Rhonda, I'm outta here!"

I reach down and start wrestling the kink out of the phone cord as if it's a pressing piece of business, wrapped around someone's neck; first aid, red alert. I wait.

Wilf clears his throat and straightens up.

"Now what makes you think I'd be so lucky?"

After a pause that feels like rolling coin with greased dimes, I drop the cord and look up. He's got his billfold out, ready to buy a lotto ticket.

"Go on," he says, "advise me. You tell me what numbers to pick. Go on, Lindy, you pick, I trust you. Let's say we win — we'll split the profits fifty-fifty, what do you say?"

"Right." I roll my eyes and shrug, taken aback.

He's serious.

"Five," I venture, "six, seven, one...."

When he pays and turns to leave I'm grinning, my cheeks pulled tight — you can feel the crow's feet. I know I'm as red as the fuzzy Rudolph nose in the window, and probably just as silly-looking. Cut the smile, I tell myself, quick, before he sees.

But he doesn't look back leaving, yanking the door open then shutting it behind him tight so the cold won't come in. I hear the truck idle a minute before hitting the pavement.

Well well; I catch myself in the chrome again, still grinning. Nothing ventured, nothing gained — so Ruby has always said.

Speaking of Ruby, that must be her in the kitchen, burning something. Toast, it smells like; no, something else — egg stuck to the stove? Jesus, Ruby. Once she left a burner on. She'd been frying sausages and forgotten to turn it off. A bunch of burnt offerings in the pan. I threw the whole mess out for the birds. They looked like dog turds lying on the ground; even gulls wouldn't eat them.

Rushing out back, I find Ruby doing dishes. Not that there's many. Our toast plates, the pan for poaching eggs. But not a puff of smoke to be seen; the toaster's not even plugged in. Still, I swear there's been something burning — outside, I guess.

Ruby keeps her back turned; she's up to her elbows in soap. So damned fastidious about dishes. With so few, I'd have rinsed them under the tap.

She's wearing her good dress, the teal-blue wool one, with the striped dishtowel over her shoulder — as I imagine a man might do dishes. Well, the way I recall Uncle doing them, which must've happened from time to time. When I grab the dishtowel she starts, as if I've interrupted something.

"Keep your shirt on," she says, in the same brusque way Grampa used to mutter, "Hold your horses." She looks disgruntled, as someone might having spent precious time locating something lost under their nose; I can't imagine why.

"I can manage, Lucinda," she snaps at me, snatching back the dishtowel. I notice then she's wearing a brooch, an old cameo pin of Gran's. A gift from Silas or his family most likely, Gran's own people being hard up. Poor as the dirt on Sore Finger Hill, kids used to tease her, or so she told me once, I'm not sure why; so I'd pity her, maybe; or see her in some other light, not always old or always Grampa's nurse.

But that's how the hill was named — gravediggers getting blisters chipping through rock. More reason for cremation, I'd say. But you know how people used to think, looking forward to the resurrection of the dead, the life of the world to come, etcetera. Damned hard to imagine now, people rising bodily or missing the boat altogether if they didn't die in one piece — would this be grounds to fence a grave?

I reach past Ruby's lobster claws for the dishrag, soapy and dripping, and wipe crumbs off the counter. Interfering, I suppose. But what the heck, she's already ticked off about something.

Life's too short, I think to myself, sweeping hard black bits into my hand. No time to be morbid. Eat, move your bowels (regularly, one hopes) and die is what the big go-round amounts to, and if you're lucky there'll be a smidge of loving in between. Very very lucky, I'd have to say.

"Who was that you were talking to?" It makes me jump; her voice is like a backhoe scraping topsoil.

Oh, she doesn't miss a trick, Ruby.

"Just one of them fellows from the road, is all."

"'Them' fellows, Lucinda?" She sniffs; her bottom lip twitches. She folds the dishtowel like a length of fine linen, laying it down. "I suppose if you want to dry, dear, I could take over in the store for a while. Give you some time to yourself, I don't mind. It would do us both good."

The dress, the brooch. Now I get it.

"And when you have a second, Lucinda, would you be a pet and go over my room? Just a light dusting. I don't see as well as I did, I'm afraid I might miss something. But just the rad, dear, and the dresser-top, whatever you have time for; that's lovely — for now. If I need you, don't worry, I'll shout."

Picking invisible lint from her front, she floats past, through the door to the cash. Like a yacht, Her Majesty's *Britannia*. Aware of me watching, she doesn't miss a stroke. She's got a mind like a well-lubed Merc — at least when it comes to knowing who's boss.

IV

Bingo!

I finish the dishes jig-time, get started on my second cup of "crank" — Edna Pyke's word for coffee, the times I've seen her doing refreshments at the Legion. Well, I'd best get at that dusting; it's true, Ruby doesn't see the dirt like she used to. (If I were truly slack, I could likely get away with sweeping it under the rug!) But then there's her health — not that she has problems to speak of, but wasn't there a piece in the *News* recently about dust mites? Call me overreactive, but the name brings to mind plagues: tiny winged monsters, hosts of flying pestilence. Not that I'm in any way religious; but like that story about the Horsemen, I say fear what you can't see rather than what you can.

Armed with the pink feather duster, I open the door to Ruby's room. Mother, the draft! She's got the window wide open, imagine, as if it's midsummer. "The price of oil," I feel like shouting, but she wouldn't hear anyhow, holed up out there in the store. The curtains are stiff from the cold, the panes frosty as the inside of a windshield. And there's that burnt smell. She's been munching in bed again, I expect. Except the bed's made neat as a pin, not a ripple or a speck on the pink chenille spread. The cushions are rolled like wagon wheels against her pillows.

I jerk the window shut and give the radiator underneath a quick swish. Then I start on the dresser, taking pains not to disturb her little silver hand-mirror; her blue plastic comb and bobby-pin tray; the crocheted doily with her cosmetics arrayed just so — if that's what you'd call a tortoiseshell compact, a few crumbs of powder inside like the sands of time, and one petrified lipstick, a peachy-red shade, worn down like a step. Bits of the duster break off and waft to the carpet, the new one from Sears. It's a pretty enough gold — Ruby had to wait while it got sent from Moncton, then hemmed and hawed when it finally arrived. She took forever getting me to lay it; for the longest time it stayed in the porch, like a giant sausage rolled in Saran Wrap, until at last I said, "Aunt Ruby, do you want the rug or not? Because if not, you may's well return it and get your money back."

I ended up rearranging everything to put that carpet in place, no thanks from her. Moving the bed was a chore, one of those times a man would've come in handy just for the lifting.

God. Wilf's smile winks in my head, if only for a second. I imagine his hands folding bills and that lotto ticket into his wallet, taking extra care with it; and his teeth, long and yellow but straight, very straight, come to think of it, when he opened his mouth, as if to say: "Go on, Lindy, you pick. Pick the magic numbers."

Glory, it hits like the downdraft of a furnace as I'm screwing the lid back on Ruby's lipstick, licking my thumb, rubbing off the dust: *Jesus Mary and Joseph — what if we won?*

What a concept.

Now when was the last time I cleaned under this bed? The dust bunnies will have sprung into hares, a breeding ground for germs, mites, motes, whatever. Gives you sympathy for Howard Hughes keeping that layer of Kleenex between himself and the world. When I read about him in the *News,* at the time I thought, Buddy, I'd feel for you — if I could only reach. All that dough and hoarding toenails. But it's all a matter of perspective, I guess.

The duster tucked under my arm, I hike the bedskirt and take a peek.

Oh my sacred!

I *knew* something smelled funny! Sure enough, there are more than dustballs underneath. Groping around, I find a piece of cardboard charred like burnt pastry; at least it's cooled when I grab it, ashes crumbling all over the carpet. It's a photograph! Like those in the album. A portrait, burned like a craft gone wrong — that new craft in *Good Housekeeping*, how to antique family photos. Except here the crafter's run amok, the face in the picture is so badly singed you can hardly make it out.

But I recognize the eyes, the funny airy-fairy look; the part of the mouth still visible, a pouty Cupid's bow.

It's Gran, Ruby's mum.

What on earth would possess——?

The discovery makes me jittery as a kid pinching gummi worms. Without a word I fetch the dustpan, sweep up the sooty mess — the remains of a mini-bonfire under the bed. By no small miracle the carpet's unmarked; it's that synthetic stuff that would melt at the sight of a match. The room could've gone up in the snap of a finger; five seconds more, and the rest of the place, before you could scream Jack Robinson. A tinderbox, this old building, especially with all that tinselly stuff out front.

Like a near-miss car crash, it's the what-ifs afterwards that hit you the worst. The speculating.

I march into the kitchen, that foolish duster poking from my armpit like a wing, the evidence in the green tin dustpan. I can hear Ruby out front, the *chinka-chink* of coin.

"Ruby?" It takes no effort at all to summon the right tone; I'm angry, ripping actually, and proper thing. I picture the whole place in flames, the two of us watching it burn.

"Ruby!" I shout, louder.

But she still doesn't seem to hear. From the doorway I see her neat white head bent over the register, her shoulders humped in that teal dress. She's busy counting nickels and dimes. I imagine her expression were she to turn and catch me looking — impatience? guilt? Likely that hoity-toity nose in the air, one eyebrow raised: "My, my, Lucinda — you've finished cleaning already?"

Instead of rubbing her nose in things, I do what's decent and slide Gran's picture, cinders and all, into the garbage. I make sure it's good and covered, squirrelling it away under crusts and carrot peels. But all the time there's a gassy pull in my chest, stiff as a breeze that can sink a chip bag floating on a puddle.

Those accidents of hers at night. Now this.

It's times like this I regret there being just the two of us. "Them old dolls at Clarke's store, two peas in a pod. Never had no use for the rest of us, did they? Guess misery must enjoy company."

Well. Company's one thing. But like they're always advising on *Oprah*, I could use a second opinion. Which is to say I'd appreciate a viewpoint now and then that was other than mine or Ruby's.

The remainder of the morning I pass sweeping out the rest of the apartment. Around eleven Ruby hollers in, saying if I don't mind it's almost time for *Dini*, and would I come take over. Things are flat as a pancake, she says. "The only one who's been in is the milkman," and sure enough there's a blue case of homo going sour by the cooler. I find a rag and dip it in Javex, and go at the racks inside; they're rusted and sticky with spilt milk, ripe with that curdled smell of things always being behind.

But the work takes my mind off Ruby. While I'm at it, I happen to notice the "Season's Greetings" banner above the cash, gold-fringed tinsel strung between two lightbulbs. It's starting to droop, the worse for wear, the part with the "gs" frayed and beginning to tear away.

I'm perched on my kitchen chair, attempting to tape it together, when the door blasts open. There's a swirl of arctic air and in swarm those kids. Nearly knocks me off my feet, the cold. A fine mess that would be, me sprawled on the floor with God knows what broken and those brats having a field day at the register. I think of Ruby and it hits me — *wham!* like the paperman dropping his bundle of *Herald*s every morning — how alone we are, like a pair of dumb sitting clucks. Now this is crazy, but next I think of Wilf whatever-his-last-name-may-be. Not just him but pretty well anything in pants, old enough to shave; every fellow I've had occasion to observe but never get to know. Some companionship, that'd be the thing. The chance, now and then, to sit across the table from someone other than Ruby and listen to his observations instead of hers.

I step down, graceful and dignified as poor doomed Di drifting down her wedding aisle, smoothing my sweater where it's ridden up. Keeping my eye on those kids — in particular that flat-faced boy with the earring, the one the others call Ronnie — I ask myself: Hell's bells, Lindy, where exactly was it you missed the boat?

Damned if that kid ever takes his eyes off me, round and watery-blue in that catfish face; You want to take a picture? I feel like shouting into it. Kids like him would sooner tear a chunk out of you than speak. I'd call the Mounties, I would, except it'd take them all day to get here and I know what they'd say when they did. "Loitering's no crime, miss. You can't book a kid for hanging around. Call when you've got a real, legitimate complaint; otherwise we might just charge you with mischief."

What's a body to do? Turn your back to make it easier for them to stick in the knife, then yell, "Help!"?

Ronnie, that kid with the queer eyes, slouches down back to the video games and gives a machine a kick, not hard but loud enough his buddies laugh. I've slid in behind the counter, my hands folded tight atop the cash register.

"Is there something you're looking for?"

This slow stupid smile spreads across his face, but he just gawks back. His friends, meanwhile, shuffle past the Coke cooler to the movies, digging each other in the ribs at the titles. *Dressed to Kill, Cape Fear, The Shining, The Mask, Terminator.*

"No *Mortal Kombat*?" one sneers. They roll around the aisle sniggering, bumping into things. A tin of peas clunks down and bumps across the floor, coming to rest beneath the newsrack. I put my hands on my hips, waiting, but nobody moves to pick it up. They just keep carrying on, cracked laughter rattling their scrawny chests — the laughter of boys not old enough to be men. I watch their shoulders poking like coat hangers under their sporty nylon parkas. Finally, they move like a cloud of blackflies towards me. One asks for yellow Vogue papers.

Damn you, I think. You figure I'm that stupid?

I stand there hesitating — do I sell the kid rolling papers or not? There are hefty fines for selling minors tobacco products. I have to think, do papers qualify?

The young fellow sees me pause, the whole swarm staring me down now, their sneering faces pale as moons. I've never considered myself small or short — Lord knows, being around Ruby you learn to keep your chin up and walk tall, and height runs in the family. But I feel tiny now, damned tiny, the blood pounding in my neck.

Then, outside, there's the crunch of tires. The healthy *tick-tick-tick* of an engine. Glancing sideways through the window, I see a pickup, one of the road men's. Those kids see me looking, follow my eyes. To my surprise, Wilf himself jumps out the passenger side, comes stalking in. There's a solemn, perturbed look on his face — he reminds me of Sheriff Dillon in *Gunsmoke* bursting into Miss Kitty's saloon, except this is all business, I can tell, and not play. His head's down; he barely seems to notice the boys as he shoves to the front.

"Twice in one day?" I try joking, but my voice wavers. "To what do I owe the honour——?"

"I don't mean to alarm you, ma'am," he says, so strange and formal all of a sudden, "but we came across something weird, well, something kind of suspicious, in a ditch we're digging up by the mountain. Don't mean to stir you up, but it looked to me like bones. Prob'ly a cow, who knows; it's hard to tell. Digger just came upon them, right where we're starting to grade. It's shot the morning anyways, I can tell you. We've called the RCMP, had to drop everything. 'Don't you fellows move a boulder till we get there.' 'Well, rock'n'roll,' I said, ''cause, officer, I'm in the middle of a job here. People breathing down our necks to get this road through.'"

The kids have gone dead quiet, their gum-chewing mouths slack. Having moved from the counter, as they check Wilf out even their feet seem to quit shuffling in their high-tops.

"I kind of thought you'd like to know, Lindy, that's all," he says, surveying them. "But it's not like a bomb's gone off or nothing. You know, just one of those things, a hitch; you've got to expect 'em. But there is a chance, I guess, they're human bones. Remains."

"Listen," he adds, "could I use your phone?"

I notice the cellular sticking out of his pocket.

"Battery" — he shrugs, sheepish as if asking to borrow deodorant — "dead as a pole."

I don't even think to ask if it's long distance.

The bunch of us stand there gawping, all ears as he makes his call to some higher-up. That's what I gather, hanging on his words. His face looks redder than usual as he talks, as if he could be making this up, or is waiting to be accused.

"About two feet down, yup; kind of swampy, you know the spot, well generally. That's right. Remains. Yeah. Bones. Nope. Kind of small to be a bear's, I'd say. Too big to be a dog. No, no skull. But one big enough to be a thigh—— I couldn't venture to say. Oh yeah, they're on their way. I know. Yep. It's a holdup, sure it is. A major bug up *my* arse. You know. Twenty guys standing around with nothing to do——"

By the end he sounds huffy in a way I haven't seen before, the five or six times he's come in to shoot the breeze. When he hangs up, he stamps his feet as if the whole of him has got the jitters. One hand digs for his cigarettes.

"Don't let me forget to pay you for the call," he says, lighting up.

Before I can object, he blows a blue cloud above the cash. The kids edge towards the door as I go to remind him, "No smoking, please; it's not me but Ruby who gets in a flap——" But I bite off the words when he shrugs and says, "I'm obliged, Lindy, for using the phone."

"Maybe it's some old rubby," I suggest.

"Wha'?"

"The bones," I say, willing him to stay long enough for me to explain myself. "Heck, they could be a dinosaur's for all we — I wouldn't worry. You know, a day's work — it's nothing to get in a knot about."

'Course I can just hear Ruby and her worries about the Hill.

"Pray for us," the white-painted rocks that were stuck there once read, till spruce and goldenrod blocked them out.

Pray for me too while you're at it, I think as my eyes grope around, finally fix on his. I'm wishing he'd joke about something, anything. The lotto ticket, for instance: "This a sign then, Lindy? A lucky day — twice in one morning, two trips to your store?

Double the pleasure, double the fun?"

But not a word. Instead he nods, preoccupied as the mailman delivering bills, and out he saunters. I figure this weird discovery could be serious, the biggest thing maybe to hit this burg since the fire.

A half-hour later a cruiser goes tearing up the road, the plain black van from Pyke's funeral home in Ferrona following close behind. A couple of hours after that they come creeping back at something slightly faster than a snail's pace. A respectful crawl, Ruby would've observed, had she witnessed the excitement.

But no, when I run back to tell her about the bones, she's asleep in the rocker, *Days of Our Lives* blaring to nobody but the walls.

It's afterwards that I notice things missing — half a dozen videos cleaned right off the shelf. All the ones with Sylvester Stallone, as far as I can make out, and another featuring Sharon Stone.

God damn. I could turn my knitting needles to spaghetti, slamming them wool and all against the counter.

And so close to Christmas, too.

Four or five days go by, then a week. There's no sign of Wilf, though I know the men are back at work. When the wind blows a certain way you can hear machinery, the noise of metal scraping rock; it carries across the river. The weather stays cold, that hard bitter brightness that seems to sharpen sound. I finish the red mitts, whip off a blue pair that Ruby and I drop off one night on a quick jaunt to Ferrona.

We go after supper; there's a bingo on at the Legion Hall and I've taken a notion that somehow or another Ruby might be convinced to stay. So many hours bunged up together inside, I tell her; that's what ails us.

"Nothing's ailing me," she retorts, putting on her coat over her teal dress, fussing with her navy loop-knitted hat. So off we go. On the road down, there's hardly another vehicle in sight; just the parched-looking ribbon of pavement grey and salt-stained in the headlight beams. The spruces on either side are huddled peaked and black as a coven; the only specks of brightness come from the odd streetlight that hasn't had the bulb shot out. Hunters, I imagine. Pulling up to the Legion, you can see the heads through the plate-glass window, smoke so thick you can smell the cigarettes. Laughter spiked with the caller's shouts spills out into the parking lot. I feel inside my purse for a spare dobber and hand it to Ruby. She hasn't said much the whole trip; I figure she's been enjoying the drive. But when I come around to help her from the truck, instead of jumping out she stares at me long and hard, this pinched look about her mouth, and asks: "Where are we?"

Not "Lucinda, I've changed my mind. You know I've never cared much for bingo — what was I thinking? I'm sorry, so sorry, but you'll have to take me home now, please."

Not "Oh my, we'll need gas masks to breathe in there — I don't think we'd enjoy it, do you?"

Not even "Gosh, Lucinda, I'm suddenly just not feeling up to it."

No, nothing so sensible as that.

"Lucinda" — she clears her throat, but her voice comes out a whisper — "where are we?"

"Hell*o?*"

I creak the door to, leaving it open just wide enough to poke my head in. God forbid that anyone should hear!

"Ruby," I launch in, no beating around the bush. "Listen, you know this place, the Legion. You've been here a dozen times if you've been here once. Why, just a month ago — remember? The Hallowe'en Jackpot, proceeds to the fire department? The jukebox, remember? In between rounds they played music and you complained it was too loud — *remember?*"

I don't know if it's the cold making me desperate, or what; above, the stars break out like hard little crystals up in the blue-black sky, and the air has that peculiar, burnt-soupbone smell of snow coming. There's this funny tingling in my teeth, the same sensation you get eating fudge or something too sweet; I'm clenching. I don't need this, I think. Come on, Ruby, stop being so foolish. Quit playing games, as if I'm seven again and you're saying, "I spy," or "Name the highest mountain in Africa." Testing me.

"Where are we?" she blurts once more, indignant this time, flustered as if I'd flung some insult at her — or a raft of them, like pebbles from a slingshot.

Sticks and stones may break my bones, this cool, crazy singsong comes to me as I pause to watch the players inside, their heads and faces bobbing through the steamy glass.

"I've told you, Aunt Ruby," I say in an icy robot tone, the one mothers use when their kids pester them for treats.

"There's no need to snap. I was simply asking a question, Lucinda, that's all. You needn't be petulant, dear."

...But names will never hurt me.

When I go to pat her hand, it feels limp as a dishrag in her tight leather glove; she pulls it away. And when I reach across her for the bag with the mitts, she tucks in her chin and screws her eyes shut. So much for a night out. I close her door and scurry inside with the mitts.

Edna Pyke is sharing some joke with the caller; when she looks up and sees me, she waves. I don't bother stopping to say hello, just push my way to the donations box by the kitchen and toss mine in. It's about half full, I guess. But I don't take the trouble to see what-all's there.

Back outside, Ruby hasn't moved an inch, not even to take a Kleenex to the window rime.

"You breathing hard or what, Aunt Ruby?" I try joshing to make us feel better. As I pop the choke, she sticks out her pointer and rubs a little hole in the frost. There's a balled-up tissue in her fist; she blows her nose on it, gives a brisk, hard wipe. Then she smiles at me, turning away. From the stiff, frosty silence, I sense she's been weeping.

On Christmas Eve the cold snap breaks. There's not a stitch of snow. Instead, it rains and rains. A couple of people come in to buy pop — mixer, I suppose, though I wouldn't know for sure. Ruby and I close up at the usual time and eat supper as always. Potatoes, a couple of pork chops, peas, carrots cut like boards, not coins. Sawing into my meat, I can't help thinking of work — the after-Christmas chore of taking down the store decorations, packing all the red and green stuff that never sells and sticking it upstairs till next year. Over my carrots and peas I make a resolution to move the Christmas stock out of there by New Year's, and maybe get a jump on Valentine's. I have to make way for the red candy hearts, the frilly heart-shaped boxes of Ganong's I ordered at Hallowe'en.

Maybe I seem distracted. At one point, cutting through her chop, lifting the bone like a teacup to gnaw off the last morsel of gristle, Ruby meets my eyes and asks, "Whatever's the matter, Lucinda — cat got your tongue?" She sets the bone down daintily and wipes her mouth on her serviette, a Christmassy one recycled from last year. She looks at me with beseeching concern, like a news anchor saying, "Talk to me!" or some prim and proper Fido begging for food.

"Don't mind me," I say and she nods, befuddled. For the next little while we sit in silence finishing supper, listening to the rain pounding the back steps.

"You stay put now." She rises first, laying a hand on my wrist. "I'll tidy up." She goes to the ironing board folded beside the fridge, where she's gotten into the habit of hanging things, and yanks down her apron. It's a pink-flowered print that looks faded and shabby against her good wool dress. She'll have that dress threadbare, the way she's wearing it lately. I get up to help but she says, "No, sit," and for once I'm just as happy to do her bidding. She's awfully spry tonight, unusually spry. Which is how she gets when there's something up her sleeve.

I realize she has something planned, some little surprise or treat in mind. For a while I'm content to sit and watch her, those three-quarter-length sleeves shoved up, elbows see-sawing in and out of the suds. The plates clink gently, clots of bubbles sliding off them into the drainer. She's forgotten to rinse — oh heck, her heart's in the right place. But as I think this, panic leaps in — what was it I got her for a present? Will she like it, will it be enough?

It's one of those Magic Bags advertised on TV — hope she won't be insulted. "Zap it in the microwave; presto! an instant heating pad; clap it on your neck." Except we don't have a microwave, but I figured the oven would do the trick; it's not as if she's pressed for time.

"Go on now, Lucinda — go see what's on the news, why don't you?"

Oh, she's up to something all right. Wouldn't want to ruin her surprise. So I go and sit in the parlour, one eye on *Live at Five*, the other on the *Herald*, waiting. I listen to her out in the kitchen, the squeal and thud of drawers and cupboard doors shutting, the wire dishrack being shoved under the sink. She slips into her bedroom and I hear her riffling around. There's the rustling of plastic bags, soft at first, then suddenly frantic.

"Ruby?" I yell. "Anything I can do?"

No answer, but the rustling's turned to ripping now, loud and frenzied as a pit bull rooting for something.

The TV, meanwhile, blares a feature on Christmas lights, and I feel a twinge of guilt for not bothering with a tree this year. Too much trouble. Just as easy, I convinced myself, to shut your eyes and imagine last year's or the year before's, propped in the corner, the same gold balls hung the same old.... At least this way there'll be no needles to vacuum, no fire hazard.

What in *tarnation* is keeping her in there?

The rustling's stopped; I have to go check.

Ruby's sitting on the bed, arms folded, her feet together on the carpet. But her hands are shaking, her knees too, and the room looks like a hurricane hit; the entire closet has been emptied onto the floor. There are clothes and shoeboxes spilling ancient receipts; a crusty-looking ledger, the black leather binding cracked and frayed. Grocery bags overflow with old nylons, bits of yarn, fabric scraps, magazines — I recognize the covers of some I've cut recipes from: gals on the front with beehives and white-frosted lips. Everything's spilled and tangled, one unholy mess. Before I can open my mouth, she makes a jagged lunge off the bed, her knees buckling as she swoops down after the ledger.

"Aunt Ruby," I cry, "what the devil——?"

V

Silver Bells

Ruby glares at me, scuffling slowly to her feet, all the while clasping that ledger like a Madonna hugging the Holy Infant. Reeling backwards, she flumps onto the bed, then sits smoothing her dress over her knees, staring at the dresser.

"I can't find it."

I suck in a long, deep breath.

"What is it you're looking for?"

"A surprise — for you, for both of us, you know, to brighten things up. I know it's here someplace. I had it made specially — well, since you didn't have time to get a tree. I thought it would be lovely, just lovely. But now...I've misplaced it. I'm sure it was here, why, just the other day——"

Shoving the ledger under the pillow, she shoots me this accusing look.

"You peeked, that's it, I'll bet. Why, Lucinda — you didn't like it? Well. Perhaps you didn't appreciate the craftsmanship, or it wasn't quite to your taste — but that's no reason to dispose of something, is it? To throw it out! The nerve, dear. When all I wanted was to surprise you. If you didn't *like* it, Lucinda, you just had to say."

"Aunt Ruby, I don't know what in God's earth you're on about!"

"Please don't swear."

I throw up my hands. Her eyes jackrabbit around the room, like somebody gauging a quick exit. She wrings her hands, then fixes her gaze on me, madder than a hatter's — ticked off, I mean. As if I've played some dreadful trick, and all this is my fault.

When she speaks, her tone would ice up antifreeze.

"Well, it's a tree, of course. A little ceramic one. I thought it would look nice on the TV set. It plugs in, you know — it's one of those pretty things with the bulbs set in. Oh, I ordered it weeks ago — that lady who makes them, she comes in sometimes? I don't know where you were. She makes them from a mould. Very smart, not at all cheap or homemade-looking. I thought it was something we could have — save you the bother of a real one each year."

I'm on my knees now, stuffing things into bags. Lining up shoes, putting back clothes ripped helter-skelter from their hangers. Pushing everything neatly as possible back into the closet, I notice a square white box on the shelf. Not something I've seen before, it's large enough to fit a good-sized hat. But sliding it down to take a peek, I find it's heavier than I expected — the weight, say, of a cookie jar or the dishes that used to come in detergent.

Sure enough, the tree is inside, its neat white cord wrapped around the base. Some green paint has flaked off the pointy branches, but no matter; the clay underneath looks like snow.

Ruby's eyes light, then glaze with the funny guilt I've seen so often, of little kids unwrapping DUBBLE BUBBLES without slapping down their nickels first.

"Oh Lucinda" — she tugs on the pearl stud in her soft, creased earlobe — "I don't know what's eating me lately. 'Jimmy crack corn an' I don't care'!" she tries to quip, rolling her eyes, a spurt of gaiety. "You're going to think I'm cuckoo. The way one gets, being old. Not too glamorous, I must say — is it, dear?"

She laughs, twisting the little gold band round and round on her finger.

"If Leonard were alive, heaven knows what he'd do with me."

Then she clasps her hands together tight; her dark grey eyes cloud with a stubborn, wistful look.

"Well, I'm not fit for the boneyard yet, am I? Now don't just stare — give me a hand, would you? Let's get this thing plugged in and see if it works. I'm dying to see how it looks, especially in the dark."

In the parlour I lift the tree from the box and set it beside the rabbit ears. The bulbs embedded in the little branches blink red, blue, green. Quite pretty, especially with the boob tube off and just the light from the kitchen. For a while we sit side by side on the couch admiring it, Ruby's crazy quilt over our laps. When I squint, the lights wink like stars and I can almost imagine a real fir, like one in *Tom Thumb* or *Gulliver's Travels*, with midgets scrambling around it. Anyhow, the sight pleases Ruby and she smiles and nods, and presently asks if I'll be a pet and go and get some eggnog.

In the kitchen I fill two mugs from a carton from the store, the stuff glugging out like yellow Pepto-Bismol. Sneaking a taste, for fun I dash in a capful of brandy flavouring. It's old as the hills, heaven knows how long it's been in the cupboard; the tiny glass flask is a type they don't even make any more.

Ruby cradles her mug in her lap and takes a couple of tiny gulps, wincing as if it's scalding. "Lovely, dear."

The drink hasn't an ounce of kick, I know; still, it gives me a cosy, holed-up feeling, and I put on *Fresh Prince of Bel Air*. We pass the rest of the evening watching TV, muting the ads to listen to the rain. Without let-up, it hammers the eaves all night.

"I hope we don't wash away!" Ruby jibes, rising stiffly when it's time for bed. She takes her cup out to the kitchen while I stay put, eyes on the screen but not really watching. After a bit, she shuffles in in her housecoat, props a box wrapped in silver-bell paper against the TV stand.

"G'night, dear," she says as always, turning her cheek to get a kiss. She smells of toothpowder and Dippity-Do, the crusty blue setting-gel she's kept in the medicine cabinet for as long as we've lived together, it seems.

"Don't let the bedbugs bite, Aunt Ruby."

For the briefest second I touch my lips to her soft withered face, that skin that feels like crinkled velvet, and give her arm a quick little squeeze. I feel her flinch, the brittle bones beneath her loose, warm flesh.

Oh my.

Next morning I open her present to me, a cardigan the colour of mushroom soup, with a jar of solid Avon perfume tucked inside. It smells like aftershave, but I do as she says and swipe out a fingertipful and apply it to my wrist.

"Your neck too," she urges, "all the different pulse points." She shakes her head, as much as to say: A woman your age, Lucinda — how on earth did you get this far and miss such basic training?

Don't worry, I could sauce back but don't. Between you and the *World News*, I've gotten all the education I need.

I hand her a box done up in identical paper.

"This is for you, Aunt Ruby, go on, open it. Don't mind the wrapping." All the same, she peels off the tape as if performing surgery. Sliding the box out, she folds the paper, laying it carefully aside before inspecting the contents. There's the Magic Bag, some bath salts and a needlepoint kit complete with a plastic frame, pink to match her bedspread. The scene is of kittens curled in a basket, a rather complicated pattern. Idle hands make for idle minds, was my reasoning when I ordered it from *Canadian Living*.

"You've gone overboard" is her reaction. "But everything's lovely, Lucinda. Beauteeful." And I believe she means it, too.

So Christmas passes quiet as usual, so much foofaraw for one piddling day. We cook a chicken instead of turkey — why not, with just us two old crows? The only hitch is when Ruby adds sugar instead of salt to the gravy.

An honest mistake, I tell her, heck, something anybody could do. But I decide then and there — like my New Year's resolution about packing away stuff in the store — to make her go for a checkup.

We end up closing shop the rest of the week, it's that slow. The road crew knocks off work too — a real pity with the weather so mild. The temperature bobs up and down like a yo-yo, not too unusual this time of year. Still, you never know what to expect with a green Christmas, everything balmy and wet as April. With such weather, I figure by now they could've paved from here clean through to Westchester. Nothing doing, though.

And not a peep from Wilf, not so much as a breath of news or gossip about those bones. Like Christmas itself, by New Year's they're ancient history, all the noise and excitement worn off. I ask the odd person coming in for milk or cigarettes if they've heard anything, but nope, the word's mum, as they say. There isn't even mention of any findings in the *Herald*. So I figure that's the end of it — typical, the way things come and go in these parts. Christ himself could visit and you might hear a rumour a year or two after the fact: Stay tuned for the next millennium. You'd think I'd be used to waiting by now.

Then one day after New Year's, who should come sauntering in? Jumpin's! I'm not prepared, not at all. I've just gotten up, thrown on some slacks and yesterday's blouse under that new beige sweater, which is a tad tight.

"Well, you finally decided to open, I see. Nursing hangovers all week, were you, you and your aunt?" His face looks soft, his silvery hair a bit stringy from the damp, but he's all smiles, slapping down a bill. "Your take, Lindy. Told you I'd go splits, remember? Just took a while collecting the prize."

It takes a second to register. "Oh my sacred!" I tug at my sweater to allow some slack around the bosom. "Twenty bucks. Well, that'd figure, wouldn't it? I'll try not to spend it all in one place — wouldn't want people to talk, eh, like I'm over here laundering money." My voice goes la-de-da on the "laundering" part. Pocketing his cash, I feel my face heat up. There's the whirr of the freezer starting, a humming silence behind me as if Ruby's back there someplace listening.

"Well, yeah, you wouldn't want people to talk," he mimics, scratching his neck. He seems kind of edgy, though, as if bored or tired of all the kibitzing and banter. I wonder, of course, if it's got to do with delays, the season, or those bones being fresher than he first let on — a body maybe. Not to be flip, but that would put a fellow off, unearthing something dead, a person I mean, in Wilf's line of work. I don't like to ask.

He rocks back on his heels, rubbing his palms together like he's trying to make up his mind: will it be Exports or Player's; a straight 6/49 ticket or one with Tag. I feel myself perspiring in Ruby's sweater, and pray the wetness doesn't show through.

"Is there something I can help you with, Wilf?" I finally ask, and he glances towards the hip pocket where I've slid his twenty.

"Give us another ticket, Lindy — on me. Like before, we split the profits, a' right?"

"You gonna make it worth my while this time?" Lordy knows where such sauce comes from; I take a big breath after it pops out. "Eh, Wilf?" I prompt; what the hell, I'm on a roll now. "You win ten million, say, and I get five? Well I like that, except there's a hitch; how 'bout some kind of guarantee? Wilf, I don't even know your last name——"

I've seen the movie, I feel like adding. Ruby and I watched it, the one where a cop and a waitress win a million; he buys the ticket, they split the take; then the cop's wife gets jealous and makes off with the whole bundle.

"Why" — is it really me going at a customer like this? — "how am I s'posed to trust someone I can't even attach a proper handle to?"

Lindy, you frigging flirt! Shameless hussy — that's what Ruby would say if she heard. Even as I'm ribbing him, a part of me coiled up inside is hissing, Stop it now, you're being stupid.

"Jewkes," he says. The abruptness makes me go redder, but I stick to my guns and squelch that inner ragging.

"Wilfred P. Jewkes," he enunciates. "Wilfred P-for-Putnam Jewkes. How's that?"

Raising an eyebrow, I start punching in some ticket numbers. "Like as not, we'd do better at bingo. Putnam," I say, "you got family around here?"

"None I know of. You want to give me some lessons?"

"Lessons?" My face is so hot now my eyeballs are burning. "Whoever heard of lessons for bingo? Any idjit can play. If you know how to read, so long as you can push around a few chips — B-one, B-two, B-three...." I put on a calling voice, uncannily loud.

See, I'm sure now that's Ruby I hear rustling around the kitchen.

"Teach me," he says, his eyes steady as a nail, though I know he can hear her too. "Restless, is she, your aunt Ruby?" He shrugs, saying "aunt" the flat way, like "plant". His eyes slide to my collar, my little fur poodle pin, the one Ruby made for me a few birthdays back using real mink, and for a second I swear the ruddiness in his face deepens.

"Nice top you've got on," he says, clearing his throat. "But I like the green one better — you know, that one with the cats. Now I'd say that suits you."

Who asked? I almost shoot back. Any goofing around earlier was never this forward. Honestly, I don't know what to make of it, so I change the subject to the first thing that leaps to mind.

"So. Any more 'discoveries' lately?" Since coming in he hasn't said one howdy-do about the bones — or whatever it was his men dug up.

"What was that?" He looks at me as if I'm right off my stick. "Didn't you hear? They took the bones to some lab in Moncton, the Mounties did. Figured they were about a hundred years old. Oh yeah, we found a skull too, a little later on — didn't I tell you? Well, part of a skull, bottom half of the jaw missing. The top part had a couple teeth gone, a big lopsided spit-hole. Bones were too big to be a kid, I guess, but they figured it must've been a young fellow. John Doe, far as they're concerned. Inconclusive. Some poor bastard lost in the woods, maybe. A mystery. Not enough there to piece together, I heard, so your guess is as good as mine. Only thing made me think it wasn't an animal was a bit of red rag on one part, a vertebra, the forensic fellow said — well, I'd call it red, though who's to say, something in the ground that long."

He rips off a match and sticks it between his teeth, flicking it up and down with his tongue. Pensive, you might say; watching my reaction.

"Say, Lindy, you lose anybody around here lately? Don't tell me there's no old skeletons in this place."

I roll my eyes and suck in my cheeks in a noisy, brazen way — one ear cocked for Ruby's doings behind me.

"None that I know of. But a gal can never be too sure, I guess. Can she, Wilf?" His name spills over my tongue like a drink, tasty and sweet as punch. But then I get jumpy, hoping I haven't been too chummy.

"Nice sensible business lady like yourself" — he shifts gears ever so slightly — "now what would you do if we won big?"

"Depends how big."

"Oh come on. Sky's the limit, say. Or are you too polite to tell, Lindy? Okay then, let's be more specific — what would you do with a million bucks?"

The thought of it makes me woozy, frankly. I'm reminded of that song on the radio by those husky Barenaked Ladies — a catchy enough tune, though the group's name puts me off.

"A trip to Florida? Las Vegas?" he prompts.

"Put me on the spot, or what! I'd have to think on it, of course. And you?"

"Welllllll, let's see. New sump pump for the trailer, a couple more acres maybe; a mechanical wood-splitter, a new four-by-four for sure...." He glances at the dusty ceiling, rhyming off his wish list. I find it hard to tell whether he's kidding or not. Then, out of the blue — his eyes fixed on a rusty spot, a water stain etched like a fern — he mumbles, "By the way, that is if you're not too busy, how's about us going out sometime?"

He lowers his eyes, a little smile creeping across his beetroot face, those big fingers coming up to pluck out the soggy match. At first I'm certain he's talking through his hat, more of the same old banter. But he's that direct; his eyes lock on mine and don't budge, this straight, earnest look to them.

"That was just carrying on, that bit about the wood-splitter. Now seriously, I'm asking, Lindy, if you'd go out with me some night."

"Well shit," I hear myself splutter, my bottom lip tightened down, aghast. Just like a teenager who knows Mama's listening. Except I've never been good at choking back delight.

"I'll be here" is about all I manage to get out.

Jesus Christ.

"Okay," he says, "okay."

And he backs off a little and nods, because Ruby's come up behind me in the doorway. And like a bold young pup being yanked to heel, he squares his shoulders and hightails it outside like gunfire, except there's no smoke. And for some stunned reason, I think again of Matt Dillon in his ten-gallon hat, him and Miss Kitty slinging the word "pardner". Which makes me throw my head back — never mind Ruby standing there — and laugh right out loud, like the man in the moon kidnapped by Martians. Foolish as a coot, and not giving a holy frig!

"Yessir," I shout like a baseball player as he drives off, this half-crazed, half-sober joy fizzing up inside like Alka-Seltzer. Ruby lifts her eyes heavenward and shakes her head.

As the bubbles clear, Wilf's truck dips out of sight. What I feel then is a queer kind of pride chased, the very next instant, by: My God, my *God*, girl — what have you gone and done?

The phone rings one evening in the store — the day the latest *News* arrives, one with a half-human, half-alligator baby and its mother on the front.

"Tell them we're closed." Ruby yawns, glancing up from her needlepoint. She's just opened the kit, was sighing at all the tiny skeins of wool she'd laid out on the couch just so. "My land, it's been years since I tackled such a thing — something simpler might've been better to get me started again," she says, sucking a yarn end, her fat needle poised for threading.

"Well, you've got all the time in the world to work on it," I yell back, dashing to the phone. "I'm coming, I'm coming."

The loud, empty ringing jangles the shelves; the floor creaks with the cold. I don't bother with lights; for a moment there's the brightness of somebody's high beams streaking past, illuminating the tops of cans, the withered stalks in the window. Then shadows, cast by the curlicued light hanging over the door like a big old daisy. The clunky register looks like Moby Dick under its grey plastic sheet.

I curl my fingers round the receiver, then, hesitating, pick it up. I don't recognize the voice straight off, figure it's some pesky soup salesman, or maybe the liver people looking for money.

"Hello Lindy." He coughs and there's a pause. "It's Wilfred Jewkes — Wilf — calling. I was wondering...."

The upshot is, he wants me to go with him to the dance next

weekend at the Legion.

"Oh, I don't know," I say, forcing myself to sound cool, cool as cantaloupe. "Well, perhaps." Sniff. "I suppose — I mean, well, sure — I guess I could."

I'm wearing green mules with knee-highs; my toes are already numb. Next my ankles go limp, as my brains, meanwhile, shoot off in a million directions. How will I tell Ruby? What'll she do while I'm gone?

When was the last time I danced?

What the bejeezus will I *wear?*

"Lindy?" he says, making sure I'm still there. "Listen, you can a'ways say no if you're not up for it. I won't take it personal."

"Wait a minute," I cut in, cupping the mouthpiece with my hand. Out back I hear the couch springs squeak, Ruby muting a toothpaste ad. "Gosh, no, it's not that at all, it's just" — I whisper — "well, you took me by surprise, that's what. Got to check the date, you know, hang on a sec while I...." The brand-new Esso calendar on the wall behind me winks back, utterly blank; even in the dark there's no trouble reading it. "Looks...ah...clear. I think. So, well, yeah, yeah, I would — I mean, yes, I wouldn't mind.... Um — when, again, did you say?"

Eagerly he rhymes off the date, the time and the name of the band — some group from Caledonia named Saddlebag, or maybe it's Baywulf, he says. As if I would know, or need convincing.

"I'll be up to your place about eight, then." His voice slides into the usual give-or-take, push-or-pull. But just as mine starts to thaw, panic closes like a hand around my throat.

"On second thought," I shoot back, "I'll meet you there, save you going the extra jog."

There's a funny pause at his end; the way I've said it leaves no room to argue. God, I realize, what if he thinks I'm some kind of nut, like one of those gals who used to burn girdles?

"Good," I jump right in, in a brash, cheery manner, as if it were Edna Pyke on the phone, or Charlene Mattattal, the girl who runs the bingos. "See you then," I chirp, "eight sharp. Right outside the Legion."

Which is where I tell Ruby I'm going when Saturday finally rolls around. Never mind I've hardly slept for three nights just thinking about the dance. I'm nervous as a cat all that afternoon, and manage to gyp one of those obnoxious kids by a loonie, accidentally, mind; I'm that wrought up. What dress should I wear? Heck, I haven't had one on in two years, not since a funeral Ruby and I attended up in Westchester, some old fellow she'd done business with. And pantihose! Wearing pantihose, for someone who's made a career of avoiding them, is like putting your bum in a hairnet.

So I decide to skip the dress and stick with slacks, better to dance in. My newish black ones, perhaps — they're a little snug at the waist but have nice permanent creases. And the green sweater — yes. No, I'd resemble a fruitcake left from Christmas. But something green, definitely — with eyeshadow to match. That is, if I can squeeze any out of the tube in the bathroom.

No wonder I end up overbalancing that day — not by a lot, though, just $1.27. Not enough that I need to tell Ruby, thank God. The last thing I need or want is her suspicion.

For supper she warms us up some beans and hot dogs sliced like quarters, and serves them on toast. Afterwards, I can tell by the way she lingers at the table that she wants to sit and talk. But I jump up, jostling the blue plastic placemats, clinking cups and saucers in my rush to get at the dishes.

"Bingo's at eight," I mumble over my shoulder. "I don't suppose you'd like to come."

She gives me the eye, a gentle, passing smirk.

"Oh I don't think so, Lucinda. You don't need me tagging along." The way she says it! As if to crow, "Who wants to be a fifth wheel?"

She goes to get up ("Leave those," she says, "I'll wash up while the news is on") and I half shove her back into her seat.

"You take it easy now, Aunt Ruby — you cooked. How's the needlework coming? Maybe you'll finish that background tonight, get started on one of the kittens."

Suds lap over onto the floor, my hands going like sixty. She sniffs and moves off into the parlour, turns the TV on so low I wonder how she can hear.

While I'm wiping off the stovetop, some brown bean juice stuck there, I stumble upon her note fallen between the range and the garbage. It's the weirdest message, Ruby's small neat jottings on the back of a grocery receipt.

1. Open tin — can opener in top drawer.
2. get out spoon, same drawer *large wooden spoon.
3. find pot, small one, in cupboard by refrigerator — small one with lid.
4. empty beans into pot, stir
5. turn on burner, lower knob, right side
6. stir beans till they burn finger
7. ***TURN STOVE OFF***

I crumple it in my fist and try to keep on cleaning. The clock's a-ticking, an hour and a half before I meet Wilf. I don't know what to do — I'm already queasy. I open the garbage and toss in the note.

But when I go to put away the ketchup, what's in the fridge but the old bean tin? Not just empty but rinsed clean, the label peeled off, ready for the trash.

Oh my Dinah.

I can't go, that's all there is to it. I'll have to phone him back, never mind there's no number listed in the book. (I checked one day, passing time.) Nothing for Caledonia, anyways, and I wouldn't know where else to look.

I have to go, there's no choice. I picture him standing around the Legion steps in his brown leather jacket — the good one he wore the very first time he came into the store, before the blasting got started. I imagine him clapping his hands together for warmth, other men nodding as they pass; and their wives, at least the ones not too busy checking their makeup, nudging each other, wondering what on earth that foreman fellow's doing there. "Doesn't live around here, does he?" I can just hear them.

I picture him alone under the stars in the lot outside that jam-packed hall, sitting in his truck with the heater going.

I fish Ruby's note from the garbage, smooth it out as best I can and leave it on the table, pinned flat beneath the salt and pepper shakers. Then I go and get dressed — nothing fancy, just those black slacks, a cream-coloured blouse and, at the last minute, the beige cardigan. That way, if I get hot I can peel it off.

There's no time to fuss with makeup; the green shadow oozes out yellow, a thin oily drop. But I've got a new lipstick, a deep frosted pink. The only problem's my hair, a few strands that fall flat in front. On a whim I try a dab of Ruby's gel; it does the trick, but up close, dried, it looks like dandruff. (Or nits, I worry later, starting the truck.)

"You're sure you don't mind me leaving, Aunt Ruby?" It's the last thing I say on my way out, poking my head into the parlour. She glances up from her handiwork, startled; she smiles, squinting slightly — the effect, I tell myself, of shifting focus.

"Oh, I don't care much for bingo, you know that, Lucinda; and all the smoke makes my head ache. But you go ahead. Of course I'll be fine."

As I'm zipping up my coat, she hollers, "Maybe you'll win big tonight, dear!" It makes me feel like a two-faced snake, but I laugh in spite of myself, stealing one final look in the mirror.

"I sure hope so, Aunt Ruby. Wouldn't that be the cat's rear end? Well, you never know. Keep your fingers crossed. Wish me luck."

VI

Shadows

Off she goes, that niece of mine, done up like a tart in that sugary lipstick. At her age! Why, when she looked in to say goodbye, I had the oddest sense of seeing Dora. Underneath her daughter's warpaint and wrinkles, of course. My sister. She used to be so lovely. I always envied her her looks; there was something sprightly and girlish about her, even after she married Albert. Something cool and airy, like an April breeze blowing through a fresh-scrubbed kitchen, stiff enough to raise goosebumps but sweet with the promise of spring. She had such lovely skin, Dora.

Or perhaps that was just me being jealous — the age difference, me being older. Six years is like the Rock of Gibraltar to the young, a mere bump once you're grown up, level as pavement by the time you reach my age. Not that Dora ever grew up. Not even after Albert deserted her. Albert. My blood thins when I think of him, the skunk. Leaving her alone with the child, and not even proper clerking skills to fall back on. No skills at all to speak of, none you could mention in polite company.

Skills, isn't that the word they use nowadays, in place of "tools of the trade" or "diploma"? When I was a girl "skills" applied to lumberjacks and switchmen. Which is why Leonard got his way with me, because his skills were of a higher nature. They were talents. But never mind. I was the more sensible of Dora and me; if there were any logic to things, I would've been the one who birthed the child, her actual mother.

Poor Lucinda. As if I don't know what she is up to now, roaring off in those shiny black pants. Bingo, my eye. She left with a bit of lint clinging to her rump. I should have gotten up and plucked it off. But there I was in the midst of threading my needle, and she in such a tizzy. I've heard her mooning over that man in the store, his name escapes me. A pleasant enough fellow, but a perfect stranger.

I worry about Lucinda. I always have. From the time she was knee-high to the doorstep. She's like a retriever, I know it's demeaning, but she's always so eager to please. Wears her heart like the pin I gave her, front and centre above one titty, for all the world to see. And handle too, if one desired. Why, just the other day didn't she unpin the brooch and tickle a baby's chin with it? Waited till the mother left to wipe off the drool.

That's the kind of person she is.

I used to worry Leonard would spoil her. He was that indulgent, would take her on his knee right behind the counter, play eenie-meanie-minie-mo with the sweets — round after round: *out goes y-o-u!* Reach his big hand into each jar and wriggle out a candy, pop it into her mouth like a mother robin feeding its baby. Humbugs, peppermints, licorice whips, jawbreakers. Dora used to whine he'd make her fat — when she was around to notice. I used to tell him, "Leonard, you'll spoil that child rotten, and who do you suppose is going to pay the dental bills?" But he always had an answer — Quick Draw McGraw, he was, with his tongue. "Don't be hard, Ruby. For the love of God, woman, can't you soften up, just for a minute?"

I hate to say it, but seeing Lucinda dolled up tonight brought to mind my first few outings with Leonard. I've been thinking about him more than usual lately, more than I'd care to admit, more than likely is good for me. Oh, he was a charmer, my husband; could have charmed the rings off a cobra, that man, if such an opportunity had knocked.

The first time I laid eyes on him....

Oh, but that racket from the television keeps carving up my thoughts! Especially the noise of the hockey game, blades cutting ice, and that dashing loud-mouthed commentator in his high collar and bright, bold jacket. I might have fallen for that type of man once — just as I used to enjoy the game on TV. Once I could close my eyes, listening to those sirens wailing goals and the organ bleating melodies, and almost smell the ice, peanuts and popcorn. But the fighting puts me off now, so many slashing sticks.

So off the TV goes, for a little while anyway. Such a brilliant contraption, the zapper; I hope whoever invented it made fistfuls of money. The picture fades to a tidy point of light, then there's nothing, and for a moment I sit utterly still, relishing the — nothingness.

Such quiet.

How long has it been since I was last alone, quite alone, in my own home? I feel like a bird in a nest, tucked under Mum's quilt. Lucinda keeps threatening to launder it; if she persists I guess the only solution will be to put it away somewhere. Out of sight, out of mind. A washing would ruin it, of course, and remove whatever nap's left in the velvet. Not to mention its fusty, old, comforting smell — which my niece describes as "odour", and I "perfume".

Beauty's in the eye of the beholder; I dare say the same applies to the nose. Though deep down I suspect Lucinda may be right, perfectly right, just as she was about the needlepoint. It certainly passes the time, though who can say why she chose that particular pattern? All my life I have abhorred cats, the best place for them being a barn. Why she would think I'd want them framed on my wall is a mystery.

But this quiet is delicious; it wraps itself round me like a satiny stole. If I keep very still and don't rustle the sofa, I can hear the frost at the windows. The walls creaking. It's cold tonight, they've called for below freezing. Black ice. I do hope Lucinda is dressed properly, that she wore boots and not those flimsy flat-soled pumps of hers, and remembered to put a bag of salt in the truck.

Why she didn't just have her friend pick her up is beyond me. Having her stealing around like a she-dog in heat appals me. The silliest behaviour, and on account of a man. Well. I hope his intentions are good. One can never be too cautious with strangers, especially men. And though on the surface Lucinda behaves like a live-wire, underneath she's as innocent as an April rain, and because of that I worry. I worry.

What one learns from tabloids is no substitute for experience, which is where, I'm afraid, Lucinda is sadly lacking. In certain, coarse ways. This could be my fault, I suppose; since she was tiny I've felt responsible for her, and being under my wing may well have clipped any need to fly. This time I will try not to stand in her way.

But listen to me! A tired old fool prattling on to myself like the Queen Mother after a toddy, as though Lucinda were seven years old again, a scrawny tow-headed brat burying her face in my mouton coat, seeking comfort. Lucinda is more than old enough to take care of herself, though, good Lord, it makes me blush to see her like a thrush feathering its nest for a vulture.

If *I* won the lottery, the first thing I'd buy would be a lovely black mouton hat. Like my coat, the one I wore years ago — or maybe a bit more recently. It was prettier that the one Leonard bought me as an anniversary gift: muskrat. Come to think of it, I wonder where that coat's gotten to; it wasn't in my closet the last time I looked.

Lucinda thinks too much quiet is bad for me. She finds quiet unsettling — why else would she sit me in front of the blaring TV at all hours, or make those constant overtures to accompany her to that awful hall? My husband — my late husband — would not have been caught dead in such a place.

The lovely, glorious quiet. A drink would do, to celebrate. A sip of ginger ale, yes; there's some that Lucinda brought in from the store. It's in the kitchen.

I reach on tiptoe for a good glass from the cupboard, a fancy pinwheel meant for sherry. The film of kitchen grease on it wipes off in a wink.

I raise the glass to the light, a little toast, then hold it to my ear. The carbonated hiss, next a stinging tingle on the tip of my tongue. My heart floats up to meet it, this heady, gleeful tingling. Such delight, this sudden fizzing solitude! There are dead flies in the light shade overhead, black specks against the bulb. But I don't give a whizgig. Lucinda can clean it tomorrow.

But what's this on the kitchen table? Has she forgotten something? I mustn't pry into Lucinda's business — but she's left it here for me to see. A grocery list? If bran is included, I shall cross it out. A list of unpaid bills?

Favours she would like performed?

But no, it's a list of instructions — chores, perhaps?

Heavens, the handwriting is mine, though I can't imagine——

It is a blessing Leonard's gone; he would have words about this...this.... He'd have something to say, no doubt; more than his usual two cents to throw in. He'd be the first to accuse me of...of things. Leonard. God rest his soul.

Why, something about Lucinda's friend — when he grinned, perhaps, buttering her up the other day, homing in — put me in mind of...Leonard. My departed husband, his nasty habits. I'd have thought someone of Lucinda's ilk would be repelled by tobacco-stained fingers. Oh, the very thought of them reaching for her coat, resting on the back of her chair, her sweater....

But maybe the dance floor will be too crowded. I can't imagine that man dancing, not with his girth. Perhaps they will sit and have drinks, Lucinda something soft, I trust, as she'll be driving.

Oh, bother. *Bother!* My problem is, I think too much.

The ginger ale goes down the hatch like crushed glass; probably I should let the rest go flat. While I make short work of that peculiar list. Lucinda's list, mimicking my hand. She has no idea how this mocks me. Imagine: "Stir until they burn...." Foolish girl. Filed in the trash it goes, where it belongs. Foolish foolish foolish girl, and disrespectful to boot.

Back to the parlour. I pick up my needlepoint and try once more to occupy myself. The creaking panes sound like someone trying to get in. My finger's raw from thrusting the needle in and out, in and out, the teeniest possible stitches. Next she'll have me doing the blind stitch, the stitch Chinese women lose their sight over. But I mustn't think ill of Lucinda; mustn't think.... She means well. It's the *quiet* that crowds me. Pricks me. But my needle is blunt, goodness yes, like the kind for sewing leather. It has a wide eye to fit the yarn. It's very dull. No fear of poking myself. No chance of harm from this — needle. The word itself slips and slides from my grip.

"Needle," a voice, my voice, croaks aloud.

Needle. Flu shots. The doctor. That shiny-faced young man replacing old Dr. Thingamajig.... Now I hear Lucinda's voice, deep inside my head: Book a checkup book a checkup book a——

Why?

There's nothing wrong. Nothing a bit more sleep won't cure — or a bit less sleep, depending on which day or night....

Outside, I can hear the wind rustling the dark. There's a new moon, useless. A vehicle speeds closer. I hear it, yes, rushing like the wind through a field of oats. Wild oats.

Lucinda? Make it be Lucinda.

The quiet has become a room now, a whole room, shrinking, the walls curving in.

Find the remote — the what? The remote, the zapper, the——

Press the buttons, quick. The what? Find the what and turn on the what's-it. Quickly, *quickly*. The television, the TV. Do it now, so the noise will swell and push back the walls....

Lucinda? Are you there? Do you hear me, dear? Wherever you are — good God, don't *you* get lost!

There. Noise. The TV face looms big and blustery, has a voice to match. Scenes flash: red-white-blue. Players, swinging sticks, glide and swoop in gyres like bulky crows.

Push the button that raises the volume, that's it. Make it loud. Louder. Till the music and cheering rattle the panes, fight the wind outside.

I fasten my eyes to the puck, and thank the Americans for making it show up on the screen.

The scritch of blades is like the sound Lucinda makes sometimes chipping ice off the steps....

Lucinda?

I get up off the sofa and stare out at the road; it's like a strip of grey seam-binding dotted with lights.

Come home, dear. Now, please.

I watch and watch for her, looking up, looking down, till I start losing track of which way she'll come. The direction she'll take coming home from Ferrona.

No sign either way of the truck. Not yet.

I sit down and concentrate on the puck again, going zigzag on the ice. I clasp my hands to keep them steady, but before I know it they're moving. Going like a thing, that thing you use for beating eggs. Slow at first, then faster; one over and around the other until they blur.

An eggbeater. Lucinda complains that that old one of ours sticks. She's always saying it's time we joined the twentieth century and got an electric one.

My hands. Turning like the blades of that old red-handled beater.

A Cuisinart is what Lucinda wants: a quease-in-art.

I stay fixed on that puck.

Loo-cin-da. Without moving my eyes, I roll the name over my tongue, as I have every day since she came into the world

The puck disappears. A buzzer sounds. My hands go limp.

Like the feel of an icy palm on my back, it strikes me that she's gone, she's been gone for hours.

And suddenly I can't put my finger on where.

That niece of mine doesn't come home till after midnight, long after the game is over. I've dozed off, perhaps, concentrating so hard on that tiny dark dot on the screen. Like someone out of a dream she startles me, marching in in her coat and snapping off the television. She nearly sends me out of my skin.

"Dora?" I blink. There's the tightness of dried spittle on my lips; I realize I have been asleep. "Oh, it's you dear. Home already. Did you have a nice time?"

Lucinda smiles wearily, looking every inch her age. Some of that mascara she stroked on earlier has slid to her cheeks, giving her a bruised, tender look. That gaudy lipstick is faded like a pink bathing cap left too long in the sun. But she is happy — oh yes, I can see from her eyes she is happy. Not a spark, exactly, but a glimmer. In her gloved hand is a pink carnation, the stem a bit crushed.

"Just a minute while I put this in water."

I grasp her sleeve as she starts to bustle off.

"Never trust a man who gives you flowers," I say. She looks at me with the snapping eyes of a muskrat, and helps me off the couch as one would a child.

"Win anything?" I shake her off: I don't need aid to stand on my own.

She folds her arms, that sad, frostbitten blossom clasped tight. Coy as a princess half her age, she says, "Nothing to speak of, Aunt Ruby. They were giving these out at the door. A consolation prize."

"Good night, Lucinda."

She makes no move to kiss me, afraid perhaps that I'll smell something on her. Smoke? The garlicky stink of liquor?

"Good night, dear," I say once more, catching a whiff of the Legion, that stale smell of beer, boiled tea, date squares and a thousand cigarettes. Old Spice too, I suspect, one brand or another of some foul-smelling substance men wear — or perhaps it's Thrills I smell, that strong purple gum that masks breath odours.

"Night-night, Ruby!" She squirms away from me, eager as a fox to vanish, safe, into that room of hers.

Needless to say, sleep refuses to come, the result I suppose of napping. I lie beneath the covers in my nightclothes, listening to Lucinda's snore next door.

This is the bed I once shared with Leonard — hard to imagine now, his soft, hefty body lying here. I've slept alone since 1934 — way before his accident, some eight years before — night after night, countless orbits of the moon. Until eventually I scarcely noticed being by myself.

I prefer the middle, always have. Even when Leonard was alive, I would roll against him in the night and force him to the edge. Our bodies spooned together, partners while asleep if not awake.

In through the nose, out through the mouth, goes Lucinda's breath, the most torturous sound you can imagine coming from the other room. It rattles around her sinuses, exits her windpipe with a godawful *pfoufff, pfoufff,* over and over and over again, like that truck of hers pinking, like something worn out and hardly human.

Finally I get up and shut the door, softly, but tight.

My husband was tall, a bulky man, in fact; his size was accentuated by his suit the first time I laid eyes on him. It was light green — the colour of willow buds, I think, lying here on my back; a shade crisp and cool as these sheets.

This was my impression of him, the first time Leonard walked into the store.

It was a Saturday, mid-spring. Things were quiet, most everyone home cleaning house and yard before the warmer weather. I was dusting tobacco tins, trying to ignore Father's anxious shifting from foot to foot behind the counter, which he did when time dragged.

"Bring a chair down from the kitchen," Mum used to suggest, but he considered it bad for business to be seen lounging behind the cash — a sign of laziness if not an utter lack of industry. When my legs ached from standing, he would tell me to pluck up, there was no reason for boredom or resignation. It was 1928, no one had cause yet to feel that way.

All the same, we took our sweet time serving the fellow in the suit. I caught his eye and kept dusting, waiting for Father to help him. I could feel him watching me, oh yes, as he cleared his throat and spoke up.

"Amphora, please, and a packet of pipe-cleaners while you're at it."

I was all of twenty-one years old. I had my shiny black hair scraped back with pins to keep it out of my way while handling merchandise. I wasn't used to scrutiny, I can tell you, especially from strangers, and the man's gaze made me balky and uncomfortable.

"You heard the fellow," Father muttered, moving away from the counter to empty some nails into a bin. Leaving me to it. Hardly glancing up from his work, he tried his best to sound jovial. "What else can we do ya for today? How's about an ice-cream or a nice cold drink, it being so lovely out?"

I couldn't help rolling my eyes, ringing in the tobacco and handing the man his change. He had a broad face, and his eyes looked narrow and bright as he pocketed his wallet and touched the brim of his fedora. But it was his hands I noticed, pale and small, incongruously so for a man his size.

He paused to slit the tobacco seal with his thumbnail. Father came and leaned against the big brass register, his hands inside his starched white apron.

"Do I know you from somewheres?"

I picked up the duster and started on some liniment bottles. Still smiling, the fellow shrugged.

"Clarke's the name, sir. Leonard Clarke, from over Caledonia way."

"Oh, yeah. And what's your line down there?" Father's voice was wary, remote. Like the scale weighing up dry goods: gauging, measuring.

"Cookies." The fellow tugged at his hat and nodded. Going out the door, he ducked his head in that instinctive manner of very tall people. From the yard we heard a motor turn over, the gentle crush of tires.

"Leonard Clarke," said Father, speaking, as he often did, without looking at me. "He's the one runs the big bakery down there. Makes dough hand over fist, I hear." He sucked in his cheeks, smiling at his little pun. "Done pretty good, too, from what I hear — a fellow his age."

You would know, I thought. The man looked to be in his mid-thirties, but in Father's opinion anyone in business under the age of fifty was "young" and therefore to be admired for his single-minded tenacity. I'd worked steadily in the store since finishing school, not to mention days and weekends from the time I was old enough to count. But in Father's mind I was simply his daughter, forever a child. My helping out was more a matter of duty than an effort deserving praise. Dora of course would have none of this, and being younger she was somehow exempt.

A few days later Mr. Clarke dropped in again, this time in shirtsleeves, without a tie, his collar loose and open. I was cutting a length of gingham for somebody.

"Cigarettes today, and a vanilla cone." He tapped his box of matches against the counter as Father slid quickly behind the register.

I pretended not to see him, intent on helping my customer find the right colour thread. When he left, though, I watched through the display of rubber boots and fishing tackle in the window. He got into a big blue car and handed the ice-cream to a girl in the front seat. From a distance it was hard to tell, but even to me she looked awfully young, high school age perhaps. His daughter? I thought not.

Another week or two passed before he returned, dressed once more in his suit. I was outside helping Father pile sacks of feed when his car pulled up. He smiled when he saw me brushing dust from my apron.

"Any idea where a fella can get a tankful of gasoline?" he wanted to know, looking right through my father. I started giving directions to a place a few miles past Ferrona while Father pushed up his sleeves and began mumbling apologies.

"You should put some pumps out front," Mr. Clarke told him. "Loads of people travel this road nowadays. I bet you'd do all right here. That garage in Hopewell is a bit of a hike." It struck me funny the way he said "graaage", like some of the farmers who'd come into town to order parts for their Massey-Harrises.

"Gotta spend money to make money," he went on, and I could see Father bristling. "People always got to have gas, Mr. Lewis — good excuse for staying open longer, too."

"Longer hours don't mean people've got more to spend, now," Father tried to joke. "Can't spend money they don't have."

"Credit."

"A'ready give them plenty of that."

"Well, give 'em more and charge int'rest." I could tell Mr. Clarke was enjoying this. He glanced over and winked at me busy sweeping up spilled grain. I wasn't so busy, though, that I missed the look Father gave him.

"That's the way she goes these days, Mr. Lewis."

"Silas," my father interjected. "This here's my girl Ruby."

"Well, if you can't sell me gas I guess I'll take a Fanta," he said, hardly batting a eye. "Could use a drink for the drive down to Hopewell." Oh, the way he said it, as if he were being forced to travel by foot through wilderness, to the absolute ends of the earth!

He followed me into the store, left the coins on the counter when I put down his change.

"Keep it," he said, "and get yourself a soda. Looks like you could use a nice cool one too."

I pushed the money towards him. His fingers brushed mine as he went to pick it up. He grinned at me, this time with the intentness of a serious shopper, someone with a certain product in mind, not just a tire-kicker. As though he'd made up his mind what he wanted, had already run up the figures.

So I wasn't all that surprised when he showed up the following Saturday. He motioned to my father and asked if he could "borrow" me for a minute, to step outside with him for a breath of fresh air. What did surprise me was Father saying, "I s'pose," as if this were someone we'd known our whole lives, and not some stranger off the road.

Outside, he leaned against the fender of his shiny big Ford, lighting a cigarette while I slowly untied my apron and watched to see what he'd do.

The sun was brilliant, crocuses were splayed and fading under the maple in the yard, the breeze was filled with the smell of grass burning in the field opposite.

He clenched his cigarette between his teeth and reached through the window, brought out a bunch of daffodils wrapped in pale blue paper.

"For you," he said offhandedly, waiting for me to come closer.

"Why?" I blurted, embarrassed, my hands flying up to fix a stray hairpin. You don't even know me, I was about to protest, when out of the corner of one eye I caught a movement, the jerky blur of someone in the shade beside the building. A flash of reddish hair. My sister, Dora, watching.

VII

Mayflowers

"Oh, don't be shy," he said, "I feel I know you. Not every woman would stick around helping out like this. But you, now, Ruby, I can see you got ambition, you got a lot upstairs."

Tapping his temple, he loosened his tie and smiled again, this time almost shyly, reminding me of an overgrown schoolboy. With crooked teeth, I noticed, crowded together on the bottom, a big gold filling on one side.

"I bet your old man has no idea how much you put into his business."

I stepped back up onto the stoop, waiting for Dora to come around to the front and start teasing about the daffodils. They were a clammy weight in my arms, the petals sticky and wilted from the sun. I was wondering how on earth I'd explain them.

"It's a family business," I heard myself pipe up. "I expect to be running things one day."

"O'course."

I remember Leonard squinting then at the smoke wafting from the field across the road; shrugging, and bending down to inspect one of his tires.

"I s'pose it does pretty good then, only store like it for miles around. Must be worth your while, bright gal like you. Worth hanging around for, I guess."

Offended, I stepped down and thrust his bouquet at him.

"Maybe you should keep your daffs, Mr. Clarke. Perhaps they'd do you better someplace else."

I can't believe my pluck; I'm not even sure I can explain it. But without a glance back, I fled into the store.

"Leonard, please call me Leonard," he shouted after me, and I could just imagine my sister later, mimicking him. Peeking through the fly rods in the window, I watched him take off his hat and stand there a minute, those limp flowers in his arms, before he got into his car and backed onto the road.

"You off your head, or what?" Father muttered, staring after him. "That Clarke fellow is one force to be reckoned with, Ruby. You could do a lot worse than him."

For a whole month Leonard stayed away. I tried my best to forget about him, would click my tongue in disgust any time my father or Dora brought him up. "Where's your fella, huh, Ruby?" She'd flutter her lashes and fling her wrist to her brow in giddy mockery. "Isn't he awfully old, Ruby? What-all do you s'pose is under that suit? Huh? And wouldn't you just like to find out?"

"Go jump in the swamp." She was a gigantic bee in my bonnet. A fifteen-year-old bundle of highjinks, bouncy as an Irish setter, and pretty, pretty as all get-out, with hair that same glossy red. But silly, constantly silly, and strung like a wire fit to snap.

"I don't know who you're speaking of, Dora. You're talking through your hat."

I was completely unprepared when he strode in one afternoon, a sheepish smile on his face, holding that fedora in his hands. He came and leaned against the counter; the wireless was blaring full-blast from the office out back. Father was beside me, listening to the ball game, the Yankees playing the Red Sox. Babe Ruth had just hit a homer.

"I hear the mayflowers are out down by the river." My father gave me a nudge. "Why don't you and Mr. Clarke go take a little walk?"

I was scowling, trembling a bit in spite of myself, as I laid down my apron and went outside, not waiting to see if he followed. I was wearing a pink short-sleeved blouse, my arms folded against the chilly breeze. Without a word, I led him through the shortcut across the field to a bend where the river frothed like rootbeer. Limbs of trees and pieces of wood skimmed past, and chunks of earth spiked with frost. But I kept going, knowing where to look, finally stooping at a spot where the sun warmed the bank. I started rooting under the dead leaves for some shiny new ones.

Leonard reached down — Lord, with my eyes closed I can see the fine red-gold glint of hair on the backs of his hands — and plucked a tiny sprig of sweet pink blossoms. To my amazement, he took a whiff and stuck it in his lapel.

"Too bad a fella can't bottle that."

I shielded my eyes for a better view of him.

"Yes," I said, startled. "I...I'd venture to say you're right." It sounded just like Father, and I couldn't help but let out a twitter almost as girlish and silly as Dora's. Leonard scratched under his hat, not quite sure what he'd done.

"So. Can I at least getcha to call me by my first name now?"

Already I was ahead of him, picking my way over rocks and fallen branches, but I turned and glanced back.

"I imagine," I said, "I imagine I could do that."

Leonard started coming around regularly, often driving the twenty-two miles from Caledonia three, sometimes four evenings a week. Mum began asking him to supper, which we always took late, after everything was closed up for the night. As spring stretched into summer, we'd spend the long, warm evenings upstairs in my family's flat, the windows thrown wide to cool the place off. My parents and Leonard and me; I don't know where Dora took off to, skipping supper. Out lounging around the bridge perhaps, with the other teenagers. She never could stay still, let alone spend a summer's night inside.

Leonard would sit sprawled on the horsehair settee, loosening his tie in the stuffy heat while Father discussed the day's profits and Mum served tea. It was usually too warm for hot drinks, and Leonard and Father would set theirs down to cool. Then baseball would come on and Father would turn up the radio, the two of them craning forward, listening, until their tea skinned over, and Mum or I would get up to take it away.

In company Leonard was quieter, more modest, his large body awkward and out of place somehow in our comfortable but somewhat cramped quarters. After supper he'd move cautiously from the table to the lumpy settee, as if the rooms themselves were too small for him, the fancy moulded ceilings too low. I assumed his care was due to the number of knick-knacks, of cabinets crammed with Mum's china vases and ornaments, fancier items that hadn't sold downstairs. Once settled, Leonard scarcely moved until it was time to leave, except to stretch his legs and shift his weight. Then I would see him below to his car, where he'd bend and gently kiss my cheek.

My parents never mentioned our difference in age — maybe because around them, shedding his bravado, he seemed younger. What's more, he seldom suggested the prospect of us spending time together alone, or passing our evenings any differently. Going to a movie down in Caledonia, for instance. Or making an excursion in his car: north, along the river to Westchester, to the falls beyond the railway pass; or south to the Bay of Fundy, to sit and watch the tide. There were so many places we could have got to, things we could have done.

Yet I never feared he'd stop coming to spend these long, slightly uncomfortable evenings; and he never indicated that my parents might be in the way. He sat quietly through his visits, listening politely to Father's advice on retail. Only once did he respond with advice of his own. "Give any more thought to puttin' in those gas pumps, Mr. Lewis? You got to think of your customers' needs, you know."

Not long after, British Petroleum arrived to install two tall red glass-topped pumps in the dirt out front.

"Good on your head," said Leonard on his next visit, ignoring my father's complaints about more work, about the interruptions running back and forth to fill people's tanks.

"Fill 'er up," he quipped to Mum pouring his third cup of tea, which he sipped, grinning at me. I had the good sense, of course, to keep quiet. It suited me to be excused from a new line of operation so obviously men's work. Mum was careful, too, to stay out of these conversations. She'd flit around instead, arranging the big bunches of dahlias Leonard brought in appreciation of her cooking.

But more and more often the flowers would be for me. I couldn't help blushing, filling the vases with water. For in the mornings there would be Dora slouching at the table in her nightgown, picking off showers of petals, leaving the centres bare as plucked hens. "He loves me, he loves me not." And I would think what a lucky thing it was that she had her friends and made herself scarce on those evenings.

Sometimes I tried to imagine what might've taken place had my parents been absent, not always there with us in the same room. But Leonard was such a gentleman, curiosity took a back seat to my confidence in him.

As summer wore on — twilight coming earlier and earlier, and baseball season heating up — our evenings together seemed further circumscribed, any chit-chat cut short by the radio. Yet, once established, the pattern didn't change; even on the muggiest days, Mum cooked as though it were winter, or as if we'd toiled all day in factories and fields. Leonard would sit back and watch as she filled his plate and passed it over, then tuck into the meal as though he'd driven all the way from Caledonia to enjoy it. I'd slip my shoes off under the table and wiggle the kinks from standing all day out of my toes, and try to eat with small dainty bites even if I was starving.

During supper no one spoke much, beyond polite requests to pass the salt or the butter or the green tomato chow-chow; we were too busy eating to ponder conversation. Afterwards, Leonard would retire with Father to the parlour while Mum and I cleaned up. If Leonard had anything to say about his own business, he found little opportunity, but this never appeared to bother him. He seemed content listening to my father's talk broken only by an announcer's patter. The way Leonard dressed and brought flowers assured us that things were going well at the bakery, very well indeed.

Heavens, what time is it? At least that blessed racket from Lucinda's room has finally ceased! But now I hear her rustling in bed — the covers being thrown back? She gets up and next I hear her in the bathroom, running water; the squeak of the medicine cabinet. Perhaps that *was* liquor I smelled when she came in, and she's paying for it now.

Lips that touch likkah shall nevah touch mine.

Dora? *Dora?* Sweet Moses, her voice travels back to me real as can be, as if through an open window.

Her fifteen-year-old's voice haranguing, always wanting to *know*. Daring me, tempting me. That night, for instance, after one of Leonard's visits: he and I standing outside by the car in the moonlight; it was a fingernail moon canted like a bowl in the sky. Leonard reaching into the glovebox, bringing out a small silver flask. Whisky, rum, who knows where he got it. Taking a swig, then offering it to me, a restless, edgy look in his eyes. And Dora's voice wafting down from somewhere — who'd seen her slip inside? — sweet as pie, mocking:

Lips that touch likkah....

I didn't accept his drink then and I wouldn't now, not even if Leonard came back from the grave.

Shame on that niece of mine, my sister's girl, drinking and carrying on like a hussy.

"Lucinda?" I call out, to make sure she's all right.

"It's nothing, Aunt Ruby," she trills. "Go on back to sleep."

Nothing, indeed. I reach for a tissue on the night table and give my nose a good long blow.

Skulking around just like your mother. Shame, shame on you, Lucinda.

Things changed around Labour Day. One evening Dora and I were tidying up the kitchen. We'd had pork roast, and she'd stuck around long enough to dine. Anxious to be off with her friends, she kept sulking, giving the dishes such a desultory wipe that afterwards I had to get them back out and dry them properly.

From the doorway I could see the others in the parlour — my father and Mum on the settee, Leonard in an unaccustomed seat in the corner. Father, the saucer balanced on his knee, was sipping his tea as if through a sieve. Leonard had his hands folded, the sleeves of his blazer pulled up above his narrow wrists. His head cocked towards the radio, he was listening to an ad for Lifebuoy soap. His face looked open and smooth as a child's, flushed with the lingering warmth of Mum's scalloped potatoes. A shaft of dying sunlight lit up his reddish glistening of beard.

"Mr. Clarke's got something he'd like to ask you, I believe," Father prompted, and Leonard's eyes leapt up, warming as I came and stood in the doorway, a tea towel full of forks in my hand. He had half risen and started to open his mouth when Father cut in.

"If you were to get married, you could both take over the business."

Mum smiled into her teacup. I just stared at Leonard, waiting for him to say something — anything — and for my parents to disappear to the kitchen.

"Excellent idea, I think. Whaddya say, Ruby?"

Leonard stalked over and took my hand in his. His fingers felt clammy; little white beads of sweat stood out above his lip. My parents stayed sitting. Father had a pinched expression on his face. Through the window I heard a car driving past, the restless chirr of crickets. I pulled my hand away and smoothed the waist of my dress — it was a mauve dress, I can still see it; the shade a little matronly for me, yet quite becoming....

If only he'd stooped, I thought afterwards. Gotten down on one creased knee and eyed me beseechingly as they did in the movies; or said something, something as simple as his remark about the mayflowers. Thank the Lord, though, that my sister wasn't present. Imagine the snickering and carrying on had she been there!

I could feel my parents' gaze, their eyes upon me in the twilit room. Father started in with his list of complaints — having too much to do, getting too old to be running the show and putting in every waking hour behind the counter. Since we'd gotten the gas pumps, business had increased, it was true; and lately I'd been working extra time ordering feed and yard goods, filling in bit by bit where my father seemed to slacken. As summer had progressed I'd noticed his lack of attention, even when men came in off the road and stood around smoking pipes and talking. Men jawing away till they happened to notice me behind the flour bin, or straightening the medicines and tonics. And they say it's women who gossip.

All of this ran through my head as Leonard squeezed my hand.

"Well," I said, when at last I summoned the nerve to answer, "I guess we'd make decent partners." Mum raised her cup in relief.

"Good, then." My father nodded, perfunctory as if closing a hardware deal, and went back to slurping tea.

"To a long and profitable life together." Leonard laughed uncomfortably and gave me a quick, rather slippery kiss on the lips. Mum suppressed a wistful smile.

"There now, Ruby," she said, "Looks like you'll have life by the tail, my girl — a business *and* a loving husband. Who on earth could ask for better'n that?" She made it sound like bringing in a new nutbar and selling out at top dollar.

Father got up and went downstairs — we could hear him through the hot-air grate, unlocking the backroom safe. He returned with a bottle of sarsaparilla, and sent Mum scurrying off for glasses. He poured himself and Leonard each a fair-sized toast which they downed in a couple of swallows.

"To your good health, Ruby, and to your fiancé. A better mate you wouldn't find!"

Leonard didn't flinch at the way Father said "feeancee" or at this display of glee. In keeping with his relegation of chores, it seemed suddenly natural — indisputable — that Father should so happily hand over the reins.

Two months later we were married, at the little Baptist church in Ferrona. On our wedding day, Father signed everything over to Leonard and me. Dora barely took notice, preoccupied like any young girl with her hair and the length of her hem. Mum's only concern was that the ceremony wasn't closer to home, our old church in Arcadia having burned down in the fire and none having been built to replace it.

Outside the chapel my groom beamed from ear to ear. I was all in white, my arm looped through his. It was a brilliant October morning, the sky a perfect cloudless blue, scarlet maple leaves wafting and swirling along the road. We had a photographer come all the way up from Caledonia. He took such a lovely picture that Leonard wanted it hung in the store — at which I laughed, of course, and said no. The King, perhaps, but no politicians and certainly not family!

Until Lucinda took over, I did keep a little portrait of the Queen — that fetching one from better days, her white shoulders bared, purple sash slung over her gown and jewelled tiara on her head. It hung for years behind the cash, right above the doorway. But after much hinting, Lucinda talked me into moving it to the parlour — which isn't so bad, I suppose, as the lamplight brings out the diamonds, the richness of that sash....

But the wedding photo — oh my! For a while Leonard was quite insistent.

"It'd be kinda nice, don't you think? Give customers a feeling of stability, you know, that just 'cause things have changed hands doesn't mean——"

"They don't need to see my mug to know we're here to stay. Yours neither, Leonard Clarke."

Oh, I could see he was hurt, though I meant no offence.

I scratch my head in wonder now, I do, at how I used to stand up to him.

At the time I figured this whole foolish debate over a photo was his notion of flattery. But he was serious. And soon enough I realized just how full of ideas Leonard was for boosting profits. Nice little touches, nothing mean or calculating — or so I thought. In the early days, I put everything down to his business sense, the fact that here was a man who could build something out of nothing. His cookie business, for instance, had started as a one-room bakeshop during the Great War, when Leonard was barely out of his teens. He never did explain how he got the money to start up. But by the time we met, he'd gone into cookies exclusively.

"The cat's whiskers," he told me once, early in his visits. "A quick, modern snack — and everybody likes 'em." At the time I was skeptical; who'd buy something everyone and their dog could make at home for half the price?

"Don't be old-fashioned," he used to tease. "Can't you see, Ruby? Convenience — the cat's *ass* nowadays!" He could get deliberately coarse if he thought I was being stubborn.

On one rare occasion during our courtship, he drove me down to Caledonia and showed me around the bakery — a factory really, abuzz with workers in white aprons and caps, and on a Saturday yet, filling huge ovens with sheets and sheets of cookies. Oatmeal, raisin, molasses — and gingersnaps, the loveliest ones, so spicy they made the tip of your tongue tingle. I was a bit put out, of course, that we hadn't used the afternoon to *go* somewhere — to a matinee, perhaps, at the Bijou; to see Ronald Coleman in *Two Lovers*, or Greta Garbo in *The Mysterious Lady*. All the same, I couldn't hide the fact that I was impressed.

That summer his business did so well that Leonard was able to pay another man to run things while he took time off to be with us. This was part of his deal with Father — between them, they decided that the hours Leonard spent away from the bakery could be put into the store. Longer and longer hours, as it turned out, by the time he and I set up house in the rooms behind the store.

As for my folks being just upstairs, Leonard never seemed to mind particularly. Oh, in the evenings we'd hear them creeping around up there like mice, muffled snippets of their conversation — raised voices, later on, when it was discovered that Dora had a fellow, that fellow being Albert, whom it turned out she was meeting nights down by the bridge. She was all of seventeen or eighteen and by then I was happy enough to turn a blind eye and deaf ear to her doings.

If Leonard and I were eating supper and an argument erupted upstairs, I'd glance at the ceiling, then give him an apologetic look. It always worked, even when Dora was being defiantly shrill. We'd hear her talking back, slamming doors and tripping downstairs. Leonard would say diplomatically that it was good having my family handy in case something arose in the store requiring Father's know-how. As for my parents themselves, well, sometimes after Dora's outbursts, Mum would tiptoe downstairs, white-faced, with a ham or a pie. She'd say how lovely it was to have an agreeable son-in-law, one so patient, whose head hadn't swelled from all that success.

So, despite the turbulence upstairs, for the first couple of years we managed very well — the store and the cookie business, that is. Then one day Leonard got a telephone call from Halifax. I thought nothing of it, being quite content to keep out of Leonard's affairs as the store took all my attention. To be honest, I never thought too much about anything in those days, besides ringing up flour and cutting lengths of broadcloth.

Good thing, too, since any expectations I may have had about married life went out the window, quickly as the smell of one of Mum's roasts after supper. It's not as though I was some giggling young slip of a thing, never mind my age. I was no crashing beauty, of course, though Leonard was hardly immune to the charms I did possess — I know that. My shiny hair, my level-headed quickness.

Before marriage I had done some reading. I would be the first to admit that on that muggy afternoon driving down to Caledonia, I'd glanced across the seat at him and wondered, not without calculation, what he might look like under those nicely pressed clothes. Once he caught me looking and pulled onto the shoulder, taking my chin in his hand and kissing me long and deep — well, longer and deeper than he ever managed after we'd been married a while. But then he stepped on it and we were on our way again, suddenly shy with each other, at a loss somehow in the strange, palpable absence of my parents.

"Oh Ruby." I remember him clicking his tongue, gazing into the rear-view mirror. "What would your father say, huh?"

Of course, I thought once we were wed he'd be as curious as I.

Next door Lucinda starts making that noise again, that long, wet snore. Sound asleep, she must be — yet how can she make such a racket and not wake herself up? Oh dear. That wide, loose trap of hers, I can picture it, like a door blowing open and shut.

Leonard accused me once of talking in my sleep. "I don't think so." I was very quick to set him straight. "It was simply your imagination, dear."

"I'll bet your sister wouldn't do that," he said, "wouldn't rant and ramble on like that while she was snoozing. While she was under...."

He hardly ever mentioned her, Dora; this was one of the few times he did.

He was lying right here, in the middle of this very bed. The mattress had such a sag he was practically on top of me; I had to push with both feet to get enough room.

"What do you mean by that?" I asked him. And he rolled over then, let out a big *hmph,* cheeks puffed out in disgust, arms folded. His fleshy white back to me.

"Wouldn't you like to know."

VIII

Sex

The darkness at the window begins to pale. Dawn, slow as syrup. It's January.

Lovely winter light melts like butter through the curtains. There's silence now from Lucinda's room. I curl my toes in the cosy softness of the sheets. This gentle shadowland of early morning. The day, the date, escapes me. The year—? But it *is* January. Of course. January — I know by the light.

I'll lie here a while longer, till Lucinda wakes. However long that is. I'll pretend to be asleep while she rises and does what she needs to in the bathroom. I'll lie here till the coffee's made, till the smell drifts in, sweet yet bitter, a smell that reminds me of burlap and dubbin and stained oak floors. I will lie here until I remember it's time to get up....

After the service we drove all the way to Halifax, Leonard and I.

"Take a couple of days now, enjoy yourselves!" Father said. "A fellow only gets married once — can't be all work, can it? Got to have some play too. Don't worry, Effie and I'll mind things while

90

you're gone." If I hadn't been so preoccupied, I'd have thought he was trying to get rid of us.

Leonard had booked a room at the Lord Nelson, opened just the week before. The best place money could buy in 1928. From somewhere, and goodness knows I hate like the dickens to speculate, he managed to wangle some real French champagne. He had a waiter bring a bucket of ice upstairs with our bags — his brashness still makes me shudder. In the room he pulled the bottle from his suitcase and insisted I try some, which, given the occasion, I admit I did. I wasn't too sure about the taste, however; it must be an acquired one. The champagne made my eyes sting, made me want to sneeze.

Leonard was sitting at a small mahogany table by the window. "To the future," he said, raising his wineglass. He stood to gaze at the cars and people in the street below. I set down my glass and sat upon the bed, fingering the green and gold brocade spread and trying to imagine what it cost. Leonard stayed at the window, clasping his glass by the stem. I took off my shoes and stretched out, smoothing the crisp netted skirt of my going-away frock. After a while he drew the shades — goodness knows why, I thought, we had to be five storeys up; the only ones able to see in were pigeons and gulls from the gardens across the street.

The rest unfolded much as I had deduced from books — books a customer had special-ordered once from the States. I'd skimmed them before wrapping them up in brown paper and handing them to the man, an unlikely-looking farmer from Westchester, when he came to make his purchase.

In his undershirt Leonard was fatter than I'd expected, his chest white as halibut beneath the patchy reddish hair. His stomach rolled slightly over the waistband of his pants, I noticed, when he finally unbuckled his belt.

I had hoped at this point he would proceed slowly, as I liked to imagine lovers doing between scenes in movies: dashing Douglas Fairbanks, Sr. carefully undressing sweet-faced Mary Pickford, undoing a button here, planting a kiss there. Instead Leonard was quick and perfunctory, though not as athletic, I decided, as a batter stealing bases. That's how I pictured it, my eyes fixed on the porticoed ceiling as if I were hovering there, somehow outside myself observing the pair on the bed below.

I thought of us in the parlour with my parents while Babe Ruth cracked the ball into the radio outfield, the fans going crazy.

Afterwards, Leonard got up and finished off the champagne, still wearing his underwear. When he crawled back into bed he touched my shoulder and asked if I'd like to get dressed and go down to the ballroom. There was an orchestra, he said, a swarm of reporters, a gathering of doctors for some sort of Dominion-wide convention. "Don't you want to be part of the hoopla, Ruby? Enjoy the novelty of all this stuff?"

I'd even had a pale blue pongee dress made especially for dancing — no mean feat, living under Father's roof. But I begged off, telling Leonard I was tired. And he put on his pinstriped suit, rather creased from the trip, and went downstairs alone. Shortly after midnight he returned, yawning and smelling of cigars and whisky.

Later, after we set up house together, I was too busy learning how to keep ledgers to feel disappointed or fret that I might be missing something. Many nights Leonard would fall asleep the second he hit the pillow; he'd mumble how tired he was running two businesses. Of course, as time proved, I was the one with the greater interest in the store. Especially after the blow-up with Dora, set off by her demands for a place on the retail side — a regular job that, Mum interceded, would allow her less time for catting around with Albert Hammond and more for serious pursuits. But Leonard said no. The truth was, he didn't feel like paying someone for things I already did for nothing. But after this, I became the person to whom Father passed advice.

The first year or two I fancied having a little baby, like those happy mothers depicted on boxes of soap. At first I was hopeful despite my husband's lack of interest. But as the months passed and it grew clear that a baby wasn't in the offing, a bit of a load came off my mind. I didn't see how I could run the store and take care of the apartment and a child too. Though Mum had managed well enough when Dora and I were small, helping Father out by doing chores he hadn't time for. Dusting, stocking tinned goods, cutting material, rolling pennies. Mum had managed, swinging

Dora in a cradle behind the counter and later, when Dora started to walk, cleaning up the messes she made of Mum's shelves.

To be truthful, the question of children never actually arose between Leonard and me. There wasn't time our first year together, after the trouble with Dora; and all too soon, the very next fall, came the market crash. Then, for the first time in my memory, we had to struggle to keep things out of the red, and not long after, the cookie business went under. Just like that, like the puff of smoke from a burnt batch of brownies, or our earliest shipments of Coca-Cola: here today, gone tomorrow. The bank in Halifax started calling and calling; Leonard was driving back and forth from Caledonia daily. Too late. Luxury items, people said, treats. The first things to go when money is short.

Losing the bakery was a blow, and Leonard took it hard. Towards the end, he laid off the fellow he'd hired to watch over things; by then, of course, there wasn't much to oversee. Leonard began staying overnight in Caledonia — to save on gas, he told me. Though I suspected it was to drink and spare himself the drive home. Even after the bank stepped in and repossessed the big brick building, he continued going down there two or three days a week. Tying up loose ends, he said.

It wasn't till a few years later that I discovered there was more to it than that. One day I was weighing brown flour, a half-pound for a lady with a coupon, while exchanging some tea with someone else for a dozen eggs, when I happened to hear two men over by the pop cooler, talking. They were fellows I hadn't seen around before. Leonard was out back unloading some sacks of sugar when his name came up; I couldn't help hearing it over my customers' banter. One of the men, a rough-looking sort in overalls, seemed to leer as he spoke. Something about Leonard and some girl at the bakery, someone named Jeanine. I had to struggle to remember her — a skinny, surly-faced girl whose job was packing sugar cookies in boxes once they'd cooled.

The woman trading eggs made a grab for them — just in time, too, as I spilled half the tea on the counter.

If those characters knew I was Leonard's wife, they never said. When they came over and asked for tobacco and rolling papers, I completed the sale avoiding their eyes. As they shuffled outside, I cracked open a roll of pennies. The egg woman patted my hand in gratitude. From the register I watched the fellows shamble out of sight along the dusty roadside. I never did find out who they were.

When Leonard stomped in lugging a big white bag of sugar, I made no move to help. I just stood there with my arms folded as he filled the bin and licked the stickiness off his fingers. I replaced the flour lid, steady as could be, and started slicing up a wheel of cheddar. But the knife slipped and bit into my hand; with a stunned calm, I watched the bright blood bead and trickle, sticky and warm as melted ice-cream. It was as if it were someone else's, the sight somehow amazing, cheering.

Leonard dashed over and tied his hankie around the wound, led me to the kitchen, where I held it under the tap till the water ran icy pink and numbed it. Afterwards, he brought a chair into the store for me and made me a cup of tea, which I took in silence. For the rest of the day I wouldn't speak, felt no reason to. A blinkered ass would've known something had happened, but he carried on as though nothing had. For more than a week I scarcely spoke beyond a mere yes or no when he asked, for instance, if an order of something had arrived, or whether we were having such-and-such for supper.

It wasn't easy continuing to share my life with Leonard while harbouring this awful suspicion about him — especially with my family so close by. The last thing I wanted was them suspecting things weren't right between us.

"You've got to put yourselves behind the business a hunnerd percent," I could just imagine Father grousing. With things so uncertain, up and down like a yo-yo, he'd grown crotchety about spending so much of his time upstairs, his fingers slipping steadily from what he feared was a mishandled, badly divided pie. Mum had her handiwork, of course, and kept busy knitting socks for farm children on the Prairies — though in those days, from what I saw in the store, there were plenty going barefoot under our noses.

As for Dora, no amount of coaxing could diminish her infatuation with Albert, who was working by then as a stationhand down at the railyard. She was almost twenty-one, had never worked a proper day in her life, not really, unless you counted testing face-powder and sampling confectionery. It was always her looks, poor thing, that got in Dora's way. My father considered her too flighty to be trusted with cash. Leonard felt the same — another reason, perhaps, for hedging on hiring her.

"All anyone's ever wanted of me is to look nice," I heard her once raging at Mum, their pitched voices shooting down the hot-air vent into our parlour. This was their last big kerfuffle before she ran off and married that deadbeat. To shock my parents, to tie their tongues once and for all — I'm sure that's why she finally did it. Flew off to Caledonia one evening with him, then called next morning to say they'd gone ahead, she and Albert had tied the knot, and there wasn't a ruddy thing Father or anybody else could do about it.

"That creature, why, oh why — of all people?" Mum sat at my kitchen table the whole next day, sobbing. The only time she took a break was when Leonard waltzed in with a box of fat Archies from Ben's, the big all-purpose bakery down in Halifax, and set a plateful in front of her to go with tea. That quelled her crying, nothing I said or did. "She could've had any fellow in the world, Dora could've. Any one she wanted. A girl like that, men would lie down in the road and get run over for!" She was still carrying on, long after I'd escaped to the store. To his credit, it was Leonard who stayed and listened, stroking and patting Mum's wrist, attentive as any son.

As for his attentiveness as a mate....

Well, a body can only go so long being partners with somebody and not speaking, not *really* speaking, and eventually I gave in and tried my best being civil and kind to mine. "My husband", I still called him if anyone asked, though by the time my sister gave birth to Lucinda, Leonard and I had stopped sharing a bed. This wasn't long after he complained of me talking in my sleep. "If you got something to say, Ruby, why don't you just spit it out, eh? Instead of mumbling on at night, whatever it is bothering you. You're disturbing my rest."

I made no bones about it, went right ahead and ordered in a mattress, single, and a fancy iron bedstead, white enamel with little gold touches. Very pretty, especially when things around us seemed so grim. "Leonard's a terrible sleeper," I told Mum.

I had my new bed moved into the little room off the kitchen;

I got a bolt of the best chintz in the store and spent one whole afternoon running up some curtains on Mum's old Singer. Spent an entire Saturday hanging the prettiest wallpaper we carried, a swirling pattern of ferns and daisies in maroon and cream, with a little striped border around the ceiling. I thought my arms would fall off, reaching up for so long, and me minding heights, perched on a chair. Leonard stayed out front the whole time, tending store; I heard him telling people I was spring-cleaning when they asked was I sick.

"Ruby's all right," I heard him say, brusque and chipper as if everything was hunky-dory, business as usual, and he solely in charge. "She's got her housework to catch up on, that's all." As for me having my own room, his only remark came after I'd finished decorating, when he stuck his head in for a look. "Pattern's kinda big for such a poky little space." He said "pat-tron", as I suppose he always had, except that now it irked me the same as if someone had licked the drip from the molasses, or broken a jar of pickles without paying. He should know better, I thought. I believe this is when my heart truly started to harden against him, bitterness coming in dribs and drabs at first, then steady as rain. Yet not without guilt. Both of us should've known better, I eventually saw, sharing as we did the same abode and place of livelihood. It wasn't as if ours was the normal way a married pair should live.

Good grief, to think I was only twenty-seven years old. Like Dora, I could have had any number of fellows interested — well, at least before I took the plunge and fell for Leonard. Or so it occurs to me, lying here in this sharp white light.

I wish Lucinda would wake.

I'm not saying I was beautiful, but pretty enough, what some might call striking. I was tall, tall with creamy pink skin; with a high forehead and my hair pulled back tight, I had a perfect widow's peak, my part just to the side of it. I had Father's long straight nose, Mum's fair complexion and, thank heavens, none of Dora's freckles. Why, there must be a picture somewhere, one taken before my wedding day. But not in the album, the old one Lucinda would sooner throw out than treasure. She's always been ignorant when it comes to family, though her heart's in the right place. "Why would I want to get to know a bunch of dead people" — that's her line — "when there are live ones I'd rather meet?"

"They're gone, Ruby, all gone." That's always on the tip of her tongue; she doesn't bother to stifle a yawn. I feel like telling her, "Maybe to you they're gone, but to me they're just, well, waiting."

I suppose today she'll sleep in forever. But it's a Sunday — yes, I remember now — so there's no real harm. Though once upon a time we'd be racing to get to church. Yes, Father, Mum and Dora and I in the buggy, closing our eyes passing the Catholic church, St. Bridgid's, not opening them till we'd stopped at the Baptist one next door; this would be before the fire, of course. Father's eyes would bulge a little from the tightness of his collar, but otherwise he was handsome, upright in his thin, meagre way.

Not a single church left now. Not a solitary place of worship, unless you consider the Kingdom Hall. The Jehovah's Witnesses in their red-brick bungalow beside the highways depot, hocus-pocus religion slotted next to the snowploughs. To me that doesn't count; not that it matters.

Speaking of kingdoms, hell could freeze over by the time Lucinda rouses herself on a day of rest — not that we observe them. Cold comfort to me, that woman. At this age my body's like that old truck of hers: you don't get it started, the parts are liable to seize.

But I don't need her to get my breakfast. I'll get it myself. And while the kettle's boiling I'll get dressed. Something gay for a change; my rose flowered dress, a chiffon scarf at the throat to hide the wattles.

Life is a gift, and I don't plan to spend what's left of mine lying down.

In the bathroom I give my teeth an extra cleaning; the smell of toothpowder brings back the days when I felt this lively every morning. Invigorated, refreshed, as though anything were possible despite the odds, the irritations. The way I felt when Dora was nursing her baby — the difference between us then! Poor Dora with her black-circled eyes, and weepy as a leaky tap. Poor Dora. I shouldn't laugh. But considering how motherhood weighed her down, in those days I was like the younger of us....

A few months after I got my own room, Dora gave birth. It was the longest day of the year, June 21, 1934. You should've seen my sister, all through pregnancy. Big as a horse, huffing and puffing everywhere she went, and cooling herself with these fans I'd make folding old torn-out catalogue pages accordion-style. As she fanned, you'd catch a glimpse of ladies' drawers here, pots and pans there.

Such a sight, though, Dora walking the road each day on her way over here to Mum's, her big cotton smocks billowing out each time a car passed. Pathetic, really, this gangly young girl so obviously in the family way, waddling along the ditch. Sometimes people would honk and stop to offer her rides. Strangers, mostly, since folks from town knew she and Albert lived only a hop and a skip away.

Towards the end, her hips spread so wide they looked almost comical, like hot tar under those smocks. She had to give up wearing the stylish little shoes she favoured, and she took to walking flat and square on her heels. Her ankles were so swollen that her stockings bunched and strained around them. I tried not to imagine her stomach, pale freckled skin stretched drum-tight. Disgusting, really. I'd try not to gape when she visited, though in truth her appearance filled me with awe — revulsion, more precisely, not easily disguised.

But there was one aspect of Dora's condition that agreed with her. By the end, it thickened her hair. She let it grow out (how typically Dora, given the mugginess that time of year), a solid glossy wave of red. Perhaps that's what attracted those drivers pulling up behind, not seeing her belly at first, or the slovenly set of her jaw, until it was too late.

Every morning she would climb the hill to see Mum. She'd stop into the store for a soda pop, and Leonard, uncommonly kind, would invite her to sit for a minute to catch her wind. Once when she raised the pop bottle I saw bruises, four neat bluish marks like fingerprints, high on one arm where her cap-sleeve flipped back. She noticed me looking and blushed, and her eyes went hot.

"I was shooting off a rifle, would you believe it? Albert was down at the station — God, it must've been midnight — and I heard this noise out back. So stupid of me; see how the thing kicked back? I thought I knew what I was doing."

Leonard glanced at me and said, "We never heard gunshots up the hill here. You should call us if you got trouble." Chummy as could be, he was, though all three of us knew he had no time for my sister. "You better tell that Albert to keep his shotgun locked up proper, where it belongs. A gal in your shape — who knows what creatures are out and about in the woods. A woman all alone like that; no telling who could up and walk right in." He shook his head, tut-tut, solicitous and sweet as all get-out. Dora gave him the eye, and me the smuggest little sneer that only I would pick up on. Then she barged right around behind the cash and through our kitchen to trudge upstairs. She was like the *Titanic*, that ocean liner of a body squeezing through a fjord.

That was about all we'd see of her, that one little stopover first thing in the morning. The rest of the day she'd sit upstairs with Mum passing her recipes, perhaps, or any secrets she might've possessed for helping Dora through this child bearing business. Being in the family way didn't suit my sister, not one bit. You could tell by her face; her expression was like a filly's — with a tire forced over its head. Oh, she knew how she looked. What's more, she acted as though the world were responsible and she herself had had nothing to do with it.

"We all have to pay for our fun, don't we dear," I heard Mum telling her once. I was upstairs dropping off some soap Mum needed, a yellow bar of laundry soap. Dora was sitting on a kitchen chair, watching Mum scoot from the stove to the washboard in the sink. A thick silence followed Mum's words, nothing but the thudding music of her fingers rubbing stains out of one of Father's shirts. Dora sat like a boulder, her arms folded on top of her belly. The look on her face was as if someone had just pried up the fresh-painted boards from under those swollen feet of hers.

Yessir, my sister dragged her condition around with her like a sled through a sand dune. But if pregnancy did anything besides fixing her hair, it closed the rift between her and Mum, the tear that was like a cloth ripped in two when Dora ran off and married

Albert. Somehow the prospect of being a mother wiped Dora's slate clean, as far as Mum went. I don't understand it myself. But for a while that spring and summer, those two were thick as thieves, trading what they called "war stories" and diapering tips. If anyone felt on the outs, it was me.

A baby.

Until Lucinda's birth, I'd pretty much shelved any hopes of having one of my own — at least with Leonard. Frankly, the moment I laid eyes on Dora's infant, I was scared skinny — and relieved. Yes, relieved, that such a creature, such a fate as caring for it, was not mine.

Dora's labour was deadly — no accident, perhaps, that it took place on the longest day; for all we knew, the gods planned it that way. Albert dropped her off on our doorstep around dawn that morning, saying he had something urgent at the station, and to call when there was news. Even at that hour you could smell it off him, some sort of liquor. He looked as though he'd slept in his clothes and had forgotten to shave. A handsome demon, you hated to admit. He was lean and dark, a little on the swarthy side — his looks quite the opposite of my husband's. His fine dark hair was always overly long and unkempt. If I could've put his dishevelledness down to Dora's distress that morning...but no, any fool could tell he'd been on a bender.

Dora was scared as a rabbit. Poor Dora. You could see she hadn't slept, no doubt up all night worrying about *him*. Her hair was a rat's nest, her face ghost-white; it would wrinkle up every time a pain took hold. She looked like a bleached raisin out there on the stoop in that tender, early light, her mouth pale and open, ready to holler until the next pain came and snatched out the sound. Of course, with Dora you never knew how much was histrionics.

You know what I thought, pushing her up the back stairs to Mum's? *Better you than me, girl*. Now that's a dastardly, selfish thing to feel, but I'd be lying if I pretended otherwise.

Near the landing something trickled from her, a few straw-coloured drops on the ochre steps. I thought she was wetting herself, but next the poor thing started clutching her stomach, crying out, so I let on as if the wetness were nothing. But as Mum opened her door there was a gush, soaking the back of Dora's dress and the roses hooked into the mat. A drop hit my shoe. I know it sounds callous, but all I could think was: Quick, find a rag, wipe it off, while Mum rushed my sister to her room. Dora's old room, with its narrow spool bed and its yellow quilt, and her cracked china doll, Tillie, on the pillow. What choice was there but to get dragged along too? As though Dora were a magnet, and Mum and I a couple of safety pins.

"I have a feeling Leonard needs me downstairs."

Oh, I tried worming out of it, compelled by the stuffiness of the room, the smell of whatever kept leaking from Dora. Hardly the rush of an open faucet I'd expected from the whisperings of women discussing confinements. But it was pink and fishy-odoured, foul with something Mum worried was from the baby.

A dry labour — this was the term bandied about once the doctor arrived. By then Father had slipped downstairs to sit with Leonard and read the *Chronicle*. I would have given anything to join them, to lug flour, scrub bins, even pump gasoline — to be anywhere but at Dora's bedside, gripping her damp, clawing hands, hearing her wails. The doctor came and went, came and went, it seemed, until we lost all track of time. Once — late in the afternoon, I believe — Leonard came stomping upstairs, thrust his head in.

"How's a fella to conduct business with the caterwauling up here?" he tried to joke. "Like a bunch of she-lions — a goddamn herd!"

"Pride," Mum muttered under her breath absurdly, pressing ice to my sister's brow. Dora looked barely human, her face and neck knotted, every line and pore wet. She looked unhinged, as though the person inside had run off, leaving behind this writhing misery of flesh. It was awful. Witnessing it, I promised myself that no man would ever put me in such a predicament, render me the likes of some half-witted, shrieking animal.

I was starving by this time, having eaten nothing since the night before. But I had no appetite at all, no stomach for so much as a biscuit or cup of tea. When the doctor finally came and stayed for the duration — sometime past midnight it must have been — the whole scene was like a nightmare. This creature I scarcely recognized panting on the bed, her body being turned inside out.

And the odour — like the meat chest between cleanings, the same sweet, raw, bloody smell.

I grew dizzy with hunger, so faint with exhaustion I barely heard Dora's screams when the baby finally emerged. It landed in the doctor's arms like a grappling, gasping fish, its red face screwed into a howl. Its skull looked bruised, the cord an unearthly glistening white. Vomit rose in my throat at the hideous plop of something — the afterbirth? — into a pail.

I was gagging by then, about ready to die, I'd say. The smell, the godawful smell! And the sound of Dora still panting, sobbing, but finally calm, and Mum tearing around like a hen with its head lopped off.

In one neat motion the doctor thrust the child at me. I wasn't ready. It almost flew from my arms, like a big slippery tongue.

Oh my God.

It fell to me to bathe her. Those wary but trusting blue-black eyes staring up at me; her shocked, frightened cry as the water licked her skin. My hands trembled fit to drop her.

This was my niece.

The doctor weighed her, this shivering little creature, in a scale like one you'd use to size a turkey.

"A healthy seven-pound girl; there's a reward for your efforts." He spoke soothingly — to Dora, I assumed. "You shouldn't have too much trouble keeping her warm now; it's a hot one tonight." To prove so, he mopped his forehead with a hankie, shuffling off to clean himself up. Mum bound the baby in mint-green flannelette and tried putting her to Dora's breast.

But by then Dora was sound asleep, past caring. From the stillness of her face, the cool, uncanny peacefulness, you'd have sworn that we'd lost her, that she'd gone and passed from us.

IX

Visiting

My land! Here it is ten o'clock and still no peep from Lucinda. A body could starve to death waiting for her to get up. Then again I'm not that hungry; oh yes, there was that bit of cereal I had — there's the bowl beside the sink, a mush of cornflakes stuck to it.

This awful confusion. It descends sometimes like a fog, falling out of nowhere and hanging over me the way mist hugs the fields on salt-damp days....

I'm up now, washed and dressed. My teeth have that scraped-clean feeling from the Pepsodent powder, same as when you take tea stains off with a sprinkling of baking soda.

Baking soda and vinegar always worked wonders for me.

My teeth feel so clean — I *must* have done them after the cereal. But I haven't had a drop of tea or coffee yet, something to get the blood moving. I know because there's no cup....

If I stop to plug in the kettle, Lucinda will come out here and interfere. She always does, lately. Watches me like some sort of owl or hawk, flitting and hovering.

If she spies me putting my coat on, she'll stand in my way. She will. Stop me.

It's Sunday, of course it is.

I'd just have to tell her, "You can't keep me from paying a social call."

"For goodness sake, Aunt Ruby." I can picture her rolling her eyes, throwing up her hands.

Sore Finger Hill. Of all the undignified names.

There. I put on my blue coat with the black mouton collar. Gloves. My navy knitted hat. A fur one to match my collar — that's what I covet. It would look so much more "pulled together". Isn't that the phrase they use in magazines, advising one how to dress?

Not that I ever needed to be told. I always have had decent taste, been perfectly capable of making myself attractive, of choosing colours that suit me. Green. Pine-tree green; it complemented my fairness, my hair before it went white.

I'll pull on these gloves, that's it, then slip out quietly. Before Lucinda wakes and wonders where I've gone.

I won't be long. Back in a jiffy. A quick breath of fresh air is what I need. Stretch these stiff old legs.

She won't miss me.

No one will.

I pull the porch door to, ever so gently so it doesn't creak. Such a heavy old door, panelled in the outline of a cross. A Christian door. Father would have wanted every door in the house to be like it.

Saturday, Sunday. Solomon Grundy....

The clear, cold air stings my face, my eyes. Tears well. I feel them spill onto my cheeks and stiffen.

All quiet out here on the road. There's a stubby brown beer bottle smashed in the ditch, left from last night? Shards of glass. Drinkers.

A grey half-ton speeds past. The backdraft sends me wobbling on the rough shoulder. Gravel bites into my soles, a draft of icy air gusting up my legs. Slacks would be warmer, more practical. But I prefer not to leave the apartment in them. There's something common about women wearing slacks. Though Lucinda does. Good God, she wears them so much you could mistake her for a man!

Silly, silly. The rough, rough road. A rough row to hoe. Sharp grey stones. Dig into my——

Feat — a feat, it was, to get outside like this without her hearing, without her coming after me....

Don't hold your breath. That could well be her I hear, her old truck rattling and growling down the hill.

Don't look back.

The Hill. I can just make out the gravestones stuck like teeth in the side.

A sudden pain knifeblades into the ball of one foot. I stare down; the road's shoulder is like a blue-grey brook of crushed stone. My eyes fix on my feet. My old blue slippers soft and gay as a May morning, and just as innocent, next to the cracked asphalt. There are grey bits of ice sticking to the plush.

Oops. Boots would've been better. But who's to see? To care?

Hurry, hurry. The fuzzy blue is like some sort of beacon amid all this grey. Quickly now, before Lucinda spots it.

I stop, toes frost-splinted, the wind swirling. A dancing duststorm of cold hard grit. Branches sieve the sky, gnarled fingers pointing. I feel a frozen weight to my limbs, yet the spirit-urge to dance. A lithe and lively two-step up the stony track.

Here. Turn right at what used to be the Templars' Hall. Rotted clapboard, paint peeling like blistered skin. Better days. Dancing feet.

No card-playing, no drinking and especially no dancing — not on the Sabbath.

Father.

Blue jays screech. Their rusted-pulley cry stirs brittle, twisted deadwood.

Come on, old tootsies. Push like a pair of tugboats in these ragged blue mules.

I watch them move as though they don't quite belong to me.

My heart pounds, a wingbeat inside a metal cage. My lungs are solid with cold. Such a struggle to go faster without the slippers falling off. Bare-stockinged feet on the bluish needled grass.

What would Lucinda say?

But I make it. There's nobody here so I squat on a little stone tablet. My kneecaps look knobby white through the tender-beige nylons. Disrespectful, knees showing. The name on the stone is scabbed over with lichen scaly-silver as psoriasis.

I should have brought something to place on Mum's spot. That pink carnation, the one Lucinda left by the stove, the petals curled and turning brown. No. Something longer-lasting, something plastic. Weatherproof. Next time.

This is just a quick visit. Just dropping by.

Stone flowers. Fanny's grave — Mum's sister. From the time I was small, her tombstone enchanted me.

On it there's an angel — well, Dora and I used to call it an angel — falling headfirst into a fistful of flowers. That's what it looks like, a doll or a child carved in white marble, a grainy Thumbelina. You can't see her features, only the halo of curls, tiny stick legs poking from her tulip dress. Falling from the sky, she is. An angel, yes, diving towards a fist clasping daisies. A closed fist — the plain pure hand of God?

The angel's so tiny most people wouldn't notice her, stumbling past the grave. They might take note of Fanny's age, however. *Twelve yrs old, departed this life January 4th, 1888. Beloved dau. of Enos & Adeline Cox.*

There's nothing about her birthplace, or how she ended up here. No mention of what took her. And not a word about the rest of the family, some seven sisters and brothers, or how close she and Mum were, only a year and a half apart. No, to look at the stone a stranger would gain nothing of that child's stint on earth, a time Mum used to talk about — sometimes as though Fanny were still around, just living elsewhere. Out of sight, but never far from Mum's mind. Though when Dora and I mentioned the falling angel, she'd get snappish.

"Don't be silly," she would say. "It's not an angel, not even a girl, it's a flower. A stray one." As though we'd hit some nerve deeper than the sting of losing her sister — a dull ache by the time we came along, surely, her other memories grown faint. Still, sometimes she'd sigh and ask, "Why couldn't you two be like Fan and me?" She could even get sarcastic. "Oh, but there's your age difference — and I s'pose that's my fault!" The next breath, she'd launch into the story of her family emigrating here, sailing up Cobequid Bay. She and her sister leaning over the rail, the water mirror-still; the mudflats pink as slabs of ham, she said. And for a second it'd be as if Fanny were standing right next to her, whispering in her ear. And I'd picture her as that girl or angel or whatever on her gravestone, hurling herself towards that smooth white fist.

Mum used to say the door to heaven's like a needle's eye. Well, if there is such a thing, I would liken it to that fist: room for only the righteous to squeeze through. Those dreamy enough to believe.

"Lord knows what Fan would've thought of these things if she'd reached my age, seen what I've seen" — Mum had a tendency to harp, especially at my sister before Lucinda was born — "which isn't much, according to you girls."

Oh, Mum thought of heaven, all right: golden gates, pearly clouds, trumpets, waxen wings — not that any of it rubbed off on Dora and me. How Lucinda sees heaven is another thing, beyond me, of course, but then that's her worry. I'm too old now to be concerned with the ply of her soul. All I can be sure of is the thickness of my own, never mind where it ends up. It's a bit late to envy or take comfort in the thinness of Mum's or her sister's — how much bulk can a soul acquire, in twelve short years, a spirit as slim as smoke? Not much, I'd say, which is why — even if I were superstitious — Fanny's falling angel cannot bring me to tears. Unless I think of *my* sister. If not for what became of her, I might laugh and rejoice that Mum and Fan and all the others have one up on that angel, being safe somewhere — in the palm of Providence? If one were so inclined to believe. Rocked to sleep in God's right hand, swift and steady as the tides that carried the Coxes here from England. No returning.

The spin and spit of gravel from the road.

Do not disturb.

It's nothing. Just wind rattling branches.

But the trees have eyes. The spruces at the edge of the graveyard, their boughs an unruly fringe.

There's the lumpy rise where St. Luke's stood before it burned, a tipsy rock wall where the steps were. The view from up there sweeps the valley. Like the view from a pedestal — if one dared risk breaking one's neck.

From there you'd be able to see Leonard's stone, if you wished. Way down at the foot of the hill, far from the Lewis plot. A salmon-coloured marker, with a space beside his name for mine. Except the ground down there is swampy, being too close to the river. And there's my fear of floods and sudden thaws.

No thank you.

"You never visit Uncle's grave, Aunt Ruby. How come?"
The gall of Lucinda to ask me, once. Goading. Her eyes so bored and wary. How old she looked that day, old enough to be my peer. A shock to me, yes, it was, since the niece in my mind is ever young.

Until lately, I'd have said the same for myself.

I'm not afraid to die. Nor do I look forward to death. Though to an outsider it might seem I'm taken with it; a silly flirt. Like an aged ballerina hobbling closer, toes poised. *Jeté.*

"Next you'll be serving them tea." I can just hear Lucinda mocking my bonds with the departed.

She'll know soon enough. That all that separates us is a sagging fence, like the picket one dividing our yard from the next, its wood so soft in summer that carpenter ants travel it like a turnpike. What bars us from the other side caves in, crumbling and falling into the weeds.

"'For now we see through a glass, darkly; but then face to face,'" Father used to parrot — not without sense, though, despite other things you could say about him.

I see no boundary. Little division, now, between Mum and me. Mum and Fan.

I read somewhere once that what links a family's genes passes through the females only, mother to daughter. For all her faults, I would stretch this to include myself and Lucinda. Though she gets me down sometimes, Lucinda is blood.

Till death do us part. It's always had a sickly ring, the sweet sad caul of death. Not hard or cold, the silence of the grave — no, no; I imagine it's more like the roar of wind in your ears. If it has a smell, perhaps it's that of spring: of mud and ice breaking up, or of Vicks VapoRub.

And if it has a look?

Well, the look would be of hands, of course, clean and white.

❦❦❦

Mr. Pyke's hands, the time I had Lucinda take me down there, to the undertaker's. Ten years ago now, it's hard to believe; I'm still breathing. I had it in mind that I should pre-arrange, to avoid a new tax coming in on funerals. Lucinda was being a wet blanket — just entering the lobby made her weak.

My appointment was for ten o'clock. We let ourselves in; there was nobody around to greet us. In the entrance were a couple of withered plants: a yellowed, leggy dumbcane, a philodendron trailing from a polished stand.

The carpeting was thin and mottled orange — just vacuumed, you could tell by the streaks, as yet uncrushed by shoes. This put me at ease somewhat — the cleanliness, and the fact that even at that hour, with no one around, the place seemed well-lit. There were two chandeliers and, on both sides of the hallway, crystal sconces to match. The flame-shaped bulbs inside cast everything in spiky shadow. Along the walls were dinner plates depicting churches, gleaming as if whisked from a table, but too high to let you read the names.

Despite the glitter and sparkle there was a certain gloom, as though the light of day was soaked up by the carpet.

"Are you sure about this?" Lucinda pinched my elbow, helping me out of my coat. A cleaning lady must have heard us, for she came scurrying from nowhere. She showed us into Mr. Pyke's office, brought us weak coffee in styrofoam cups.

Maxwell House, that's what the place smelled of. Not death.

At least there was nobody resting at the time, or no one we were aware of.

"Give a call before you drop by," Mr. Pyke had advised on the phone. "Mrs. Clarke, in my business you don't know minute to minute what might come up."

A handsome man, I thought when he finally appeared. Neat and well-groomed in his natty black suit, though rather short and stout — more so than his father, who had buried both my parents and Leonard. This fellow's hair was a silvery brown that looked faded against his broad, tanned face; you could see the marks from his comb along the part. When he smiled he had lovely white teeth, so even as to appear false. They were his own though, I decided, because they matched his hands and his fingernails, pared and squarish with perfect half-moons. Lovely hands, despite their paleness compared to his face; I couldn't help staring as he folded them on his desk. They looked almost bleached, as if the tan had been scrubbed off under the lacing of fine, greyish hairs. His palms reminded me of a monkey's, creased and leathery. He was wearing a ring, a wedding band, which made me think of his wife. How could anyone marry a man in this line of work?

"I like to get things out of the way," I said, clearing my throat and setting my cup aside. I shifted in my leatherette chair; Lucinda was perched on the edge of hers, looking squeamish. The only light was a torchiere that kept flickering. "Not that I'm in any great rush," I added, straightening my purse upon my lap. I meant it as a little joke.

"Whatever you wish, Mrs. Clarke." He eyed Lucinda, then smiled at me. "You're smart to plan ahead; that way you get exactly what you want. In the crunch, there's no telling what can go awry. Getting down to brass tacks, ma'am, there's no two funerals alike, I've been in this business long enough to know. It's an awful stress for the family, having everything left up to them. You would not believe some of the squabbles. But with pre-arrangement...."

"Let's talk dollars," I cut in. "How much for cremation? And traditional?"

"Now, first you have to consider the advantages," he began, avoiding my eyes and addressing Lucinda. "If travel's involved, cremation's ideal. You know exactly where Mom is — in your suitcase."

For some ungodly reason Lucinda snickered — out of nervousness, I assume. Whether he'd made a mistake or spoken in jest, he should've known better. I didn't find his remark funny.

"First off, Mrs. Clarke isn't my mother," Lucinda sputtered. He grinned; he seemed to appreciate her sense of humour.

"You've got to be open-minded in this profession," he said, still grinning though his eyes were earnest. The lines around them reminded me a little of his father. "Oh yes, my wife and me, we deal with the families. We see their wants. Their desires. You've got to respect them, the living. But you have to remember the loved ones, too. You have to think of their wishes. Their wishes, Mrs. Clarke, are my business."

He looked at Lucinda. "You'd be surprised at some of the requests."

"What's the cost of a basic cremation?" I asked, but he didn't seem to hear. He was too busy gazing at my niece.

"Take hunters, for instance," he said. "If Pop was into hunting, he might want his ashes put in shells and shot over his favourite moose grounds." Lucinda gnawed her lip and yanked a Kleenex from her purse, wiped the corners of her eyes. Her shoulders were moving: she was trying not to laugh.

Mr. Pyke leaned closer to tell us how a fishing chum with river frontage kept finding crematorium tags washed up. "Like lost lures," he had the nerve to say.

Lucinda must've found this sobering, somehow. "Makes you think of the Hindus," she said, "you know — the Gandhis, dropping poor old Indira's ashes from a plane." She sniffed, chewed her lip some more. "Is that legal?"

Pyke rocked back in his chair; there was the squeak of vinyl. "Look," he said, laying his hands out on the polished desktop, "I seen a man once who...."

I stopped listening then, realizing there was little point. Hell could freeze over before anyone with grammar like that handled *my* remains. *Ashes to ashes, dust to dust....*

I coughed and stood up.

"Would you like to see the showroom?" he asked, clearly startled. Lucinda nodded enthusiastically. I glared at her.

"Not today, thank you."

"Why not, Aunt Ruby? Just a peek?"

"I know what a casket looks like, Lucinda."

"Ah," Pyke interjected, "but the choice nowadays! There's one particular model you really should see." He could have been discussing automobiles.

"I think not."

"We aim to please, Mrs. Clarke." He sounded regretful. Hurt, almost. "It's a family enterprise," he said to Lucinda. "If you're not happy, we're not happy."

If I'd disappointed him, he quickly recovered. Showing us out, he gave my old paw a long, vigorous squeeze — as though our appointment had left me rattled and needing comfort. If I felt any emotion, it was glee at not having arranged or signed anything. I figured that when the time came Lucinda would be better off having something to do, to take her mind off things.

The second we got home, I went straight to the sink and washed my hands. Still, despite my good mood, I didn't feel much like eating the ham sandwiches Lucinda slapped together for lunch.

That niece of mine — where is she?

Home, asleep. That's no excuse. Why hasn't she come tracking me yet?

Snoozing.

Hog-wild, she must've gone *hog*-wild. Out last night. Conked out.

Just when I could use a lift.

My toes are frozen. Like lumps of iron cast in mud. Frozen mud. Solid flesh, numb. Too numb to feel—

Snow, white. Rags of it sift down. Linger on my coat. Like the time Lucinda washed my sweater and forgot a Kleenex in the sleeve.

A soft wet thickness on my lashes.

The weight of a kiss.... Leonard's kiss. Prickling on my cheek. A champagne tingle.

Try to dance now. Down the frozen track, ruts frosted white. Like sugar-dusted gingerbread. Sugar-sweet.

A cold metal taste on the tip of my tongue.

Softness falls, a thin white sheet. My hobbling, slippered feet....

The woods. Such silence. I must. Turn my back. Like a sprite. Tiptoe away. Leave no footprints.

The pavement: a wet black ribbon. Clear-cut as a chickadee's stripes. The white dissolving. No tracks, just my slipper-slap.

Same dirty blue as the holes in the sky.

Lucinda. How could you. Not know. Where I am.

Come for me, come now, comeforme, comfortme.

The wet *slap-slap* of my soles; the sound shimmies up my legs. My heart chugs. Face burns. Icy spit on the backs of my shins.

The cold pinches me. Pushes me past the ditch. Past a fence.

Up the hill. At the crest, the old white building grows. Gabled, solid as an iceberg.

A dull red berry decorates one toe.

Panting. Heart pulls. Lungs burn, a kind of heat that leaks out the ends of my poor old nipples. Heat like milk, maybe.

A flash of mint-green, a dishevelled brown head stark as horse-flesh against the air: Lucinda, running towards me in her nightie. Rubber boots on her feet, bare white legs over the tops.

Flakes fall and melt on her shoulders, her hair. She is close to me. She's shaking. Titties jiggling under thin nylon.

Flurries wisp now like mosquitoes.

Lucinda. I'm crying. Go inside, please, and make yourself decent.

Her arms come around me. Tight, tight. A stale smell, body-warmth, sweat. Crow's feet, her hard scowling mouth. The bite of her hand on my wrist. Dragging me in through the door like a thief.

"You wouldn't dare hurt me," I rebuke her, my voice cracking. Pleading.

She lets go and falls to her knees, rocking back on her heels. Sliding the slippers off my feet. One at a time, gently. A mother undressing a toddler. Except there is rage in her face. Yes. Fear and despair, too. A grainy redness to her chest where the nightie's lost a button, above that jiggling crack.

"What in the name of Christ do I do with you?" She sighs, her eyes averted. Wobbles to her feet, her face turned away. Slippers on her hands like bath mitts. She yanks them off, slaps them down on the rad. Icy bits ping everywhere.

"How dare you. Speak that way. In my kitchen," I waver, settling down, elbows first, at the table. Snowdrops bead and shine, roll off my sleeve like little silver cake decorations.

Lucinda sobs, on her knees again. She's got the dishrag. She's scrubbing hard, fist knotted. Cleaning up a thin red string on the floor. If the room tilted, she'd look like a climber scaling a cliff.

"I don't care what you say, Ruby. We've got to get you in to see somebody. I don't know what in the Jesus is going on here, only that I can't handle it no more."

"Any," I correct her. The word comes out a squawk.

If it didn't mean getting up, I would go and strike her. I would. A swift sharp crack to the side of the head.

That brassy dyed hair, the dull patches showing through.

"Get up, Lucinda," I order her. "Get up now, please. You look plain pitiful, down there on all fours.

"Pity-ful — do you hear?"

X

Fire

Lucinda swishes in with a blue basin. It's full of cloudy water. My eyes squeeze shut, a glimmer of light coming through the lids.

"Did you remember to add the salt?"

No answer. She corrals me with pillows. Lays a palm on my chest. Eases me backwards.

"Not too far now — that's it, just comfy." Her voice is flat and far away.

She stoops, flimsy green nylon straining over her thighs. Reaches up, unhooks my stockings. Rolls them down, dirty brown rings round my ankles. Like a man removing a prophylactic.

Leonard.

She yanks them off.

"Skin the rabbit," she jokes. No smile.

I don't want my feet to get wet.

"Just a soak, okay?" she coaxes, unctuous.

"It's all right," she keeps saying. Seizing my heels, dunking them into the too-hot water.

I jerk away. Water lops over the sides. She sighs, mops the carpet with a towel. A pink towel, stiff from outdoors.

The salt stings. The sea in a bowl. My toes thwunk the slippery sides, the nails thick and yellow as a comb. A tortoiseshell comb. Skin like pickled raisins. Delta of veins. Calluses like dried cod.

"Stay put — that is, if you're able to." Raw fingers circle my ankle, her other hand pushing down upon my knee.

"It's for your own good."

I shut my eyes, grit my teeth.

The weight lifts from my leg. The room empties — there's no whirr of her presence, or even of her leaving: a pulse of air. I can hear her, though. Somewhere out there, whistling a tune through her teeth. Terse as wind through a ripped screen. I hear her pressing buttons. Cricket chirps. She's calling someone — who?

No talking. A click. A sigh as she puts down the phone.

"Try finding someone who makes house calls!" The air before me fills with her face. A brave face, a brave smile that means no smile at all.

She squats again, the pink towel in her lap.

"What are you trying to do to me?" I stare down at her. Lift one foot, dripping. Obedient. Watch her dry it off, then the other.

I study the bridge of her nose. Two red dents where her glasses dig in, the glasses she wears in the parlour, reading. Watching TV.

"You ought to wear those specs of yours all the time," I sniff. "The better to see what's going on."

If you're so anxious to keep tabs on me.

She chews her lip. Jerks one of my feet up to the light, squinting. My back kinks like a knot in a chain. I hold hold hold my breath as she paints on iodine, fussy as if it's nail varnish. Pain sets like a bee sting, spreads like a stain.

"Thank you kindly," I say in a voice that is almost Father's. Her eyes bulge but she says nothing. Just swings out of the room with her basin. Her bottom rippling under that nightie like mice under a carpet. Or clouds shifting on hills....

"Dora?" I call, but she doesn't turn.

The door shuts.

My feet look like driftwood against the rug. Like river-scoured tree-roots. She's stuck a pink Band-Aid to one toe. Out of sight, out of mind. No hurt.

I get up and limp to the closet. Such a jumble of things. A

musty mothball smell seems to rise through the floor.

Look for it. Now.

My hands shove aside boxes stacked on the shelf. Shoebox lids tied down with twine. A hat-box. A Pot of Gold box. A jagged, crooked pile, everything out of order. Misplaced. Lucinda's fault — or Dora's. The result of her meddling.

Old receipts. Accounts received, accounts payable. Some old store ledgers. Yes, here's the one, at the bottom: brittle black binding, pages that fan and crumble at the touch. Pages lined the same pale blue as a summer horizon, embroidered in Mum's crabbed hand. That spills past the margins, shrinks to fit where it's out of bounds. A special ledger for yard goods, notions. With fine-point curls and serifs, the early entries; a sweet, refined efficiency. Then scribbles, later; dribbled ink. A diary of sorts: "February 18th, finished two quilts!!! No special pattern but good for girls' beds. March 3rd, darned socks; March 20th, started rug. April 4th, mended. April 6th, 7th, 8th, mended. June 7th, finished smocking Ruby's dress. Dora wants one too...."

Skip a few pages and there's a letter. A long, long one that wends its way to the end of the book. The craziest thing, it begins, "Dear Fan"....

Oh, we saw her scratching in it once, Dora and I. Bent over the counter, elbowing us away. Father out back, totting up bills; do not disturb.

"What are you writing, Mum, a story?" Dora was seven, bony-kneed, shrill.

"Of all foolish notions——" Mum thumped the book shut on her thumb. Her eyes shifting from Dora to me, her hand dipping deep for licorice babies.

"I'm taking stock, dear, can't you see, just keeping record——"

"Of what, Mum?"

"Don't be so silly, Ruby. Big girl like you. Run along now, take your sister, you hear? You run along now, the two of you, and play."

I never saw the book again till the day of the fire; I forget how much later, weeks maybe.

But that's how Mum did things. She seemed almost sneaky at times, furtive as some thief in the night, as if anything of *hers* had to be carried out under cover. As though Dora and I were waiting in the wings to come mess things up. She was that way with her sewing. Long after Dora quit crawling and climbing and putting things in her mouth, Mum kept her sewing basket way up high on the very top shelf of the buffet. She was always on guard, always worried anything unprotected would come to harm. Like Leonard in this respect, Leonard lighting a cigarette. He was always so careful to cup his hand around the match, never mind he kept a whole darned box of matches in his vest. It was as if he feared the slightest draft would put out the flame — or fan it out of control.

"Don't tell Father," Mum said, when we found her writing. "It's nothing anyways." Her hand loping over the lines, a daisy chain of letters, the dotted i's like jumping sparks.

That's how they say the inferno started: a spark from someone's chimney, a big double house down by the chapel bridge. Three weeks, no rain. The shingles were like split kindling. The spark hit the roof next door, fanned by wind dry and hot as a sirocco racing through town. That house went up, then the one next to it and the next, flames roaring with the wind straight up Church Street. The fire like a pen tracing dot-to-dot. More big dwellings caught, then the company icehouse, the company store, the company houses. By the time it was over, four churches had succumbed, the Baptist, Presbyterian, Catholic, lastly the Church of England. The school, St. Bridgid's Hall, the glebes and rectories. The Scurrah Hotel, the Waverley, the old bank, McIlwaine's store. Forty-seven buildings in all, gone in a matter of hours, when finally the fire burned itself out.

It was a Sunday morning, the second-last day of May....

The smell of dust was at the window; you could almost feel the chalkiness on your hands. Mum was in the kitchen braiding Dora's hair. We were getting ready for church. I was in the front hall tying on my hat; it was flat and of navy straw, a tad childish. I was thirteen. I had breasts by then, under my cornflower-blue dress; I worried the world could see. My face in the mirror was narrow, gloomy. Bored.

Dora whined as Mum tugged and elbowed and moaned at

her, "Keep still!"

"Where's Father? What's keeping him?" I wanted to know, peeking through the lacy curtains. Expecting to see him out front leaning against the buggy, stamping his feet in the dust.

Heat ripples rose from the roof across the street, and it wasn't yet eight-thirty.

In the kitchen I tugged at the front of my dress.

"Isn't he coming?"

Mum dipped the comb under the tap.

"Must be waylaid up the hill. The walk'll do us good. He can meet us up there, at church."

It wasn't unusual, Father working Sunday mornings before service. Preparing for business next day, checking for trouble over-night. The cost of separating life from work, he used to grouse, the years we lived in the centre of town, when living so far from the store made it harder keeping an eye on things. "So far" — from our tall white house on Broadway below Foundry Hill, across the bridge and up the opposite slope to the top of the hill. A fifteen-minute walk at best.

I went out to watch for him from the veranda.

It was then I heard the first shrieks. The faint smashing of glass, the timbers squealing. The roar, like a locomotive grinding, chugging closer, closer. Funny, but I didn't see the smoke at first, though I could smell it. Sweet almost, grassfire.

The black cloud swept from the bridge, flames stabbing the sky like orange blades piercing the rooftops. The blaze rolled up Arcadia Avenue. A fireball like a comet, something descended from the heavens. To foolish, frenzied shouts of "Fire!"

Flames devoured the houses below ours, engulfing fences, grass and gardens. The street became a river of people screaming, running, swept by gales of crackling heat, dust, embers. I heard the bray of dogs somewhere, trapped inside.

There was no time to save anything. Flames cartwheeling to our roof. Leaping like acrobats from windows, gliding down drain-pipes. The heat was so savage it felt as if our eyes were ablaze.

Mum still had the comb in her hand, pulling Dora down the steps and into the street. Dora was crying, tearing at the loose locks on one side of her head. Somehow Mum had managed to snatch her crazy quilt, something wrapped up inside it. She thrust the bundle at me. I peeked, I don't know why, as the three of us fled, gusted along in the throng. It was her old black ledger.

Dora lost a shoe, and I my hat, racing up Foundry Hill ahead of the flames, past the abandoned works. Above town we hugged the gorge, following the river branch upstream. Below the falls, where the river widened and its banks lowered, people spilled into the stream. Some waded to their waists in the chilly swirling current, their arms laden with a flea-market jumble of crockery, photographs, bits of clothing. There was a child with a fat white cat in her arms, the creature's wails like a strangling infant's. Women knelt, the water carving their skirts against their thighs, rinsing soot from their cheeks.

Not a single person perished — a miracle. But scores were left homeless. By ten o'clock, the flatiron heart of Arcadia had been razed to a smoking heap of cinders. The only places that survived were those on the other side of the bridge — our store and the five or six houses nearby.

So much for our competition.

People said we were damned lucky, to have somewhere to move into. The old tin-ceilinged flat upstairs, where Father and Mum had lived with his parents till he bought the house on Broadway.

A good thing, a fortunate thing, yes; we had somewhere to go — amid the free-for-all of squatting, burglary and theft that followed. Decent folks and wastrels alike took over houses, whatever could be found on the outskirts of town, as far out as the end of Station Road. Places abandoned years before, when the last of the pipe and rolling mills went belly up.

The squatters took over like mice. "The right of adverse possession" was how the town excused it. I always felt this was wrong; it can't be proper for a tenant to dwell rent-free in a home not rightfully his. It's as absurd as a house taking over its owner — simply not right.

The body is the temple of the soul. *In His house are many mansions;* so Father used to say.

The walls of such a dwelling — I wonder, are they fluid? Like the walls of a cell, of an amoeba, never still; are they that easily crossed? Invaded? I picture a squirming inner brilliance leaking out. An absence, an empty vessel, like the store emptied: lights on, nothing left inside.

In the temple, my temple....

My stomach growls, a deep, caving hunger. My toe throbs.

I am thirteen years old again. I lug Mum's ledger to the bed, burrow down under the covers with it. I am Mum's child. I am. Mum.

My soul floats, liquid as a drink.

Poured from a vessel, half full. Half empty.

A punch bowl. The one at the hotel. Our honeymoon....

A sculpted block of ice, the sweet pink liquor inside melting its way through.

I didn't see it myself. Leonard told me about it afterwards. Raved about it, last thing before going to sleep.

Whisky on the pillow.

I should've tried harder with Leonard. Loved him. Forgiven him. Let our spirits merge and in the bargain maybe, like a symphony, allowed mine to swell.

But no.

How, exactly, do mountains move?

To some queer silent music, perhaps, that nobody can hear. Not the kind I'd like to listen to, anyway, or used to, as a child. Sharp, swinging brass. There was plenty of music like that here in town when I was a tot. Summer nights, in the bandstand just off Furnace Street. Trumpets, French horns, clarinets; gliding gay melodies trimming the air. On harsh winter nights, they used to hold symphonic band concerts at St. Bridgid's Hall. There were lady violinists, two of them wearing spidery lace; a soprano decked in flowers. And the men — oh, the men, with handlebar moustaches, dressed in tails. I suppose I was no more than four, but Mum and Father always took me along. By the time Dora arrived there was no more music, nothing but hicks sawing fiddles. The company had shut down most of its operations, forcing half the townsfolk to pull up stakes and leave. With them went the finer things.

Leonard and I never attended concerts. We never danced.

Oh, a couple of times we went to Caledonia to watch Fred Astaire and Ginger Rogers on the Bijou's big screen. I loved the chatter of their feet accordioning up and down stairs, but the music itself made me edgy. I wanted them to stop singing and get on with things. Even when musicals were all the rage.

By then I wasn't much for music.

Neither was Leonard.

And then came the thirties, when things got to him. The constant strain of staying afloat through those years, despite glimmers of hope once the war was on.

People started buying things again, with cash instead of barter: ready-made clothes, not just rubber boots and long johns. Toiletries, fly rods, other fancy fishing gear; taffeta instead of plain worsted. Farmers roundabout were starting to think bigger, our trade in farm equipment was on the upswing. The store's cut in mail orders rose, too.

Leonard had signed deals with Massey-Harris and the T. Eaton Company the day he went off the road.

The doctor came from Caledonia, too late. There wasn't much left of the Ford topsy-turvy in the ditch. Two boys from up Westchester way found him. Seemed he'd struck a tree. Poor fellow was still clutching the wheel, what you could see for the blood. This I heard later in the store; the things folks say when they think you're out of earshot.

The doctor's report gave me the biggest jolt. From what he deduced, it appeared Leonard suffered some sort of attack, tooling along; his heart, or maybe a seizure. There was no evidence of him drinking or speeding. No skid marks to suggest he'd swerved to avoid something, a child on a bike, perhaps, somebody walking too close.

This was what I found hard to get over: that a man of forty-nine could be struck down, out of the blue. In bitter moments I would think: Serves him right, all those days and nights he spent at the bakery and didn't have to. Then something would remind me of mayflowers, that sweet, one-off scent, or the stiff, creeping tingle of champagne. And my heart would dissolve like a spoonful of seltzer.

Like the blood that day I was cutting cheese in the store, the pain amazed me.

Dora was no help. By then she had her own crosses to bear — though when Albert finally disappeared I'd have to say her burden lightened. She was drinking, raising Lucinda on what little Father gave her. He and Mum pretty much kept to themselves upstairs, and offered no comfort. Father had divorced himself from the store, later becoming confined to bed on account of his legs. Mum spent all her time knitting socks for soldiers and refugees.

So that left me. The whole town looking to Clarke's for their gas, goods and whatnot. Though with more and more cars on the road, there was always the chance that people would feel less troubled going the extra few miles to Ferrona or Hopewell. I had to keep up.

When she turned thirteen I hired Lucinda to work the pumps on weekends. I wanted to save myself the trips racing in and out of the store, not to mention all the handwashing between customers. That was a waste of time; but I never could bring myself to make change with greasy fingers. Even for some of the hicks and roughnecks who'd pull in for a fill-up, from God knows what part of the woods.

More and more I preferred staying put, safe behind the counter. Plus, there I could listen to the radio. Afternoon dramas; Red Skelton, George Burns and my favourite, Gracie Allen. And you could carry on a decent conversation with whoever happened by to chat. Not that there was much to talk about, really, besides the weather and the goings-on in Europe, though the war had seemingly little to do with my life.

One warm, windy day in late May — oh, three years after Leonard died — I was sorting penny candy when a blue car pulled up and honked. I dropped what I was doing and ran out. The woman wanted gasoline, so I put in a ration's worth. She handed over the card and some money, trailing me inside as if she couldn't quite trust me to bring back the change.

The woman was skinny and had a sallow complexion; there was bright red lipstick smudged above the bow of her lips. But what caught your eye was her outfit. Despite the weather she was decked out in gloves and a pretty but cheap-looking suit. It was peacock blue, same as the ink Scheaffer was pushing for its pens. She wore a pillbox hat to match, a bit of black net drooping over one eye.

Odd garb, I thought, for a drive in the country on such a warm afternoon. Dust devils swept up from the road like miniature tornadoes each time a car passed. I figured she must be from away. A war widow, perhaps, gussied up to meet the poor fellow's family somewhere out in the sticks.

But she wore no ring, and when she spoke I knew differently. She had the same flat, unaffected voice of most everyone else in this county. Only her clothes set her apart.

"You must be Mrs. Clarke," she said. She smelled faintly of cigarettes and damp nylon, as though she'd been sitting too long in the car.

"That'd be me," I said, "Ye-es?"

She asked for a cream soda. I popped the cap for her and rang the drink up with the gasoline, and laid down the change which she dropped into her purse. When she said nothing, I turned and screwed the lid back on the humbugs, careful not to let the grease on my fingers rub off. I did the same with the licorice shoelaces, aware of her standing there guzzling from the bottle. She hadn't budged.

"Is there something I can do for you?"

She shrugged then, forcing a grin, her lipstick smeared.

"Not really." She gave a long sigh and I could see her tongue stained pink from the soda. "I just seen this place, passing through a couple a times, that's all. Wanted to see for myself, you know, what it looked like inside."

"That so."

I waited, figuring she was working up to something. Through the ceiling I heard Father's cane tap the floor, signalling Mum to bring him more water.

When the woman stayed silent, I gave her a quick dismissive smile — the kind reserved for window-shoppers who, chances are, won't be back.

"So then, missus" — I sniffed, breathing in lightly and working up to Father's silly old ploy — "what can I do you for?"

Well. She looked for a second as though she might cry. Those bright lips of hers went pouty, like a little child denied a Popsicle. She tugged at her gloves, the nylon stretched almost sheer at the seams.

"Nothing, thanks." She felt around inside her purse for her change. "There's not a thing you can do for me. Not now, anyways."

Then she turned and clicked out of the store, her flimsy high heels wobbling a little as she reached the door. Or maybe I just imagined it, watching her sidestep the sill and hurry to her car.

Before I had the lid back on the chicken bones she was gone. Out of there like a shot, leaving nothing behind but the splutter of an engine, and dust. A long yellow funnel of dust spinning down the road towards Caledonia.

Who'd have thought that a few months later my father would be gone, Mum too, one right after the other? Father died that September, my mother the very next January.

Not to suggest that that woman coming in that day had anything to do with it. But, had I been paying more attention, perhaps I might've marked that day as the start of the doldrums for me — not so much a spate of bad luck as a slow, winding loneliness of a kind I hadn't quite known before Leonard's death, and haven't since.

Dora was hounding me to take her on as a partner — in other words, split the profits with me doing all the work. She'd gotten slovenly; though she had no trouble keeping her figure, after Albert's desertion she lost her prettiness. Scarcely a day over thirty-five, and a face like baked clay.

On Lucinda's eighteenth birthday, Dora dropped the bomb on me. I went down there that evening for cake and tea — she still had the place on Station Road, hanging onto it by her teeth, I'd say. The paint was peeling, the porch lattice caved in. Leaves from the fall before were matted like cardboard over the excuse for a garden. Usually at that time of year — late June, trees in fresh leaf, the lilacs out — in the softest summer twilight, the shabbiest greys can be excused, forgiven. But that evening it was all I could do to walk up and tap on the door.

Lucinda's cake was tunnelled and lopsided; Dora must've forgotten to add something. The girl put on her bravest face. ("It's okay, Ma, don't worry, Ma — it's the thought that counts!") Dora was in her dressing gown, eight o'clock in the evening. Her hair was in curlers.

She was going out, she said; she had a date in Caledonia. Not even sunset and you could smell the booze off her, overpowering the Evening in Paris. She smoked a cigarette while Lucinda and I chewed through two small wedges of cake. Before we were finished she jumped up to get dressed.

"Go on over to Ruby's with her, why don't you, Lindy? You could spend the evening together — God knows you're over there all the time anyways."

After that crack, I couldn't very well leave without Lucinda; could hardly expect her to spend her birthday alone, could I? And this was the first of many nights Dora forgot to come home, as it turned out. Not that Lucinda was a baby any more; a week later and she was finished high school. But she had no plans, or none she confided. So I offered her a full-time job in the store. A good thing, too, for by August her mother was off every waking moment on these mystery trips to Caledonia. Scarcer than fillings in a set of dentures, Dora. And loose.

One day I said, "You're here all the time anyway, Lucinda. Why not save yourself the walk back and forth, and move in? Time is money, dear — what's the point wasting precious minutes going to and fro, when you could be here helping me stock shelves?"

I made it sound as though she was doing me a favour — which in a way she was, I suppose, by smoothing over my guilt. Somebody had to keep an eye on her. That mother of hers was useless as Mum's old knick-knacks trapping dust upstairs.

By August we knew it was a man Dora was seeing in Caledonia.

I thought, what an example. And what a terrible thing if a girl of Lucinda's mettle were to turn out like that, sneaky as her mother, using the same poor judgement — the kind of judgement I was afraid might run in the genes.

So it wasn't charity, my taking her in. But yes, I felt responsible for her. Thus began our living arrangement — the icing on the cake, really, of all that had grown between us since Lucinda's birth.

It was good timing, too, because two months to the day after Lucinda's graduation, didn't Dora take off with that fellow of hers to Toronto? I should have counted my lucky stars, seeing the last of her. If she had stayed there.

Good God. The days in my life I've wondered how she and I were sprung from the same pool! Or how she begat a daughter like Lucinda, sensible, with her head screwed on properly — most of the time. That was something to be valued, even if she was an awful tomboy.

We could've taken the upstairs flat. Lord knows it was roomier and available. But at the time it seemed too much of a chore to move. And I didn't want to make Lucinda feel she owed me more than she already did. But the door was always open, I used to tell her. I gave her an out; was it my fault she chose not to take it?

The downstairs flat needed some redoing. I took back the big room and bed I'd shared with Leonard, and gave Lucinda my little one. We sold off some of the bigger pieces from upstairs; for a while I had this foolish notion she might want to go to the normal school in Caledonia, and become a teacher; or to business or nursing school down in Halifax.

"No, Aunt Ruby. Why would I leave? I aim to stay right here, with you."

Perhaps I made it too easy, selling off that stuff: Mum's oak sideboard, the dining-room set, the settee from the parlour. I gave Lucinda the proceeds, which she socked away, then one day up and used them to buy herself a car.

I had plans to rent out the upstairs — the store went through a rough patch after the war — but never did get around to it. I didn't like the idea, anyway, of strangers up there sleeping in our old beds, cooking in our kitchen. Then there was the problem of what to do with the rest of the stuff. Not the furniture — a dealer from Caledonia snapped it up as if at a fire sale — but Mum's personal effects. Her dishes and silverware; all her lovely handiwork: runners, doilies, shams. Not to mention other odds and ends, chiffoniers, cupboards and drawers full of sewing things: embroidery hoops, needles, chalk, a rusty tracing wheel. Kitchen items: her tin sifter; her rolling pin, its red handles faded to the shade of iodine. Then there was her journal, of course, which I found in her dresser, in the top drawer. This was just after her death; I was sorting what to give to charity, what to keep, mostly for the ragbag. I was picking through shrunken slips and chemises, a mess of un-ravelled lace, yellowed cotton and greying wool.

The ledger was at the bottom, underneath a packet of letters bound with twine. My fingers grazed the cracked, grainy leather. I didn't recognize it at first, until I flipped back the cover and saw Mum's writing like a cast, floating line. It reeled me back. To the day the town burned, the last time I'd laid eyes on it.

I didn't have to read it; and I could have burned it, later. I simply lacked the heart.

I burrow down now, in my bedsheet tent. The pain in my foot a tiny drumbeat....

I'll start at the very beginning, a very good place to start.

I can just hear you, too, Mum: your tidy singsong voice, like the lady in *The Sound of Music*.

XI

Passages

To all dispersed sorts of ARTS and TRADES
I writ the needles prayes (that never fades)
So long as children shall be got or borne,
So long as garments shall be made or worne....
Yea, till the world be quite dissolv'd and past;
So long at least, the Needles use shall last....

"The Prayse of the Needle",
by John Taylor

April 4, 1920

My Dearest Fan,
It says in Hebrews: "Now faith is the substance of things hoped for, the evidence of things not seen." Things in the heavenly realm, this surely means. Well, there's not a soul in the earthly one in whom I will confide, so I write placing all hope and trust in the belief that — somehow — you can hear me.

My urge is to seek solace on paper, the comfort of holding a pen. The kind-hearted would understand; the cruel I'm sure would jump to call me mad. And justly so, if faith borders lunacy. Sometimes I doubt that they are different.

But I am utterly within my senses. I no longer give a fig what others think — and likely this is madness, in this vale where it's best to keep some convictions under one's hat.

I say this with confidence, for I feel your presence. Of course I do. Our lives were entwined, once, like a bobbin wound with two shades of blue. Like words that share a meaning.

You must remember the morning we sailed in, that morning in 1887. The bay looked like a big pink funnel — your words exactly as we stood at the rail, taking everything in. Mam and Pa were so frantic seeing to the little ones and the baggage, they had no time to stand on deck and watch the land grow closer. The cloven shoreline, mist-covered hills and trees thick to the shore. All that green, and amidst it rooftops, steeples — remember? — white houses and churches such as one never saw at home.

Never dreamed of in the old country, Wiltshire — a world away after two weeks at sea and nothing but wrinkled blue ocean. You were eleven and a half; I had just turned thirteen. My monthlies started the week we embarked. "The visitor," Mam muttered when she found me crying on deck, scared as a cat dangled over water. It was fear of the unknown plaguing me, she figured at first, my worries about leaving, until I admitted the trouble. She rolled up one of the babies' flannels. "Don't tell nobody," she said, "'specially not your sister. Last thing she or anyone else needs right now is something else to get in a flap about."

The blood was bright as a flag on my drawers, the new ones Mam had sewn: two pairs for you, two for me, just for the trip. Goodness knows why, unless she feared we'd be lost and therefore should be decked in our finest. "But Mam" — oh, I can hear you yet — "what if the ship sinks while we're sleeping, or in our old ones?"

To think of it now, the crowd of us travelling to a place we'd hardly heard of. Until that day I started bleeding, I thought of everything as an adventure. Now what I recall most are the cramps, the queasiness I mistook for longing, longing and dread, that seemed to cling to my shoulder like some awkward bird for the length of the trip.

Sailing in, the first things we noticed were those big white houses with their widow's walks and cupolas facing out to sea. Captain's houses, the cabin boy told us, leaning beside us as the pier loomed. He couldn't've been more than a year or two older than me. His arm brushed my sleeve; for a second he stood so close I could smell him, that salty odour of hemp and sweat. You didn't blink holding onto your hat, a faint hopeful smile on your face. You were so pale. I moved closer till my arm touched yours, and we stood there like, well, two peas in a pod. Except you looked sweet and delicate as a flower, I like a stick in my wrinkled dress.

The excitement felt like a bone stuck in my throat. I looped my arm through yours while we watched the boy hauling a line. You could see the muscles jumping in his scrawny arms. He glanced over at us and grinned; there was a black hole where his eye tooth should've been. Then he swung off, looking just like a monkey as he disappeared down a hatch.

"Quit making eyes," Mam would've said, and pinched me, had she been there and not below herding the others. She was so harried with the babies — Peter only two months old and Mary not yet walking. We were always minding the four bigger ones, but this day Mam gave us a rope's length of freedom. You were so sick coming across, she was likely relieved having you out taking the air for a change.

Most of the crossing I spent watching you and the others, stuck in that corner of the hold. But sometimes I'd go up on deck and do cross-stitching on that sampler I'd brought, if the wind wasn't too strong. Not that handiwork made the days go more quickly; time did queer things out there. It rolled like the ocean itself, but only the sun's slant gave it shape.

Thank heaven we had fine weather. It was July and the company that brought out Pa and the other men wanted them working by early August. When we first got wind of our leaving, in June, Mam was all for it, had heard of plenty who'd gone to the States and found all sorts of work, mostly in mills in Massachusetts — women too, working for money! The United States of America, the Dominion of Canada: it was all the same country to her, one big place where work reaped reward. We'd heard about the winters, the cold, but Mam put that down to healthy exaggeration, concocted to ease the sorrows of those left behind.

Once, when you were napping, a man on board showed us a map. Mam's eyes lit when he pointed out Bournemouth, our port of departure, then glazed over as he dragged his finger to the reaches of Canada, a claw of land stuck out in the ocean. "You see?" she said, laying Peter over her lap while she straightened her dented hat. "How could it be any colder when England's the place farther north?"

Rolling up his map, the man told some tall tales about storms and hurricanes, waves as big as Salisbury Cathedral. "Oh, he's just having a bit of fun, trying to scare you!" — Pa dug Mam in the ribs. She sniffled and put Peter on her shoulder. The ocean looked like a carpet that day, a soft breeze riffling the hairs straying from under her hat.

Then the man told us about a ship, the *Mary Celeste*, built on the very bay where we were headed. It was found a couple of years before I was born, he said, deserted and drifting under full sail off the Azores. There was food on the table, a baby's cradle still warm. But all hands were gone, never to be seen or heard from again.

"Now there's a corker for you, a likely, likely story!" Pa said. But Mam went white as muslin. Clasping Peter, she grabbed my hand.

Half-baked as the story sounded, I wasn't sure what to make of it. None of us had even seen the sea until the day we left from Bournemouth. Pa was the only one to whom it wasn't a stranger; he'd lived near the coast in Cornwall.

Remember how he used to leave Mam in charge of us and that patch of land we rented in Chalford Road, to go off and work in the tin mines down there? Until I was nine he'd been a slagger at the ironworks nearby; when they shut down, he followed some other men to the Lizard, after the tin. Every few weeks we would get a letter. I can still picture our house behind the Bell pub — that tiny red-brick cottage at the foot of the hill, with its garden at the back, its bit of pasture along the footpath. In summer that path was a tunnel of blackberry canes; at the end of it was a lovely view of the White Horse that Pa used to say King Alfred had carved in the cliff, celebrating his victory over the Danes.

For a while Mam kept sheep, till the Biss mill switched from wool to cotton. She was determined that you and I go to school — she had plans for us, that we'd end up more than the daughters of a slag man. So for a few years we did attend, until there was no place left around to buy her wool. I believe that's when Mam lost some of her pluck, though she wouldn't've been more than thirty then. All of a sudden she seemed to slacken off, claiming most things worth knowing you could pick up by yourself. "Take needlework, for instance: practice makes perfect," she started saying. "And lookit them poor ducks next door — I b'lieve they both went to school as chillern, and lookit them now!"

The poor ducks were the Cockells, our neighbours in the other half of the house. They were old, their children all gone but one. Albert, his name was, a burly fellow with the mind of a little child. He used to call to us sometimes from the window if we were out in the garden; he'd call and call, babble mostly, nothing you could make out, till Mrs. would come and slam down the sash. Even with the window shut you could hear her inside scolding him. In all our years on Chalford Road — and think of it, Fan, every blessed one of us was born in that little house — we never saw more than his big stubbled face through the panes. Until that one afternoon, not long before Pa got his moving orders, we spied the poor fellow helping his ma out back, shelling peas. You and I were crouched behind the butterfly bush — remember? Mrs. would run her thumbnail down the middle of each of the pods, then press them one by one into those clumsy fists and guide his poor fingers to snap them open. His tongue lolled like a slice of ham as he picked out each pea and let it roll away in the dirt. Once Mrs. must have heard us giggling, for her head swivelled around. As she turned back to her son, the anxious look on her face melted. But you could hear her sigh as the last pea went under the step.

Heaven knows why I've put this down; it's just that my other memories from back then are a blur of helping cook and clean — and you and I only children!

Just before we sailed, a position came up at Horesham, the big manor house at the top of the road. Lady Philby was looking for a girl my age, "clean and reliable and honest"; reading and writing were appreciated, it was stated, but not essential. Mam didn't want me to go, and put up a half-hearted fuss saying my help was needed at home. But no denying she was finding it harder and harder to keep bread on the table. Then, the very day I went up there — the only time I was privileged to pass through those tall iron gates or stand inside that huge stone kitchen — didn't word come from Pa that we were bound for Canada? The company was sending men to its works there, paying passage for whole families and promising wages double what anyone made at home.

That night the table was stacked with dishes but not much besides biscuits and cheese for supper. Mam had the baby to her breast; her face, it seems to me now, looked smoother and softer than it had in a long, long while. Or it could've been the light, I suppose, the stillness of evening.

Buttoning up, she went next door and asked Mrs. Cockell to mind you and the others. You'd been peaky all day, running a bit of a fever, so Mam thought better of leaving you in charge. She told Mrs. we had an errand, she and I. Mrs. balked at first, saying her husband was sleeping off his afternoon at the Bell, and she hated to leave Albert alone. But she gave in to Mam's mood. "No girl of mine, Lizzie, is goin' into service," Mam kept telling her, "and we've got some straightening out to do." Finally Mrs. consented to come and plant herself in our kitchen — ears no doubt cocked for sounds of trouble next door — and off we went to deliver our "news."

Had Mrs. quibbled further and delayed us, who knows but Mam and I might've missed the business we witnessed later that evening. It was past twilight by the time we reached the top of the road. The chalk horse on the hillside above gleamed white under the three-quarter moon. Dampness rose from the hayfields around us; the ditches were alive with voles. As the moon climbed, it glazed branches and fenceposts with a silver so bright you could make out every pebble and leaf.

A big row of oaks hid the house from the road. When the fancy gates came in sight, we picked up our pace a little. Mam had her arms pinned across her bosom, fighting off the tingle, I imagine, that signalled she was due to nurse. The gates were open. Mam was a step or two ahead of me, anxious to have our "straightening out" over and done. But as we went to turn in, the two of us beheld something that prevented us from continuing — or ever telling the Philbys of my change of fortune.

Coming down the drive, drawn by two black horses, a black hansom cab sped towards us. There wasn't one creak of a wheel, one snort or crack of a whip; not a single hoofbeat upon the cobbles. There was nothing but perfect stillness.

Mam yanked me out of the way, her scratchy old shawl brushing my cheek. The driver's face was a shadow. He didn't so much as slow or nod as the cab rushed past like a swath of velvet through the dusk. At the gates the cab turned and kept going, away from the village, towards Bratton.

Mam's hand was ice-cold, gripping mine. Tripping over her hem, she pulled me along down the hill, not uttering a word until we reached our cottage. Inside, Mrs. Cockell was pacing, a child in each arm.

You were upstairs in the bed we shared with Sarah and Mary, when Mary wasn't in with Mam and Peter.

Mam sank into the rocker and started fumbling with her buttons, poor tiny Peter wailing in her arms. Mrs. gave her a look and cried, "Addie, what in the name of mercy——?" just as a pounding came on the wall. Patting Mary on the head, Mrs. grabbed the biscuit she'd been chewing and dashed out.

As for the Philby household, Mam refused to have either of us set foot near it again, even in daylight. "Don't you tell the others what we seen," she warned me, leaning so close you could see the blood vessels in her eyes. "Don't even mention it to 'em." As if doing so would tempt fate.

Which is why I never told you about it, Fan; I didn't want to frighten you. Because the next day it was announced that Lord Philby had died in his sleep.

The afternoon of his grand funeral, our pa arrived home, grimy from his final shift and two days' train ride. When we glimpsed him coming by the garden, we ran to meet him. He was hauling a black trunk on his back, worn out, you could tell; the lines around his eyes were traced with dirt. He set down the trunk and swooped the younger ones up. Mary made strange, of course, leaning out of his arms and reaching for Mam. Each of the boys got a quick box on the ears. You and I each got a kiss, you squirming away from the burn of his whiskers. Holding onto Mary (Peter must've been asleep), Mam laid her free arm across his back and led him inside. It would've been a good seven or eight months since they'd last seen each other, I suppose. Usually Mam would've acted girlish, maybe even set aside the wash till Pa got settled in with his tea. But this day she seemed skittish and standoffish, as if it were some stranger come to call. Instead of getting herself a cup and sitting with him a spell, she went straight for the trunk, pulling out the contents. There wasn't much besides a couple of old shirts and a pair of ragged trousers, and some oddments he carted back and forth to Cornwall, a lunchpail and his heavy atlas of the world. Imagine hauling around a book like that, full of places one had little hope of seeing.

"Never mind them things, Addie — come and sit, would you! Let me see you — seems I've near forgot what you look like. Them clothes can wait; no, pitch 'em, Addie, for pity's sake. We'll all be fit for new ones, once we get to Canada."

Canada. The way he said it, Fan, put me in mind of someone choking, taking a bite of some costly new food and not quite knowing how to swallow it.

A week or two later we left. It took no time to clear out our possessions; what wouldn't go in Pa's trunk and the tea crates he'd managed to wangle from somewhere, Mam gave away or threw out. She got jittery and short with us, parting with things only she could see the value of: britches with the knees out, cracked teacups, boots with no soles. Pa brushed off her fears with promises of better to come.

Our last morning in Chalford Road, we left the key and what rent we owed on the mantel, under Mrs. Cockell's watchful eye. She didn't seem awfully sorry to see us go, but gave Mam a quick buss on the cheek and waved from the doorstep as the cart we'd hired pulled away, hauling us and all our worldly goods to the train for Bournemouth.

I felt a bit guilty not explaining myself to Lady Philby's housekeeper, though I don't imagine I was long on her mind: little Effie Cox, the waif who'd enquired about a job as cook's helper. A dozen girls would've given their eye teeth to work at Horesham, so I reckon she had no trouble finding someone. The only one to suffer disappointment was Mam, denied her chance to look the woman in the eye and say there were better things in store for me.

But no doubt it was this hope that kept her going those days at sea, with everyone sick and crying. I can still see us, you and me helping Mam rinse and string flannels up to dry all around that tiny cabin.

The sickness I'll never forget — just thinking of the smell makes my innards rise. But the worst was at night, wasn't it? The darkness, as though we'd been swallowed like Jonah! That hold was "a bleedin' dungeon", I heard Mam complaining once. You were sound asleep. "Now, now, Addie," Pa tried to console her, reaching down from his upper bunk to stroke her arm — remember how she and Peter nestled together in the one below?

All those nights, the ten of us holed up in that cramped space, slotted and stacked like pieces of mail in our bunks one atop another. The youngest ones doubled up: Mary and Sarah, who'd just turned three; and the boys, Joseph and Ezekiel — Joseph was just seven, Zeke five. Willie, being almost ten, had the bunk above them, a crawlspace tight as a pantry shelf. We were lucky, you and I, to have our own bunks.

But those nights! The mice — no, they must have been rats, they were that big, scurrying around. The slither of their tails across your skin! And the air, Fan! Sticky and warm as the baby's spit-up and just as sour-smelling, mixed as it was with the stink of tar and kerosene. The minute Pa put out the light, we'd lie in a sweat praying for slumber. We soon learned to sleep with the covers drawn up to keep out the critters. I would try my best not to think of the cold black fathoms below; I took pains not to mention my fear, because voicing it would've made it worse. But I know it weighed on you too, the notion of all that water; oh, I could tell by the way you'd lie so still up there above me. Yet I could usually tell by your breathing that you were awake, though sometimes I'd have to climb up to check, and there you'd be with those peepers wide open.

"Pity the buggers in steerage," Pa would whisper in reply to Mam's rustlings below him; she was always waking to make sure Peter was still breathing. "We've got it good compared to them poor souls, Addie. Thanks be to Christ we ain't in with a bunch of strangers, men, women and chillern all jumbled up together like so much luggage." Sometimes his hand would reach down, but she'd yank hers under the blanket. "Could be a damn sight worse," he'd mutter, then groan with the effort of rolling over.

Some mornings the glare of daylight made your head ache whenever you ventured outside. What a sight I must have been, my skinny braids in a rat's nest, a spot scrubbed nearly thin on the back of my skirt. (The stain never did come out of my drawers.)

It's a marvel that cabin boy looked twice at me, Fan, that miserable boy with the downy smudge above his lip. "Plenty of critters like you where I come from," I might have said to him, had he addressed me earlier in the trip. But that last morning, standing there with you watching the treetops grow bigger, I rather envied him despite his seediness. He'd seen all those trees before, you could tell; and for a moment or two I wouldn't've minded being in his skin, filthy as it was, surveying things through his eyes. When he scampered off, my heart slipped a notch or two, just like the anchor when we finally made port.

Remember the noise when the ship nudged the pier? Timbers groaning, and that long, loud shuddering like thunder? That flock of birds bursting from a nearby marsh — the formation of their tiny bodies shimmered like a razor over the bay! I grabbed your sleeve. The two of us watching with our mouths open till those birds were just a pencil mark above the mauve horizon.

"Gotta git 'er unloaded before the tide falls, b'ys," someone yelled, and as folks sprang to action it was like a scene unglued — one of those sailor's valentines made of shells: mother-of-pearl, angel-wings, the daintiest of periwinkles. So many bits and pieces spilling on deck, then down the gangplank, along the wharf: families and crewmen. A flood of people lugging steamer trunks, crates, blankets and babies, all going off to meet new lives someplace in those woods.

Lord have mercy, when I think now of what awaited us! The little company house near Furnace and Main — two miles from the train station but at least it wasn't far from the centre of town. It was built of wood, the same reddish brown as all the others along the tracks. That old paint made of burnt iron ore — red ochry — mixed with oil. People used to slap it on anything with four walls, the only exception being places of worship.

Arcadia Mines was a far cry from Spenceport, where we'd landed, with all its fine white houses. Still, compared to Chalford it was a veritable city. My land! There were three hotels, a choice of apothecaries, dress shops, jewellers, milliners, twelve blacksmiths, eight saloons; more grocers, confectioners, bakeries and general stores than you could shake a stick at. And churches! Just up the hill was St. Bridgid's; you used to say it reminded you of a wedding cake with all those tiers of windows and the pretty scalloped shingles on its bell-tower. Beyond it was St. Luke's, sturdy and solid as the company manager's mansion but not nearly so grand as the Romans'. Remember the copse and the little pasture separating the two houses of God, full of wild rose and goldenrod? Mam was forever scolding you for losing yourself in that field and being late.

You must recall the buggy ride that day we landed, those six long miles travelling inland, straight north. There was barely room for us children, everything we owned heaped around us as we followed a string of other folks similarly burdened. That long red road winding over hill and dale! At first it snaked along the river, stony and yellow through the spruces; you said it looked like a tiger's eyes.

It didn't take long to lose sight of the bay, that coppery gleam behind us. The mosquitoes were fierce despite the sun; Mam kept flicking them away from the baby as we headed deeper into the woods. You and I were perched behind her, a child or two straddling each of our knees, the whole herd of us swatting and scratching till any bare patches of skin were raw. Pa kept scraping his cap back and forth on his head. His hair underneath was in wet strings, his face so red he looked fit to melt. Mam just kept staring off into the trees, the shadows under her eyes cast greenish-grey by her brim. She looked as though she'd misplaced something, yet couldn't bring herself to name it. Peter's little fist was curled around her thumb. Once she caught me looking at her and turned away, as if peering through those dense, webbed boughs.

Heaven knows where or how Pa had found the driver — that

hunched, reedy man who scarcely spoke, and spat tobacco when Pa asked him how much farther.

"Ohhh, it ain't too bee-ad," he finally answered in that odd, flat voice; you and I had to cover our mouths to stop the giggles. We were bone-tired and giddy, perhaps the only reason we found it so funny. Then Peter started to fret and Pa offered his finger, shaking his head as the baby latched on and made loud smacking sounds. For a minute I thought Pa would laugh too, which might've provided relief from all the heat and crowding and nerves. But no; you and I were the only ones who found anything comical. Mam never took her eyes off those trees flying by, her cheek muscles twitching, she was trying so hard not to cry.

XII

Valleys

And though from earth his being did begin,
Yet through the fire he did his honour win:
And unto those that doe his service lacke,
Hee's true as steele and mettle to the backe.
He hath I per se cye, small single sight,
Yet like a Pigmy, *Polipheme* in fight:
As a stout Captaine, bravely he leades on,
(Not fearing colours) till the worke be done,
Through thicke and thinne he is most sharpely set,
With speed through stitch, he will the conquest get.

Remember our first view of the town, spread below that rise in the road where the woods thinned? Beyond it, the low purplish mountains were pocked with the scudding shapes of clouds; at their foot lay a scorched-looking maze of buildings and belching stacks. Just above us the sky was a pure perfect blue, but over the valley it hung in a thick pink haze. In the distance, above the horses' stamping, you could hear the roar.

I can see it yet, the thin smile on Pa's face as he pulled his finger out of the baby's mouth and pressed Mam's hand. For the first time in many days she shed that distracted look and appeared almost smug, though she couldn't have been too comfortable. She must've been wilting in that dress, her good black one, the bodice so stiff in places it shone like watermarked silk.

Settling in Arcadia Mines, what took the most getting used to was all that space. Not so much open space as forest sloping towards us, hemming in the town. The valley itself looked like a black and green bowl lidded with smoke. Our house was shabby and plain, with a privy out back. When we moved in, a film of soot covered everything, and the walls were steeped in the odours of previous tenants — smells of boiled meat and cabbage and coal mingled with the yeastiness of layers and layers of old paper. Still, it was more than we'd enjoyed in England; you and I got to have that little room above the porch to ourselves.

We'd brought precious few household items: a few pots and dishes; our blue-and-white pitcher and wash basin, which got chipped during the crossing; and Mam's square cake-plate. Wrapped in a shawl at the bottom of Pa's trunk, it survived without a nick, as unmarked by our passage as the babies. A lucky thing, too, as that plate was all Mam had of her own ma's, what I knew of at the time. It was thick white china with a faded blue tree painted on, a perfectly shaped willow dense with leafless twigs branching into ever tinier ones. Mam kept it safe on that shelf high above the dry sink.

Those first scorching August days, you and I helped clean and scrub. Sometimes Mam would stop in the middle of what she was doing and untie the rag around her hair, and gaze out upon the hill behind the outhouse, at its blackened bank of coke ovens and the woods beyond. She never said much, did she, Fan? Who knows but she was thinking of Chalford and our old life. She didn't read or write, so there was little exchange of news between her and her people. She had our uncles back there, all with big broods of their own; both her parents were gone.

Not long after we settled, while Peter was napping and Pa off at work, she asked me to sit and take down a letter. You were washing rags in the tub out back, wringing them and hanging them to dry. It was a hot afternoon, not a bit of wind stirring the dust in the yard. Mam had been cranky and short all day, her hands raw from cleaning. She looked fit to crack me if I refused, as if it were my fault she couldn't put the words down herself. I found a pencil and a scrap of paper. *My dear brother*, she began, her eyes red-rimmed, gazing at me, not blinking. *We are settling nicely into the new place....*

In the corner Peter started fussing, little fists waving from the dynamite crate Pa had rigged as his cradle. Mam ran over and snatched him up. She stood there with her eyes closed, kissing his tiny ear and rocking him, her drab old skirt swishing the side of the stove. And she seemed to forget all about her brother, whatever message she'd wished to send.

To make things shipshape we needed furniture, of course, every stick purchased on time from the company. Its store was the only one we patronized — that tall false-fronted building on Church Street, near the river. Once in a blue moon we'd go to Lewises' up the hill. By the time we arrived summer was practically over, so it was too late to put in a garden. Walking the baby up and down along the fence, Mam would study the neighbours' vegetable patch, carrots and turnips bursting from the greyish-pink dirt. Perhaps she felt, for the first occasion ever, that she had time on her hands, such as it was, having no weeds to pull, nothing to put up.

Pa worked from dawn to dusk as a puddler. There was that time he sat us down, explaining what he did: melting pig iron and stirring it till the carbon burned off, turning out bars of it to be made into steel. He couldn't've made more than a dollar-fifty a day; he got paid once a month. Whatever we needed went on our bill at the Arcadia Mines Store, everything from beds to bags of flour. After our first week or two of sleeping on the floor, Pa had decided there'd be no more doing without.

"What's the difference?" I can still hear him, can't you, dumping out his first pay, a few pennies after the store had taken its due. "Whether you're in hock to the Philbys or the Steel Company of Canada, it's all the same. No such thing as a free man, in this world or the next, Addie."

Mam would flit like a moth around the kitchen with its smells of strong tea, fresh bread and biscuits, and all of us children milling about, starving. When Pa got that way, weary and slack-jawed, slouching at the table in his boots, the little ones clambering over his knee, she would clam up and keep her distance. She'd go about the chores like a machine, one of those hammers or presses Pa was forever describing.

He was always going on about the works. That Dr. Siemens and some other company man, Sir This or Sir That, bringing in all the latest in steel. The cream of the empire, these men of science, he'd boast on their behalf, showing an odd respect. Sometimes we weren't sure whom he was addressing, himself or us. You and I found little of interest in any of it, Mam the same. It was a man's place up there amid the smoke and stink of Foundry Hill, men's doings as queer an alchemy as iron-making itself.

Pa took pains trying to make us understand how lumps of ore could be transformed into smooth black metal; stranger still, into something shiny and clean as steel. It was hocus-pocus to you and me. The only things we saw were the lines in his face and hands, the tar he'd cough up at sunrise, traces of it left in the wash basin.

But he loved talking about iron. The ways of making it strong and malleable, the word he used. One night in the parlour I listened to him telling Willie and Zeke how molten metal got cast in sand. They were all ears, while you nosed deeper into your book, the primer you'd brought from England, and I into my needlework. Mam would glance up now and then from nursing Peter, feigning interest, when any fool could see her mind was miles off. But the boys were spellbound. The next day you caught them in the ditch trying to set fire to some rocks with kindling snitched from the stove.

"An' the grass so dry it'd go up like that!" Mam snapped her fingers and hollered, dragging them inside by the ears. "What in the name of God were you thinking?" She was right; they could've done a load of damage, with the fields like a tinderbox that summer. The air was so dry it turned your hair to straw. It made Mam long for England. When her mind wandered, you could almost see in her eyes the dew-soaked hedgerows and ridges of mist above the horse on the cliff.

At night we'd lie in our new yellow spool beds, whispering about Chalford, about poor retarded Albert Cockell and girls we'd known at school. We whispered less and less, though, as those first weeks wore on, savouring instead the quiet; the creaks of the house settling into coolness; the night sounds of wind and crickets coming through our tiny, hinged, diamond-shaped window. For the first time in our lives there was nobody hovering behind the outer wall; no strange but familiar clatters or thumps; no muffled yet audible voices. Now that we were lacking the distraction of other people's doings, silence tuned us more intently to the goings-on inside our house.

Mam was skittish at first about letting us go out and about on our own. When we weren't busy helping her, we hung about the house trying to keep out of her way. At least it was cooler inside than out, so long as the fire wasn't going in the kitchen. But then Mam would start cooking; the heat would drive us out to the yard. That big poplar tree out front — we whiled afternoons away sitting under it, bored as sticks. You'd dress and undress your rag doll, with me beside you sewing, mostly darning: threadbare socks and drawers forever handed down from one of us to another.

The people next door were from the old country too, the Sculls, and down the road that other family, the Elkinses. They'd come out the year before. But neither had girls our age, so you and I stuck together in the yard. From behind the red picket fence we'd watch the passersby. There were plenty coming and going, Arcadia Mines being full of people like us, everyone from someplace else. It was nothing in those days to see hordes of young men just off the train with bundles on their backs, heading towards Foundry Hill. All were seeking work, some of them rough-looking characters in ragged clothes. I'd shimmy in closer to the tree as a few passed, whistling our way and making eyes. I was tall for my age, which made me look older; it was likely this that seized their attention.

In September we started school. There was no question but that we'd go along with the rest of the children in town. Nobody had planned for the flood of new pupils who had arrived that summer. By the first bell both classrooms were packed solid, the biggest students slouching at the back, the youngest squatting in front of the board. Every inch of floor space, every surface but the pot-bellied stove, was strewn with primers and slates. You and I managed to get a desk, sitting wedged together, wearing those blue pinafores Mam had cut down from one of her dresses. We dared not open our mouths, scared the others would mock our west country accent.

Some of them came to school barefoot, their shins scabbed over with fly bites and scrapes. Some looked shifty and sullen and had eyes like spitballs; you could feel them sometimes on the back of your neck, or sliding across your sums. Occasionally Mr. Slade, the schoolmaster, red-faced and harried, would bring his pointer down hard on their knuckles, the *crack* enough to send me out of my skin.

By the third day, you wanted to quit. On the way home we stopped by the river where it branched between the schoolhouse and the end of Furnace Street. You took off your shoes and put your feet in, bunching up your skirt to crouch in the yellow shallows. Soft gold sunlight lit the top of your hair — I'll never forget it — the green-gold reflection dancing on your face. All around you, wasps and darning-needles flitted and thrummed like tiny, blurry stars. Tossing in a stick, you stood up, wobbling a little on the round, slippery rocks. The hem of your skirt dipped and dragged in as you looked back at me minding our books on the bank.

You swatted a dragonfly buzzing at your ear. "Careful!" I shrieked. "It'll stitch your lips if you don't watch out." I'd heard the children at school say so. But you just pouted.

"I'm not goin' back there, Effie," your voice danced over the stony gurgle. "I wooon't, and I don't care what Mam says!"

But you did go, the next day and the next, and all the rest of that term. Of course, if you had stayed home, the chores would've made school seem pleasant; you'd've had to mind Mary. She was one almighty handful, walking by then and getting into the coal-bin, the pots and pans, even Mam's sewing basket if given the chance. I caught her once rolling spools of thread across the floor, about to fill her mouth with pins as she'd seen Mam do. Another time she nearly got her hands on the hankie I was tatting for your birthday. After that I learned to keep my work up high with Mam's plate.

As for either of us playing hooky, Mam said if anyone were to stay home it should be me, since I was the handy one, and you more bookish. Oh, I got along all right, had no trouble with schoolwork, though at that time I wasn't much for reading, unlike you. No. Until lately I suppose I've always preferred handiwork, things that keep the fingers as active as the mind. Though I would never have said so to you — or to Mam, of course — all my life it's been in the back of my head how much less I'd have gotten done had my nose been in books. Oh, I like sums all right, and figuring — my knack with numbers is what carried me through high school, that and writing. I used to enjoy essays: theme, proof, conclusion; now it's more need than pleasure prompting me to hold the pen.

Two years later the town got a bigger school with twice as many rooms as our old one, and I was able to continue through grade twelve.

Not that you ever had the chance.

You made it to that Christmas; even sang in the glee club concert at St. Bridgid's Hall, against Mam's better judgement. You had been ailing since November, when the weather changed. Such a shock, the coming of winter, after the leaves dropped and the cold arrived. The sky turned a constant grey, the sun as remote as Jupiter, after beaming down relentlessly that August and the first half of September. It stuns me now that we didn't pay more attention to the signs, the earliest snap in the air, the first frost on the grass. But one morning we awoke and the water in the pitcher was solid, the cat's milk skinned over with ice. We started wearing our dresses one on top of another, two pair of socks squeezed into our shoes — imagine!

You came down with a cold, then a fever, the cough rattling inside you like an ore cart down a hill. In our room one night you made me lie beside you, my ear to your chest. Through your thin white nightie I could feel your skin burning up, could hear the sickness inside filling you bit by bit the way a leaky faucet fills a pot. Mam came in and shooed me over to my bed; I watched her hold the back of her wrist to your forehead, then wring a cloth from the pail of cool water on the floor. She sat for a long time washing your face, lifting your pale hair to get behind your ears. When you shut your eyes, the lids looked bruised. I slipped over and laid my hand on Mam's arm, the two of us peering down at your face. It was smooth as a candle, with an odd ghostly flush, like rose petals trapped in wax.

Mam got up and blew out the light. "Shush now, Effie," she said. "You must leave her be now, she needs her rest."

You slept the rest of the night; I lay watching you through most of it, till sometime towards dawn I heard Pa rise and go off to work. I must have dozed then, because when I woke you were sitting up, hollow-cheeked, your eyes like marbles in that steely light.

"Where've I been, Eff?" you wanted to know.

"You've been awful sick, girl. Don't you get up now — Mam'll have your head if you do."

"But I'm better now." You spoke in a scratchy whisper, lowering your feet to the floor. They jerked upwards as your toes hit the boards.

"Get back in there — Mam'll put your neck in a sling if she sees you out of bed!"

You gave me one confounded look, as if I'd gone plain off my rocker. But it was a dreadful fright you'd given Mam the night before. "You should've seen 'er, Fan!" I said, "Poor Mam. I'd get back under those quilts if I were you!"

"But tonight's the concert, ain't it, Effie?"

"Hmph," I said, and put my hands on my hips, just like Mam. But you wouldn't give up.

"I'm a'right. The fever's gone — see?"

I stumbled out of bed and got you out of your nightie; it was damp with sweat. I helped you into your blue dress.

"You're gonna catch it from her, Fan," I tried one last time. But you were already at the landing, Mam striding from the kitchen, frowning up the stairs.

"Lord in heaven! Fanny Cox — what in the name of God——?"

Behind her, Peter started howling and some sort of ruckus erupted; something must've spilled and scalded someone — a bowl of porridge, perhaps.

You went with me to school that day. And that night we crowded with half the town into the Roman hall to watch you and some classmates sing "It Came Upon A Midnight Clear" and "Joy to the World". Poor, dear Fan in the front row, centre stage — your mouth a perfect earnest O, your eyes aglitter in that jumpy gaslight.

A boy got up and played "Away in a Manger" on his violin, the glee club joining in on the chorus. It must have been a hundred degrees in there, people squirming in their seats, pressing forward for a better view. The air was positively steamy, laden with the smell of damp wool and hair tonic.

When at last everyone filed offstage — boys tripping each other, grabbing at girls' hair ribbons and bows — you glanced into the audience and gave Mam and me a little smile. Even at that distance we could see you shivering.

Afterwards Mam put you straight to bed; you never did get up again. Dr. O'Hanley came the next morning and prescribed a tincture of balsam to help your breathing. He told Mam that it was pneumonia and that apart from praying there wasn't much we could do. It was best, he said, to sit back and hope God's mercy prevailed, and in the meantime try to make you comfortable.

When Mam showed him to the door, he advised giving you lots of water and keeping the room cool to control the fever. Despite the gravity of things, this last request seemed almost comical, the world outside so cold and grey, and us doubling up on clothes to keep warm.

It still hadn't snowed. Remember how we were like birds on a wire awaiting the first snowfall, the drifts and driving blizzards people kept talking about? The little ones could hardly contain themselves, though Mam and Pa would get a look like scared rabbits whenever mention of snow arose.

Christmas came and went without a flake. The sky was like a steely shroud, the wind raw and damp with a cold that would grind bones. In our socks hung by the stove, each of us got an orange, firm dimpled fruit that fit neatly into one's palm, its skin warm to the touch, so smooth and perfect I hated to peel mine. Its juice stung the corners of my mouth as I sucked it, section by section. Those oranges didn't last us ten minutes. But you barely touched yours, despite Mam's coaxing and holding pieces to your cracked lips.

Finally at New Year's it snowed — small wispy flakes at first, wafting like shadflies past the window. As the wind picked up, they whirled and gathered in thickening blasts, and soon covered the yard. The boys ran outside, fine fluffy whiteness filling their shoes and turning fingers and cheeks bright pink as they rolled and whooped and stuffed handfuls of it down each other's necks.

Outside, I held my face up and stuck out my tongue. Of course we'd seen snow in England, but not like this. I cannot say what I expected — a sweetness, like sugar? I just recall my disappointment when the sudden melting wetness tasted vaguely of the sky, of metal and soot.

Later, Mam and I got you up to watch the snow falling past our little window. By then it was almost dark; there was a ruff of white on the sill, and smaller tufts were frozen to the pane. You stuck out your finger and squeaked moisture off the cold black glass. Tiny pearls of perspiration stood out above your lip. Mam helped you back into bed, tried feeding you the rest of your orange. But you turned to the wall, the outline of your body trembling under the covers.

All night it snowed. Next morning the fence was practically buried, snow drifted and pooled around the tops of the pickets. From the window the town seemed transformed, even the sheds and furnaces blanketed white, the landscape a rolling sea swept and bleached of colour but for the odd pinprick of black or red. You lay in a fitful sleep while Mam readied the others for a trip to the store. The lot of us had to be fitted for boots, the ones we'd brought being thin and leaky as sieves. Mam left me to keep an eye on you while they trudged outdoors, the little ones shouting with glee, trailing behind her.

Upstairs I pushed the window out and grabbed a handful of snow. Slipping to your bedside, I held it to your cheek.

"You've got to get better, Fan." Could you hear me?

I held the snow till it was a knot of ice melting into the pillow. But you didn't open your eyes; I don't even know if you felt it.

Pa summoned Dr. O'Hanley that night and again the following day. But each visit he just shrugged, avoiding Mam's pleading looks, and patted your hand lying limp on top of the covers. She hovered at the foot of your bed, biting her cuticles, her cheeks sucked in, until Pa showed the doctor out. Then she sat like a scarecrow beside you, listening for snatches of gruff, polite talk below: Pa's murmured thanks, the doctor's curt apologies.

The third day after the storm, your breath grew shorter and

shorter, your chest heaving like a sparrow's, as though you were fighting for air. Or drowning, as if struggling from the depths of something fathomless pulling you under, little by little. Not once did Mam let go of your hand, as if she thought by hanging on she'd keep you from washing down into whatever flashed or glinted beneath those poor purplish lids.

For even now I cannot let myself think you weren't glimpsing something as you slipped like that from Mam's grip, from Pa and me bent over the bedside. It's impossible to believe a child could take her leave without someplace to *go*, however dark and distant, without someone or something waiting on the other side.

It's purely sentimental, a part of me knows. But how could I feel or think otherwise, watching you leave us?

The others stayed downstairs with Mrs. Scull, who'd come over to help when word of your sickness travelled next door. She kept everyone in the kitchen during the doctor's last visit; I marvel now that Mam and Pa allowed me to stay upstairs with them. They must've needed my company, or known that you did. Or else, in their miserable silence — the clock ticking below the only sound in the house besides your racked, raspy breathing — they forgot I was there; forgot I was only a child myself.

At the end you didn't open your eyes or speak. So all that business about what you might've seen in your mind's eye is but conjecture, my imagining. Maybe it was all blackness — no recollection or speculation; nothing but darkness sweeping in like a neap tide.

I can't tell you the moment the breathing stopped and your spirit took flight, your small face becoming smoother in death than in life. Mam seemed to shrivel up, her fingers laced through yours. Pa pressed her shoulder, stooping to kiss your cheek. Then he stalked out. I could hear him on the landing, crying, such a queer harsh sound in the icy stillness; that and the deepening hush from the kitchen as he crept downstairs.

I laid my cheek against Mam's back and felt her sobs, an empty shuddering inside. When at last I was able to touch you, your face was still warm.

I don't know how long we sat there, Mam and I. After a while I heard the stern but gentle sounds of Mrs. Scull herding the others next door, Pa going out to fetch the undertaker. It was so quiet I swear I could hear the *whisht* of his boots through that powdery snow.

Mr. Rushton arrived with his little black bag. It took both him and Pa to coax Mam from the room, so loath was she to leave you. I was told to go make tea while she and Pa sat in the parlour. What a strange relief when the kettle boiled, for a moment blocking out the rocker's creaking, the choking sounds coming from the next room. But as I rinsed the teapot, death's cold, graceless magnitude descended; it really was as if something had swooped unseen from the clouds and plucked you away.

Mr. Rushton returned later and helped Pa set the pine box on straight chairs in the parlour. Mam crouched by the stove, refusing to leave the kitchen. Once Mr. Rushton had gone, Pa nailed the lid shut, with a gentle *tap tap tap*. Not till after she'd gotten the little ones to bed did Mam venture into the room. Weeping, she kept running her hand over the splintery wood, like the blind reading Braille.

"It's no good, Addie," Pa whispered, drawing her back into the kitchen. "You got the others to think of, maid. You mustn't forget them."

"Not one flower or scrap of lace, no picture of her or nothing," Mam moaned over and over, making an awful sound through her clenched teeth. "Not a bit of prettiness for my sweet little girl."

XIII

Misdemeanours

And more the Needles honour to advance,
It is a Taylors Javelin, or his Launce;
And for my Countries quiet, I should like,
That women-kinde shoulde use no other Pike.
It will increase their peace, enlarge their store,
To use their tongues lesse, and their Needles more.
The Needles sharpnesse, profit yeelds, and pleasure,
But sharpness of the tongue, bites out of measure.

Had it been summer, we'd have put flowers on the grave — a
bouquet of daisies or our favourite, pansies. But in the depths of
winter, just getting the hole dug had Pa nearly twisting off the
ends of his moustache. That night it snowed again, and even Mr.
Rushton was concerned. I heard him discussing the arrangements
with Pa; Mam was out in the kitchen pouring tea, thank the Lord.

"Soil's so thin on the Hill it takes three fellows with crowbars
to dig a grave in July, let alone in the dead of January."

It sounded like a warning — useless, since the only other cemetery was the Roman one, the big level space squared off with

trees behind St. Bridgid's. Everyone else, Anglican and dissenter alike, was consigned to the stony ground overlooking the river.

But all was managed. The morning you were laid to rest, two men came for the coffin in a small black sleigh drawn by a single black mare. Mr. Scull was waiting in the yard, his team hitched to his bright red one. Numbly, we piled into it. The wind made our eyes stream, snapping like the whip Mr. Scull used on the horses.

We followed Rushton's sleigh. Their mare snorted in the cold, puffs of steamy breath above her blinkers. Her hooves made no sound in the rutted snow. In that frozen stillness we pinned our eyes upon the skimming runners ahead, the steaming clots of dung. Anything not to look at Mam pale and stiff in her thin black coat, her hands hidden inside Mrs. Scull's ratty black muff — the bleakness of her face even harder to bear than her weeping.

On the Hill, we stood stamping our feet while listening to the rector, his dry white lips burbling words of prayer and comfort, cold comfort. The grave gaped like a cut in the soft white drifts. I shut my eyes as the men from Rushton's lowered the box in — shut my ears, too, against the icy spatter of stones and dirt. My heart was clenched like a fist. And yet I felt it sliver, as though parts were being chiselled off and sunk into the ground with you, stowed away forever.

Mam was the same. She never got over it, Fan. For a long time it was as though our world had stopped like a ball of wool unfurled under a chair. For weeks, perhaps months, we went about barely speaking, tiptoeing from room to room as if the floors were of glass. At first, Mrs. Scull and the other women on our road sent pies and loaves and dishes of food — mashed potatoes, turnip, even a roast of pork. As their offerings petered out, once again Mam took up cooking and cleaning and minding children, of course. Though with neither the same quick tongue nor the same coaxing patience. She seemed even more distracted, as though she were no longer completely with us, had her sights placed firmly elsewhere. As if all the whining and pouting and whizgigging in the world could no longer touch her.

It took Mam and Pa a couple of years to place the headstone. They had to travel to Caledonia, you see, to choose it; to hear the carry-on, Peter and Mary's howling when they left on their errand, you'd have sworn they were off to another country.

Mr. Rushton could have ordered the stone; it wasn't a monument for an official, a company man or Member of Parliament or some other bigwig. I'm still not sure why all the to-do — perhaps Pa needed the trip, to view the countryside beyond our blue hills. Or maybe he was simply humouring Mam, who wouldn't trust Rushton's to do their best by you.

This left Willie and me to mind the others while she and Pa spent the night in Caledonia. I was all of sixteen, old enough, I suppose, to handle a houseful of youngsters.

We stood at the gate seeing them off. It was a fine Saturday morning; Mam had a flush to her cheeks, which made her look nervous, hanging off Pa's arm as they left on foot to catch the train. I had Peter wriggling in my arms. He was a bit big now to be held like that, but he squalled after Mam as she strode up the hill alongside Pa. She looked small and stocky in her grey frock; dressed in his old black suit, Pa wasn't much bigger, the pair of them stooped yet sturdy-looking in their dull, serviceable clothes.

When they reached the crest, their heels stirring the dust, you could scarcely tell one from the other. I've heard it said once that people married awhile come to look alike. I don't know how much store I'd put in that, except when I think of Mam and Pa going off that day to choose a tombstone. They even shared the same short, determined gait, as if they had more in mind than this one sad errand.

There wasn't a return train till early the next day. Mam had given me the lowdown on getting the others to bed, seeing they were clean and fed and tucked in tight while she was gone. I have to say my heart sank like birdshot as she and Pa disappeared over the last rise, and Peter's arms circled my neck like a rope. "Mind you help your sister," Pa had instructed Willie. But Willie was off like a jackrabbit before they got out of sight — off with his friends, I assumed, some boys from over town.

I hadn't time to wonder where he'd taken off to — the river, maybe, to catch frogs; or outside the Waverley House, watching men shoot the breeze and hawk tobacco juice onto the dirt, or peering inside at folks eating ice-cream. Willie might've passed the rest of the day fooling around outside Lewises' store; he had chums from up that way. I was too busy keeping the peace and hulling strawberries to give a hoot where he'd disappeared to.

By afternoon the day grew so hot the air pressed down, sticky as the sealer on a Mason jar! Mam had left a slew of berries to be washed and hulled for jam; already they'd started to blacken in the big enamel basin. I was working like the devil to get them done while the little ones played back in the field. Every now and then I'd glance out and see their heads bobbing like gophers in the long, bleached grass. It was nearly four o'clock — any second they'd be in, clamouring for bread and molasses — and I had quarts and quarts to go. My fingers were stained red, the back of my shirtwaist was stuck down with sweat. The room swam with murky sweetness, the smell of berries and kerosene. But at least it was quiet, the lovely stillness of an empty house, which, if one could assign a colour, would have to be pale, pale blue. The only sounds were the odd ping of my knife against the bowl; the faint, shrill shouts of the children just far enough off. Flicking hulls into the sink, I watched as a couple of crows perched outside on the shed roof, cawing before flapping off. Two crows joy, I thought, sweating and licking juice from my fingers.

I dumped sugar on the clean berries mounded in Mam's yellow bread-bowl, stirred it in until they glistened. In the parlour the mantel clock started chiming, like the scratchiness of a key in a rusty lock. Without warning, as if out of nowhere, came the thud of boots upon the veranda; a light, frantic rapping. "It's open — let yourself in!" I yelled, figuring it was Willie. When the tapping kept up, I slid off my stool, pushing sticky strands of hair out of my face, all set to give him a raking-over. But it wasn't Willie at the door; rather, it was a stranger, a dark, gangly fellow in filthy clothes.

"Don't mean to trouble you," he said in a drawl, a slow, shy smile working across his moon face. "But I was just goin' past when I wondered if a fella'd be so lucky as to get a drink of water."

He couldn't have been much older than me, but he was taller — so tall he hung his head to speak. The toes were worn clean out of his greasy boots; gaps in his buttoned shirtfront showed the smooth brown skin underneath. Despite the heat he was wearing a cap, a dirty woollen one which he didn't remove ducking past me into the hall.

I didn't move an inch; I couldn't. Instead, I stayed pinned to the wall, sweat like snowdrops between my shoulderblades. Later, I could've kicked myself for lacking the brains to up and run next door. But all I did was stand and watch as this ragged, lanky stranger stalked to the kitchen and helped himself to Pa's tin mug. The *hee-haw* of the pump seemed to go on forever, the gurgle and splash rending the silence as he leaned over the sink, his chin cocked, guzzling.

Then, as if remembering me standing post-like in the hall, he flung down the mug and plunged his grubby hand into the berries. Stuffing a fistful into his mouth, he started towards me; he wiped the dribbling juice on his sleeve. Peering at me through the gloom of the hallway, he tipped his cap. His face looked flushed, feverish. Slippery as stove oil, his eyes slid over my face, my front, with no hint of a smile any more. I crossed my arms, gripping both elbows to quell the trembling.

"Obliged to you, missus," he said with the most absurd politeness. His eyes skimmed the floor as he sidestepped me; his sleeve brushed mine. "A fella gets an awful thirst, out on the road." When he spoke I noticed he had two teeth missing. Greasy locks curled behind his ears. His jaw was smooth, with the faintest smudge of down and little pinkish rivers of dirt.

"I'd be rightly grateful if you kept this to yourself, missus, this little visit. We'll call it a secret, eh, between you an' me? And don't forget, 'cause now I knows where you live, I kin always come back for another look-see."

He reached out to seize my arm, perhaps even to give it a pinch, but when I shrank away he stopped himself, and the next I knew he was out the door and through the gate, his footsteps lost in the road.

A few minutes later the children piled into the kitchen, Sarah hauling Peter, and Mary scrabbling after the berries. If I was shaking, they never noticed. To quiet them I gave each a dish of berries to eat out on the stoop while I calmed down enough to start supper. I don't suppose they noticed my hand wobble as I doled out each sweet portion, much of my afternoon's work, or took up my knife to start scraping potatoes.

We'd just sat down to eat when Willie rushed in like a puppy tripping over its own feet, so agog with news he could barely catch his breath. Something about a holdup at Lewises' store, two fellows bold as day sauntering in off the road and cleaning the till of every nickel. "Me and John Landry," Willie gasped, eyes shiny as spoons in that freckled face, "we seen everything, like something out of a dream 'cept speeded up jig-time." Mary, Sarah, Joseph and Zeke were all eyes, their little mouths open like a fish's, the cut-up scraps of mutton hardening on their plates.

Willie leaned forward on his elbows, describing the robbers in their torn shirts and britches, dirty red bandanas tied over their mouths. Their muffled jeers; the rifle jabbed up under old man Lewis's Adam's apple. Gave us the blow-by-blow, Willie did, us listening as if it were some dandy entertainment, spectacular as sparks from the forge showering the sky. Never mind that the little ones were scared skinny — me too, for that matter. I forgot the beans in the oven till they started to smoke. Not one of us lifting a finger or chewing till we'd got the whole story, how it was Silas Lewis, the merchant's son, who finally opened the register and handed over the money, his arm shaking like a dead branch.

Malcolm Lewis must've balked — Willie said the old fellow slid his eyes past the gun barrel towards his son — because just before Silas surrendered the cash, the robber rammed the butt under the father's chin. You could hear his teeth break like china, Willie said. Apparently that's when Silas flung the money at the thieves.

They made a grab for it and ran out, nearly knocking over a woman in the doorway, I gather. Like himself and his friend, Willie said, she'd just walked in. From the sound of things, nobody'd had any inkling of the commotion going on inside until they found themselves in the thick of it. It seems at first everybody just stood around dumbfounded while the old man slumped there spitting blood. Willie said he and John were scared to move. According to him, it was Silas who ran to fetch the sheriff. By the time Lem Mattattal arrived on the scene, the robbers were long gone. Into the woods up Westchester way, most likely, headed straight for the hills — or so it was surmised, Willie told us. And sure enough, next day a red hankie was found in the ditch up past the forge.

Rumours spread that the same two fellows were seen a fortnight later, pulling similar heists in Springhill and as far away as Moncton. Crazy as it sounds, however, nobody — not even the Lewises — could come up with much of a description. The men's ages, whether they had blue eyes or brown; their hair colour or the shape of their jaws under those grubby masks. Nothing to print on a poster or to set the law on a fruitful trail. So no one was ever caught, nobody we heard of anyway. And I never did find out if one of the bandits had missing teeth.

As for old Malcolm Lewis — well, once he got back on his feet and dusted off the seat of his pants, I gather it was business as usual. People said what Lewises' lost in a matter of minutes they recouped in a day. If anyone was shaken up, it would've been Silas. He was a year or two ahead of me in school, hardly what you'd call a big strapping boy; I don't suppose you would remember. But I wager he took the brunt of his father's ire for letting that money go so easily — almost as easily as it was made in the first place, some said. But what else could Silas have done? What would any smart-thinking person have done?

Well, if the robbery didn't interrupt the Lewises' business, I wish the same could've been said of mine. Mam and Pa would have walked the twenty-three miles home from Caledonia had they known of it. I was on tenterhooks all that evening, nervous as a cat lurking around, double-checking locks and windows. I shut the place up tight as a drum, the others watching and whining about how stuffy it was inside. All the while I tried hiding my jitters, which worsened once the dishes were done and the shadows outside lengthened, the sun a shrinking ball atop the hill.

All I could think of was that fellow in our kitchen hiding out in the woods, blending with the trees. His slippery soles quiet as an Indian's on the spruce needles.

If you'd been here, we might have eventually lapsed into nervous giggles, fearful shivering become tittering glee. It would have helped, I know.

Darkness fell too quickly, though I took my sweet time getting the others to bed. Once they were asleep, I undressed and put on my thickest nightie — despite the others' complaints, I felt not the heat but a chill. As I tiptoed downstairs to finish up the berries, fear crept from the small of my back up my spine. In the kitchen I lit the lamp and put the last of the fruit on the table. It was now soft and purple. Starting in on it, I stopped to draw the curtain — a veil against the drafty darkness at the panes, the deep violet beyond. My thumb left a pink print on the white tatted cloth. From someplace out back I heard someone whistle for a dog; the throaty trill of peepers.

The light flickered, filling corners and nooks with soft pitch shadows — a velvety dimness that would've been soothing, had I had company. I'd grown to like evenings best, Fan, when the house was finally settled and I could sew and sip tea in peace with Mam and Pa. Their gentle quiet; Pa's talk, the creak of Mam's rocker. The click of my needle against the thimble.

But that night all I listened for was the sound of intruders. I knew they were out there somewhere, those two men. Knowing it made me stand straighter gripping the knife, breathing from the tops of my lungs — as if drawing too much air would be like throwing down one's defences. Unlocking the door, inviting *them* in.

Above in their beds, I heard Willie turning, Peter's faint snore, Mary murmuring softly in her sleep. Outside, the wind rose. I heard it whoosh through the poplar out front like the river running its banks. Clinkers settled in the stove; the cat wailed to go out, the same pitiful cry as a newborn's. Wiping my hands, I eyed Pa's shiny Marlin rifle hung on a peg above the coal scuttle. I'd paid it no heed since the day he'd bought it at the company store, after a notice in *The Week's Doings* advised, "Protect Your Homes!" He'd joked to Mam that a gun might come in handy felling ducks and rabbits to feed us, but so far it hadn't been down off the wall.

Out in the yard, Puss kept up her caterwauling, her cries half squelched by the wind, then shrilling to the shrieks of combat. The moon had risen, a pale egg hatched from the clouds. The cats quit their squalling, perhaps skulking after mice instead.

I stood on a chair to get the rifle. You would have marvelled at me cradling its dull weight in my arms, metal cool and heavy as clay. Holding it like a baby, I stood for a time at the kitchen window, then went into the parlour.

There I slid to the floor, huddled with my back to the wainscotting, the gun laid across the scuffed boards at my feet. I sat like that all night, till the lamp in the kitchen burned itself out and the sun came up, filling the room with weak light. Out back the cat clawed to come in, and upstairs the children began to stir. In the silkiness of dawn, Pa's rifle looked greeny-black, stupid and cold as a watersnake.

Soon I heard Mary on the landing, and I got up and hung the gun back in its place before she or the others could notice. Without any more to-do, I put on water for porridge, another big potful for the washing. Mary climbed onto the bench by the window, whining for Mam, and before long the others came trooping downstairs, Zeke in wet pyjamas. I had my work cut out, I could see, before our parents got home. But being so grateful for daylight, I didn't growl — just dished out breakfast, holding my tongue when the little ones turned up their noses.

I was out back, Fan, up to my elbows in Mam's big grey washtub, when Silas Lewis and Lem Mattattal sauntered round the side of the house. Sniffing out some sign of reasonable life, it appeared — I suppose they'd gone to the front first, then come around back when they heard the crying and brawling over something or other inside. Willie was supposed to be in charge while I did the wash. I guess he'd wandered off again.

I happened to glance up from the greyish suds as they appeared, Sheriff Mattattal portly and impatient, dangling his watch-fob from one pocket. He was sweating, a trickle of moisture along one ruddy, pitted cheek. Silas stood beside him, tall and red-headed, skinny as a rake, with his pants hitched so high the tops of his boots showed.

He was a grade or two ahead of me, as I've said, though till that day I'd never paid him any attention. Except when the teacher, Mr. Slade, asked tricky algebra questions. Silas was always good with figures, all that business of x's and y's. The girls would roll their eyes and snicker into their palms — the boys too, those still in school and not working in the mill — whenever Silas rose to give the answer. Two bright spots would light up his cheeks, normally pale as a pickerel's belly. There was nothing to make you want to look at him — I mean *really* look — when he stood there gazing at the board, rhyming off equations. I cannot say I took much notice of him at all till that moment he came around back with Lem, and caught me humming "Be Thou My Vision" only half under my breath.

Mattattal looked about fit to string him up, as if it were Silas who'd committed some misdemeanour and *I* the long arm of the law being required to pass judgement. This unnerved me — I must have appeared dumb, standing speechless, my hands dripping. Finally, Lem spoke.

"Effie Cox, aren't you? You fellas seen any odd goings-on around here the last little bit? I seen your folks heading out to the station yesterday — you wouldn't want trouble hereabouts, girl, especially after what they've been through up to Lewises' place." He turned and nudged Silas hovering beside him, looking vexed.

"Now Silas, you tell Effie what you seen — I don't mean the robbery itself; figure by now the whole town knows the details. I want you to try and tell her what those two felons looked like."

Silas blushed and stared at the pair of drawers I'd been swishing out, as if their appearance might spark some recollection. From inside the house came a squeal, the racket of something crashing to the floor — Mam's bread-bowl, I feared.

"Like I told you, sir, I can't remember what-all they looked like," he sighed, his eyes moving from the washwater to my red, red hands, then up to my face.

The sun was baking down, high and strong as the day before. I could feel brackets of perspiration under my arms.

"C'mon there, we don't have till Christmas. Why, those fellas are probably way past Folly Mountain by now!" Mattattal sucked the ends of his moustache, let out a beleaguered sigh. "Like I told your father, we're gonna need all the help we can get!"

Silas shrugged, looking at me.

"One of them was kind of tall, I think — about my height, maybe? The other had a scar on his thumb, a scar about an inch long, I guess, curved like this, in a crescent——"

The sheriff shook his head, shifting from foot to foot, fingering his watch chain the way a Catholic would his rosary.

"I'm sorry, I can't help you," I finally spoke up, my eyes on Silas. "No sir, we haven't noticed one thing queer, not today or yesterday or the day before, far as that goes." A half-hearted smile skimmed Silas's face, fleeting as a bird's shadow.

"Well, I guess that's it then — for godsake. I s'pose we'll try next door and see if we have better luck." Patting his pockets, locating a packet of snuff, Mattattal leaned against the house; the faded, peeling shingles were the same shade as Silas's hair. "Them folks of yours aren't gone for long, I hope. Asking for trouble, you ask me, young lady like yourself all alone with that brood."

By now Peter was hanging in the doorway picking his nose, soaking all this up like a rag. Mattattal slapped his thigh and nudged Silas. "Better get on, boy — that old man of yours is gonna think I've got you locked up!"

Then off he went towards the road, Silas trailing behind like a long-necked crane. Or that heron we saw, you and I, one time at dusk, in the marsh downwind of the mill. Its wings looked orange, remember? You insisted they were pink.

When the one o'clock train pulled in, Mam and Pa had their purchase with them. Wrapped in canvas, it was heavy as lead; it took two freightmen to haul it off the baggage car and onto a waiting cart. Mr. Scull came this time with his wagon. Riding home, I was so happy to have Mam and Pa back that I almost forgot what was under the cloth.

In the kitchen we couldn't help milling around Mam. While she shooed the others from her purse, Pa pulled treats from his pockets and handed them out. There was pink-and-white striped ribbon candy that slivered like glass when you bit into it, the hard, sugary crackle digging straight to the roots of your teeth.

You would have loved it, Fan. You'd have asked for more.

XIV

Spooning

A Needle (though it be but small and slender)
Yet it is both a maker and a mender:
A grave Reformer of old Rents decayd,
Stops holes and seames and desperate cuts displayd,
And thus without the Needle we may see
We should without our Bibs and Biggins bee;
No shirts or Smockes, our nakednesse to hide,
No garments gay, to make us magnifide....

A month or more passed before I laid eyes on Silas again. He'd finished grade twelve that June and, I suppose, was working for his father full-time — not that he was the type you noticed much, coming and going. We bought most of our necessities at the company store, had little occasion to shop elsewhere. But one afternoon towards the end of summer Mam sent me up to Lewises' for rolled oats and Epsom salts advertised on special in *The Doings*. She needed the oats for bread she was in the midst of making.

Silas turned pink when I entered the store. He slid closer when I stopped to peruse a display of medicinals. From the office to the rear, I could hear the old fellow yammering on about some stock gone missing. Silas laid his bony hands upon the glass countertop, rolling his eyes at his father's grousing. Some customers bustled in, foundry men with their sleeves rolled up, wanting tobacco. He seemed in no hurry to help them, their grumblings apparently no more urgent to him than a horsefly's buzzing in the window. His watery eyes locked on mine as he handed me the little blue box of salts. Haltingly, he went and measured the oatmeal.

"What's a fella to do for some service around here?" one of the men bellowed. Silas slung down the bag of oats, grabbing my money as fast as greased lightning, and, before his father could come out and reprimand him, handled the surly customers.

"See you round, Euphemia," he called, his voice rising as it followed me to the door. "You-pheem-ya" was how he said it, in the tone a minister might use. Until then I wasn't even sure he knew my real name.

I pretended not to hear him, imagining his look, having got my attention: hope awash in those eyes guileless as a cow's? His eyelashes were so pale, his lids so pink, he almost looked as though he'd been crying; the thought of his eyes made me squirm. So without turning I hurried outside, pulling in my skirt to avoid something sticky on the steps, a dribble of molasses or syrup that had wasps circling. But as I stalked away, Mam's bag of oats a warm weight on my arm, I was suddenly aware of each muscle, each movement jumpy and tense as a ratcheting flywheel. I found myself wondering when Mam would need me to go to Lewises' again.

Then one October evening, in that gilded dusk when the leaves are all yellow, I ran into him while out walking. Perhaps I should say he ran into me.

I was behind the school, picking wild asters, when the notion hit me to place some on your plot. Once the headstone was laid, it seemed we took great pains not to visit it — and after all the to-do over a fitting marker. Too fitting, I'd venture to add, since placing the stone only picked the scab off Mam's grief. To us, the Hill became a place to avoid — where, passing by, we ducked our heads and thought other thoughts. Unlike the Romans, crossing themselves every time they came within a stone's throw of St. Bridgid's or its churchyard. It's almost foolhardy to recall, but for a long, long time it felt as though all those lying in that rocky dirt had the power to reach up and pull the living down with them, beneath the burdock and thistle.

With my weed bouquet I started up the shortcut by the river, the steep dirt track winding through the yellow birches. It was just after supper, the sun low but bright. The air was perfectly still, the woods a blaze of gold; leaves swished at my feet. All was so still that I hunched a little as I climbed, as though to make myself smaller, less intrusive. It seemed as if the gaps between the leaves were eyes, Fan, shifty as sunlight through the twigs.

Near the clearing, where the gravestones stud the hillside, I heard the bushes move, heard a half-swallowed shout. There was Silas, of all people, a short distance away, marching towards me up an adjacent path. Catching me up, he yanked off his cap and held it in one hand, gazing at his feet as he spoke.

"Queer place for a stroll, don't you think?" The other hand disappeared in his pocket, jingling coins at a fevered rate.

"No queerer than running into you, Silas Lewis."

"Oh, I wouldn't know about that."

The sleeves of his jacket were too short; when he bent to pick something up, a birch switch, his shirt's smudged white cuffs rode up to show the reddish hair on his wrists. I had to look away as he twirled his cap on one end of the stick before flinging it like a spear over some tilted stones.

"My grandfather's buried here, his father too. Baptists, right up alongside the Methodists and Church of England. All in the same boat now, no matter how you see it. Perhaps the Lord's not too picky — at least, for their sakes I hope not. What do *you* think, Effie? Euphemia," he corrected himself softly, as if mulling over the sound of each syllable. I gave him a look and didn't reply.

"Who'd of ever thought I'd catch up with you here, Euphe — or is it Effie?" Even in the fading light I could see his colour rise.

I went and laid my flowers on the grass beside your stone.

"Mind if I walk back with you, then?" he called in a hoarse, high voice. "When you're done, I mean." As if I were browsing for soap or perfume!

"I suppose not," I muttered, mortified. Yet I felt the rush of blood behind my ears, a sudden, peculiar shyness. Making for the road, we quickly descended the hill. I kept my eyes on the leaves and pebbles at my feet as Silas shambled along at my elbow.

We cut across the field. Up close he didn't seem quite so gangly, his legs scissoring through the goldenrod in step with mine. A couple of times I glanced sideways, felt myself ease slightly — enough to speak.

"So how come you're not working?" I finally uttered, to make conversation.

He gave a polite but nervous guffaw. "Not like we're open round the clock or nothing — the father does give me the odd time off, you know." He sounded so earnest that I felt something inside me give, like the laces of a corset slackening.

"I'm sure," I said, uncertain of what else to say. By then we'd reached the crest of the hill, where Main Street ascended from the Chapel Bridge. In the distance, near the foot of Church, the gabled peak of St. Bridgid's Hall cast the surrounding houses and storefronts in bluish shadow, their rooftops a greyish glint in the dying sun.

Just across the road from us was Lewises' store. The blinds were drawn, its big front window an orange-golden glare. In a window above, a light came on; I glimpsed a woman through the limp, lace curtains.

Silas removed his cap again, his eyes jittery and bright.

"Well, I guess I'll be seein' you," he said, a nervous grin lighting his face as he stared past me, past the bridge, past the Merchants' Bank, the promenade outside the Waverley just visible beyond its stone façade. His elbows cocked like a turkey's, he stood looking for all the world as if, from this safe and distant vantage point, he was willing something to happen — brawling drunks to spill from the Waverley onto the street, or his father to appear out of nowhere.

The curtain twitched in the window above.

"Like as not," I said — a tad more shrewishly than I'd intended, racking my brain for something else, what other girls would say in a similar position. *See you up the hall, maybe, next time the brass band plays, or next time you're out for a walk or down the ball field for the next game.* Or, if all else failed: *How 'bout St. Bridgid's, the next boxed supper?*

But none of these would have applied, since neither he nor I attended many sporting or social events.

The upstairs light went out.

"Guess I'll see you next time there's a sale," I finally said, sounding so stupid I turned and started running down the hill towards the river. There were no goodbyes or good nights. I figured he would head inside then. But at the bridge I glanced back and he was still there, a dim string-bean shape in the arc light outside the store. He lifted his hand and waved.

The chances of running into him waned, of course, as people began stocking up for winter. The poor fellow, I suppose his father had him going full-tilt till Christmas, working out front and in back too. Maybe that's where he was the one time I ventured in, on the pretext of buying ribbon and some thread for Mam in a scarlet no one else carried.

For my errand I put on a clean shirtwaist — had to stoke the fire twice getting the iron hot enough to press it. Cursing the cold and my shabby brown coat, all the way over the bridge and up the hill I rehearsed what I'd say. *Long time no see. Business must be booming, I guess.* But when I got there he was nowhere in sight; there was just the father, cagey and stern as ever behind the cash. He gave a curt nod as he counted out my ten cents for the purchases, not once opening his mouth. Notwithstanding my new-found...charity towards Silas, I'd relished a peek at those black stumps left after the run-in with the robbers. But no; Malcolm Lewis never said a word. If he had, I might have plucked up the nerve to enquire after his son.

Over Christmas I expected to meet up with Silas somewhere — if only to catch a glimpse of him. At the band concert, amid the droves flocking to St. Bridgid's. But for all I knew, he might as well have left town. By New Year's it occurred to me that perhaps he had, fear of this settling upon me like the grippe. For a week or two I lost heart in almost everything, school and needlework alike. Twice Mam cornered me, after Pa was in bed, wondering why I'd gotten so peevish. I might have told her, too, had she not looked so suspicious. Her concern made me feel silly, foolish and irked at being in knots over something I figured no other soul could see, let alone understand. I barely understood it myself.

Not Silas! Silas Lewis? Malcolm Lewis's son? I could just hear Mam. "For the love of God, girl," she would've chided, had she known. "Not that Lewis boy! Nothing against him, now. But that family, with all their money and their holier than thou's.... Oh, I seen him in the store and he *seems* pleasant enough — not like the father. But homely? Think of the children he'd spawn! And anyway, don't let them plain looks deceive you; it's under the skin what matters, and there I daresay he's a Lewis, through and through."

That winter there was little snow. By the time the real bitterness set in, the strong-arm cold of January, I had resolved to forget Silas. I'd sit in class rubbing my hands to warm them, and look around, surveying the boys' stiff, ruddy faces. In my mind I was picking and sorting through them like buttons, the ones Mam snipped from worn-out clothes and saved in a tobacco tin. There was Reggie Cuthbertson, Isaiah Rushton, Bert Putnam — they were the choice ones, the ones girls swooped their eyes at. They were like the fancy brass buttons Mam cut from a jacket of Pa's, shining amid the dull old ones of bone and Arcadia-made iron.

It was our last year in school; in a way you had to credit all these boys for finishing, and not following their dads up Foundry Hill. Yet when you saw them sprawled in their seats, legs thrust out in the aisles — heard them laugh and joke whenever Mr. Slade paused to put wood on the fire — any lustre they might've possessed quickly rubbed off. I could picture them, the sour cut of their mouths, the roughness inherited from their fathers, as soon as they graduated and started working.

Once Bert Putnam held the door and walked behind me up the street, shouting a compliment when I turned off at our row. Something like "That was some good answer you give today in history" or "Whoever thought a gal could be so smart, almost as smart as Buddy Whasisname used to jump right up with the answers — the math-e-matical weasel!" I bumped our gate wide with my hip and marched up the steps. The ache I felt for Silas was like that of a bad tooth.

Perhaps the entire town thought I had feelings for Silas — and why not? His people had money. Regardless, I longed for what set him apart — a quietude despite that stumbling, stolid way of his; a quietude bred of certainty, yes, security. The security of his faith. He made me think of molten iron cast in sand, just as in Pa's descriptive ramblings: bubbling metal cooling, taking shape, turning strong and eventually unbendable. Any awkwardness, I believed, resulted from Silas living with his father. His oddness I saw as a show of mettle, his shyness perhaps a mark of distinction.

Our chance meeting at the river one evening proved me right. It was February; a three-quarters moon lit the frozen stream, the ice shiny and black as cut coal. I'd gone there with girls from school, two sisters, Ruth and Peggy Grandy. They were flying around on their skates, scarves and coattails twisting in the wind.

I'm no skater — never was and Lord knows never will be. But Pa had come home this day with a new pair of Starrs; someone at the mill whose wife had run off had given them away. The Grandys had promised to teach me to skate, so I agreed, to please Pa; also to get out from under Mam's gaze, the way she'd taken to watching me lately.

"Arse over teakettle" was how the Grandys described my efforts once the wretched blades were strapped to my boots. Wobbling to my feet, I slipped and landed on my rump, stunned as a cow, the cold spreading like a bruise through my drawers. The others grabbed my arms and helped me up, took turns leading me around stiff as a plank. Soon they grew bored and glided off, leaving me on a rock. Shivering down to my innards, I closed my eyes and listened to the sound of their skates like knives cutting glass, and the burble of the river beneath.

Off they flew towards the bend, where the sky and trees melded into black. A muzzy wheel ringed the moon overhead, tinged with an orange glow from the mill. Aided by its pale light, I gazed down through the ice at dead leaves, even a lily pad, trapped there as if floating in blackness. I lost sight of the girls, their shapes blending with the spruce. Sucking in my belly, I stood up, tried pushing off with one foot. I'd just managed another little push when he called out. Silas, I mean; his awkward voice ringing over the river.

Rigid with cold, I was too timid to move. He slid towards me, skates slung over one shoulder, his arms going like windmills. "My land," he said, "when did you take up skating, Phemia? I don't recall seeing you out here before." I must've looked like a tot learning to walk, my feet braced wide, with not another soul in sight. He was laughing at me.

"It's a free world," I snapped, then caught myself. Something let go inside me. "For the love of heaven — *stranger!* I reckoned you'd left for Timbuktu!" He looked startled; then he did something most unexpected. Skidding closer, he reached out and poked my cheek with his finger. His glove was cool and butter-soft.

"Might as well have. Father's got my life cut out for me these days up the store." He coughed, eyeing me with that earnestness I'd begun to hanker for. "A fellow could say the same for you, you know. Some might wonder where you've been hiding yourself too."

The sound of blades whisked closer. There was the chilly echo of laughter.

"It's Silas," one of the girls hissed as they snowploughed up to us. I tried to wiggle away but my feet skidded out from under me. Silas grabbed my arm. The Grandys were all eyes, taking this in.

"Found yourself a new teacher, have you?" Their cackling seemed to crack the air as they flitted off, twin shadows.

Flurries started wisping down. Holding both arms out like broomsticks, I stamped my feet. They felt frozen to the river.

"I take it you've had enough, have you? I s'pose there's something you'd rather be doing?"

Skating was for the birds, I felt like saying. But he was busy watching the girls, a look of stubborn clumsiness returned to his long white face. I could see it, that and the faint scrub of whiskers on his jaw. I was waiting for him to put on his skates and glide off, leaving me marooned like the puck I'd seen frozen to the surface, lost as those leaves trapped underneath.

Instead, he took my stiff, mittened hand in his — mind, this was Silas doing this! I let him tow me to a rock, where he undid my blades. Gripping his gloves in his teeth, he had to work at the buckles. His fingers were shaking — from cold or nervousness, I'm not sure which. Somehow it didn't matter, his shyness, I mean. Because that made two of us, and I resolved then that it was something we'd get over, soon enough.

The wind rattled the trees as he walked me home. My toes and fingers were numb, but I didn't care. I could have lost them to frostbite, it wouldn't have mattered. Especially when he leaned over the gate, as though to retrieve something he'd dropped, and kissed me just above my mouth.

His lips were rough as tree bark, Fan, but gentle and warm too. I kept my eyes open, watched his lolling under the lids like a baby's at the breast. His breath was dry and a little sour, like old apples; perhaps he had a troublesome tooth. But I didn't mind. I wouldn't have minded if his mouth had been full of stumps, or he'd tried to gum me to death!

Pa did, however. He and Mam were waiting in the kitchen when I came in. Mam sighed and clicked her teeth. "Not right, a young girl out on her own this late with a fella. No tellin' what could happen." She said it with a faint, rather smug smile.

"What became of them girlfriends of yours?" There was an ugliness to Pa's voice. "You don' know what kind of creatures might be in them woods at night, girlie."

I hung the skates on a nail.

"I seen what you were up to, Effie. And it don't matter who the fella was, if it was that Lewis bloke or whoever. I expect you to act like a lady, is all, and what I seen out there by the fence was not what I'd have any girl of mine doing. Lewis or not, these young fellas are just out for one thing. And where, my girl, would that leave someone like you? Eh?" He squeaked his chair back and hunched forward, those big hands knotted between his knees. He pinned me with his eyes.

"I'll grind his bones, I will, any fella lays a finger on you. You hear me? I don't give a goddamn who he is, neither. No girl of mine'll be made a whore of."

He got up and strode out, his footsteps rattling Mam's cup and saucer. She took a deep breath and gave me a weary smile.

"Girls'll be girls, Effie. I know how you feel — I ain't blind, so don't you think I can't see it for myself." She reached over and pinched my earlobe, then rubbed it softly between her scratchy fingers.

"He's a nice enough fella, too. Got a nice way," she said, which kind of took me aback. Your pa'll see that. He will, in time. He's gonna have to, I guess. Sooner or later."

The next night at supper Pa barely looked at me; he made a point of asking someone else to pass the salt and pour him another cup of tea. After I helped Mam clean up, I grabbed the skates and ran down to the bridge. Just as I hoped, Silas was there, swooping over the ice like the wind as if it were something he was born to, all clumsiness whipped away.

The rock underneath me was cold as Greenland, but for two hours I sat and watched him, and then he walked me home. Mam and Pa were waiting in the parlour this time. Mam tapped Pa's arm when it looked as though he'd start in. Without speaking, he stomped up to bed while I went to get a cup of tea. Mam nodded when she came out to see what I was doing. She gave me that same tight smile, as if she were the one with a secret — a secret she wouldn't have minded disclosing, just didn't know how or where to begin.

"Watch your p's and q's" was all she would say. Which at the time seemed kind of hollow, as she had never learned to write. "And mind you don't shame or hurt your father." As if nothing I did could shame or hurt her.

And so I kept meeting Silas on the river, and he kept walking me home. A fortnight of clear black nights, just the two of us in the moonlight. I would wear the skates long enough to make it truthful, explaining to Mam what I was doing. This helped smooth over any guilt about the part I omitted: with whom I was doing it. I also hoped to win over Pa, letting him think the hand-me-down Starrs were a wonderful gift. Which in a way, I suppose, they were.

Though neither Silas nor I said it, we both dreaded spring, dreaded the river breaking up, the days lengthening. It was Silas who chose to declare our friendship more than a mere testing of the ice. One evening in late March, when the fields and roadsides were a welter of mud, he came calling. The children were in the kitchen doing homework, wrestling over a pencil. I had taken some darning into the parlour in order to escape the noise. Pa was dozing in his chair by the fire, his tea gone cold. I was holding my needle up to the lamp to thread it when the knock came. Mam dropped the broom to answer it.

"You got company, Effie," she announced, a mix of impatience and amusement on her face. Showing Silas in, she resumed sweeping, only faster, as if the dust and dirt were embers. Stirring, Pa glanced up, his eyes fixing on Silas slouched in the doorway, his cap in hand. He twisted out of the way as Peter and Zeke roared towards him. Bending slightly, he stared in bemusement when Peter began rolling a marble over his boot.

"Won't you sit for a minute, have a cup of tea?" Mam brushed past, tipping a stack of mending from the one unoccupied chair.

Pa's gaze was like a rattlesnake's. He waited till Silas sat down stiff as a poker opposite me; then he spoke. "So, what business is it brings you to see us, eh? I wouldn't suppose it's your father sent ya out collecting I-owe-you's."

His jaw twitching, Silas glanced towards me and grimaced. His cheeks burned in the lamplight. Mam scurried in with his tea, sloshing a little into the saucer. She'd given him her best china cup, a pretty one with yellow roses, a tiny chip in the bottom from the others' shenanigans. Silas thanked her, then stared at his lap, holding the cup as if it were dynamite.

"It's Miss Phemia I've come to see, sir." He choked and cleared his throat. "And might I add, sir, our family settles all its business by account."

Pa straightened, the lines around his mouth tightening.

"You don't say. Now what, you figger, would your family's business have to do with mine?"

I jabbed my needle into the sock. The darning mushroom rolled off my lap, clattered under Pa's chair.

"Come in the kitchen now, won't you, and meet the others." I bounded over, seizing Silas's cup. Nodding to Pa, his face a mask, Silas unfolded himself from his seat and followed. The space behind my eyes stung.

Zeke and Joseph glanced up sullenly from their books. Willie's gape became a smirk. In the kitchen's brightness, Silas looked pale as the curtains. Beads of sweat glistened on his brow.

"Don't mind him," I said loud enough for both parents to hear, swallowing my dismay. "His bark's worse than his bite, and Mam says he'll come around — eventually. So help me God."

I clattered his cup as I dumped out the lukewarm tea and went to pour some fresh.

"A drink of hot water would be just as good, Phemia. If you don't mind. Personally I don't as a rule take tea, or coffee neither. N-not that they're sinful themselves. But Father says they pave the way to ruin — tobacco and card-playing. They weaken the spirit." He blushed as he said so; still, I could tell he was serious.

Mam bustled in and pushed aside the boys' books; began wiping down the table in big wide arcs. Silas pulled his cap from his pocket, clutching it. His knuckles looked shiny.

"Then perhaps you'd offer your friend a little lime cordial, Effie — it goes good with a glass of water. He might enjoy that."

"No thank you, ma'am, I don't think my folks would take too kindly to——" He faltered, twisting his cap, a sheepish smile creeping over his face. "It's just to see Phemia that I came by, and to...to have a word with you and, er, Mr. Cox. You see, ma'am, I'd like to make some time with her, ma'am, if I may. If it's all right with you, I mean."

Mam started to laugh, then clapped her hand over her mouth, her eyes wary. "Not much I can do to stop you, is there?" But she held out her hand for him to grip, and Silas — so relieved and so jittery I swear, Fan, you could hear his bones knocking — gave it a hard shake. I saw her bite her tongue, stifling laughter as she jerked away from him and finished tidying, exactly as she'd do when a child's antics struck her as funny.

Later, before I went to bed, she muttered, "When they made that one they threw away the mould, all right." I must've looked hurt, because on my way upstairs she reached through the banister and tugged my sleeve.

"Don't be so touchy — I think your fella's a fine one, Effie. So don't let Pa sway you."

INTERCESSION
Timepiece

The snow finally comes, a thick white coat covering everything. In the store window Lucinda has put up little red hearts cut from the side of a Coke carton. Up close you can see the swirly lettering, *oke* and *ola*. I can't help noticing, waiting out front while she starts the truck.

The sky is so bright it hurts my eyes, the hillsides and snowbanks reflecting it; everywhere a blinding vista, blue and white. It's comfortable here in the shade of the stoop. I could stand here all day and look at the view. But Lucinda has something up her sleeve. She's taking me to Caledonia, she says, to see the doctor.

He's a polite enough young man, though a little too youthful to be altogether trustworthy. I would prefer someone more like Doc O'Hanley, yes. A silver-haired gentleman in a clean white coat. This man — I forget his name — wears a plaid shirt, a green tie that looks like snakeskin. He is handsome, sort of, though I don't like the shadow on his jaw, as though he hasn't taken time to shave properly. It makes him look shifty. I keep wanting to call him Dr. Eugene, Doc O'Hanley's son, who took over the practice when I was first married. A character, he was. Not like his father, but rather forward, a little too familiar. Always nosing into your business.

Always hinting around at "getting to the bottom" of my "problem" — Leonard's problem — our lack of children. The "bottom", all right. I was happy when he closed up and moved his office to Springhill.

This new fellow asks me all kinds of questions.

"I'm Dr. So-and-so," he says, "and what is your name and where do you live and when is your birthday?"

None of your ruddy beeswax. I glare back at him. "Why do you ask?"

Then he wants me to draw him a clock, of all things. "You're pulling my leg," I say, but I see he's not. He tears a sheet from a pad. Lucinda digs for a pen. He hands me a yellow pencil.

I draw the damned thing, perfectly round as I can make it. "Hickory dickory dock," I say, and push the paper towards him.

He pushes it back. "Now, Mrs. Clarke, make it say two o'clock — can you do that for me?" He's sweet and patient, as if urging me to take off my brassiere! Unctuous, to boot.

Lucinda's face burns. Shit would melt in her mouth.

I pick up his yellow pencil and draw in the hands. "The clock struck one, the mouse ran down, hickory dick——" I let the writing stick roll over the desk to his forest of pictures. They look like framed paper dolls. His loved ones. A blonde, smiling wife, two toddlers. The girl in a pink dress, the boy in a bow tie and tartan weskit.

"Satisfied?" I want to snap at him. But there's Lucinda on the edge of her seat, that big boxy purse of hers like a toolbox on her lap. She's looking at him, all eyes. Puppy eyes.

"Good news, doc?"

Please tell me auntie hasn't lost her marbles.

Forgetful, he says, absent-minded. No sign of stroke.

His eyes don't move from me.

"How's your diet, Mrs.——?"

"Why don't you just snap a picture?" I tell him. "It would last you longer."

Some absent-mindedness, some confusion — normal at this age, he says.

"Forgetful, all right!" Lucinda laughs like a woodpecker. "But hey, look who's talking — I mean, who isn't?"

He says nothing I don't already know.

Outside, the bright blue light makes me dizzy. The sidewalk tilts and I have to grab Lucinda's arm for balance. We stumble along a wide, paved street. The snowbanks look like brown sugar. The buildings are brick and jammed together like teeth.

"What place is this again?"

She gives me a look and shakes her head, stepping over a splatter. Pigeon dirt. The sidewalk is like a sheet of yellow barley candy. She skids and slides, almost takes the two of us down. Like a drunken waltz. The brick façades slant down, windows blazing blue.

"For the love of God, Ruby! That'd do it, now wouldn't it, the two of us old dolls with broken hips."

"Who are you calling old?" I bat my eyes. My dear, I almost say, you must be mistaken. I don't know about you, but myself...I'm twenty-two. Or three. Hick, hick. Hickory, dick.

The sun feels strong on my face, a coddling warmth. I'm feeling so...liquid, lithe; so happy, in a way I haven't in such a long time.

But now she's got me by the sleeve, rushing me along. Skating over the clear-candy sidewalk. I'm afraid she'll let go and I'll find myself spinning into the slushy street, the glittering hiss of passing cars. I whimper.

"Why didn't you ask the doctor where we are? He might have been able to give us directions."

"For *shit*sake," she says — under her breath, she thinks. But I hear it, all right.

"Don't be coarse, Lucinda."

Suddenly she erupts. Spills over, like a pot of boiling noodles!

"You're just doing this, aren't you? Please tell me, Aunt Ruby, you're just doing this to get my goat. To be obtuse!"

"The hands on the clock — was I correct? Two o'clock? Hickory dickory, thank you so much, Lucinda. If ever there was someone obtuse! An obtuse angle" — I hear Father's voice — "or angel." I shake off her grip, my head held high. "*If* you please."

Beside the parking lot is a building. It looks like stucco with bricks showing through. A theatre, with that roller-coaster marquee.

There are lightbulbs missing: smashed, plucked out; empty eye sockets. Black letters slip and slide like intoxicated ants. LETHAL WEAP_N, STAR-ING — the names mean nothing to me, nothing at all. But the way the sun slopes off the façade, the odd jagged bulb flashing like a diamond.... There's something, yes, something about the sign, the doorway, its porthole eyes; the empty glass wicket....

The sweaty warmth of a hand. I *am* twenty-two.

Leonard's voice:

"Dancing — hmph — that all they can do? Seen one of these shows, you seen 'em all. You'd figger, now wouldn't you, Ruby, they'd come up with something different now and then. How 'bout old Fred jumpin' Ginger's bones, eh? Try that on for size. Huh?"

Born crude.

I'm not listening, Leonard. No husband of mine....

Dancing dancing dancing.

"The Bijou!" I exclaim, the sun cracking my face into a smile. Warmth fills my mouth.

"What? Yeah, well, so it is — I guess."

Lucinda doesn't stop. She yanks me across the lot, stuffs me into the truck like one last bite of sausage into a waiting maw.

"But I thought we were going for a doughnut!" I cry as we speed down the street. Past those buildings now dingy, faceless; all the same. "You promised, don't forget."

That's how she talked me into coming, travelling all this distance....

On our way out of town, she sighs and pulls off into another lot, parks beside a squat brick building. It's different from the others, low and newer-looking, smoked glass windows hung with huge close-up pictures of food. "Home of the Hole," says the big orange sign, the o's dripping yellow, like honey.

"Coming in?" she snaps. I don't like the look of the place; inside I see a cloudy haze, people wearing ballcaps.

"I'll just wait, dear. Are you going in? Perhaps you'd bring me a little treat, and I'll have it out here. If you'd be so kind."

"What d'you want?"

"Surprise me. Look — there's money in my bag. Take it." I push my change purse across the seat but she sighs again and slams the door. I can see her inside waiting at the counter, then sitting by herself, her head bent, drinking something from a paper cup.

Good Lord, she takes forever in there. When she finally comes out she hands me a little brown bag streaked with grease. Inside is something sticky sprinkled with tiny bright specks every colour of the rainbow. It looks like something a child would order, and there's no hole.

"I was hoping for a doughnut," I tell her in the mildest tone possible.

"Oh Aunt Ruby!" Exasperated, she jams in the key, races the engine.

"Where's the fire?" I gasp as we peel onto the highway. She doesn't answer, of course. And after this I refuse to speak; she needs to see that I won't be treated this way and stand for it.

Trees and hills float past like clouds. Where in creation is she taking me now? I want to ask, but won't. Instead, I bite my lip until there's blood, that sharp, tinny taste.

Gripping the wheel, she sees me looking at her sparkly gloves. She reminds me that they are new, a present from somewhere; they massage your fingers while you drive, she jokes. La-de-da. As if I give a sweet damn.

"Home sweet home," she announces at last.

"Cuppa tea?" Her smarmiest, sugared voice when we're barely in the door. Before I've even got my coat off.

I don't answer, just trudge in my boots — with a cosy shmursh, *shmursh* — across her shiny floor. I shut my door and go back to my reading.

Now where were we, Mum, when *she* so rudely interrupted?

oh mother what a web you weave
with your l's and m's and p's and
cues to act and so believe in
tricks of needlework and pies
that love should lie and bind
with ties that none
in her right mind
contrives....

XV

Tackle

Wilf's kisses taste like sauerkraut and Scope — I mean, that would describe Kiss Numero Uno, after the dance. You should've seen Edna Pyke and her friends, those ladies doing refreshments. Could've put Edna's lip in a sling, it drooped so. We were out in the parking lot, see, leaning against my truck. It was late; inside they were starting to tidy up. Edna came out with a big Tupperware tray of leftovers. That's when she spotted us.

I was unlocking the door; Wilf had me pinned up against it. Well, I exaggerate — a little. We'd both had a few. I don't usually drink, no more than a beer or two, that's my limit. But at the time...the Legion was so noisy and smoky, and when the band played — mostly songs too fast, too jerky to dance to — it was just plain too loud to talk. Well, unless you count shouting at each other across the table: "How ya doing?" "You okay?" "Having a good time?"

Somebody had gone to a lot of trouble decorating the place. They'd covered the bingo tables with white paper to hide the burn and dobber marks, and made up little centrepieces. Each table had a candle stuck to a tuna-fish can decorated with pasta bows, the whole works sprayed gold. A cute enough idea — except when

Wilf leaned over to yell something, and his sleeve nearly went up. It was right after that he excused himself and went outside for a bit; when he came back in, he went straight to the men's.

Like I say, we didn't dance. Given the tempo, I was just as glad, and put it down to Wilf's good manners — or sense — that he didn't ask me. When the band finally quit sometime after midnight, my face hurt from all the smiling and straining to hear. He walked me to the truck, steering me by the elbow. It was then Edna came out.

Brazen as can be, he put his hand on my shoulder and pulled me close. His lips were cold and tingly-feeling. I was too stunned to do much besides stay put. And all the time I'm thinking, Look at you, stop acting — what kind of woman — at your age, Lindy — get a grip! — when he stops to come up for air and my mouth is numb, my lips too rubbery and slick to speak or move or do anything, and he says — does he really say it or is this my imagination gone berserk? — he says, "Wanna unlock this?" Or I think he does and I'm so charged up I don't have time to stop or wonder what he means or give a hoot and God it happened so quick I'm going out on a limb to bring it up but — he slipped me the tongue.

I was shocked. For a split second I almost gagged. But like I say, it was over so fast, and what could I do but stay still, lips glued to the spot? And I felt so hot and bothered and ashamed but happy too. Like the last twenty or thirty years were tiny marks on a Magic Slate and — whup! — he'd just flicked the page. And you know, I didn't give a tinker's damn for Edna or anybody else tiptoeing past with their cracker crumbs.

From out of nowhere he pulled this gorgeous flower — a rose, a carnation, what's the difference? All I saw was pink. It could've been plastic for all I cared. By then I felt so wobbly I might have been on my feet all night in the store, up and down, up and down, bending kneeling dusting. When I finally went to drive away, my leg was shaking so badly I nearly popped the clutch.

I put his flower on the dash so I could keep an eye on it the whole way home, the words to "Mustang Sally" crashing around my head. Get a grip, get a grip, I kept telling myself. You're practically a senior citizen. But then I'd look at that flower and think: So, who gives a goddamn?

Aunt Ruby was waiting up for me, if you can believe it. "Win anything?" she wanted to know, and I had to think for a minute what in God's acre she was talking about.

Then I slept — Lord, did I sleep, worn out with all the excitement, the anticipation. The sheer crazy lust, the *accident* of it! At my age.

Must've been the body's way of preparing for trouble, my sleep-of-the-dead that night. Like a bear finding a deep, cosy cave. My last decent sleep, it seems like. Because wouldn't you know, the very next day my troubles with Ruby started in earnest.

But to all troubles there's a silver lining — that, I would have to say, being Wilf and his kisses. Three in total now.

The second was on Valentine's Day. I hadn't seen him since the dance — gosh, a fortnight or more. Not that I was keeping count — who could, with Ruby giving them the royal runaround? A three-ring circus, that woman — you talk about a mind playing tricks! Dancing bears and elephants — and dogged? Dogged as a tiger jumping through a flaming hoop! And me all of a sudden ringleader, master of ceremonies, and not a light to see by in the Big Top.

So, as you can imagine, I was in a bit of a stew, the store a shambles, when Wilf showed up. I'd gotten behind putting out the Valentine's stock, half of it still in cartons behind the counter. Fancy heart-shaped boxes of Ganong's; glittery red pens on cords, nice enough to wear as pendants. I'd spilled a box of hard red cinnamon hearts — they clicked like buttons underfoot — and was just sweeping them up.

Poison little buggers, I kept cursing, hunkered down with the broom. To make matters worse, the place was hopping with those teenagers again, going at it with the video games — what else was new?

Wilf caught me, the words on my lips as I struggled up. He was laughing, looking kind of sheepish but pleased with himself, a skinny red parcel behind his back.

"Well if it ain't the lone stranger."

"Long time no see, Lindy," he shot back, though really it hadn't been. Like I say, time flies when you're having fun. Then he said, "These are for you."

Mint patties, I figured, by the shape of the box.

"My waistline," I blurted. "Really, you shouldn't have." I could've bitten off my tongue for sounding so grumpy.

He set the package down on top of the register. You could tell he'd had it gift-wrapped in that shiny red foil, the bow as big as the box. I knew then it had to be more than candy.

It was a scarlet pair of spandex gloves, Isotoners, one size fits all. The Zellers price tag was X-ed out in ballpoint.

"I don't know what to say." I could feel my face turning red as his present; the *bleep-bleep* from the back of the store, the *chunka-chunk* of the machines eating quarters, filling in my loss for words.

"No need to say much of anything, Lindy." Clearing his throat, he cricked his neck and glared at those teens. "Come on now, put 'em on. Let's see how they fit."

Who could credit what he did next? He leaned over the counter and gave me a great big smooch, right on the lips. Thank the good Christ Ruby wasn't there to see! "At your age, at any age! Really, Lucinda, behaving like some fallen woman. Some fallen woman of the night." I was just imagining her saying it when another sound came wafting from the back. A snort, a hiss, above all that electronic burping.

"Check out the sex kitten."

I'm sure it was Ronnie, that obnoxious one with the earrings — there's more metal on his face than in my truck. But I kept my eyes shut, puckering up to make that kiss last just a split second longer, Wilf's warm, cabbagy taste linger on my lips. He missed all this, of course. If he'd heard, he might've wanted to smuck the kid between the eyes, the miserable bit of pond scum!

But, do you know, I didn't care. At that moment those young twerps could've said anything, could've set the place on fire, and it would've meant diddly. Flatulence in a gale.

Which might well be how my kisses taste, for all I know. Turnip wind and Colgate.

Maybe I should've been more careful. But right in front of that noisy crew I leaned forward, looking straight at Wilf, and asked, "What did you say you're doing for supper?"

He was busy that night, as it turned out — for the best, actually, since Ruby had a doctor's appointment next day. Took almost three weeks to convince her to see somebody; Lord love a duck, I said, what would you do if you were dying? I had to close up shop one entire afternoon, by the time we drove to Caledonia, waited, saw the fellow, stopped for coffee and drove back.

The time I had, just getting her in the truck. Had to bribe her, as you would a kid. And then to be made an arse of, a complete arse.

Once or twice she called the fellow Doc O'Hanley. She even started to get up and leave when all he wanted was a rundown of some of her wackier doings. "Got a week?" I tried joking, wishing I'd written them all down. But how could I have told him with her sitting there sober as a judge, eyes like tacks? Without looking at her, I mentioned the list, the map, her directions for navigating the store.

"It's not exactly Casa Loma," I said, "or Buckingham Palace."

"Perfectly normal to be somewhat absent-minded at this advanced age." He looked me in the eye, then turned to her and smiled, the warmest sweetest there-there-it's-all-right-don't-you-worry-about-a-thing smile you'd ever want to see. He kept lacing and unlacing his slim, tanned fingers. "This is your aunt's manifestation of the normal ageing process."

"Me? My what?" she piped up, as if shaken awake. "Why, there's not a thing wrong with me, young man. I know Miss Hammond means well but, you see, my niece has always been a bit of an alarmist. You'll have to excuse her."

With all her bluster, I forgot to mention the burnt-up picture, her slippered adventure. That's how frazzled I felt, as if these things had flown straight from my head.

Before we left, he had her draw a clock. No problem. Then, to shame us both, to add insult to injury, at his bidding didn't she go and recite the alphabet backwards — twice.

"My advice to you both is, wait and see." The doctor shrugged and shook Ruby's hand and told us to come back in a few months. On our way out he drew me aside. "It's up to you, Miss Hammond, to monitor and make note of anything you find odd, any changes in your aunt's behaviour."

What do you think I've been doing? I felt like saying. Playing Donkey Kong?

"Where do you s'pose he got his licence?" I couldn't help myself as the door shut behind us. "Kingdom Hall, or Khan's Variety? Sheesh!"

By then I was just about crazy to get on the road, though it was too late in the day to even consider reopening. Helping Ruby along the sidewalk, I started to daydream. I pictured myself and Wilf out someplace. A steakhouse, maybe; somewhere nice. Cold beer in tall flimsy glasses, not those ugly steins; real cloth napkins. Two juicy T-bones; bread in a basket. Wilf tucking his napkin into his collar, reaching under the table to pat my knee....

When we finally got to the truck, Ruby looked for a moment as if she wouldn't get in, so I had to help her. I no sooner got her buckled up than she started feeling peckish, asking about a doughnut or something I must've promised. Selective memory, I'd say. By this time I just wanted to be home, to put my feet up, maybe catch the last twenty minutes of *Oprah*. I kept hoping Ruby'd forget her craving. But no. Halfway out of town I gave in and stopped at a Tim's. Figured a coffee wouldn't hurt, for the drive home. Then damn, after all that, if she didn't go stubborn on me and refuse to come in!

Fine, I said. So I went and treated myself to a double-double, and took my sweet time, too. Had to, to calm down. Figured I was doing us both a favour, being in no shape to drive. You can do stupid things when you're upset, especially behind the wheel. I must have looked frazzled; twice the cop at the next table glanced over. You want my licence or something, pally? I felt like snarling. But then somebody dropped a plate out back, and he and his buddy started clapping.

I got Ruby a "rainbow", double-dipped, but when I took it out she turned up her nose. "That's not a doughnut," she said, and look, it was all I could do to start the truck, and keep from snatching the thing and eating it myself.

Drawing a clock, indeed.

She barely spoke the entire drive home. Just like another time, a year or two ago, when we went to Caledonia to get her watch repaired. She'd had the thing since the fifties, I swear — a gold Bulova with most of the plating worn off its bracelet. She'd overwound it; that's how old the watch was, one you had to wind.

Before we made the trip to town I had a look at it. The little knob wouldn't budge, the spring inside wound tight as one's innards feel after you eat too much spicy food.

The watch-repair fellow wanted a hundred dollars to fix it, no guarantees. "You could buy a nice new Timex for half that," he said, shrugging, just being honest. "The nerve of that guy," she whispered when he disappeared out back for something. "This is a good watch, good when I bought it — what in creation would I want with a new one? When I bought this, I meant it to do me."

In the end the man agreed to repair it. The entire drive home, she fretted about the money. "A hundred dollars! It only cost twenty, new. Imagine!" But by the time we reached Arcadia, she'd decided that it was worth it; that if you did the math, a hundred dollars wasn't so bad for five more years. Which she figured would just about do the trick. "I'd be wasteful, silly," she said, "to fork out money for a new timepiece, this late in life."

"You, Aunt Ruby? A spendthrift?"

At the time I found it kind of comical. Perhaps I should've read the signs, seen all this coming.

So now it's almost Easter, early this year — just in time for mud season. The time of year that fills me with hope, crazy as it sounds. Except I could do without the religious hysteria, the hype that bursts forth every spring, like crocuses from the frozen ground. I'm thinking of those nuts you hear about in foreign lands, parading around with skewered hands and feet.

The headline in the *News* this week read: VOICE OF THE BEAST HEARD BY MIR. Honest to Pete. Sure, I say. Tell me another one. Tell me Ruby's not the only person hearing voices. As if that would make a difference.

But come to think of it, if there is a God out there and he's listening, I wonder, would he mind keeping an eye on her for me? Just the odd afternoon; every bit counts. And while he's at it, do me another favour — send chocolate; no, supper — I'm up to my eyeballs in bunnies and hens. A roast of pork, maybe, and applesauce made fresh, not from a jar; potatoes, too, glazed with drippings.

If he's the type pays any attention, he'll know I haven't time for cooking, spending every waking moment watching Ruby. Worse than minding a little kid.

And feeding her — that has got to be the worst. I tried fried bologna with peas one night. "I don't like that. What is it anyway? Dogs' dinner? I'm not eating it. You must be crazy if you think I will. And what's more, you don't fool me. Not for a minute, missy. I know what you're trying to do. You're trying to poison me, aren't you? Well, you won't succeed. Because I shan't, I won't, I WILL NOT eat that!"

Tried fish sticks and succotash another time, an old favourite of hers. No luck. Ham and potato scallop the same, nothing doing.

Not even steak, nice pan-fried blade with lots of onion. That's what we had the evening Wilf came for supper. Finally. I'd asked him three times and each time he had some excuse. I wasn't pressuring him. Gosh, no. I just wanted to reciprocate, you know, for the dance, the gloves.

I think now he was trying to spare me embarrassment. Not that I'd told him much about Ruby — for godsake, the last thing I wanted was him thinking it might be catching, or might run in the family. I must've been dreaming if I thought she'd change her tune, be on her best behaviour for company.

It began the minute he came into the kitchen. He was all spruced up — he'd been putting in longer and longer hours on the road, and had driven all the way home after work to shower. I noticed where he'd nicked himself shaving, above the collar of his fresh, checked shirt. His hair was shiny clean; you could see comb-marks where he'd slicked it back. And he smelled nice, too. Old Spice. In his hands was a brown bag from the liquor commission, a bottle of Cold Duck.

That's what set Ruby off, as soon as she spied it. I poured out a glass for each of us, those fancy little sherry glasses she keeps on the very top shelf. Should've known better and filled hers with tomato juice instead, because she stormed to the parlour and cranked up *Empty Nest*. She stayed in there till supper was served, the food going cold while I coaxed her to come and sit. The onions were burnt, the carrots a little too crunchy. Ruby started in, poison this, poison that; wouldn't take a bite. I was so mortified I almost choked on some gristle, had to excuse myself and run to the bathroom to spit it out.

Wilf was great. "Ignore her," he whispered across the table, his shoe nudging mine. "Take her plate away, give her time to forget — maybe try again later?" He drank his wine very slowly. When his glass was empty I filled it again, too full, right to the brim. I barely touched my own, however, wishing Ruby would just get up and go back to her TV.

Wilf rocked in his chair, stifling a belch, polishing off his second glass of wine a little faster than his first. It was as if he'd picked up on the need to get rid of it — put it out of sight, out of mind — for Ruby's sake. Sawing into his last bit of steak he said, "That's one tasty slab of beef, Lindy." I could see him eyeing Ruby's untouched on her plate. But he didn't mention it, of course, this being a date. Our second — which put me in mind of our first, the dance. His big burly arm at the small of my back, the taste of mouthwash, his smell of Brylcreem and woodsmoke, a smell that makes me think of maple syrup.

No kisses that night, not even later, with Ruby sitting there in her armchair, eyes glued to the tube, and Wilf and me on the sofa, a mile apart. I let him finish off the Cold Duck, and once while I was doing the dishes he came in and put his arm around my waist, even rubbed his chin on the nape of my neck. But then Ruby coughed and muted a commercial, and I swear the man jumped two feet from me. And when *Fresh Prince of Bel-Air* came on he got up off the sofa and said he had to go, he had to be up at five next morning. I offered to make him a Nescafé for the road, seeing as how he'd drunk that bottle of wine, but by then he had his jacket zipped. So we shook hands in the porch, where I stood while he got into his truck, and watched him drive off. And stunned as it sounds, part of me wanted to run out after him and yell, "Wait a minute — aren't you forgetting something?"

Our third date — if you can call it that — comes right before Good Friday. The snow's gone, what precious little we've had, so things are uncommonly dry, drier than you'd expect, though the wind's still raw. He takes me for a ride up to Westchester to see the road — well, the new route being cut through the woods.

He comes in at noon and asks, spur of the moment, if I'd like to take a gander. Of course I'm sick at leaving Ruby, even just over lunch hour, but I tell myself, What the heck, she's been okay alone all morning with me busy rolling dimes. She seems content enough, dozing in front of a program.

"Half an hour, tops," Wilf says, talking me into it. "She'll be all right — don't think she can give away the store in that short a time, do you?"

I feel like a foreman myself, riding up front with him in the truck, a Conway Twitty tune rattling over the radio. There's a brand new leopard-skin cover on the seat, still creased from the package — a good buy at Canadian Tire, he makes a point of mentioning. The interior's neat as a banker's office. And though he's a smoker, he won't let anyone light up in his truck, himself included.

"Filthy habit," he says, a Player's dangling from his lip as soon as we jump out and find a spot overlooking the construction. The wind combs the smoke away. Hands thrust in his pockets, he hunches away from me, neither of us saying much, just watching the work going on below. I'm wishing he'd come closer when he stamps out his cigarette and gives me this funny look.

"I want to tell you something, Lindy. I'm gonna be straight with you. What I'm looking for is — companionship," he says, out of the blue. His tone is exactly what you'd imagine if he were ordering a load of asphalt.

"Companionship?" What in heck does *that* mean?

"Come on" — he sucks in his cheeks, nudging me — "lemme show you around the site."

So I stumble down the hill after him, the site being acres and acres of tree-roots and boulders rousted up like giant potatoes. The spruces still standing are ribboned with surveyor's tape like the stuff police use cordoning off murder scenes, or runners burst through in marathons.

It's about as exciting to me as a root-canal — the stink of diesel wafting up the hill, the rusty old-socks smell of dirt and chewed rock. On the grade below, men in yellow hard hats spread gravel; from a distance their labours appear leisurely, the new road-bed soft as a nubbly red scarf.

We're far enough away that no doubt the men mistake me for one of them. The wind flicks Wilf's steely hair off his temples, and in this raw, chilly light, this ripped-up landscape, he looks craggier, too. His forehead is wide and square, setting off his hawkish nose, his eyes deep set as creeks cut through a marsh.

"What I'm trying to say...," he pipes up again, louder now on account of the wind, the diggers and 'dozers grinding over the earth like prehistoric Dinky Toys. "It seems you and me have got a few things in common, don't we, and, well — far be it from me to go putting words in anyone's mouth, least of all yours — but I'd call that lucky."

He's still speaking as though ordering truck parts — a new axle or tires for his pickup? But then he reaches out and squeezes my arm. I can feel the warmth of his hand right through my quilted down sleeve. He leans over and gives me a peck on the mouth — in broad daylight, for all the world to see. A couple of fellows leaning on shovels glance up, and I think one of the flagmen slaps his thigh, jerking his hard hat towards us. But no, it's just my imagination. My nerves. This queer, panicky gurgle in the middle of my gut is like a gas pain. What in hell's acre are you doing, Lindy, you crazy old sleeveen?

That's Kiss Number Three.

He runs me back to the store, shakes my hand as I'm sliding out of the truck. I turn and wave when he pulls away; he doesn't notice, he's too busy watching for traffic. But I see him gawking in the rearview, oh yes I do, and he puts up his hand like a Hollywood brave: How!

"Back at one," says the cardboard clock hanging from the doorknob; sweet Moses, it's ten after.

It's then I notice the window, the big round bugger of a hole the size of a fist smashed right through the glass above the lock.

Panic grabs me by the throat, forget my indigestion.

Ruby? RUBY? Where the bejeezus——?

My hand shakes so hard I can hardly fit the key.

Ruby? Oh sweet Jesus, let her be all right.

Inside, I find the rock on the floor, a mug-sized chunk of sandstone.

Ruby? I pole-vault behind the counter, never mind the mud

from my shoes. A shelf full of Pepsi bottles rattles and rubs the wall with a dull, heavy *glub*.

She's in her room, sitting on the bed, her feet in the new mint-green slippers I bought to replace the others. Calm as Hillary Clinton, she studies herself in her little blue hand-mirror — examining a mole, perhaps? The glass is all steamed up.

"For the love of Pete, Aunt Ruby — are you all right? Didn't you hear?"

She looks up, aghast, when I explain. "A stone? No dear, of course I didn't notice a thing. Perhaps I've been asleep, have I?"

She follows me out to the store, helps pick up glass — I don't want her to, but there's so much; it's everywhere.

"Well, be glad it wasn't the whole durn window," she says, sighing; ticked off, yes, but calm, calmer than I'll ever hope to be. For a few blinking moments she's herself: good old reliable Ruby, picking slivers from the pink baskets and eggs in the window display. "Tut-tut-tut, well I never," she mutters, brushing dirt from a faded purple bunny while I rush around finding duct tape and cardboard to patch the hole.

"That'll have to do," I tell her, for some reason feeling guilty — guilty as if it were I who pitched the rock and owe an apology. "Well, nothing for it, is there, but a trip to town for some putty, a sheet of glass? Sooner the better, I guess, eh? How 'bout tomorrow?"

But she's not listening, cradling the bunny under her chin. Her eyes have a vacant, baffled look. And she says, "Lucinda — where'd you put the fishing gear? First signs of spring, dear, folks will be looking for it."

We quit selling that stuff in 1973, I start to say, then change my tack. "Oh, it's on order, Aunt Ruby. Rods, reels, fly-tying gear — you name it. Sure, it'll be here any day, that stuff."

This pleases her no end — you can see the smile, not so much on her face but in the way her eyes light up. And it's a good thing, because I've got my work cut out for me, and it gives her something to ponder while I think about calling the Mounties, and figure out some kind of booby-trap for Grampa's safe.

XVI

Anglers

Thus is a needle prov'd and instrument
Of profit, pleasure, and of ornament.
Which mighty Queenes have grac'd in hand to take,
And high borne Ladies such esteeme did make,
That as their Daughters Daughters up did grow
The Needles Art, they to their children show.
And as 'twas then an exercise of praise,
So what deserves more honour in these dayes,
Than this? which daily doth itself expresse,
A mortall enemy to idlenesse.

Well, it wasn't long before Silas started coming around regularly. He'd nod at Pa in the parlour, then come back to the kitchen and sit with Mam and me, the three of us chit-chatting above the children's racket.

"I'd've thought you'd have work after hours keeping you busy," Mam would tease, watching him blush and stare at his hands before looking over at me. I believe she was testing him, sounding out the depths of his feelings — perhaps trying to cosy up, too, that being her way.

At first Silas didn't know what to make of Mam, but he soon caught on how to answer. "Well, no, ma'am. With respect, the store's not like a house. My own mama, she says a woman's work is never done — well, the store's a handful all right, but it's not *that* bad. Some things can wait till tomorrow, though my father mightn't agree. But there have to be allowances, ma'am, when a fellow's got other business to attend to."

Mam smiled, same as when Joseph or Zeke came out with something comical, but you could tell she was pleased; she looked smug as if one of our brothers had said this. It made me squirm a little — not her teasing, but the way any fool could see she'd been won over. It was almost as if she were young again, despite all her travails, and both of us vying for the same fellow. Still, this was better than Pa's sulking in the next room, a mood you could almost smell. And Mam never said boo when Silas rose and asked if he could take me for a stroll or to the Waverley for ice-cream.

Outside we breathed more easily, turning our faces up to watch the stars come out one by one. We'd take our time lolling along the road, leaping muddy ruts and potholes shimmery with rainwater. Usually we stopped on the bridge to lean over the railing, admiring the rocks round and dark as the snouts of fish beneath the current. Neither of us spoke much; we were too busy listening to the knee-deeps' trilling in the duckweed. Silas would throw pebbles, with sharp flicks of his wrist.

"You know I'd never do anything to hurt you, Phemia," he ventured once, his voice soft, unsure. "I think your ma sees that. But your pa" — he let fly a good-sized rock — "it'd take a prophet to know what he's got agin me. I've got to say it makes me more than a tad edgy, his sitting so quiet while I'm around."

"Don't mind him," I said, starting as his arm came up and brushed my waist. Next he took my hand, his fingers cool as grass, and drew me down the path below the bridge. Moisture from the spongy ground squished between my toes.

He let go and leapt out upon a rock, squatting among the reeds. I thought of you, Fan, that day with the wasps and dragonflies. Waving at me to keep still, he shot his hand out and clapped the surface, scooping something up. He nodded to me to come closer, a solemn delight on his face. Opening his hands a crack, he showed me the creature inside, its throat pulsing, eyes bulging green. Crouching, he released it; with a tiny *pop* it broke the surface, vanishing.

We scrambled up the bank and again he took my hand. Sidling close, he kissed me on the mouth, his lips wet and bumbling. It lasted but a second. Then he was pulling me back towards the bridge.

"Chocolate or vanilla?" he asked as we crossed, still holding hands, and headed up Main Street. He laughed with a naked kind of relief. "Well I don't s'pose you could tell I was waiting all evening to do that," he said, almost to himself.

I wiped my mouth with my fingers, delicately, so he wouldn't notice. "You might say I had an inkling." I tugged his hand, then dropped it as we neared the Waverley. Outside on the veranda were some fancy gentlemen in bowlers, chewing tobacco; a couple of wild-looking girls with deep painted lips and flyaway hair. One of the men spat a long stream of yellow juice into the mud as we climbed the steps. Making a face, Silas gripped my elbow and steered me past the saloon to the café.

"My treat," he said. "Get whatever you like." He watched as I spread my skirt around the wobbly little seat. Looking back, I suppose that's when it first dawned on me that the two of us might spend our lives together, that it was "meant to be". Fate, Providence — whichever you prefer to call it.

By June we were scarcely apart except when Silas was at work and I at school, finishing up. After dismissal, I'd march straight up the hill to Lewises' and sit on a stool behind the dry goods while Silas waited on customers. His father turned a blind eye — he couldn't've been too crazy about my being there, distracting Silas and generally disrupting business. Tryphena Lewis, on the other hand — Silas's mother — enjoyed having me around to help with the ladies if she wasn't available. They perked up when they saw me; they'd come right over and whisper their requests for "delicate things", as Tryphena labelled tonics and potions for such things as monthlies.

Nobody — least of all his father — could deny the change in Silas: the spring to his step when he scooted out back for an extra sack of feed or flour; the way he'd smile and wish people well, handing back change. It was no accident that business picked up, with more and more townsfolk stopping by, even if just to chew the fat. The fact is, Silas was learning the ropes — beyond the taking in and laying by at which his father was so proficient. For all his shyness, Silas had a way with people, which surprised even him once he got onto it. Maybe, deep down, customers felt as I did about his earnest manner. After the old man's surliness, it was like a long, cool gulp of water on a muggy day.

As for his cheeriness — well, anyone with eyes could see I was the reason. So his father tolerated, perhaps even came to expect, my presence while Silas tended shop. Business as usual; I wouldn't have had it any other way.

One afternoon — it was the first day of summer, so hot I felt useless, fanning myself with the cover of an old pattern book — Malcolm surprised us both by letting Silas off early. Out on the road the air was thick as dust, so through the woods we went in search of a breeze.

At a spot where the river widened, Silas's father kept a little white rowboat hauled up in the bushes. Beyond the reeds, you could see where the water deepened, slow dark pools ringed by snapping trout.

It was Silas's idea to go rowing. He dragged the boat into the shallows, steadied it as I boarded. Wading alongside, he nudged it towards the current, water foaming like ale around his skinny thighs. His wide-legged trousers slapped to him like paint — oh, he used to favour such pants, loose as a sailor's, that whisked when he walked.

Grinning, he heaved himself aboard, dropped the oars and began pulling hard against the current — you could feel its heaviness at the bow. He rowed and rowed, till sweat trickled down his face, his mouth pressed in a thin straight line. His hair looked nearly as wet as those pants dripping a puddle at his feet. Along the banks, swallows flitted from the willows; the silky beat of wings and the hum of bluebottles were the only sounds above the gurgling water.

Here the river slowed, languid and dark as kerosene under the mossy shade of overhanging branches. Silas shipped the oars, the boat swinging in a lazy gyre. He smiled at me, ducking leafy switches as we drifted backwards, hugging the bank. I shut my eyes, felt leaves cool as fingertips on my face.

When I opened them he was reaching for the oars, still smiling. It was then I heard a noise — a giggle, a throaty sigh, coming through the trees. Close, unmistakeable, yet soft enough to be a whisper. Deaf to it, Silas had started rowing again. But as the current snagged us, I saw. A flash of skin amid the green. A rump. A boy, dark hair falling over his face as he turned away. His smooth white back. A girl beneath him, laughing, her skirt hitched up. In that split second I saw. Her face was pink, her mouth crushed-looking. I recognized her — Ada Skoke. I'd seen her outside the Waverley, evenings Silas and I went strolling; boys at school made crude and wicked jokes about her.

I must have gasped with the sheer, ugly surprise of it. But Silas noticed nothing, pulling upon the oars. As we eddied away, I felt the queasiness of shame and something else, a shortness of breath, a queer, sombre longing at the top of my chest. In seconds we were moving upriver once more, the coolness off the water like a poultice drawing out the guilt at what I'd seen. I said not a word to Silas; it was easier to stay quiet, to keep a dirty thing to myself.

At a spot shaded by elms, Silas stopped again to rest. Dragging the oars aboard, he cupped a handful of water and splashed his face. He had an odd, apologetic look, as though it were sinful to sweat in a girl's company. Cautiously he unbuttoned his shirt, just enough for me to glimpse his pale, shiny collarbones, and commenced rolling up his pantlegs. Grunting a little, he squeezed and rolled, squeezed and rolled, till the puddle at his feet spread, sliding fore and aft and licking at my shoes. Unlacing them carefully so as not to jostle us, I took them off and set them beside me on the seat.

"Any sign of fry down there?" he said, staring at my toes through the damp grey stockings. Holding onto the gunnel, I craned over, gazing past my pale reflection into the river. Its darkness masked any dart or shadow of minnows.

Silas had managed to roll his pantlegs past his kneecaps, so knobby and white they could've been an old man's. Reaching into the tin box beneath him, he pulled out a spoon wound with green twine fitted with a hook. He leaned forward and flung the line in — too preoccupied, or so I hoped, to catch my eyes lingering on his knees, the blue-veined flesh of one thigh and the soft bulge higher up. Shame, I thought, shame, feeling myself redden.

He was facing me, the dripping hook dangling from his fingers. A darning-needle hovered nearby. I glanced off into the elms, praying to God he hadn't seen me looking at him.

"Want to give 'er a try?" he asked. His mouth open, tongue showing slightly, he rewound the line around the spoon, methodical as if rolling coins. As he passed it to me, the front of his shirt gaped and I glimpsed the hollow of his chest, the flat pinkness of a nipple. The string glided through my fingers; a shiver passed between my shoulderblades. Of happiness, perhaps; anticipation? A premonition, it may well have been, of things to come.

"Feel anything down there yet, Phemia?" His eyes were hopeful and eager as the children's, Peter's or Mary's, when I'd return from doing Mam's shopping.

"Nope," I said, just as the hook snagged. Tightening, the line bit my hand.

"Haul 'er up, quick!" he shouted, and I tugged. Harder and harder, but it would not budge, caught on Lord knows what on the bottom — a rock, perhaps, a fallen bough.

Silas seized it and started yanking, pulling and pulling, with no better luck. Giving up, he threw his head back, laughing, a loud, hiccupy chortle.

"Well, you've done it now, Phemie! Go for trout and you hook the durn river." And he let go, the tangled green line lassoing the surface, floating light as a mosquito for moments before the current dragged it under. The spoon flashed like a fish, wafting down.

"Got more line where that came from, don't you worry. Only one who'll mind is Mama. She was hoping for a nice big rainbow for supper." Unrolling his pantlegs, the brownish twill creased and almost stiff now, he sighed and dunked the oars.

"Speaking of which, I s'pose it's high time I got you home, isn't it?"

Silas's mother was just as her name would have you expect.

Tryphena: it reminded me of butterflies, which churned in my stomach the first time he took me upstairs to his family's flat. We had passed plenty of afternoons together in the store, of course, but it was a good while before I was invited into their abode. The invitation didn't come until weeks after that day in the boat. Perhaps Silas's shyness had something to do with this, but more likely it was the old lady, Tryphena I mean, adjusting to the new development in his life.

I call her old, though, looking back, she and Mam would've been about the same age. The difference was, Silas being an only child, his mother had a plenitude of time on her hands. In some ways she didn't even seem like a married woman. No, from the first she struck me as almost spinsterish, surrounding herself with busywork and a soft, stuffy quiet that filled the space taken in others' lives by children. Except that she had Silas, who, to her, could do no wrong; and she was never lonesome. I doubt it would have occurred to her to feel lonesome; lacking Silas and his father, she had God.

She was a churchgoing woman, Tryphena: possessed of a fervour and devotion you never saw in our house, or church either. It was from his mother that Silas got his notions, the sense that God was always watching. You mustn't get me wrong, Fan. From the start, I reckon it was such faith that set Silas apart, something I found enviable. You and I were raised knowing that God's eyes wandered, that despite his best intentions things occasionally blocked his view. Sure, of necessity he turned his attention elsewhere when you were peeling potatoes, using the privy or otherwise tediously indisposed. It was only natural. As I figured, God didn't have time to keep a constant eye on everybody — the way Tryphena would've kept hers on Silas, had he not grown up and found his own place in the store. A guardian angel: had she been Roman, heaven forbid, that's how she'd have fancied herself. Oh, such a big strong woman of faith in that dainty china teacup of a body. So help me, Fan, my immediate thought when Tryphena took my hand in hers was how tiny the bones must be under that soft, yellowed skin, that rustly dress; how tiny and frail and easily snapped.

Not that I mean to be critical. Thirty-odd years later I still mean it when I say she was "good"; one who looked for the best in people, turning aside at faults as if at unpleasant smells, and looking blithely the other way. She was willing to overlook evil, yes; to turn the other eye, if not cheek, and keep going.

I think Silas feared that's how she'd treat me. Instead, Tryphena seemed to like me straight off, started right in spoiling me like the daughter she'd never had. This was especially so once I got religion, her religion, when she could look at me and know that, like herself, her husband and son, I was saved. It must've been a relief to her, believing that.

Until I came to know Tryphena — by that I mean sitting almost nightly at the Lewises' dining-room table, my belly growling while she said grace — my feelings for Silas were but girlish and flighty, like a kite jigging beyond reach in the sky. Sharing his faith attached a string, a tail too. It reined me in, yes; fastened my feet to the ground.

You see, until I tasted his mother's pork roast and helped with the dishes (so many matching pieces, bone china so thin you could see your hand's shadow through it!) and sat with her afterwards in their spotless, velvety parlour — well, Fan, until then I never fully appreciated Silas, the life he could afford me. The articles — the rewards, if you like — of his faith.

Picking through her satin-lined sewing basket — an endless array of sterling thimbles, tiny heart-shaped cushions porcupined with pins, spool silk and Anchor crochet-cotton in riches of colour I'd never imagined — Tryphena would talk to me of God. Of miracles and gifts and love, divine love, and how it could manifest itself in a child. One's very own begotten child. It was talk I'd never heard before, not so shamelessly anyway, especially the parts about love — never mind from whom or whence that love came.

Tryphena opened her heart to me. Her sewing basket, too. One Saturday night while Silas was downstairs taking stock, she and I sat on the cut-velvet settee poring over a stack of *Harper's Bazaar*s from the store. They were full of patterns for crazy quilts pieced with goods I'd scarcely dare dream of: velvets, silks, satin brocades. I could picture the colours: purple, gold and russet-brown; emerald, scarlet, burgundy; the pieces feather-stitched with gold, embroidered with flowers, fans and spiderwebs, names, dates.

There was a place you could send to for fancy silk scraps, another for instructions on appliquéing blossoms — pansies, yellow and violet, delicate as ones pressed in a book.

"Ohhhh," I must've sighed, thinking suddenly of you. Due to Silas, perhaps, you'd been creeping into my thoughts less and less those past few months. Forgotten? Of course not; you were always there somehow in the back of my head. But fainter — yes, I have to say it — my memory of your face softer and blurred at the edges. Fading.

Tryphena glanced up from her magazine, curious. Quizzical. She was never quite what you'd call nosy.

"My s-sister," I tried to explain, "I had a sister once who——"

But she was already licking her thumb to turn the page.

"All the rage in Boston, I gather, these quilts." She watched my face. "A trifle gaudy, I think, don't you?"

"They put me in mind of gypsies and wild ponies," I blurted, overcome with foolishness, imagining the soft heavy slither of velvet. Tryphena's look warmed from distaste to pity. "There now," she said, patting my hand. Sly hope added a quickness to her small grey eyes.

"Well. We could send away for a pattern if you like, dear. Seeing how you're so taken with these things. Perhaps tomorrow, after church, we could see what's lying around the store — remnants, you know, odds and ends; get you started on something, anyways."

Oh, you could see her mind working, her faint eyebrows arched, her prim, dry lips pursed.

"Yes, of course that's what we'll do. Just you and me, after the service, dear. What do you say?"

It was as if she were offering something on one of her pretty dessert plates, holding it out to me like a slice of raisin pie. Oh, I knew she had more in mind than the ragbag downstairs, no matter how gay and gaudy its scraps. More, too, than friendship, the kindness of one woman to another albeit years younger and rather less favoured.

I could have declined, you know. Even as she mentioned it, I knew I could say no. Oh Fan, I may have been young and wanting, but I knew clear as sin what she was offering. Her world, one that included not only her son and the store, but the entire fold of the chosen, well-heeled or not. I could've garnered scraps for a crazy quilt from elsewhere — though it might've taken years. Cigar silks, hatbands; scraps scrounged from jumble sales and the poor box at the Templars' Hall, castoffs from women like Silas's mother. I could have saved and hoarded them like money till there were enough, though Lord knows by then I'd have been too old for such fancy-work.

As for the rest of what Tryphena held out to me? Well, only a dullard would have declined. And funny thing, the faith I found going Baptist won Pa back too, indirectly. Even if only a little and, at that, a bit late. Oddly enough, what finally brought him around was the Lewises having religion. On account of that, he tried to overlook what the town said about Malcolm Lewis being such a skinflint that his palms squeaked when he rubbed them together.

Of course, Silas's people weren't folks our parents would've mixed with themselves. Any notions Mam and Pa had of his parents came from the odd occasion glimpsing them about town — not crossing paths, by any stretch. Though, for all anyone knew, our pa and Silas's might have shared some interests. The lectures at St. Bridgid's, for instance, put on each Thursday night by the Geological Society.

Tryphena dolled herself up like royalty for these events, sitting up front in her black plumed hat with her husband, waving a black silk fan. I know because once Pa went and afterwards described to Mam who-all had attended. A scientist from Montreal had spoken on the wonders of Arcadia iron, praising its strength when used in artillery. It never occurred to Pa that Mam might've enjoyed being there too, an evening out, though it meant listening to foreigners debate grades of ore.

The British army used our iron for guns, Pa was quick to boast. And, as if passing on an equally prideful piece of information, he relayed to Mam details of seeing Mrs. Lewis as well as the wives of some company bigwigs, sitting straight-backed and serious, looking engaged. "Imagine," Mam said, not altogether amused. You could tell, though, that seeing Silas's mother there had made Pa uneasy. But, like pulling a stone from a foundation, in a way it may have helped loosen his grudge against Silas.

Yet what changed his mind about *us* was the fact the Lewises were churchgoers — though Pa himself was not. You must remember — each Sunday from the time you and I could walk — Mam herding us to service at All Saints', the big stone cathedral in Chalford, at the centre of our old village; then here, to St. Luke's up the hill. Pa was from a family of dissenters, Mam told us once, as if to excuse his absence. He always stayed home; no one had the gall to ask why or what he did while we were gone, points that Mam made a habit of avoiding. We figured he stayed in bed, remember, judging by his crankiness, Pa creeping downstairs in his long johns upon our return home. It was always as though we'd just woken him up.

"He's jealous, your pa. Sees things in others maybe he's scared he lacks himself," Mam whispered, the first Sunday I went to church with the Lewises instead. I'd expected to catch it from her later: her stone-cold silence and weary, pained looks, as good as saying, *You've gone and done it now, girl, turning your back on your own and all you were brung up to; off seeking greener pastures.* To use Tryphena's expression, I expected hell and castigation from Mam. That whole morning in church, dread gnawed at me like hunger.

Though I did my best to cover up, Silas's mother noticed me fretting. After the service she laid her hand on my arm, light as the stem of a rose, all the while smiling and nodding to the rest of the congregation spilling down the steps. "'He that loveth father or mother more than me is not worthy,'" she said in a soft, breathy voice. Steering her towards the road, Silas's father bowed his head and added, "'he that loveth son or daughter more than me is not worthy of me': Matthew 10:37. 'And every one that hath forsaken houses, or brethren, or sisters, or father, or mother, or wife, or children, or lands, for my name's sake shall — inherit — everlasting — life!'"

Their way of offering comfort, I guess.

To my amazement, Mam showed no signs of vexation or repining when I got home. Rather, she seemed resigned, as she did sometimes, throwing down her apron, asking me to keep an eye on things to give her a moment's peace. She seemed sad, too. But almost relieved, as some are, once the inevitable comes to pass. As if she'd known all along it was only a matter of time before I cast in my lot with the Lewises. Perhaps she figured I had their way in my blood already.

XVII

Salvation

The use of Sewing is exceeding old,
As in the sacred Text it is enrold;
Our Parents first in Paradise began,
Who hath descended since from man to man:
The mothers taught their Daughters, Sires their sons,
Thus in a line successively it runs
For generall profit, and for recreation,
From generation unto generation.

The Lewises had me to supper that evening, after leaving me to spend the afternoon with Mam. It grew late, and I figured Tryphena had forgotten about us going below to pick through bolt ends. But she hadn't. After the dishes were dried — plain ones this time, to match the simple meal of cold meat and scrambled eggs — Tryphena got the key from Malcolm and the two of us crept downstairs. Off the pantry was a little stairway leading to the back room where Malcolm kept his accounts. Fussing with the lock, Silas's mother led the way.

It was the first time I'd entered this office of sorts, wide and lofty like the store, with the same fancy ceiling, but cluttered and dusty. In one corner, opposite a desk piled with papers, stood a woodstove big enough to cook on; also a large enamel sink, indicating the office had at one time been used as a kitchen. Two smaller rooms branched off to one side; they appeared empty but for some tea chests and burlap sacks. A door in the centre of the room opened into the store, dark and cavernous as the hold we'd slept in, years before, crossing the ocean.

"Malcolm lived down here, dear, before we married. His parents had the upstairs suite. They'd have preferred it if we'd taken over down here and fixed things up. Malcolm would've been happy enough, but oh, I found it much more suitable upstairs. Too cold down here in winter, and when you're in business you need *some* privacy. He saw my point of view, once we started trying for a family." She sniffed and laid the key atop a stack of ledgers. "Though it wasn't all roses, dear, let me tell you, living with his folks. Heaven rest their poor old souls!"

Whispering like a thief's, her voice seemed to burrow into the shelves. She flicked a brass switch and like magic the lights flooded on, the neatly arranged merchandise leaping into view. I tiptoed after her to the yard goods section, to the metal rack limbed like a tree with bolts of cloth. Headless wicker dressmaking forms rested like birdcages behind the counter.

Tryphena knelt and started rooting through something, a box heaped with odds and ends: mostly short fraying lengths of plain, practical goods — burlap, broadcloth, gabardine.

"Mercy!" She shoved it aside and reached for another box. "Now where could that stuff have got to? Why, I'm sure there was velvet, just the other day; black, a good foot or two. I cut it myself, you know, for Eliza Peck's sister. And some cream-colour satin too, come to think of it. Oh for pity's sake, don't tell me Malcolm sold them!"

Rummaging faster, under the strong yellow light, she looked quite piqued. She started digging through a shoebox of ribbon scraps and tangled skeins of embroidery floss.

"Now don't despair, Euphemia. Perhaps we're in luck after all. Good things come to those that wait, dear, don't they? And oh yes, there's that batch of hatbands from the factory in Caledonia, out in the other room, mustn't forget. Goodness knows how they ended up here; I s'pose they were ordered, then someone never had the courtesy to pick them up. I'd have to ask my husband, of course, but they might be of some use to us."

I watched her sort the most promising scraps from the dullest.

"If you see anything, dear, don't hesitate."

Turning the rack, I couldn't resist rubbing my hand over the flat, stiff bolts. The only satin was plain white, suitable for a fancy chemise or petticoat.

"Mustn't give up hope, Euphemia. We'll send to *Harper's* for a pattern, that's what. By the time it arrives I'm sure there'll be more to choose from. Sometimes we just have to be patient, dear, that's all. But that's the *joy* of sewing, isn't it? If one weren't patient, one wouldn't make much of a seamstress — would one, Euphemia?"

She seemed to feel a need to repeat my name — to commit it to memory, or perhaps simply get used to it. Smiling, I locked the door for her and followed her back upstairs. Disappointed, yes, but cheered too.

Settling into the parlour with some needlepoint, she grinned at me, stifling a yawn with a dainty flutter.

"Well dear, I suppose it's time Silas took you home. Your mother will be wondering where on earth you've got to, won't she? We wouldn't want her to worry."

As Silas helped me on with my jacket, she came and stood in the archway above the stairs, her stitchery tucked under one arm.

"Don't you fret." She squinted at me. "There'll be something pretty for you by the time that pattern comes." Then, as if recalling some vague, cloying detail, she said, "That sister of yours — the one who's with the Lord now — was she a seamstress too?"

It took me aback, Fan. I had to stop and think.

"Fanny? Oh no, not really."

She patted my arm, reaching up on tiptoe to kiss my cheek, a dry, quick peck with no warmth to it at all.

"We must remember her in our prayers — she never knew Jesus, I s'pose." She looked pained, her smile fading. "You must ask the Lord to forgive her sins, Euphemia. It's up to you, dear. You must ask, and he'll listen. He always does. The Lord answers prayers, you won't forget that, will you?"

I don't suppose you recall the Baptist chapel — the red clapboard place down the road from the big churches, not too far from the store. People said the meeting house was built with Malcolm Lewis's seed money, whatever that meant, profits made off tobacco, shoe polish and Chamberlain's pain liniment. At the town's expense, some argued. Once or twice after you were gone, Mam tried rousing Pa on a Sunday morning, urging him to pay a visit there while the rest of us trekked up to St. Luke's. But he refused. Not because of the Lewises — Lord, this was before Silas entered my life! — or because Pa was sour on God. No. My guess is that he needed the sleep more, that bit of quiet for an hour a week. Not that he had anything against church or religion or people who believed; it was just that he himself had no such longings, though sometimes you sensed his envy of those that did. When he heard about me going to church with the Lewises, something in him eased up, odd as it sounds. Like a rusty cog with a fresh coat of grease.

Mam wasn't crazy about my consorting with the Baptists. But as I've said there wasn't much she could do, except purse her lips and turn aside when I quit attending St. Luke's with her and the others, to sit with Silas and the Baptists at their meeting house instead. If, before, old Malcolm had cause to look down his nose at me, by my second Sunday anyone could see his grim, smug pleasure having a new recruit in the family pew. Silas's mother took it upon herself to introduce me to the other ladies, to Reverend Freeborn Peck and his wife, Eliza. All of them beamed as though I were some poor lost cur hauled in off the road.

And me? I figured that if I quit, Silas would think me unworthy and lose interest. Though, goodness knows, there might have been any number of fellows willing to step in and fill his shoes. Bert Putnam, for instance — though after grade twelve I'd look right through him whenever we met on the street. Once I noticed him outside the Waverley with a girl; she was common-looking and frowzy, judging from my glimpse at the back of her dress. I didn't get a look at her face, but from behind she might've been Ada Skoke.

If there were other boys interested in me, I had no inkling. So I can't tell you how or why a girl my age back then could've felt so decided, so mule-stubborn fixed on any particular fellow being the right one. I guess there's no limit to what the young and soft-headed will do for love. Love, oh yes, years later there's no denying its power. And by then I was convinced there was nobody else for me but Silas. The moon rose and fell on him, far as I was concerned.

After a year or so devoted to the business, he gained confidence. And he started to fill out, putting flesh on those bones and dressing fit to assume his father's place. He took to wearing crisp white shirts with black garters pushing up the sleeves; well-cut, boot-length trousers. If you'd seen him behind the counter, Fan, you'd've thought: Now there's a fellow with his life in hand, knows what he's after. Unlike the others in town — Bert and his friends who ended up at the works, forsaking all ambitions but blindly feeding the company's fortunes, just as Pa had done. It's wicked to say, God rest him, but for all his fascination with science and steel, our pa was tied to the mill like a dog on a rope. Not one of these fellows had a hope of clean work, work where they wouldn't come home sooty as if their shifts were spent walking in hell. Or inside a furnace, where indeed Pa might have toiled; Bert too, since Pa said they worked together for a time. Though for all Pa's talk, none of us was ever sure what they did there.

Not that I was too interested. Not even the day I went home and found Bert at the table, drinking spruce beer with Pa. He still had dirt around his eyes, ringed like a raccoon's, and he knocked his mug getting up to greet me. I didn't know where to look, Fan; all I could think of was his hand at the small of that girl's back, his fingers tweezing gauzy, wrinkled fabric. He asked how I was and I looked at his hands, the dirt around his nails, and I wasn't sure what to say. My mind was outside the Waverley, recalling that evening out of many: the scent of pomade and ice-cream and spittle stamped into the dirt, the smell of fresh paint on the curlicues and spindles on that wide veranda. I remembered the rough, scratchy sound of the girl's laugh. But I could tell by Bert's eyes that he had no recollection. In front of Pa he was all politeness, with no penchant for teasing or coarseness; I tried not to flinch at his "I seen's" and "you ain't's" and, worst of all, "Your pa here, he learned me."

When he was leaving, Fan, I wanted to shake his arm and say, "You could do better," thinking of the times he'd followed me from school. But I couldn't bring myself to go close enough to touch him — not because of the dirt on his sleeve, but because of that girl. And when he was gone, Pa said, "Now there's a fellow," but to be truthful, all I could think of was Ada Skoke, and the seat of Bert's chair and his empty mug smudged with soot. No amount of hot water could scour that mug clean enough for me to drink from; I noted a chip in it and remembered to let others use it, never myself.

Talk about letting the devil inside one's door — which is what Silas might've said.

And I'll advance now as plainly as before: compared to Bert, Silas had a certain appeal. It made me see past his habit of totting figures and gazing skyward, beyond the rafters if we were in church, as if consulting spirits holy and otherwise. So I took his religion — not because of his mother or the store or anything else, but because I was in love. Not with God, of course, but with Silas. And he was smitten with me, and desperate, yes, desperate, that I be his. In mind, body and spirit.

It meant sacrifice; no debate there. That first time I accompanied Silas to service, in between bouts of nerves I chewed the insides of my cheeks raw to keep from snickering. I was wonderstruck. The behaviour of those Baptists in a house of God! I saw why — despite anything Mam might have said — Pa had so little to do with dissenters, especially this kind. The wailing and mewling, people weaving and staggering in the pews, their eyes screwed shut. Some had tears streaming down. The whole congregation swayed like trees, trees or tipplers: arms aloft, waving, waving and reaching as if for God's hand. Some had a downright foolish gleam of peace and calm on their faces, everybody flushed and sweaty in the stuffy little room.

"Praise the Lord!" they mumbled and muttered, wagging their heads and smacking their lips as if surveying a big feed of some sort. A picnic: plates of ham and pitchers of lemonade spread under a tree. No doubt that's what the poorer ones were picturing:

food, a glorious feast. Or their Sunday dinner; the gristly joint at home, roasting while they prayed.

And Silas — to this day I haven't forgotten how he looked, praying. Eyeballs roving under his lids, pale stubby lashes resting on the hollows above his cheeks. Murmuring gently to himself, only half shy, like a little child playing make-believe. And all the while a faint blush of pride on his face, threatening to break into a smile. I saw him biting his lip so nobody would catch him out.

For Silas took Reverend Peck's talk of the Holy Spirit to heart. After our second or third session in church, he'd stand with his eyes closed, a flat, bland smile on his lips, palms lifted as if waiting to be showered with gifts. He seemed hardly aware any more of me beside him in the flounced green dress Tryphena had helped me sew, taking it for granted that I was as present in spirit as in body. Which perhaps I was; by then I'd overcome my squeamish-ness at people's moaning and mumbling, their rustling like cooped hens catching a fox's scent as the Spirit descended. I forgot my urge to laugh, watching men's faces melt as Reverend Peck led them in prayer, the room abuzz with their shaking and muttering.

"Can't you just feel Him working, dear?" Tryphena would hiss, leaning past Silas, smiling, her eyes flooding light. "Marrrvellous, marrrvellous!" she rejoiced, settling back, beaming at him. Once she reached up to brush his lapel, then caught herself. Malcolm fixed her with one of his lingering stares. They took this all so seriously, the Lewises. But then I guess so did I.

Because after a while I felt it too, when I shut my eyes. Felt something moving inside me with the sharp, tinkly chords of the piano, the reverend's raspy, naked voice. The Spirit, a gentle buzz-ing in my ears, a soft hazy glow swelling inside like nothing I'd felt before. Perhaps it was love, like the warm secret tingling I felt that day in the boat, when Silas wrung out his pantlegs. Except now it was centred high up in my body, soothing away that feeling lower down — if you can sense what I mean.

Sometimes, wrapped in the warmth of those Baptists praying, I'd open my eyes, Fan; watch the feathers in women's hats shaking ever so slightly in that soupy air. The Spirit moving. It was down-right catching, infectious as a summer grippe, being held and rocked like that in the Lord. Something I never knew before. Not at St.

Luke's, with its righteous smells of polish and wax. And certainly not at home, amid the messy, squalling closeness that drove you to the quiet someplace inside your skull. No, being in the chapel gave me a noisy, raucous peace, a feeling that blurred and hummed beyond my skin. It gave me hope, Fan; do you see what I'm saying? It made me believe you were *there*, only invisible.

And so I trusted myself to the Lewises, giving thanks and praise to God that they'd found me and brought me to this. Washed in the blood of the Lamb, they called it. And so I hoped I was, allowing faith to fill in where reason lapsed; believing too, with a certainty beyond knowing, that Silas and I were meant for each other.

My fourth trip to church I gave myself to the Lord. One muggy night in July, the Baptists held a revival meeting, the little building filled to bursting. Half the town, it felt like, turned out to hear a travelling preacher, the Reverend Lenfest Vans. The moans, the wailing — the heat was enough to make you swoon, like a pot fit to boil over, a fever pitched to lift the roof off its rafters!

A short burly man in a black suit, Vans danced and spat as he preached. Starting soft as a hum at the back of the room, a noise grew and fanned the crowd like a hot wind, roaring overhead like flames towards the front. An awesome noise, it burned my ears, blowing itself into a wild, frantic hectoring — gibberish, like some foreign tongue; not French or Greek or Arabic, or any language recognizable by shape or sound. But a lolling, frothy roar like the multitudes gargling — the noise you'd imagine Leviathan making, swallowing ships.

We were on our knees; Silas had me by the wrist. He pulled me to my feet and I slid behind him into the lineup snaking to the front, a ragtag queue of sobbing men and women sliding, stumbling from the pews. I moved forward just like them, too jubilant and full of Spirit to look back or take stock of who else was in line. When I reached the stage, the evangelist squatted, capped my head with his hot, sweaty palm. Closing his eyes, he muttered, "Thank you Je*sus* thank you Je*sus*!", the corners of his mouth specked white. I crumpled like a ball of paper, half blinded by tears — tears of joy and gasping, reckless relief, as if I'd run some bumbling distance race and won by a hair.

"'Get thee behind me, Satan,'" he hissed. "'Blessed are the

dead which die in the Lord!' 'For he that is dead is freed from sin' — the lusts of the mortal body — to walk in newness of life!"

Reverend Peck was crying too, tears glittering the length of his nose. "Welcome to the Kingdom," someone whispered, taking my hand, leading me back to my seat. It was Malcolm Lewis, soon to be my father-in-law.

Afterwards, walking me home in the gentle darkness, Silas hung behind his parents. Even at a distance, I could see his mother's shoulders trembling through her eyelet stole. His head bowed, he fumbled for my hand. And he asked if I would humble myself to marry him, Fan. Me not even eighteen, and Silas barely twenty. It was God's will, he said, a halfwit could see.

"Yes," I answered, without a moment's pause.

"Together forever in the body of the Lord," he mused, and we both smiled, mulling it over. My sense of *rightness* was so complete there seemed no need to speak further of it.

"Amazing, isn't it, Phemie," he piped up then, perhaps afraid I was having second thoughts, "the way things are unfolding, one after another, like a neap tide covering everything — perfect! — mud, rocks, sand an' all!"

What a funny way of putting it, I thought at the time. Though I shouldn't've been surprised; occasionally Silas travelled to Spenceport in his father's stead, meeting ships carrying Irish linen, West Indies molasses. He knew the ocean's business in ways I wouldn't've cared to.

"Crabs; starfish; sculpins; mermaid's purses," he went on listing things, me so happy I scarcely heard. "Why, you'll get to see 'em for yourself, Phemie, all these critters!" And he promised to take me to the bay for our honeymoon.

But first there were my parents to be told, and the more urgent matter of my baptism.

Mam kept very quiet when Silas asked for my hand. Pa told him we'd have to wait till my birthday, at least.

"Just as well," Silas agreed, the picture of equanimity, "since we've got to wait anyways; can't do much till Phemie's baptized."

Mam opened her mouth, a haughty, wounded look in her eyes.

"Baptized! But Effie, my girl, you been christened!"

Pa yanked her sleeve. "If Effie's got a new religion, that's her choice. Not as though she's a kid no more, Addie. A bit of churchiness never hurt anyone; sure, that shouldn't prevent two folks being man and wife." He raised an eyebrow. "Seems you're not far off saying that yourself. So if this is Effie's choice, I don't s'pose we got much call standing in her way."

"S'pose not." Mam crossed her arms over her bosom and stared at the ceiling. Peter and the rest had gotten sent upstairs while we talked; the thumping up there was fit to bring the house down. Mam looked at me, her eyes hard.

"Well. I guess you'll do what you're gonna do. Nothing I say will change your mind. Baptized, indeed. As if *their* water's holier."

She glanced at Silas all got up in his best suit, his neck chafed red from his collar.

"But at least you won't be wanting, and I won't have to be worrying about you no more." With that she marched upstairs; we heard her barking at everyone to simmer down. Pa went and stood at the door, eyeing Will outside splitting wood; sighing, he slammed outdoors and watched him stack it.

After Silas left, Mam came downstairs with a little blue bag, its satin dull and spotted with yellow stains. Shaking something out, she held it in her palm. It was a ring, the gold worn thin and pitted, set with a small blackish stone. A garnet, she said, holding it pinched between her thumb and forefinger, up to the light. It was the colour of pigs' blood, blood we'd found in a bucket once behind the butcher's shop.

"'Twas my mam's, see. When you were born, she wanted you to have it. S'pose you could say I've been minding it for you. Till the time came."

I pushed it back at her. "Maybe you'd best keep it, then."

Squinting, she held it up again.

"Oh, someday you'll change your mind, girl, once the holy-roller charm wears off. Someday, when you start seeing things as I have." She tucked the ring back inside the tiny sack. Then she stepped forward, prodding my cheekbone with her finger. Leaning close, so close I felt the heaviness of her bosom against mine, she kissed me. A soft cool kiss, faint and gentle as a fly lighting on a screen before the wind blows it off.

"Good luck, my girl. Though you'll have *his* family and all their worldly goods and all the Bible-thumpin' in the world on your side, you're still gonna need it. Every blessed bit of luck you can lay your fingers on. So don't ever think you got it made, Effie, like some do. Because that's not the way of the world, whether a person's been dunked or not."

So much for her blessing. Of course I wanted to shout back that she was wrong, dead wrong; that Silas and I had the Lord on our side. *His* benediction. But there was no use objecting; I wanted only to get away from her, Mam and her gloom and doom. It seemed beyond her to be grateful or happy — as if any joy in her had up and left and never thought to come back. Enough to give you hives, her behaving as though she knew things others didn't, always taking it upon herself to give warnings. As if she wouldn't be around later to bail you out — which in my case came, more or less, to be true.

XVIII

Union

Thus plainly, and most truly is declar'd
The needles worke hath still bin in regard,
For it doth ART, so like to NATURE frame,
As if IT were her Sister, or the SAME.
Flowers, Plants and Fishes, Beasts, Birds, Flyes, and Bees,
Hils, Dales, Plaines, Pastures, Skies, Seas, Rivers, Trees;
There's nothing neere at hand, or farthest sought,
But with the Needle may be shap'd and wrought.

My day of baptism, Mam made herself scarce, Pa too — as if, succumbing to something bigger than themselves, they chose to hide. Mam said she couldn't endure the carry-on that would accompany such a spectacle as a public dunking, before the whole town, to boot. Pa merely bit his tongue — proof, to me, of God's healing grace, the miracles he wrought.

That bright Sunday, not one of our kin came to watch from the riverside — only my new family, the family of God. The "dunking" itself took place before service, in the cool of early morning. The leaves were still a tender green; there was a pale scrap of moon in the high blue sky. Robins sang from the elms beyond the steep, rocky shingle where the congregation gathered, the spot where garter snakes would coil and sun themselves once the day grew hot. Past the round pink stones, the water rushed, reeds and eelgrass streaming like ribbons. I was gussied up in a pale blue dress that Silas's mother had helped sew for the occasion. It was of real silk from the store, her gift. "Only the best, the very best, is sufficiently suffice for someone meeting her Maker," she insisted.

The dress had a fancy dropped waist that I'd stayed up all hours finishing. I couldn't help wondering how deep the river would be and how long I'd have to stay in it. I worried how, wet, the silk would sag and cling; that the curls Mam had grudgingly set with rags would wash out. I was so afraid of what Silas would think, seeing me drenched as a duck-dog fetching a stick — not to mention the simple concern about how I'd breathe while Reverend Peck dipped me under. These were my thoughts as I stood there shivering, trying to look joyous — any notion of God about as near and dear just then as that fading scrap of moon.

Grinning like a coot, Mrs. Peck helped me into a long white smock like the choristers at St. Luke's wore over their clothes. Silas's mother hung about, stooping to straighten the hem, the sleeves, the buttons, ensuring it wouldn't float off during my immersion.

The water raced past as I waded in, the tinkly coolness seeping through my shoes, engulfing my ankles. I let its rushing fill my head, rinse away my cares. Reverend Peck plunged past, his black frock billowing as he trudged waist-deep, his limp black Bible held aloft. Lurching to keep his footing, he turned and beckoned me to follow, smiling, unmindful of the cold as if the river were a milky bath the Lord had drawn.

Creeping forth slowly so as not to lose my step on the slick, slippery stones, I felt the current snag and lift my skirt, the white gown swirling, bloating up under my arms; the iciness like thorns. Wading towards him, I fixed my eyes on the reverend's; they were the same colour as the river. I heard myself gasp and squeal like a baby as the cold bit my ribs.

The Bible clenched under one arm, Reverend Peck reached out, his lips barely moving. One of his hands cradled my head, the other the small of my back. I felt my knees buckle as he yanked me backwards and held me under. Up my nose, through my ears, the water flashed and bubbled. *I baptize thee*, his voice spilled and tumbled like the river, *in the name of the Lord*.... I felt a sparkling, clear as mercy; in the one split second I opened my eyes, caught the sun's blinding glitter. A splintering light, as though the firmament were a mirror smashed and shattered in a trillion dazzling pieces.

"Amen," I cried out, bursting up for air. Choking, wading ashore. "Praise God!" thrummed the voices on the bank, a solemn steady hum like the sound of grasshoppers. "Hallelujah! Hallelujah! Blessed is he who comes in the name of the Father!"

"Blessed are those washed in the blood of the Lamb — they shall inherit the earth!" I heard Reverend Peck sing out, triumphant, rocks grinding and clattering under my feet. The weight of dripping silk dragged me to my knees.

"Praise the Lord!" I cried out again, shuddering and sobbing with heartsick joy. I stumbled into Silas's arms, my teeth and bones knocking together so loudly I swear I could hear them. But I didn't care — not a whit — about the cold, the dress or Mam and Pa's absence. You see, Fan, at that moment nothing of this world mattered.

All these years later, writing of it makes my skin prickle. For no matter what came before or has come since, I know that on that day I was blessed. Oh yes. Even if for just one quick second, I believe I glimpsed God.

Our wedding took place on a blustery day towards the end of that October. Half the town was present, Mam and Pa included, though they kept well to the back of the chapel, sitting by the pot-bellied stove near the door. I felt Mam's presence like a weight upon me the entire service; felt her eyes roving from me to the splintery pews, the whitewashed walls, the makeshift pulpit. "This is no house of God," I imagined her complaining.

Part of me might've agreed, considering the shabbiness, especially contrasted with my attire. Silas's mother had gone all out, no denying. My dress was creamy satin with leg-of-mutton sleeves; seed-pearl beaded bodice; a wasp waist. Tryphena had ordered the goods from New York; had had Miss Laura Beveridge, the best dressmaker in town, make it up. I can't tell you the number of fittings I endured; the week before the wedding I had nothing but oranges and clear tea, and still I was forced to suck in my breath to keep from popping the stays. The entire service I feared I'd faint; I kept my eyes on the pastor's and breathed as shallowly as possible, butterfly breaths from the top of my chest.

Reverend Peck presided over us with hands outstretched as if we were two little children. Following the vows, Eliza Peck thumped out the wedding march on the piano as Silas and I strolled down the aisle — a short hike, though it seemed to take an eternity. So it felt with the eyes of the congregation upon us: some shifty and sore as though being present amounted to consorting with the devil; others smiling in blissful beatitude.

"Beatitude", that was another of Tryphena's favourite words which she'd drop like hankies whenever I shared her company — which was most of the time, after Silas and I decided to become man and wife, or "join in holy mat-rimony", as she preferred to say.

Following the service, we repaired to her parlour for little cakes and "cord-yal" served with ice in crystal glasses. It was actually Dominican lime juice ordered for the occasion. For those few guests not members of the chapel, there was a small pitcher of cham-pagne soda and a silver urn filled with Lyman's coffee. Mam and Pa stayed long enough to siphon down a thimbleful of each. They took the "coffee" black and scalding, passing on the sterling pitcher of cream, the dish of cubed demerara proffered by Silas's mother.

True to his word, Silas took me to Spenceport for our wedding night, borrowing his father's blonde mare and hansom for trans-port. By mid-afternoon the weather turned dirty, spitting drizzle, the wind whipping the last ragged leaves off the sugar maples. Tryphena saw that we were well-bundled with rugs for our trip, though it was only a few miles downriver to the Stinson hotel — a big, square, galleried place as grand as the Waverley but (as Malcolm Lewis said) spared the hoi polloi. Silas was given two days off so we wouldn't have to hurry back.

It was quiet as a morgue in the lobby, fronds of two big potted ferns barely moving as we passed. A bald man sat behind the desk, his back to a row of shiny keys hanging from hooks. He showed us up a wide, polished staircase lit by a chandelier. At the landing was a huge stained-glass window patterned with lilies dimmed by the greying sky.

Our room overlooked the Bay of Fundy, its flinty surface a shade lighter than the sky, and the slate-coloured smudge of hills on the opposite side. Above the water, clouds roiled, squalls blurring the distant shore; in the middle of the bay, steely planks of sunshine broke through, reaching down like fingers.

"The hand of the Father, praise be!" Silas observed, his arms circling me from behind. Gently he pressed himself to me; his belt buckle nudged my spine. His breath smelled of cucumber and lime, brisk and cool on my neck. "Speaking of hands, let's have a look at that ring," he said, and lifted my hand, rubbing my palm with his thumb, running it over my wedding ring. It was a plain gold band that had belonged to his father's mother, engraved with her initials, A.L. —A for Azalea. Tryphena had decided I should have it.

Silas let go of my hand and went to perch on the bed, a high, wide affair with dark twisting posts, a wine brocade counterpane drawn up to the bolster. On the night table stood a tarnished vase of chrysanthemums, their gold petals slightly brown and curling. Silas reached over and plucked one, then another and another. "She loves me, she loves me not, she loves me," he teased, then tested the mattress as if bouncing an India rubber ball.

Shyly, I turned back to the window and watched some cows grazing on the olive-green banks of the river below. It idled like a serpent through a bleached spread of cattails, and through a stark stand of elms. Their bare, silvered branches looked like bones against the dove-coloured clouds. Everything was washed grey, even the large white houses, the dark sprucewoods lit here and there with lingering flashes of yellow.

I reached up to undo the topmost buttons of my going-away dress; they were tiny, a dozen and a half in all. Tryphena had helped cover the entire row with matching rose silk. At the time, I'd thought, Heavens, it'll take till Doomsday to get out of that thing! Of course I had said nothing. But now that the time had come, I found myself half glad of all those buttons.

When I glanced over, Silas was untying his shoes, careful as if helping somebody in the store. Bent forward, his neck looked the same splotchy red as it had a few hours earlier, when he'd cleared his throat and boomed (in a voice that surprised even Reverend Peck): "In-sickness-and-in-health...I do so take this woman, Euphemia Cox, for my lawful-wedded-wife."

Slipping closer, I plucked a handful of petals and sprinkled them over his head.

"What God has brung together let no man tear asunder," he breathed, drawing me down beside him. He arranged himself so as not to crush the yards of rosy silk spread between us. A shred of grey light fell through the drapes, the last weak bloom of afternoon. For a moment motes danced and sparked — fairy dust — till the room dimmed blue. Under the long row of buttons I felt my heart thumping, wondering what should come next.

You may think I was shy, Fan; longing to be elsewhere — with you, perhaps, out of this body, watching all unfold as from a distance. But no. I wasn't shy, only anxious.

Silas sat up and peeled off his frock coat, laying it neatly across the foot of the bed. Leaning on one elbow, he began unbuttoning his shirt, his eyes never leaving my face.

"Perhaps we should wait till dark?" he whispered, eyeing his hand upon my waist as if it were another's. "Oh, Phemie."

He put his face to my hair, still frizzy from the wind, slowly unravelling the loose braided knot Mam had fussed over. Oh, Fan — it was like being tickled to death, the waiting, the wondering; my willing his hand to move.

As the light dwindled, our fingers wandered, skittish as mayflies at first, then bolder. Our mouths hungry but frightened too, as if tasting something new, some hitherto forbidden fruit. After a while his breathing grew hitched and ragged. Mine too; it may have been *his* pulse pounding in my ear. Our hands were deft and slippery, working at his mother's buttons.

In the darkness his body gleamed white and smooth; his hipbones were etched like saw-blades. I lay perfectly still, wanting so badly to look at him. Instead I kept my eyes closed. Like a thief his hand sought and found its spot, and they flew open then to glimpse his face. He'd turned slightly to the side, his eyes squeezed shut as if he were dreaming. His breath came in hard, sharp snorts as he entered me blind, parting my flesh like a bee probing a blossom.

He let out a gasp and fell away. After a few moments he opened his eyes, regarding me with a strange, glistening gratitude.

"God bless you," he muttered, kissing my cheeks, my eyelids. Then, naked as an infant, he slid to the carpet; kneeling, he buried his face in the counterpane. Hands clasped in prayer, he begged the Lord's forgiveness.

"Silas!" I rubbed my hand up and down his arm, up and down. "Oh, Silas, you mustn't, you must not——!"

Till death do us part, I thought. He lifted his head and for one awful second I glimpsed tears. "I love you, Phemie," he blurted, a pronouncement more like God's word than anything passing the lips of a mortal. "And I aim to do my best to honour you, I promise; long as I live, so help me Lord."

I knew he expected me to bow too, and likewise promise obeisance — to God as well as to my husband. But something in Silas's eyes made me still, snuggling deeper into the gamy warmth of the sheets, of what we'd just done. With our souls as much as our bodies.

And it struck me, Fan, that the body itself wasn't awfully different from the spirit, once you let it have its way. For however long it, the act, lasted; like giving yourself up to the Lord — if only on loan. Knowing, of course, that one's sojourn in this world is but temporary; except when you're eighteen, and the body breeds its own faith.

I was Silas's forever now, that's how I saw it; as much his as Christ's. I figured then, still do, that being married amounts to the same as trusting in the Lord. Both boil down to an awesome leap, whether it's Someone or Something filling you, body or spirit. So I couldn't quite grasp Silas's guilt, though it pained me to see him upset. Especially when he rose from his knees and skulked to the washstand: the sight of his haunches as he washed his hands, scouring his nails as if to cleanse them of a day's work.

"Perhaps, just perhaps — well, if you think about it, I mean," he said, climbing into bed in his chilly, creased nightshirt, "the Lord does turn his gaze from...*certain*...things. On occasion, that is." He leaned over and patted my cheek, as if to show he was feeling better. "Probably these...things...get easier, maybe, with time, would you say? In God's eyes, I mean."

"Don't worry so." I reached under the covers for his hand. "Maybe the Lord only sees what he chooses."

It wasn't altogether the right thing to say, but it did appear to soothe him, enough that he shut his eyes.

When I was quite sure he was asleep, I got up and slipped on my nightdress, Mam's wedding gift to me. It was flounced white eyelet trimmed with hairpin lace; I'm sure it had come from McAdam's, the newest store to open up in town. I drifted off, trying not to think what it must've cost.

Silas was the first out of bed in the morning. When I awoke, he was in his clothes, sitting at the window. I rose and dressed while he went downstairs to arrange breakfast — orange juice and tea-cakes which we devoured in the big empty dining room overlooking the mudflats. There was tea in a samovar, which I resisted. The day was grey, a fine drizzle coating the windowpanes, but warmer. So we got into our coats and went walking, past some huge houses with cupolas and widow's walks, towards the docks.

I tried to remember the pier at which we'd landed, Fan, that lifetime ago. But all appeared changed; the tide was so low, ships at wharfside sat high and dry, the deep-veined mud strewn with shells and seaweed. Descending to the beach, I marvelled at the smoothness of the seabed before the water's distant pinkish shimmer, a shimmer the same as rags of kelp strewn here and there, mirroring the sky.

Below the tidemark, a lace of blackened seaweed marked the sand from the mud flecked with shards of mother-of-pearl and broken shells. Mussels, moonsnails, false angel-wings; Silas named them all. Sloping towards the water — the beach itself a vast red prairie — the mud deepened; smooth and thick as custard, it sucked at our boots.

"Where does all the water *go*?" I mused, squelching along; reddish clots flew up, spattering my hem. Plodding on, his head down, Silas didn't answer; he was on the lookout for shells, ones intact, unscathed by the sea.

Some still bore the creatures inside, clams and periwinkles; others the claws of hermit crabs protruding, groping the air. Silas picked each one up to show me, tossing it back to search for others. Poking a stick through rubbery clumps of Irish moss, he stooped to retrieve a sand dollar thin and round as a communion host; the skeleton of some tiny, lost creature. A perfect disk in the palm of his hand — he rubbed away some mud and held it up so I could see.

"Look at this," he said. "The whole story of Christ, in one itty-bitty shell."

I bent closer.

"In the middle there's a star — see? The Star of Bethlehem, Phemie. And them five little holes at the end of each point? The four nail holes, praise be to God, and the spear wound in his side!" He sank back on his heels, beaming.

"I see a flower," I said hopefully, trying for the life of me to credit what he saw.

"An Easter lily!" he said triumphantly.

That second it could've been his mother talking, I swear; the two of us in her parlour, Tryphena glancing from her needlepoint to smile at some little observance of mine — about the air in church, for example, coming alive with the Spirit.

"Praise God!" I waited for him to declare, with his mother's mix of humility and pride.

"The flower of his resurrection, Phemie!" He shook his head, snapping the shell into pieces, letting them fly. Five tiny, white, bony pairs of wings scattered over the mud.

"Five doves of peace, don't you see? Flying off to spread his word!"

And he swooped down to grab another sand dollar, perfectly formed but smaller, and pressed it into my hand.

"For good luck, Phemie — we'll keep this one, all right? For better or for worse; what do you say?"

The crazy quilt pattern was waiting when Silas and I went home the next day. I'd almost forgotten about it, to tell the truth. It took so long to come from the place in New York, and so much had happened since we'd sent away. I say "we" though it was Tryphena who wrote the letter, filled out the form and handled the postage. ("My treat, dear, don't fret so, it's nothing!")

The pattern's arrival was somewhat lost in the hubbub of our homecoming, the two of us set to begin newlywed life — in his parents' abode.

Right after the wedding, Tryphena had had new paper hung in Silas's bedroom, olive-green floral with a wide, striped border round the ceiling. His jaw dropped when he saw it. To my mind it made the room overly dark. There wasn't much we could say, seeing the trouble she'd gone to — out of the goodness of her heart, and her husband's pocketbook. I knew it was meant to welcome me.

But Silas wasn't too pleased, coming home to find things rearranged, his belongings packed away to make room for mine. Ours, I should say, including gifts that trickled in from church and other acquaintances. Hard to credit some of these, especially the ones from people who didn't know us. From the manager of the Merchants' Bank, where the Lewises did business, we got a souvenir plate picturing the town with the mill, furnaces and church spires in the background, and no sign of the river. "A prosperous, modern place," read its gold lettering.

The Pecks gave us a white leather Bible that locked, with a page for our names and those of future children. "With wishes for eternal life together," said the inscription, in Mrs. Peck's tiny hand.

Another present was a velvet-backed photograph album, spaces for the pictures edged with gold leaf and bluebirds and garlands of pink roses; the sender escapes me now.

Waiting on the dresser was an amethyst glass scent-bottle, specially made at a factory in New Albany, part of the trousseau Tryphena had helped prepare for me. Flanking it were a small silver hand-mirror and two tortoiseshell combs — these were from Silas.

Loveliest of all, though, was a velvet lambrequin, maroon and tasselled with gold — a gift from Silas's relatives in the States. It was meant for a fancy mantelpiece, but the only such fixture was the one in Tryphena's parlour, already trimmed with crocheted lace.

"Oh, well," she sighed, layering the present with tissue, packing it away "for later".

The lambrequin was gorgeous enough to wear, truly; exotic and sumptuous as a queen's apparel — the Queen of Egypt, I decided. It gave me more than a twinge, laying it away. You see, in all the goings-on, no mention was made of Silas and I having our own place, decorating our own parlour. As if we weren't quite mature enough to undertake such responsibility, and would do better under his parents' wings — for the first little while, at least. Though it was never discussed. And who could predict how long a "while" would be? As long as they'd have us, I supposed.

XIX

Domestic Bliss

Moreover, Posies rare, and Anagrams,
Signifique searching sentences from names,
True History, or various pleasant fiction,
In sundry colours mixt, with Arts commixion,
All in Dimension, Ovals, Squares, and Rounds,
Arts life included within Natures bounds;
So that Art seemeth meerely naturall,
In forming shapes so Geometricall;
And though our Country everywhere is fild
With Ladies and with Gentlewomen skild
In this rare Art, yet here they may discerne
Some things to teach them if they list to learne.

His mother made room for my clothes in Silas's mahogany wardrobe, his matching chest of drawers. Our first evening, I unpacked my new nightgown, limp and slightly soiled from our wedding night. I had just tucked it away when Tryphena tiptoed in with a little sachet she'd embroidered. Before I could speak, her wiry, nimble fingers were upon the drawer. Jerking it open, glimpsing inside, she made a face.

"Oh dear — I guess you'll be needing something cosier, won't you? Goodness knows I don't mean to criticize, but I don't think, somehow, that Silas's father would approve. I doubt you'd be comfortable in such a...thing. Here," she started to say, but smiled instead. "Come now, let's put you in one of mine, shall we, till we can find you something...appropriate." Decent, she meant.

A second later she appeared with a thick blue flannel nightie over her arm, and an itchy-looking robe.

"These should do, for the time being. Come, you can try them later. But for now, there's the Lord's business — hurry, dear; the fellows are waiting." The fellows? She spoke as if Silas and his father were suitors calling.

"Prayers, dear." She fluttered her eyelids. "In this house we pray together every evening before bed. Come now, you mustn't keep the bridegroom waiting."

Silas clasped my hand as I nestled next to him on the settee. Leaning forward in his wing chair, his father opened the Bible upon his knee. Tryphena whisked in, fussing with the shades, the antimacassar behind us, before kneeling stiffly on a needlepoint stool at Malcolm's feet. Then Silas's father reached out and dimmed the glass-globed lamp, and formed a steeple with his fingertips.

"In thy holy name we ask," Tryphena began to pray, her voice wavering at first, then stronger, resolute, "that you bless this household, oh Lord — and all who dwell in it. As we give praise and beg of you *keep* these young ones *safe* from harm and the world's e-vil ways."

Her eyes opened a crack and she beamed at Silas slumped forward, rubbing his brow in meditation.

"Pleeeease, dear God — make theirs a long and happy union!"

She paused, looking up at her husband deep in prayer. His face danced with licks of flame flashing through the grate. Sniffling, she succoured herself for the finish.

"And preserrrve them always oh Lord in Je-sus' name, and give them strength in reviling *lust*, and keep them whole in their union with you!"

Sighing, she rocked back on her heels, eyes squeezed shut. There was another pause. The father coughed — clearly it was the first time they'd opened this nightly circle to a newcomer — and started praying aloud, a low, monotonous rumble.

Our Father who art in heaven — I let my mind wander, wrapped in words cosy and soft as an old quilt. *Hallowed be thy name.*

Malcolm's voice droned on, rising and falling to the accompaniment of Silas's murmurs, his mother's breathy ah-mens.

"...And let them prosper Lord in this world and the next when they go to sit with you at your right hand and in your heav'nly home...."

When I opened my eyes, Silas's father was staring at me, his ice-blue eyes hangdog, almost teary.

"Daughter," he muttered, as my gaze dropped to the carpet and Silas's fingers, clammy as cold ham, squeezed mine.

Silently he raised me up and led me across the room. He hung back as I bent to kiss his parents — first his mother, her cool cheek smelling of cloves; then his father, with his fusty odour of well-handled pennies, his sandpaper jaw.

"Sleep well, my darlings," Tryphena called as we fled down the hall, adding in a dry voice, "I trust you won't find the bed too rigid, Euphemia."

"Thanks" was all I could muster, a chilly rectitude settling upon me.

And so began my days of domestic bliss, days I now recall as a time of hunger. Not of spirit, goodness no. Lord knows that was well taken care of; Tryphena saw to it that our souls were given constant refreshment. Prayer before breakfast, lunch and supper, washed down with those nightly soirées after she and I laid away our handiwork.

Nor was it a hunger of the belly, quite, for God knows she took it as her duty to feed me. Not only feed me, but ensure that I learned her way of managing food, following her recipes, her methods: how to make pot-pie with crust as tender as hers; potatoes scoured just so, each eye gouged out with the tip of the paring knife.

No, my hunger was more a mix of the bodily and spiritual. It was a longing to know Silas as I had that first night in Spenceport. Just Silas, without the creak of his parents in their bed next door, or his mother creeping down the hallway.

Tryphena was a poor sleeper, I soon learned. At all hours, Fan, you'd hear her getting drinks of water, asking Malcolm to fetch her smelling salts or spoonfuls of tonic for this and that. Dr. Wilson's Herbine Bitters for headache; Hanford's Balsam of Myrrh, Chamberlain's Liniment for back pain and lumbago; Lydia C. Pinkham's Remedy for Women — "A baby in every bottle," read the label.

All these medicines she kept in a locked cabinet in the lavatory. But one morning when I got up to relieve myself, there they were in full view, lining the shelves in their reddish boxes.

"Never you mind, dear, it's nothing," she said when she found me looking. "I just like to be prepared, don't you?"

Prepared for what, I did not ask.

"Some small complaints the Lord hasn't time to help us with," she chided, steering me towards the breakfast table already laid with marmalade and toast — a stack of it, thin-sliced, cut in triangles. Silas and his father had eaten, of course, and begun their day downstairs. Some mornings, it was the register's clang that woke me, the far-off ringing of the till opening, closing; the pitch of their voices wishing customers well.

Sometimes — more and more often as the days rolled by, once I'd quit tallying the hours of marriage, the days; quit feeling wonderstruck, as if it weren't quite real, my being someone's mate — I would stay put in the bedroom until Tryphena went out. I'd listen for her traipsing quietly down the back stairs to Malcolm's office; then I'd don Mam's nightgown, creased but scented with lavender. I would unwrap the wedding-gift lambrequin and drape it round me, its velvet rich and heavy as the day we'd received it but less lustrous somehow, the nap chewed-looking in spots, as if already the moths had found it. I'd pin up my hair and sneak into the parlour, study myself in the tall bevelled mirror above the mantel. I'd tell myself how gorgeous I looked, and how lonesome. Almost as lonesome, Fan, as when you first left us.

Once, so dressed, I happened to peak down into the road in time to glimpse Mam marching past with Peter and Mary, baskets on their arms. I tapped twice but I guess she didn't hear me; or perhaps she did but was in too big a rush to stop.

Not that I missed her, particularly. I could've gone home any time to visit. No, Fan, it wasn't homesickness or missing Mam that made me lonely. The one I missed was Silas, never mind we were rarely more than a storey apart. Even lying skin to skin, we were never really together, not really, not with his mother and father a whisper away; not since the night we first knew one another.

Things started to sour between Tryphena and me. Not overnight, mind; not like a jug of milk left out, not that quickly. Rather, it happened like a stitch being dropped here and there in a piece of knitting — nothing at the time, you think, till you go to cast off and find the whole sweater skewed, the front too short for the back.

So it was with my mother-in-law, every little thing I did somehow a disappointment. Every tiny, nitpicky thing counted and totted up, till after a while it seemed nothing I could do would please her.

The last straw came one snowy day after Christmas, when she and I were making lemon pie. Lemons had come in that week, fresh from the tropics; she'd set aside the best two. The pie was for the Ladies' Fellowship that evening, being held in our parlour. Perhaps that's what had her so riled up. Riled, I say, though she was more like a pot on a hard boil, that saintly patience and goodwill of hers barely keeping the lid on. My method for making dough finally made her spill over.

"Mercy! Who*ever* heard of mixing pastry with a spoon, dear! Euphemia, child, I shouldn't have to tell you — for heaven's sake, use a fork."

At first I thought she was joking, her face pale under splotches of flour, hands shaking as she dusted the rolling pin.

The pie was served after prayer circle, the ladies holding hands for grace. They made cooing sounds, smiling expectantly as Tryphena went to the sideboard, started cutting. Teeny-tiny slivers, Fan, so everyone could have a taste. From my seat I could see her having some trouble, her cheeks going pink.

I handed round the portions, scarcely able to wait for my own, that sharp syrupy tang on my tongue.

Taking the smallest mangled piece, I sat poised for the first bite. My fork slid through the golden fluff of meringue, the custardy yellow goo, hit the crust — hard as the ground outside. My heart sank like lead, then bobbed to my throat, caught there. All I could think of was the proverb I'd read in that week's *Arc-Light*: "Beware man who praises wife's cooking but uses her doughnuts as fishing-line sinkers."

Eliza Peck had her plate balanced on her knee, dabbing lemon from her mouth; her lips pursed as she tried prying off another forkful. She'd almost succeeded when the utensil slipped, sending her piece flying to land face-down on Tryphena's Chinese carpet. For a moment the entire room stopped chewing, staring at the mess stuck to some tapestry birds.

"Oh my!" Tryphena was on her knees faster than you could say "praise be" or "pass dessert".

"Mercy!" Mrs. Peck sank down beside her, retrieving hairy bits of pie. Like a child, she held out her sticky fingers to be wiped.

I fetched a rag soaked in vinegar, started working on the stain.

"Can I offer you something else, Eliza?" Tryphena asked in a shrill, quavering voice, her lip trembling.

"Let me put the kettle on," I said, dashing to the kitchen; then realized there was little point, unless the ladies liked hot water. Unlike any normal household, there wasn't a leaf of tea in the cupboard.

The rest of the evening Silas's mother refused to look at me. When the last of the company left, she held her wrist to her temple and staggered off to bed, leaving me to tidy up.

Silas was still awake when I finally crawled in beside him.

"Something the matter?" he whispered as I turned to the wall.

"Do you think," I whispered back, mincing my words, "do you think someday we might have our own place, Silas?" I lay still, waiting for him to ask why, not daring to say it was because of his mother.

"I've already started saving up, Phemie. And Father's promised me a raise in a year or two. If you'd just be patient...."

He looped his arms around me.

"She means well, you know. She does."

The headache kept Tryphena in bed till suppertime the next day. In silence the four of us picked at our food until dessert — what remained of that blasted pie. There wasn't much, yet no one had the heart to throw it out. Tryphena pushed hers away when I placed it in front of her. Silas, bless his heart, tucked into his like the devil deprived of sin.

"Dee-licious!" he said with his mouth full, and reached for his mother's piece too.

"Tasty, ladies, very tasty," Malcolm muttered, picking crumbs from his moustache.

Tryphena forced a smile.

"Well, you can thank Euphemia. It's her pie, certainly not mine."

I waited for her to get up and go back to bed. Instead, she went into the parlour and lay on the settee; she called for Silas to come and tuck the afghan around her. By the time I finished the dishes, she was sitting up — "Much improved, thank you" — and in better humour.

"Euphemia? Whatever became of that crazy quilt patt-ren?" she wanted to know. "You haven't lost interest already, have you? Bring it out, dear, and we'll have a gander, shall we?"

I went and felt under the bed. There it was, the packet glossy and crisp as the day it arrived, only slightly furred with dust.

"Splendid," she said, as I unfolded the sheets of paper. "Just the ticket to pass these bitter evenings."

Foolish as it sounds, Fan, it was the quilt that kept the peace, per-haps even saved my skin. Not that she wasn't eager to leave her mark on it. I'd given up waiting on whatever remnants material-ized downstairs; had pretty much given up on doing the quilt at all. But then, for a surprise, Tryphena sent away for a package of scraps — fancy, specially cut ones you could purchase to go with the pattern. She must've given those dawdlers in New York heck, for within a fortnight the parcel arrived. It contained a slew of pure silk brocade and velvet squares, triangles, fans — in shades that transported me.

"Oh, Mother!" I couldn't help myself, Fan, sorting through the patches. Tryphena folded her hands, watching like a fairy god-mother; it was all she could do to keep her hands off the fabric.

"I don't know where to start," I couldn't help gushing, beaming yet wary.

"Well," she said, "it'll give you something to do, dear. You know what they say about idle hands."

Spreading out the pieces on the settee, I waited for her to come and start rearranging them. Instead, she stayed put.

"You might try laying them out on the dining-room table — light's better in there. But mind you don't scratch it; if you're working with pins, best find someplace else."

After a while she came to inspect my progress, adjusting her spectacles to admire the fabrics' sheen.

"Takes such care, doesn't it, working with a nap?" She kept her hands clasped behind her, bending over my arrangement: shiny, lighter shades interspersed with darker, denser ones; florals with solids. What I had in mind were the varied shades of dusk, embroidered with golden stars. I hadn't thought to worry whether the goods' grain ran the right way.

"Is this what the patt-ren calls for?" she asked, reaching out to stroke a scrap of velvet over and over, as one would a kitten. It was a dull silken gold, a colour that made me think of a lion or some other exotic beast. "A thing of beauty's a joy to behold," she sighed. "Well, that's good; now you've got your work laid out, Euphemia."

I expected her to help me transfer the whole kit and caboodle to the kitchen table; at least offer to help pin some pieces together. I was almost disappointed when she didn't run for her sewing basket, or take up my pins, hold them bristling between her lips, fingers nipping and tucking, deft as insects. But giving approval seemed as far as she could go. Without another word, she left me to my handiwork and returned to her own, a cross-stitch sampler she was making for our bedroom.

"God Bless Our Abode," it said in green and yellow letters twined like vines around tiny twigs. I don't suppose she relished our wish for a home of our own; although we were careful to keep it under our hats, she must've divined it.

On the coldest, blackest night in January I started the patchwork. Every evening for the rest of the winter, from the time the dishes were done till we gathered for prayer, I'd sit in the parlour and sew. One fan to two triangles, one trapezoid to two diamonds.

It was slow and piecemeal work, and tedious for a manufacture of such whimsy. Piecing, basting with the smallest running stitch — the monotony and fussiness were enough to make one crazy, or blind.

Tryphena would sit across from me, bent over her needle, her tidy grey hair tarnished yellow by the lamplight. Every now and then she'd squint over and nod.

"Patience," she'd cluck. "Remember what the Bible says. The Lord rewards those who are patient, Euphemia; good things come to those that wait."

I didn't remind her that the quilt was my handiwork, not heaven's. I wouldn't have dared, with Silas and his father in the room, their noses in books — mail-order catalogues, mostly. Thick, flimsy volumes of hardware, for example, featuring every variety and description of hinges and screws. That's what they pored over, catalogues and the Bible. And a leather-bound copy of *The Red Badge of Courage*: I recall now that's how Silas occupied himself that first long winter, though it's a mystery how that volume found its way into Tryphena's household. Perhaps someone had ordered it, then declined to purchase it.

Tryphena didn't hold with books, especially works of fiction — untruths, she scoffed, no doubt noting Silas's choice of reading as a sign of backsliding. "But then you are a married man," she sighed, as if consoling herself for his undoing — which was, of course, on account of me. She never said so, but you sensed what she was thinking by her pinched expression as she stitched at her sampler. Silas would pretend to ignore her, cradling the book in his hands, seemingly engrossed in its pages.

From time to time his father would grumble about the new price of something, nails, for instance. Tryphena twigged to his tone like a bird on a clothesline, reserving comment but chattering half to herself about So-and-so from church, "this one" or "that one" hanging about the store. Silas would glance up when she quit talking and give me a dogged yet rather absent grin, as if startled to see me sitting there. Eyes trained on my sewing, I'd press my thigh to his — a sudden, flighty movement like a spoon knocking the side of a bowl, quick enough that his mother wouldn't see. And so we'd pass the evenings, my eyes aching from staring too long at the same small scrap of fabric, my cheeks from the effort of smiling.

Night after night, week after week, the quilt kept me busy, till it seemed its very colours began to fade, their magic dimmed by the endless task of straight-stitching. Before my eyes emerald turned olive, russet the shade of dried blood and chocolate the colour of the road between rains. Perhaps it was the poor light, the effect of so much time stuck indoors; maybe, plain and simple, it was my eyes.

To pass the days I started helping in the store. It was a chance to be with my husband, if only to rub shoulders or exchange looks at the register. A good deal of the time it was just the two of us serving customers, while his father filed accounts and filled orders, and Tryphena flitted around, dusting and putting things right. Not that Silas and I got much chance to converse, but at least we were together — in the same room, I mean. Somehow, we felt more intimate surrounded by patrons than we ever did upstairs, after business hours. And in the store I caught glimpses of the world I missed in church and within the flat's musty walls.

Funny, but it was my working downstairs that helped the quilt take shape. Not all at once, mind, nor of a piece — sewing was never that simple — but gradually. Sometimes, sorting spools of thread or counting pillboxes, I let my mind wander. I'd work out new patterns, ways in which one pre-shaped piece could be trimmed to fit another. Out of Tryphena's presence, my imagination took flight, winging its way from the store, through the woods to the bay, and from there across the seven seas and parts of the earth I'd never hope to glimpse.

One afternoon a man came in enquiring about some pipes from the foundry. He pulled a maraca from his pocket of all things, shaking it to get Silas's attention. Tryphena hung in the office doorway, ready to press the alarm bell Malcolm had installed after the robbery.

"We don't handle foundry shipments, sir," said Silas, calm and measured as the day is long. A big, swarthy man with leathery skin, the fellow seemed in no hurry to leave; he leaned against the counter and started telling Silas of his travels. While he chatted he kept toying with the maraca; he'd gotten it in Mexico, he said, or somewhere near the Caribbean. Its fast, itchy sound turned customers' heads, like a swarm of insects ticking against a window. It made me want to jiggle, to dance and stamp my feet.

That evening in our room, I unpinned a black velvet square and cut a maraca out of it, using my darning mushroom as a guide for size. Begging a stomach ache, I sat up in bed and stem-stitched a flamingo on it — a delicate, long-billed bird on one bent leg, in gold floss pilfered from yard goods. Who cared whether or not flamingos lived in Mexico? I had no idea, though I'd seen a picture of some in *Webster's Illustrated Dictionary*, the one book besides the Bible that Tryphena revered. Correctness hardly mattered; the truth was piddling compared to my satisfaction as the bird took shape.

Around nine o'clock, when I was nearly finished, Tryphena rapped at the door, offering one of her remedies.

"Prayer in ten minutes, dear. May I suggest a liver pill, just in case you're not quite up to it——"

"I'm much better now, Mother, honestly I am. Don't know what got into me; perhaps it was the candy I had today in the store."

"For heaven's sake," she chided, waltzing in. "I wouldn't touch those licorice babies — they do dreadful things to the digestion, not to mention one's waistline! Suffice to say I wouldn't feed those sweets to a dog."

INTERCESSION
Lament

When I was an infant, Mum used to hold a mirror to my lips while I slept, to make sure I was breathing.

I know because she told me so.

She didn't do this with my sister. If she had, I'd remember, or you'd think I would. I was six when Dora came, six

years

old...

...I'm lying on my back on the patch of lawn behind the store. The wild pear is in bloom, snowing petals: confetti. The sun pulls my skin, so bright and so hot I cannot open my eyes, but feel it through the lids, through my frock. It's the colour of buttercream, this dress. Buttercream splashed on the sticky-warm grass.

I force my eyes open; squint at the sky so blue it burns. I hear the petals waft, touch down — a sound sweeter than robins' song; a thrum, a pulse deeper than the earth's.

I can feel it, this sound, the same as the singing whisper of Mum's footsteps through the grass, the chilly distraction on her face.

I know there's a baby coming; she told me so, Mum did.

Her hand reaches down and strokes my forehead, warm but

cool, cooler than air: separate. Her shadow blocks the sun, shades me. Folds of green-striped cotton, folds of pale, pale blue; the whoosh of her clothes. I hear her breathing, a scratchy, rasping sound; her stifled complaint as she rolls to her knees; the grunt as she curls on her side upon the grass.

I take a good look at Mum's face: her round green eyes, the blotchy colour in her cheeks.

She could run out of air, I think; the baby grinning inside, stealing her breath....

But she laughs and strokes my hair; she doesn't see my fear, because she is detached, and she says, "Look at us, like two poor hounds sprawled out on the ground, Ruby. The dog days, all right, wouldn't you say? Pray your pa doesn't look out and see us, love; a woman in my shape. A woman in my shape, indeed."

I want to curl into her, against the hardness of her belly, but she is breathing, apart from me; and there's the baby, too, the lump hard as rock she says is its head. And she tells me everything will be fine, just fine; the same only better.

But I know different; I know what's coming: the baby, Dora. I know...but when I try to tell Mum, she's not listening. She just laughs, because she is separate, and nothing she says or does can make us one again, the same. Not even when she rolls, grunting, and sticks a petal on the end of her nose and rubs mine Eskimo-style. Curling closer, wincing, to hold me tight....

XX

Safecracking

Damn this old strongbox anyway, worthless heap of metal! Turn to the right — click — twice to the left — click! Of all things, "Little Sally Saucer", that childish verse, pops into my head: "Turn to the east Sally, turn to the west! Turn to the very one that you love best." Once more to the right — bingo!

A stunned monkey could crack this thing; confound it, the money inside is about as safe from thieves as cowpats from flies. I know, I know, I should go to town to make the deposits. But you have to consider the time, the gas. And this is how Grampa did things, and his father before him, keeping the profits locked up. Fort Knox it isn't, a clumsy cast-iron box next to the stove — in roughly the same spot my great-grandfather kept it when this was his office. Queer thing to have in a kitchen, where most folks would put their microwave. Guests must do a double-take, spotting it the first time — not that we have many of them, besides Wilf; and he hardly batted an eye that night he came for supper. Too polite, I guess.

Though just before he left, he whispered, "Lindy, think it's a good idea keeping dough in the house like that? To my mind, it's a bit like laying a picnic for bears."

He doesn't usually give advice; I'd say he's not that kind of fellow. But I know he's right.

Now the sucker's finally opened, I've a little trick up my sleeve. Oh yes; I aim to fix whatever twerp makes for my money — our money, the store's take. I'll teach them to mess with my mustard.

Here we go: a bonus-size pack of disposable razors, pink Lady Schicks. Too bad we don't carry loose blades any more; the blades are all I need.

The cash is in an old canvas bag Uncle Leonard used to take his deposits to the bank. It feels like a brick inside, the neat, flat stack of bills.

"Lucinda? Looo-cinda?" Ruby calls from the store, bless her heart, still seeking out slivers of glass.

"What is it?" I yell back. "Just give me a minute."

"Looo-cinda," she keeps calling, "Looo-cinda!"

I open the bag. There's a fat bundle of tens, another of twenties — has it been that long since my last trip to a wicket? Small change to some, I suppose; life savings to others. Ruby'd have a bird if she knew how much money's in here; more than she's laid eyes on in a while, a long while. It's like Monopoly money, all those pretty bills, if you let your mind wander. This way it looks like more, a lot more, than the figures would on paper.

"Lucinda?" she calls again, her voice levelling.

"I'm in the middle of something, Aunt Ruby!"

I have to take the hammer to those Lady Schicks to get the blades out. An awful waste — but if you want an omelette, you've got to break some eggs. And it's worth it, to protect my interests.

There, you little bastard, whoever you might be!

I slide five neat blades into the sack with the bills: one for each thieving finger. Like a snakebite — oh, the surprise! I can just imagine the culprit wince when he sticks in his hand, greedy fingers closing around those bundles. Of course, the cash itself might get messed, but heck, money is money. I've seen places accept bills ripped in two, with Sir John A.'s face X'ed out in pen. So what's a little blood? The bastard still gets the money, but my point'll be made. That rotten bunch of kids, I know it was one of them put that rock through the window — I know the way Wilf knows roads.

Maybe I'll see who's responsible, whoever comes in wearing Band-Aids; catch him red-handed, so to speak. "Want to tell the Mounties where you got them cuts to the hand?" Son of a bitch.

"Looo-cinda? Looo———"

Ruby'd kill me if she knew what I was up to. "Of all the low-down, dirty tricks," she'd say.

"Lucinda, dear — there's someone to see you!"

And Lord knows how Wilf would react: slap his thigh in admiration, or head for the hills. Better not to tell, so I'll keep it a secret, though I can't help smiling. It's like those cartoon booby traps: trip on a vine and the ground opens under the bad guy. Gotcha! And before you can say Jack Robinson, the bandit's up to his neck in quicksand — or *merde*, deep *merde*, which is what I have in mind for whoever....

"It's Mrs. Pyke, dear. She's got something here, some stuff she'd like to———"

I snap the door shut, give the knob a twirl. Safe. Lockstockandbarrel — for now.

"Coming, Ruby, I's-a-coming — just give me a sec," I yell, wondering what in heck Edna Pyke could want. I take my time tidying up, stuffing all those cracked pink handles into the trash. I'm just putting away the hammer when Ruby shuffles in, making for her room.

"That lady's still waiting," she says and slams the door. I hear the bedsprings creak, her long, weary sigh, and before you know it, the crackle of pages. Back to her reading, the old duck, as if there's no tomorrow. No today either, for that matter — no smashed glass or window; no Edna Pyke out there wanting service. As if nothing concerns her.

That must be some book she's reading, lengthy as the Bible, juicy as a V.C. Andrews. Whatever, it keeps her out of my hair. For how long, who knows?

It's dreadful but, like an evil afterglow, more wickedness jumps into my mind, that campfire chorus — "Boom-boom ain't it great to be cra-zy! Boom-boom!" — with all the rollicking glee of Girl Guides belting out their "Titanic" song: *Oh it was sad, soooo sad.*

"Lindy? You there, dear?" Edna Pyke's voice pitches in. "It's me, Lindy. Look, I was in the neighbourhood — hope I'm not interrupting — I'll only take a second———"

"Edna!" I say, as if pleasantly surprised. Her flushed, pinched face looms in the dimness — Ruby must've unlocked the door to let her in. The lights are off, the place dark as your arse; it's nearly time for *Oprah*.

She's about my age, Edna, but that thin, wiry type looks as though she smokes. A sharp dresser, gets her nails done in town — Lord knows where she finds the time, running bingo, not to mention keeping the books for her husband plus minding everybody else's business. Her kids are grown and live out west; I don't suppose she sees much of them.

She hefts a green garbage bag onto the counter; a lot of strength in that scrawny wrist. Right away I'm on my guard.

"What's this?" I ask. "Some mending you want for the box?" I start to tally those mitts I knit, then explain how my time's eaten up these days with Ruby.

"An' who else — huh? I saw you at the dance, Lindy, I did; looked like you were having a grand old time, too!"

"That so, Edna? Well, I was indeed," I say, feeling myself blush. I wait for her to ask Wilf's name, but she doesn't. She opens the bag instead, starts smoothing whatever's inside with her bony hand, those nails that look like claws.

"My sister-in-law passed away last week," she says, as matter-of-fact as if totting up a bingo loss. "She was about your size — well-built woman, Lindy. Took care of herself, pampered herself, really, till the sickness got her. Liked to dress, you know; always took care of her clothes. Good clothes. So when I came out today, I thought, rather than throwing them out———"

I don't ask what the woman died of. And though I'm a teeny bit insulted, I'm curious, too. Edna pulls a pair of navy slacks out of the bag, still with the dry-cleaner's tag. She shows me the label — 100 percent wool — the legs creased perfectly, knife-blade sharp. I can't help myself.

"Well, if you think no one else wants 'em, Edna, I s'pose———"

"No, no — take 'em, Lindy, they're no use to me. No one else I can think of's Dorilda's size. She'd feel better, knowing, you know. What doesn't fit, you can throw away; don't feel bad or nothing. I just thought, rather than giving them to a stranger———"

"Hold on a minute, you're sure you don't——? I mean, there must be something you'd like to keep for yourself, Edna. I appreciate your kindness and all, I'm sorry for your trouble, but——"

She backs away, smiling so as to make me wonder what germs are in the bag. But then these people, the Pykes, being around death all the time, likely they see it differently....

Edna keeps smiling all the way to the door.

"They'll look good on you, Lindy. Sure they will. See you at the next dance? With your fella, eh, Lindy? With what's-his-name?"

That evening after work, Wilf comes in for a Coke. I've got on one of Edna's sister-in-law's blouses, this low-cut little number with shoulder-pads; too bad they show through the sheerness. I've been trying on the clothes, see, sorting which to keep. He doesn't even mention the window, duct tape flapping in the draft.

"Woooo-ee, Lindy!" He can't keep his eyes from sliding down my front. At first I think he's eyeing the wattles of my neck, but by the way he reddens I know that's not it.

He sniffs at the air and pulls a face. "What's that smell?" he says off-handedly, which causes me to stew, thinking it must be the blouse — the scent of Bounce, maybe, or poor Dorilda's Tabu.

"Off? Muskol, maybe?" I joke. "Gal my age, I'm too old for perfume."

He takes this in, pausing to consider it.

"Well, lemme ask you, Lindy" — he sniffs again — "what is it you're waiting for, then? Like someone always waiting for the bus——" He winks at me, leaning forward, hands clasped, till his eyes are about level with my cleavage.

"To make a good-lookin' corpse — that what you're after?"

It strikes me as kind of cruel but funny. I'd like to mention the blouse, but he's set me off laughing.

"What's that s'posed to mean?" I manage, giving him a coy look, one hand over the deep V, I'm that aware of the jiggling there.

"I'll be calling," he says, his eyes on mine, dead serious. "Don't you worry."

When his truck roars out of the yard, I lock up and go back to trying on clothes. The pants fit, sure they do, not too tight across the rear. And there's another blouse like the one I'm wearing, plain but feminine. Womanly. The kind of fabric gives you goosebumps across your shoulderblades, it's that cool and slithery. Not a bad little windfall, if I do say so. 'Course, it worries me a little someone might spot me out in my glad rags and ask, "Haven't I seen those before?" But for now all they need is airing. And on second thought, if Wilf wants to know, I'll just tell him I went shopping.

Supper's late on account of the clothes, not that Ruby notices, picking at her meal. I get the dishes cleaned up, her cup of tea made, when she asks, "When do we eat, dear? I'm famished."

"Extra hungry tonight, are you?" I try to sound cheerful. "Must've been all that exercise, picking up glass. Eh, Ruby?" She stares back at me as if there's nobody home.

Before bed, I help her with some lotion the doctor prescribed ages ago for psoriasis — as if it's her skin giving her trouble. There's a little dry spot on her arm that won't clear up. Twice a day she's supposed to rub on lotion; why, I've caught her lately applying it three, four, five, sometimes six times an *hour*. When she's not reading, she's treating a rash — but what the heck, if it makes her happy.

Except going to bed I get the smell in my head — not the sister-in-law's perfume, but Ruby's prescription. It reminds me of asphalt: the tarry odour of the pond below Foundry Hill, of railway ties splashed with pee.

The tracks ran through town when I was small; cut right past our house by the station where Daddy worked. There was that smell of creosote under the freight shed the time I found some kittens — a mess of them, dead, frozen stiff. The mother, a stray, had hung around our steps for days. "Don't be feeding her, now, that's just looking for trouble," Ma said, kicking at the door when the poor critter clawed the screen. "G'way, you filthy thing. Don't you touch it, Lindy, you hear? If you do you might get sick; God knows what diseases you could catch off of it!"

I petted the cat, threw it a piece of chicken skin under the stoop. It was cold out, being March, and raw. The cat was white, part of one ear missing, a big crooked patch of black over one of its round yellow eyes. It kept meowing and I followed it along the tracks, right to the shed, the big peeling barn where the railway stored goods from the furniture factory. The cat kept rubbing my leg, letting out these mewling wails.

Then I spied the kittens, matted black and white lumps like rats or guinea pigs. Their eyes weren't opened yet. I crawled under to get a better look. They were hard, hard as stones; they didn't budge when I nudged them with my boot. They were frozen right to the dirt.

When I ran home to tell Ma, she was at the table having some coffee, waiting for Daddy to come home for his dinner. Still wearing my boots, I went and stood on her feet, rubbing my hands together and bending down to whiff the hot, milky steam from her cup. But there was something about it almost sweet, medicinal, that stung my eyes like iodine if you get too close. And I could see she wasn't herself, wobbling off her chair, then clicking to the bathroom in those slippers with the hard-looking heels. And her words slid together like a string of boxcars when she said, "Not now Lindy I'm not int'rested in kitties hear unless you went an' touched them you didn' touch them did you Lindy the first thing you got to learn girl is you mustn' mess aroun'...."

For two solid months I avoided the freight shed like the plague. Truth is, I was scared to go back and see what happened to the kittens once the ground thawed and the mud started. I pictured gruesome things: worms threading ragged fur, insects picking tiny bones clean. I would've gone back to bury them — you know, a proper Christian burial like some kids give their pets: a shoebox coffin, rest-in-peace prayers, the works. But by the time I went back, they were gone. Daddy and a man from the furniture company were inside, drinking.

The barn itself was huge, tall as a slagheap, the sides slanting into the weeds. The furniture company made school desks, see, used to store them here for shipping out by rail. As stationmaster it was part of Daddy's job to see the desks got loaded on time — big shipments by the end of June, to be ready for September. I was only months shy of starting school myself; figured a gander at those brand-new desks might prepare me.

I knew Daddy was in there; after my supper I'd seen him going over with his friend. I'd never really been inside; had this notion of it being like a big schoolhouse. I imagined rows and rows of desks with pretend pupils sitting in them, hands folded, learning the ABCs.

I knocked first; when nobody answered I let myself in. The main floor was pitch-black, with the smell of new wood and varnish sickly-sweet as butterscotch — the same smell as the pews in Grampa's church. I followed Daddy's voice up some steep, creaking steps to the next floor.

Wings beat from the rafters — bats or pigeons, who could say; swallows, maybe. The air was hot and dusty and dry, not a wisp of wind through the bright cracks in the walls. The desks were stacked sideways in shaky-looking towers of two and three. I found one that was upright and sat down, licked my finger and squeaked it round and round the inkwell, its sticky-smooth edges.

From a door beyond the desks came guffaws, the clink of glass, Daddy mumbling a joke, the other man's raw, joyless laughter. I sat there listening, swinging my legs to the rustling above, to the quiet splash and *glug* of a bottle. I sat until the cracks in the wall turned velvet-blue and the laughing grew loud, uneven. Then the floor creaked and the door opened, flooding light over the piled furniture. Daddy took a swig and pushed the liquor at his friend, his eyes locking on me. In the darkness they shone like the greased wheels of a train.

"Come 'ere, honey," he said, wiping his mouth on the back of his hand. I stayed where I was, waiting for his question: Was it Ma sent me spying again?

Instead, he took another drink, grinning at me, and I should've felt happy because this, after all, was my daddy.

"Come here an' shake hands with my buddy, Lindy. He likes little kids, don'tcha Walter? He don't get to see 'em too much, though; don't have none of his own, poor fella. Come 'ere, Lindy, let Walter get a look at you. C'mon, he don't bite. He won't hurt you."

The friend laughed and set the bottle down by his feet, unsteadily but carefully as if it were an egg. He staggered closer, like

I was a butterfly he didn't want to scare off.

I don't know what grabbed ahold of me then — I knew Daddy would be mad, real mad, at my being rude, and that I'd catch it later, all right. But I slid out of that desk lickety-split and made for the stairs, those steep narrow stairs, and God, you know that saying "bat out of hell"? Well, that's what I felt like, bumping down those steps past those desks downstairs, Daddy's and that man's hard, crude belly laughs grazing my eardrums.

Ma was asleep when I got home. There was a half-eaten piece of store-bought cherry pie waiting on the kitchen table, dessert I hadn't had room for. I wolfed it down, thinking about my Aunt Ruby — she was the one who'd brought it over, from the bakery in town. A treat for my uncle, she said, except they couldn't eat it all.

Ma used to say Ruby and Leonard were good to me because they were jealous, having no kids of their own. "Don't you wear out your welcome," she'd say when I stopped off at the store on my way home from school. Once I got old enough, I liked going over just to hang around, hoping for a bag of humbugs or licorice shoelaces. Aunt Ruby was usually rolling coins or helping ladies decide on material or what size underwear or boots to buy their husbands. That was Ruby, all business, at the customers' beck and call — or so she let on, sending me sidewards looks while she waited for people to make up their minds. All nods and agreement, she was, serious as if the colour of blouse someone chose meant life or death. "Oh, and how about a pair of shoes to match that shade?" she'd slip in, real slick, so people would buy twice what they'd come for, thinking what a good idea.

Ruby had a talent, all right. Sometimes she acted as if I weren't there until she and her customer finished their transaction, the two of them smiling; the customer — occasionally — putting on a brave face after emptying her purse. Ruby was one shrewd cookie; she had the reputation of being lily-white, not so much kind as fair. Hard-bargaining, stiff-nosed — but honest as the day is long. And smart! Oh, Ruby was nothing if not smart.

So it puzzled me when I'd hear Ma bickering with Daddy,

saying how hard-done-by her sister was, how Leonard had wrecked Ruby's life — like Daddy had wrecked hers. That's how Ma put it, too, as though the man were the engineer, the woman the train, and he was responsible for her going off the rails.

To me, Uncle was the nice one who'd drop what he was doing, go and turn the radio off and swoop me up on his knee. He'd ask questions like what I'd done in school that day, what was twelve times twenty-two, that sort of thing. Then he'd unscrew the lid on the jelly-bean jar and reach in. His hand looked so white and rubbery through the bluish glass, I remember, like the pickled snakes and frogs in science class later on in high school.

If I gave the wrong answer — "Two hundred!" — Uncle would look at me and laugh, the red and yellow beans falling through his fingers. When I got the number right, he'd pull his hand out full of candies, slide them into a brown paper sack which he'd top up with molasses kisses.

He'd fold his arms and watch me eat, a big lump of candy inside my cheek. He'd take his time getting off his stool to wait on whoever happened in, leaving Ruby busy at the cash. There were some who wouldn't deal with Uncle at all, but chose to stand in line waiting for her to pick out what they wanted. Women, mostly, choosing personal items: little silk hankies, twists of embroidery floss, bottles of pills for ailments Ruby seemed to know all about.

Perhaps that's why she was highly regarded. The longer I hung around, the more I realized that Ruby knew the business of most everyone in town. Some of their most intimate business, I'd wager.

Yet she seemed a lonely woman, Ruby; perhaps that's how come Ma said those things about Uncle, as if he were to blame for it. Though I had no idea why when I was six or seven — a shy little girl, a bit on the pudgy side, with a spit-hole between my teeth when they finally came in.

"Takes after the Lewises, Lindy does. And a damn good thing, maybe. So she is a loner — you'd be one to talk," Ma would harp right back at Daddy when he tried blaming her for my shyness. "Look at Ruby, for godsake!" she'd say, exasperated, when Daddy asked why didn't I bring home kids from school instead of hanging around the store. As if he were there to notice.

"Bunch of stuck-ups. You make it sound like shit'd melt in

their mouths. And look how they've treated you," he'd say, shov-elling in his dinner, then heading straight out again. He'd tell Ma he had paperwork, or an extra batch of shipments needed tending. But I knew where he spent his time and how, and so did she.

And I knew he was wrong, what he said about the Lewises being snooty. Even as a kid, I knew our feeling of being set apart, different, had nothing to do with being better or worse than any-one else. Like my Aunt Ruby, I never needed other people the way some do. "In their blood, I guess," Ma would shrug, and Daddy would just shake his head. Though with Ruby you always got the sense she was holding something back. That's where she and I differed, our personalities veering away from each other like fork-ing roads.

"Too bad your auntie and I never had a little gal like you," Uncle would say, gazing right at me, not smiling but not alto-gether regretful-looking either. I'm not sure what that look was, when he ran his hand down the curve of my head, over the grainy part between my braids. Sometimes his hand would linger on the little bump at the top of my spine, as if he was busy thinking about something and forgot to take it away. He'd stop talking and, aware of Ruby at the till clinking coins, I'd wait for him to speak. One time he just sighed, his red-bristled face bent so close I could smell the tonic he used on his hair. "Leonard?" Ruby cut in. "Run out back, would you, and get me that extra bag of alfalfa seed; a fel-low's coming in this afternoon."

Uncle sniffed and yanked my pigtails, following Ruby's bid-ding. And I felt kind of gypped, as if she'd seen me snacking on something I shouldn't've had and snatched it away, quick, before anyone could say boo.

"*Wrecked Ruby's life*"— no, as a kid I could never put a handle on those words of Ma's, since it always seemed to me that Ruby was in charge. My aunt with her bright, sharp eyes — giving you the rundown on how many jelly beans were in the jar before my visit, how many after Uncle finished doling some out. Wrecked? I don't think so, or at least I didn't back then, when I still had Ma and Daddy. Before Daddy disappeared for good. I was seven go-ing on eight when it happened. One night he never came home for the supper Ma left out on the off chance he'd show up, starved and already a little shaky on his feet. Rumour had it that he had just quit taking tickets, and boarded the express train bound for Montreal. Two blasts of the whistle and he was gone.

About five o'clock that train normally made its stop. Daddy tended station from six in the morning to six or seven at night, when the last train to Halifax chugged through, dropping off a handful of travellers — fewer and fewer as time went on. Ma used to complain that if business had been brisker, Daddy wouldn't have had so much time to kill behind his wicket. By then she was used to his routine — or lack of routine, some might say — meandering off after work with the brakemen. Lord knows where they got all the booze, if it was supplied by the railway or bootlegged right there in the sooty little waiting room.

After a while Ma had stopped caring where or how he managed to do his drinking — or when he came home. So had he, as long as there was food waiting: a dried-up chop, a piece of bread, some cold potatoes on a plate. And after a while that's about all there'd be, once Ma got a taste for other people and "keeping company" of her own. That's how she put it, powdering her face with her blue satin puff, spraying on the perfume Ruby'd ordered from New York for her birthday.

The other mothers in town "kept company" at the Ladies' Guild, the odd game of bridge or euchre. But even as a child I knew she wasn't dolling herself up like that to sit in the basement of some hall, or to bat her eyes at a bunch of women in sensible shoes.

XXI

Morning Sickness

And for this kingdom's good are hither come,
From the remotest part of Christendome,
Collected with much paines and industry,
From scorching Spaine and freezing Muscovie,
From fertill France, and pleasant Italy,
From *Poland, Sweden, Denmarke, Germany,*
And some of these rare Patternes have been set
Beyond the bounds of faithlesse *Mahomet*:
From spacious *China*, and those Kingdomes East,
And from Great *Mexico*, the Indies West.

The next piece I worked was a scalloped fan cut from a burgundy triangle. It was a lovely satin material that put me in mind of a gown, tight-bodiced with a deeply cut neckline, a bustle gathered into a bow. The colour reminded me of a blood-red sun — "Red sky at night," as Silas was fond of saying, "sailor's delight."

I embroidered the edges in gold to match the flamingo I'd done on the maraca. This I accomplished by telling Tryphena that I had cramps, "my monthly visitor", as she called it. For three whole evenings I was excused.

And then I found my treasure — a scrap of indigo voile at the bottom of the remnants bin, faded to a sheer filmy violet. How I'd missed it before, Lord only knows. But it was perfect, the shade and texture exactly of a pansy pressed between the leaves of a Bible.

After seeing that the dishes were dried and put away precisely to my mother-in-law's liking, I slipped to my room with a clean scrap of butcher's paper rescued from the stove. I shut the door, whispering through the crack to Silas that I wouldn't be long; then I worked feverishly drawing the pattern, pinning, cutting. Gathering my sewing things — the raw-edged pansy-shape, my silver thimble, my best embroidery needle — I went out to the parlour and asked, bold as that fellow with the maraca, if I might take a peek through Tryphena's silks.

A hush fell. Silas looked up from his book; his mother blinked. His father cleared his throat and continued reading.

"Why certainly, dear. Though I'm not sure you'll find much. I didn't realize you were so far along as that."

Reluctantly she opened her sewing basket and let me pick through it. I chewed my lip, finding what I wanted — some tiny skeins of blue-black purple, bright yellow, cream. I took pains not to unroll her measuring tape, dislodge any pins or disturb the spools of thread arranged so meticulously by colour.

Glancing over every now and then, Tryphena watched the flower bloom from my needle — taking stock, no doubt, of which silks I'd chosen. But not once did she comment or put a question, not even to enquire what had become of my pattern or where I'd learned to do appliqué.

This diversion got me through February's silver thaws, the fiercest Sheila's Brush in March. Its results got me through the evenings of piecing. By Easter I'd finished the patchwork. Nothing fancy, mind, but the most tiresome aspect of the work over. I was so wrapped up in it, I scarcely noticed winter's ebb, slow though it was as an old fool removing his coat. As the days lengthened, the sky beyond the drapes a lingering, paler shade of violet, a heaviness overtook me — the oddest wish for things to stay put. As the world outside awoke, I yearned for sleep. Such fatigue, Fan! The sort of tiredness that settles in the bones, slows the blood. And I was eighteen years old.

Nestled beside Silas at prayer, I would shut my eyes and listen to the sombre thrum in his throat: *Thank you Jesus, thank you Jesus.* I'd let my mind drift, not to the Lord but to bed; I'd pretend I was floating beneath weightless quilts and coverlets. Sleep, *sleep*, was all I could think of, till Silas's elbow, his mother's anxious pout, jarred me alert.

"Keeping you up, are we? Heaven forbid, child — as if the Almighty weren't worth staying awake for!"

A cup of tea, a good, strong cup of milky tea; that would've done the trick. So when they shut their eyes — such holy supplication — and started in, God-grant-this and God-grant-that, that's what I prayed for. Tea. Its sweet, filmy bitterness on the back of my tongue, warming my innards.

In the mornings the craving would vanish, though the tiredness hung on like a flu. Even with the sun streaming through the panes, I'd lie in bed long after Silas left for work. Not dozing, but simply trying to quell the gnawing in my belly. It was like hunger, except I had no appetite for food.

The queasiness carried me back, Fan, to our nights in those bunks, me lying with one foot on the floor to still the seasick churning. And you up above whispering, "Don't think about it, Effie, just don't think about it. Try imagining the fishes instead, what they must do in a storm."

They lay on the bottom, I figured — and this was how I overcame my growing nausea: by imagining myself a fish knifing over the seabed. It would work, too, until Tryphena came and hovered in the hallway.

"Are you unwell?" she'd ask, her voice like a schoolmarm's piercing the door panels. As if I were playing hooky!

"Let me bring you a bite, then."

She'd slip away and fetch dry toast, perching on my bedside while I chewed piece after piece. She would watch accusingly as I forced down each bite, a sourness pooling in my throat. For a moment or two the rockiness would settle, but by the time I nibbled the crusts my stomach would be heaving.

Once, I nearly knocked her down in my haste for the washroom. She stood in the hall, a towel over her arm, as I retched.

"Oh dear," she said, "I should've guessed." Her face twitched with disgust and a kind of wonder bathed in patience, as if — like everything else that went on in her household — she had been called to have an unwitting hand in this.

There was a touch of hurt in her demeanour, too, as though Silas and I had gone and done something behind her back, and in some unforeseen way had swindled her of something.

"A nip of Lydia Pinkham's, that might help — mightn't it, Mother?" I begged, my throat dry, ribs tight as a corset.

"To make you feel better? I think not, Euphemia. With your complaint, it might do more harm than good."

Staring at me with an odd haughtiness, her lips drawn as if sucking a lemon, she pinched a fold of her skirt; pinched, twisted, then let go, the nub of cloth like a wrinkled teat.

"Well, I suppose Silas will have to be told. Goodness knows how he'll take such news." She blushed, sighing as though visited with the worst tribulation — my sickness. "My Silas, a father! God willing, of course. One must, I suppose one can only, trust what he has in store. For us. Indeed."

Silas was absolutely tickled, there was no disguising it. He was stunned, too, as a boy felling his first bird with a slingshot. He was much too gentlemanly to discuss it, of course. But that night in bed, and every night until the baby came, he treated me with the most fearsome gentleness. As if his weight on me might cause our lives to leak out.

Mam wasn't too surprised. Once the sickness eased, I went to see her. The kids were all at school. When she came to the door and saw me, her face fell, then lit with a slow, rascal smile.

"It's you," she burst out, as though at first she had needed prodding. "Come in, my darling girl — come in!"

She swept off a place for me and put on the kettle.

"I know why you're here," she said, the peaked look of my cheeks the only sign she required. "Stay, Effie; stay for a bit and take a cuppa tea with me, at the very least."

I never tasted anything better, before or since. I can still feel Mam's tea sliding down my gullet, Fan, as if it were a second ago

I set down the cup, Mam's good china one.

Then she said she had news too.

"I was goin' to come up the store," she started, "but I didn't know the best time. *She's* got you on your knees all hours, has she?"

I laughed at that, couldn't resist; hot sweet tea sprayed through my teeth. Wiping my chin, I took two of the long-john cookies she'd set on a plate; dunking them both, one in each hand, I drank in the taste of milky molasses.

"I don't s'pose you've heard, Effie," she said, picking her words, "but affairs at the company aren't good. They're talking of letting men go, see. Your pa could tell you better than me. But there's word of a new place opening up someplace near New Albany — two hundred miles away — and it seems your pa's been made an offer."

I could feel the watery milk curdle in my stomach, the knot in my womb flutter.

"Ah, but Mam, no, you can't...."

My baby. Till then I hadn't really thought of it as more than an ailment, an affliction to be got through, like gout — I believed it would work itself out, as Tryphena conceded, so long as there was someone to hold my hand through the ordeal. My own mother — though I'd scarcely considered this and would hardly have dared mention it to Tryphena.

You see, I'd assumed that when I needed her Mam would be there, the same as one trusts in God. I'm not sure why, after how I'd behaved, going off to my new life. But there you have it: I just believed she'd always be there, close enough to call.

"When, Mam?"

"First of the summer, moving's a deal easier then." She got up to pour more tea, then came and stood by me, rubbing my shoulder.

"You'll get through, all right. When the time comes. I always did."

She pulled me to my feet.

"Wait'll I shows you something, Effie, what I been working on since Peter started school."

In the parlour, stretched upon a rough board frame, was a huge spread of patchwork: white cotton flour-bags split and set among dozens of squares of printed goods, faded but serviceable. Some were a pale pink floral — one of Mary's old blouses, I could picture her in it. Others were worn blue chambray: a shirt of Pa's. There was also a dark blue twill, from the matching pinafores Mam made once for you and me. They'd both been handed down to Sarah, who was too hard on clothes to pass them on to Mary.

It was the kind of quilt that puts weight on a bed; the kind you study before drifting off, playing games with yourself, recalling each article or place the scraps came from.

"It's lovely," I said, feeling the sting of tears, focusing on the lilac buds beyond the window.

"Tell me what you've got on the go, Effie, now you're a married girl. I s'pose his mother's full of ideas, what?"

I shrugged and rubbed my belly, and didn't mention the crazy quilt, its store-bought patches as free of memories as a blank book. A clean slate, I told myself; the perfect palette. Yet, as I was leaving, I couldn't help stealing another look — if only to see whether that twill was quite as prim as I remembered.

And yes, it was, Fan, as prim and dark as a pall. And rightly so, perhaps, it pains me now to think.

By the time I started to show, I was well into embroidering. Spread over my lap, the quilt-top was like a bird's-eye view of the world: a rich rolling patchwork of fields, forests, lakes of sapphire. Tryphena allowed me all the floss I wanted, spun gold that made me think of Rumpelstiltskin. The most gorgeous purple silk with which to etch the sky.

As my belly swelled, the weariness left me — as if I'd finally awoken and crawled out from under the thickest featherbed. I still felt burdened, though, weighed down by an uncanny dread of Mam's leaving, and fear, of course, at the prospect of giving birth. But all seemed far off, the sort of cares one tucks and pins safely out of mind, worries eased by the steady flick of the needle.

As wild pear budded and bloomed, then daffodils, lilacs, I let my needle wander. I did a twining, for example, of silken strawberries on lustrous green stalks, the tiniest French knots for seeds. Even Silas's mother admitted it reminded her of a field of berries ripening in the sun. "Mercy, you can almost taste them," was how she grudgingly put it.

Next I did a spiderweb, the wee dangling spider devouring a fly. And after that, a darning-needle with gossamer wings. "Why this fascination for science?" Tryphena had to add her penny's worth, her eyebrow cocked, inspecting my stitches. Stem stitch, blanket stitch, feather stitch: two loops forward, one loop back.

"Very nice," she'd sniff. I longed to show my work to Mam except, who knows, she might've felt I was mocking hers.

Imagine my vanity, fearing that. When likely it was all Mam could do to pack up house and home, never mind fuss over my pastimes. She had bigger concerns, or thus I believed. So I put off going to see her again, choosing to keep out of her way and the others'. I didn't want to add to her worries. Perhaps, too, I was afraid of letting them see how scared I was.

They left Arcadia Mines on the first of July, Dominion Day. I was big then, so big with child it was an effort climbing stairs. Already the summer heat was fierce, though nobody else appeared to notice. Tryphena made it clear how improper it was for someone in my condition to be seen publicly; this put an end to my helping in the store. Just as well, since the heat left me wan and perspiring, my fingers so puffy my wedding band left a dent.

Stripped to my chemise, I'd lie whole afternoons on the bed, cooling myself with a pale blue cutwork fan Silas had given me. Removing it from the box, he'd spread the delicate ivory spokes as gently as one would an infant's fingers. He was so damnably careful, you see; so cautious, at first it warmed my heart. But by summer it made me want to snatch things from him and work them myself. "There!" I often felt like snapping. "You see? I'm not completely useless."

The morning my family left, they drew up outside the store in Mr. Scull's wagon. He'd offered, I assume, to take them to the station, the back of his cart piled high with chairs and bedsteads, pots and pans. The children ran along behind, though Will, a surly grin on his face, sat up front with Mr. Scull, and Mam and Pa behind, wedged between a trunk and a hat-box. It was a sight more than we'd arrived with, Fan, but no less sorry-looking and half-baked. Mam's hat was on crooked, a cheap, beaded hatpin stuck in her fine, faded hair.

My in-laws had the decency to stay upstairs while we said our goodbyes. Pa's eyes jumped when he saw the girth under my smock, gave a look as though he wanted to cry — or curse, it was difficult to tell which. He was gruff yet he seemed softer somehow; hopeful. The kids were clamouring about missing the train, excited, you could tell; happy, and itching to be under way.

Pa remained seated while Mam climbed down to kiss me. She winced a little, her breath catching. She was quick and businesslike, as if embarking on an errand, like the day they'd gone to Caledonia, just she and Pa. "Well Effie, perhaps you'll come visit. After the littl'un's born." She wouldn't look at me, climbing back up. Pa and Mr. Scull reached to help her, and then they were off, a lurching, lolloping sight that might've been comical — in someone else's life, perhaps.

That summer, a month and a half before my confinement, Silas's father sat us down and made what was less an offer than a directive. It was time we had our own digs, he'd decided. And so we moved into the home he purchased for us: a modest, hip-roofed place across the river on Arcadia Avenue, not far from the school.

A row house would have made me happy, given the circumstances, but this house — oh Fan, I thought I'd died and gone to heaven! The cool delicious silence after breakfast, while I did the dishes and Silas dressed for work, and when we'd stand at the door and kiss goodbye, Silas hunching, sway-backed, over me. I'd cup his face in both hands, dart my tongue into his mouth. Grabbing his jacket from the coat-stand, he'd look down at me with love — awe too, perhaps fear. Leaving, he'd straighten his cravat and pat the top of my stomach, as if addressing the baby and me: There, there, be still. Calm yourself in there.

I'm not sure how Silas took to living apart from his mother. For me it was a blessing, of course, like opening a window on a smoke-filled room — not that the burnt smell didn't linger. Tryphena visited each afternoon at four o'clock, to check on things, she said, though she was always careful to avert her eyes from my stomach. I'd have to stop whatever I was doing — bringing in the wash, cutting up meat — to fix lemonade. It was hot, and she'd be thirsty and flushed despite waiting for things to cool off a little before walking over: her excuse for calling so close to supper.

While I folded clothes, she'd sit at the kitchen table, her eyes on the rim of her glass, and tell me about church.

"Perhaps it'll look like Silas," I interrupted once, out of the blue, wiping off the ring left on the table by her drink. Her face grew pinched; there was a sound like crushed glass being sieved as she sucked the dregs.

"You were missed at Fellowship last evening, Euphemia. Eliza Peck was asking after you. Oh, I don't suppose it would do that much harm to be seen in church."

"Would that be proper, Mother?"

You must understand my feelings that summer: pardoned, was how I saw myself; excused; my condition like a deep, luxurious bath in which I was free to float, a watery respite from others' doings. Soon enough, I must've realized, the plug would be pulled and the tub drained, leaving me bloated and shivering on its porcelain bottom. But I endeavoured not to think of that, biding my time — and prudently: making things nice for Silas, and working on my quilt.

At the end of a visit, Tryphena would set her glass by the sink, and perhaps stop to smooth the wrinkles out of Silas's shirts. "My, look at the time!" she'd say, then: "Should you be on your feet, dear? There now, have a seat. I'll show myself out."

This is how these visits passed, except for the day she stayed and folded an entire wash and ended up making supper. It was sickeningly muggy, the sky yellow-grey; not a breath of wind in the poplars (money trees, Silas called them) behind our house. I was expecting his mother, as usual, when a few drops spattered the window and I rushed out to reel things off the line. It must've been ninety degrees, the air so sultry nothing stirred. Even the children next door were sluggish, the noise of their playing drummed out by crickets, a weird, unearthly hum above the foundry's drone. It was almost eerie, everything laden, suspended as if waiting for something to break.

I'd just thrown the last of the clothes in the basket when I heard it: three, loud, unmistakable cries — Mam's voice, calling, *Effie, Effie, Effie.* And not a soul around, not in our yard or next door, where the children had disappeared inside. Not a soul to be seen anywhere.

It unnerved me. I took the basket inside, then came out again and stood on the stoop, looking over the yards as far as I could see. In my belly I felt the baby roll, its feet jab my heart. *Effie, Effie, Effie.* It was as if she'd been right there on the grass, calling up to me.

When Tryphena knocked I was seated at the table, the tangle of damp clothes at my feet.

"Come in," I cried. The weight of the baby had me pinned to the chair — that and a sick feeling in the pit of my stomach.

"Euphemia!" she gasped when she spied me. "Gracious, shouldn't you be in bed?"

"It's nothing, Mother — a touch of heartburn is all," I told her, my voice quavering, heaving myself to my feet. "But if you don't mind, today perhaps I'd better rest."

Not long after, the telegram came from Pa. I was in the parlour drawing the shades when I saw Silas coming down the street, his mother scurrying behind. Mid-morning, it was; a Wednesday, in the midst of a downpour. Their clothes were shiny wet, plastered to them when they dashed in.

"Are you ill, Silas?" I asked, as they started to burst out at once: "It's your mother." Silas seized my hand and led me to the sofa.

The rain was pelting the windows in long grey needles, drumming the porch roof and sluicing from the eaves. Silas and his mother held their breath, waiting.

"Mam?" I whispered, the rain's blackening sound encircling me. "I know," I said. Their eyes darted like birds caught in a chimney. "I *know.*" It came out a deliberate, choking cry, a plea to seal the news upon their tongues.

Silas unfolded the scrap of paper, kept smoothing it in his palm as if to erase the words. Then he folded it and handed it to me like a dollar bill. He leaned down to swing my legs up on the sofa. Out in the kitchen I heard Tryphena opening cupboards, running water; the rain's thrashing as if the sky itself were falling. "*Mam,*" I cried, as if calling out might summon her voice.

It was her heart that had given out, from what I made of Pa's message. The little ones had found her in the front room, some knitting in her lap.

"If I'd been there," I couldn't help whimpering, the telegram's ink smudged in my fist. "Oh Silas, Silas; I should've expected...."

Tryphena entered with a glass of water; she nudged him aside to bend over me. I still remember her smell — like wet ribbon with a faint whiff of rosewater — as she held out the glass.

"Now, now, you couldn't have known, dear. No one knows how these things work, only the Lord, what he sees fit."

I shrank from her; the baby pressed on my lungs, making it hard to breathe. I felt trapped like an animal, my hot, tearless eyes upon the ceiling, my hands grasping the cushions to keep myself from sliding, slipping down. It was as if the windows and doors had been flung open, rain rushing in to replace air, the bulk of my body pinning me under its icy swoop.

Awkwardly, trying so hard to be tender, Tryphena gripped my shoulder with one hand, her other curled around the glass. "You must pull yourself together, Euphemia. For the child's sake; for the Lord. You must have faith——"

"The Lord knows criminy!" I spat, gazing at her, the proffered water dribbling on my dress. Her fingers tightened; she took a little step back. She said something wicked then, and hurtful; something unforgivable.

"If you'd kept up at church, Euphemia — if you'd kept up, this mightn't have happened. Your poor mother might still be alive."

My eyes felt like cinders. I heaved myself up, knocking the glass from her hand. I didn't mean to, Fan; truly I didn't. But she flinched as it hit the floor and shattered, the noise ringing out like one sharp peal of a bell.

"Lord in heaven," she gasped, her hand at her throat, eyeing the mess in horror, "have mercy upon us!"

XXII

Divine Intervention

Nor doe I degrodate (in any case)
Or doe esteeme of other teachings base,
For *Tente-worke, Raisd-worke, Laid-worke, Frost-worke,*
Net-worke,
Most curious *Purles,* or rare *Italian Cutworke,*
Fine *Ferne-stitch, Finny-stitch, New-stitch,* and *Chaine-stitch,*
Brave *Bred-stitch, Fisher-stitch, Irish-stitch,* and *Queen-stitch,*
The *Spanish-stitch, Rosemary-stitch,* and *Mowse-stitch,*
The smarting *Whip-stitch, Back-stitch,* & the *Crosse-stitch.*
All these are good, and these we must allow,
And these are everywhere in practice now....

Silas took me upstairs — oh, I was good for nothing by then, Fan; useless. I stood sobbing as he undressed me the way a mother would undress a child, with the same unfazed expression, his eyes scarcely taking in my veiny breasts and swollen belly, the purplish lines like rivers snaking up from between my legs. Somehow he got me into my nightdress and under the covers. Then he leaned beside me, his elbow on the pillow, whispering, "Hush now, hush."

After a moment he rose and got the fan from my dresser, and knelt by the bed, fanning and fanning as if trying to blow some sense into me.

He curled my fingers in his, so tightly his nails bit my palm. Bowing his head, he started to pray, *Please God, please God* — on my behalf or his mother's, I'm not sure.

As for *our* mother, word had come too late for me to travel to the funeral — which I couldn't have done anyway, in my shape.

Silas wired flowers, a pricey arrangement of gladiolas with condolences "from all of us". Whether or not it arrived I never knew. Pa was not one for writing, and he had his own grief to bear, not to mention the care of five youngsters, all but Willie much too young to be on their own. I would have gone — I swear I would've — to take Mam's place temporarily, had it not been for Silas, and the impending baby.

"It's not your burden, Phemie," he'd try and soothe me. But nothing Silas said helped. Guilt and worry gnawed at me, filled me like an awful vapour — though I knew he was right, there was little I could do under the circumstances.

"You've got your own family," Silas would sigh, running out of patience, as if to say, "Phemie, put a lid on it, please." Yet at night he'd keep his hand on my belly as he slept, and I lay with my eyes wide open, watching shadows that moonlight threw upon the wall. I'd count the child's kicks, which became slower and gentler the bigger it grew. I imagined it as a creature with gills: a carp in a shrinking pool.

"Little baby, little baby," I'd whisper in the dark, sending it messages: pulses of love deep and secret and nurturing as blood. And slowly, over time, I forsook the blackness around me, the airless void that the world had become without Mam, for the rich dark place inside where the baby waited. Like putting together a jigsaw puzzle, I assembled a picture of it: its cramped limbs folded, the tiny face stretched and blurred from lack of space.

While Silas slept I told it stories, how it had landed inside me like a fish fighting upstream — against all odds, a miracle. Slowly its presence absorbed the blackness, passing the boundaries of my skin as I waited, jumpy as a lizard, for it to be born.

"If it's a girl, we could call her after your ma," Silas said a week or two before my time. *Adeline Cox Lewis.* I'd thought of it — Lord knows I had plenty of time to consider names. I'd grown so ungainly, Fan, I could barely hang the washing; I was scared of falling off the step or reaching too high, causing the cord to wrap around the baby's neck.

Silas hired a girl from across the street — Ina Joseph, her name was — to come in and help with the chores. A handy thing, another instance of his goodness, though it dumped more time on my hands.

All I wanted was to have the baby *out*, to see its face, count its fingers and toes. To hold it in my arms and keep it safe, as if, too much longer in that warm secret place, and it would surely drown — miss its exit altogether and never come, as if the darkness outside were but waiting to rush in and snatch it. There was a terrible urgency to all this, you must see, my need to lay claim to this child before something else could; to have it fill the spaces left by you and Mam.

How childish, I realize now, to imagine one life as recompense for others. But it weighed on my patience, my condition did, till I was nearly crazed with the clocks' ticking, the endless, creeping spread of days and nights.

September came and went, shot through with the shouts of children dawdling past, to and from school: soft, burnished afternoons that reminded me of you, and of the first time I spoke to Silas, up at the cemetery. The children's voices fed my longings; they piqued my fears as well, the way a shoe raises a blister. Dangerous, it is, to want something so badly, to pin all hope on something, someone, so small.

Silas saw how fidgety I'd become. Goodness knows it rubbed off on him; I don't know how he managed to tend shop. As a last resort, he dragged the crazy quilt from the cupboard where I'd tossed it after Mam died. It was all but finished, Fan; just needed the backing sewn on, the edges bound with satin. But I'd given up on it, throwing myself into sewing nappies and soakers instead.

"What a shame," he said, "all that work, Phemie, then hiding the thing away where no one can appreciate it." He was right. And though I hadn't much heart for it, one morning, out of desperation pure and simple, I picked up the quilt and started back at it.

All of a sudden, I felt frantic to have it done. Lord knows why — just the need, I suppose, to finish what I'd begun, gaudy and impractical as it was.

1893, I worked in stem stitch, gold on black; the initials *A.L.* — Adeline or Adam, those were the names we'd settled on. Though when I did the *L* it came out so much like a *C* that they might have been Mam's initials. Hard to say now whom that quilt was intended for, her or the infant.

This done, I worked like the devil to complete the backing, a huge piece of gold velvet, all tucked and tufted. I remained in the parlour one entire day in order to finish the task by supper. As the final stitch was drawn, I could hear Ina out in the kitchen, peeling potatoes. Clipping the last stray thread, I draped the quilt over the sofa and sat waiting for Silas to come home.

"Surprise!" I cried, rising to kiss his cheek.

"Oh my," he said, running his hand over the velvet, careful as if measuring lye. He patted my arm. "You've done a lovely job — Mother'll be right proud of you." Loosening his tie, he then went out to enquire what was for supper.

Labour snuck up like a thief next morning, starting so gently I hardly knew what was happening. A splotch of blood on my drawers, the water breaking: a slow pale trickle along my thigh as I crept downstairs. Silas had been at work for hours, though it couldn't have been nine o'clock; a couple of tardy children were straggling past en route to school. The pains started as I watched from the window — little more than a tightening at first, a gentle pulling like purse strings being drawn, then released.

Ina wasn't due over till ten to start the wash. But as the pains took hold — still nothing terrible, not much stronger than a twinge — panic seized me and all I could think of was my being alone. A sudden shakiness overtook me, so I went out to the veranda for some air. Silas? I thought, watching up and down the street for him, as if somehow he should've known to come home. Now that this had finally started, I wanted it stopped. *Not yet*, I prayed, *I'm not ready; no, not yet. Of course; so this is what it's like,* whispered my rational side, a voice like a shadow outside myself; observing the rest of me, succumbing.

The children going past noticed me watching them. They stopped and gawked as a cramp girdled my belly and I hunched over, clutching myself.

"Please," I heard myself call, as if there were two of us standing on the veranda. "Run and fetch Mr. Lewis. The young one, not the father," I found the presence of mind to add — the sensible part of me that was Silas's wife. The other part squatted like an orphan by the door, biting my tongue to keep from crying out, It's his wife, tell him. Tell him it's time, would you run now, quick — quick! — and get him, *please.*

Dragging myself back inside, I walked the hall like a caged tiger, swaying, doubling over whenever the pains hit. The clock on the mantelpiece struck nine, seemed to chime forever. At eleven minutes past, Silas stumbled in, out of breath, to find me pacing up and down, up and down, fit to wear a path through the floor-cloth. I tried to tell him it wasn't that bad, there was no need for alarm. But that other part of me wept at the sight of him, grabbed at his hands as he helped me up to bed.

"Don't leave me," I begged as he ran to fetch Dr. O'Hanley or, failing that, old Maudie McDow, who caught babies when the doctor was busy.

Alone, I was sure I would die, that each wave of pain would wring the light from my body. Suddenly it had nothing to do with a baby — so seemed this wild tug-of-war between me and the heaving of my belly. Trapped yet loosened, detached, my spirit begged feebly to be spared. *How on God's earth do you make it through this?* my brain fluttered and flagged, knuckled under with pain when at last Silas returned with Maudie, his mother trailing after. From far, far away, I could hear her pacing beyond the door while Maudie's cold hands worked over me, probing, poking. Squeezing my hand, she spoke in a bright, steady voice, her amber eyes holding mine.

"There now, honey, it'll be all right. You'll be fine, I'm right here, I'm not going nowhere."

Over her shoulder she hissed, "Good strong cuppa tea would help; and something stronger, for after. Girl's gonna need every ounce of strength; big baby she's got in there, first time. Looks like we all could be in for a bit of it. Mister, why'n't you go tell your mother to put on the water."

I heard Tryphena creep downstairs and start instructing Ina. The back door banged. Dr. O'Hanley? No. I stared into Maudie's eyes as the pain rode up, filling me to the teeth.

"Keep breathing, Effie, that's right, that's right. That's just Ina running next door, I bet. Doc O'Hanley'll be along, don't you worry. Don't you worry about a thing now, girl."

"Mam," I whimpered, the pain ebbing.

"It's breech," I heard her tell Silas out in the hall, the sole time she left me.

The rest is a blur, Fan: my husband pacing somewhere downstairs — miles away, he might've been, any bond between us stretched thin as spider silk. Even Maudie, spectacles sliding down her nose as she rubbed and rolled my belly, trying to turn the baby: her presence veiled, transparent. Everything seemed to slip from my grasp as the pain towered, crushing the breath from me till I thought I'd suffocate. As if the world and I were a stony beach, each pebble and grit of sand lifted and dragged out by the undertow.

"Make the doctor come, make him come," I kept screaming, a distant, bodiless voice. In the trough of a wave I glimpsed Tryphena, or believed I did, wringing her hands at the foot of the bed.

"If it has to come feet first, so be it," I heard her whisper to Maudie, "the good Lord willing."

Jesus Jesus Jesus, I was gasping, praying, as if on the brink of darkness — the darkness gathering at the window, waiting to swallow me.

Mam. I want my mam.

Shhh, shhh, somebody kept saying, as all at once I felt myself split apart, like a block of wood riven with a spike, my flesh tearing open.

"Come on now, Effie — push! Get it out now, that's it. You can do it. *Push!* Stubborn, stubborn...come on, little baby; come on, Effie. Oh God, yes; I've got his heels — here he comes now, Effie! A boy, I can see. In no big rush, though, are you, little one? Keep pushing, girl, come on. Keep pushing, honey, don't quit on us!"

Maudie was coaxing and pulling when Dr. O'Hanley slipped into the room.

An instant later came a gush, the rush of blood and water and life. The doctor's hands shook as he caught the baby. There was a cold hush as he worked on it, then handed it to Maudie to bathe.

"A lovely, lovely boy. Just let me clean him up, then you can hold him," she said, a stiffness to her voice.

"Well, he's *breathing*," I heard the doctor tell Silas, "But I'm sorry; it's just a matter of time."

I never heard the baby cry, Fan.

He was heavenly, though; not a mark on his perfect little body. He felt so warm when Maudie first laid him in my arms, a warm tight bundle; a perfect rosebud mouth, Silas's nose. But eyes that would not see, I could tell even then; something about them looked different from other newborns', dim, shocked yet trusting. Perhaps he didn't have it in him to cry.

The cord had cut off his air, it was wrapped so tightly round his neck, the doctor said. The risk one took with breech babies, so long in being born. There was nothing he or Maudie or anybody could've done; nothing. Just be grateful, damn grateful, I heard him consoling Silas, that you didn't lose your wife too.

Adam lived only a few hours. I held him the entire time, the duration of his little life; lay with him in my arms, weaving in and out of — not sleep, no. More a shadowy play of light and dark, warmth and cold; flashes of seeing, not seeing — as it might be opening one's eyes underwater, perhaps. The only sure things the baby's gentle weight against me, the faint lift and fall of his chest through layers of flannelette. My lips against the soft dark fuzz of his scalp, the small pulsing triangle in his skull. My hand on his heart, its beat slow and faint as footsteps on damp earth.

I breathed in deep and slow, willing my heart to shudder, its pounding to fade, to feel our pulses mingle once more.

"Try to rest now," Dr. O'Hanley said, washing his hands in a basin Ina brought. As the doctor was leaving, Silas turned to put out the light.

"No!"

I held the baby in the crook of my arm while Maudie changed the bed and finished cleaning me up. As she bundled soiled sheets and newspapers, I tried raising myself. His tiny chest still moved against my breast, his cheeks puffing with the effort to breathe. But already his lips were blue, his little fists ice-cold, and not a blessed thing I could do to warm them.

"Don't leave me," I cried to Maudie, my voice like rain raking gravel.

Tryphena came in and bent close, a flicker of hope in her eyes, hope and pity — an awful, all-knowing pity that welled in place of tears.

"He might do better by the stove, Euphemia."

Maudie shoved the bloodied sheets into her arms. "Here you go, missus. No place better than his mama's arms, I'm afraid, poor wee thing. No amount of warmth can fix his trouble — best to leave 'em be."

And so I lay trembling till the cold little body turned mine to ice too; the stiff clean sheets a snowy nest; the tiny rosebud mouth grey as twigs in November. Like the trees outside our hotel in Spenceport — Remember, Silas? I wanted to ask, my tears sleet upon the pillow when he came to take the baby. I don't know why I thought of those trees — buying time, perhaps, or wishing to stop it altogether.

"Phemie," he coaxed, his face pale and stiff.

His mother came in, stone-faced; stood, appalled, at the bed-stead. "Come now, Euphemia — dear."

But I held onto my bundle, as if its chill might freeze my veins, spread the iciness from my toes up into the hollow beneath my heart. *Take me too,* I prayed, the throb of my pulse numb and stupid as frostbitten fingers come back to life.

Too much to bear, the thought of one so small going off on his own....

It was Maudie I finally allowed to take him, only because I knew she'd be gentle — gentle yet strong enough to see that no harm crossed the tiny sleeping form. His face, a mirror of mine and my husband's — and Mam's, my mind yielded, or my heart, grasping for something to harbour.

"Poor lamb," Maudie whispered, holding out her arms as slowly, slowly I gave him up. She stood for a moment rocking him, her big wide hips swaying ever so gently. "Poor, poor lamb."

"Better off now," Tryphena sniffled, "up there with the Maker, up where not a thing can hurt him."

The same as my sister? I wanted to shriek.

The rage I felt, Fan! It burns like a fever still, if I let it — even now, now I have my girls, my lovely girls. All these years later, when I remember losing that baby, sorrow floods in as if it happened last night.

Some said it would've been worse if I'd gotten to know him. They figured it was easier losing a child at birth than one you'd raised and nurtured — like a geranium! My girls, for instance: Ruby, then Dora, who came along after I'd given up hope of having more babies. Fifteen years I waited for Ruby, a good long time — too long, if you ask me, after Adam, and then two miscarriages.

But the Lord works in mysterious ways, as Tryphena was so fond of reminding us. "Never shuts a door but he opens a window; never hands out more than a body can take."

I don't know, Fan; I'd still have to say part of me dried up and vanished, like heat up a chimney, when that baby perished. It was a bigger part than I could put a finger on, even once I'd had the girls. My little Ruby: she was a window, all right, a wide-open window that let the world peek into my soul. A miracle, but overdue. By the time she came along, there wasn't much left in there to see.

The Lord giveth and the Lord taketh away — another of Tryphena's favourite sayings, especially when her husband passed away three years after I lost Adam, and she came to stay with us for good. Enough to make you crazy, her applying this to the piddliest things: a customer wandering out with a pencil, Silas locating a spare tin of beans; me losing a thimble and finding it under a chair.

For eleven years she lived with us. The entire time, I felt as though I was being watched. Then one night — ten months before Ruby arrived — didn't Tryphena pass away in her sleep? It was timely for me, given how things transpired. I might never have had my daughters — well, certainly not Ruby — had she hung on.

Better off in heaven, I'm sure she is, the old bird; so, will we all be, someday. I'm after finding out: I'll be forty-six my next birthday, no one needs reminding. That is, if the Lord finds anything about me worth saving, whatever's left once I'm laid to rest. I hope he's not too judgemental. For it's the thought of seeing you, Mam and my poor wee darling that keeps me putting one foot before the other, stumbling as I am towards that Mansion.

The Lord taketh, yes. I only aimed to get some back.

This is not an excuse — there's no excuse, Fan, for my behaviour once Silas and I found ourselves alone, truly alone, for the first time in our marriage. After his father died, Silas practically moved into the store, spending day and night there. At first it was to catch up, taking over all the business; later, simply to escape his mother — me as well, I see that now. What a withered pair of old raisins we made, she and I; my youth spent, our days devoted to tatting and crochet. When I lost the baby, I lost my taste for the world outside; could stomach neither the prospect of some customers' sympathy nor others' apparent lack of it. And Tryphena — well, she'd grown too frail and unreliable to help in the store.

So we passed the days together, as separate beings in separate rooms. Mornings, she kept to hers while I did laundry and dusted downstairs. After lunch we changed places; I'd retire to mine for a nap while she amused herself in the parlour, reading Scripture. When I rose, usually about three o'clock, I would make myself some tea and take it sitting with her. This didn't please her, of course, but at least by then she'd learned to mute her disapproval. And thus we'd sit and sew, making polite conversation, for an hour or two before I started supper.

There I was, not yet thirty-three and a dried-up crone — my God, with a life identical to *hers*. The only difference being that I'd stopped going to church; had quit altogether after that summer I was with child.

So perhaps I was ready, ready and desperate — I hesitate to say "ripe" — the day Bert Putnam, of all people, came waltzing up the veranda steps.

INTERCESSION
Hide-and-Seek

Oh, Mumma. Your flustered face, heat-flustered. Pale, pale yellowish skin, blotches of colour in your cheeks: the shades of a peach. The play of sunlight through the leaves, white petals floating down. The sky a net, a huge blue net.

Your arms make a wide warm hoop. You move to kiss me, but I slip through, roll away on the cool, cool grass....

You say there is a baby. I ask, How did it get there?

What I mean is, how can I believe what you say?

Shiny spikes, like tiny icicles, glitter in the dustpan. Glass, the woman calls it. "Don't cut yourself," says she, Lucinda-Dora, not Mum. Slivers, spikes, silver needles....

"Going back to your reading, Ruby?" She laughs at me. She is always mocking me. I hate her sometimes; wish to God she would go away.

Darkness falls. It's good; it wipes her out of the picture. There's only the sound of her breathing....

She tells me I mustn't get up at night. But the darkness draws me....

Only the sound of her breathing. The greyish outline of things, shapes: no colours, nothing that needs naming....

A deceiver, Mum. This must be where she gets it from — that woman, Lucinda-*not* Dora. From Mum. Telling lies. Tricking me, that woman. I hate her for it, too.

Mum's words, a load of crap. Crap, as Leonard would say, Leonard, the man I was married...am married to..."till death do us part."

Mum's lies, her filthy stitchery. I want to burn her words, all of them; set fire to the whole kittencaboodle, watch them curl yellow blue orange, then black....

But that woman, that *bitch*, has hidden the firesticks, oh yes. Unless she has some out there, in the room with the rain-needles-slivers — glass!

Mum's handiwork is so heavy, it takes both my hands to carry it. In the dark I float past shapes — the fridge, the stove — towards a plank of pale light: the doorway. I clasp Mum's word-embroidery, heavy as sin. Lay my palm on something smooth, cool, hard: the countertop. Feel for the bowl with cards of firesticks, pennies at the bottom. Leonard's idea, that bowl: "nice for smokers" — *Leonard?*

But the bowl's shiny-cool, empty. My arms laden with lies. Heavy, much too heavy to bear — bury? Berries, the colour of blood. No. Bury, lay to rest. Out of sight, out of mind, don't-mind-if-I-mind-if-I'm-mine....

The cooler! Coca-Cola red! Tall shiny shivering bottles inside: bottles filled with orange water brown water pink water green water clear water too, clear as — glass. My palm touches something flat, cold, cold as sleet but not wet.

Mum's book, Mum's words, the devil's handiwork. I bury it.

Deep, deep in the crack between the metal and the wall. The secret black crack. I stick it where the sun don't shine, as *he* would say.

That fellow — the one I loved once, I *think* he was my husband.

Leonard? Come out, now — you hear?

I *know* you're in here someplace, hiding.

Come out come out wherever you are.

Finders, keepers; losers, weepers.

XXIII

Sightings

There was a guy at the building supply store the spitting image of the King.

"Look — there's Elvis!" I said.

"Who, dear?"

We were at the checkout, Ruby and I. Honest to God, you could've sworn it was him. I nearly dropped the sheet of glass I was buying.

Elvis looked tired and thinner than you'd expect; he had on jeans and a long-sleeved checked shirt, the tails hanging out, the sleeves rolled up tight above his biceps. He was buying C-clamps, of all things; paid cash.

What got me was the hair — coal-black, slicked back with gobs of Brylcreem in a nice fat jelly-roll — and the sunglasses he was wearing. Mirrors, with see-through silver frames chain-linked like strings of bubbles from a goldfish. I've never seen shades like that on anyone from these parts — one big clue this was no normal joe.

"Ohmygod," I gasped.

At one point he glanced our way and that sheet glass nearly slid like wet soap from my arms. Fine mess that would've been, the entire store gawking at me. "Customer service, cleanup in aisle eight, *ma*jor cleanup."

"It's him, it has to be." I dug Ruby with my elbow. "That or a damn good impersonator."

"Elvis who, dear?" She looked at me blankly.

"For Pete's Sake: 'Love Me Tender'? Sideburns, pelvis? 'Suspicious Minds'! It's him, Ruby — I know it sounds out to lunch, but it's him!" I was only half joking.

I thought I'd pee my pants. Then didn't Elvis turn and look straight at us. His lips twitched; he had this hunted, nervous look, as though he was running late or behind schedule or something. Impossible, though, to see what was in his eyes behind those shades, the store lights, the red flash of my jacket, the glare of my new-to-me blouse, all reflected in the lenses.

I couldn't wait till the next time Wilf called so I could tell him about it.

"Oh yeah," he'd likely say at first, but then I would try to convince him. Still, I couldn't help wishing for another witness.

Poor Ruby — the event was wasted on her. Edna Pyke, now there's someone who would've enjoyed it, would've rushed to the front and demanded his autograph, whether or not the guy was the real McCoy. Yes, she would have, being younger than me — early fifties, I'd say. No doubt she grew up with the King as her idol.

Yup, in spite of everything, I found myself wishing Edna were there; she would've got a kick out of it. Ruby's only remark, when we finally got up to the cash, was "Awfully puny paws, that man — like your uncle. Your uncle — you know."

Well, he did have small hands, this Elvis, come to think of it — just like Ruby's Leonard — hands that made you speculate on the size of other body parts, something I could mention but would rather not.

The night Daddy quit coming home for good, I stood in Ma's doorway and watched her primping in the scratched little mirror above her dresser. "Tell your father there's peas in the cupboard, if he wants them," she said, pulling one eyelid down, her mouth dragged into a sneer, then squeezing, squeezing her lashes through that little metal contraption of hers. The whole effect was ugliness — like what kids aimed for behind the teacher's back, thumbs hooked in the corners of their mouths, pointer fingers stretching bloody eyelids. The eyelash curler always did look to me like a device for torturing mice, or for doing something else, something dirty and secret perhaps, kinky.

Ma finished curling one set of lashes, blew her nose, started in on the other.

"Where you going?" I asked off-handedly, not wanting to seem nosy. I was hoping for her usual church-basement answer, afraid of the truth — or confirmation of the rumours at school. "Your mother's an old rip, Lindeeeee! Your mother's a hooer," these two boys used to sneer, in grade five. Once, just before dismissal, the same pair leaned close enough to whisper in my face, "How 'bout that? She don't smell a bit like her ol' lady," and then, in a cruel, gassy hiss, "Whew! Somebody tell 'er to close her legs — I can smell her last customer!" I had no idea, honestly, what they meant.

A whole row of heads turned and gawked, till the teacher slapped the strap down hard on the windowsill and yelped, "All of you! That's e-nough." She kept the boys in to clean the boards, the rest of the class for extra sums; but she let me go, skimming past with the pointer, a gentle rap on my desk. "Don't forget to do your math, Lindy. Maybe you can get some practice at your uncle's store." Because, more and more, that's where I was spending my time, the more Ma went out keeping company.

Uncle would invite me into the kitchen while he took his tea breaks, fixing us plates of leftovers from whatever Ruby'd cooked the night before. Not that I couldn't've helped myself, but I liked the attention. I liked the way Uncle rocked back in his chair, thumbs in his natty blue braces, and watched me wolf down a chicken leg or a bowlful of sweet brown beans, the molassesy juice dribbling down my chin.

He looked after me in a way no one else would. "Go on, Lindy," he'd say, "fill your boots, that's it. Eat, eat; it's good for you." Then Ruby would holler in, "Leonard? For the love of Pete, if that child's hungry she's big enough she can get it herself." By now she was used to me being around. By the time Daddy left, she accepted the fact that I was practically theirs — if not hers, Uncle's. Because that's how he treated me, especially after Daddy disappeared.

Some said that my father never got as far as Quebec City, that he jumped the tracks someplace in New Brunswick or Maine, wherever it was he took a thirst. A fellow from Ferrona came to see Ma not too long after; he said a cousin of his had seen a man of Daddy's description drunk as a skunk in the club car, somewhere near Rivière du Loup. There was a woman, too, quite pretty; she convinced him to sober up, apparently. But we never found out if any of this was fact, and soon enough Ma was past caring anyway.

When Daddy first left, Ma went into a shell; that's how Aunt Ruby and Uncle put it. They set up a cot for me in the back porch, brought me over to stay with them. Since there wasn't room in the flat, they used the porch for storage — spillovers from the store. There was a shelf full of old *Saturday Evening Posts*; torn window screens; a sign from Uncle's bakery; a bunch of mismatched pots and pans. I felt like an extra pair of boots, sleeping out there.

The cot folded up in the daytime, like a fat suitcase with springs. In the night, whenever I rolled over, it would tilt and sag and thump the floor, the head or foot flying up, and I worried I'd be tipped out on my ear.

Uncle and Ruby said it wouldn't be for long, just till Ma got back on her feet.

I thought it would be a treat staying there — candy for breakfast, lunch and supper — but it wasn't. Once I stowed my things in a drawer Ruby'd emptied, it was as though they didn't quite know what to do with me. I asked if I might sleep upstairs with Gran and Grampa Silas, but Ruby said no, they were old and certainly not up to having a child underfoot.

The first night, there was meatloaf and wax beans for supper. My uncle and aunt didn't talk much during the meal. I guess they were tired from their day in the store; likely wondering what they'd gotten themselves into, taking me.

"Bedtime, Lucinda," Aunt Ruby said, when it was barely dusk. She sounded different around Uncle — businesslike, but remote, too; impatient.

Moths pinged the screens as she turned out the porch light for me to undress. I could hear Uncle in the kitchen smoking, listening to the ball game; the soft *paw-phhew* when he exhaled.

After I brushed my teeth, Aunt Ruby balanced on the edge of the cot and tried to tell me a story. You could see she was a little uncomfortable doing so; she kept mixing up details, and I was a bit too old for it anyway — something about a small fox outsmarting a bigger one.

"Like the tortoise and the hare, you mean," I said grouchily, my eyes closed, half dozing. She laughed, kind of embarrassed. "Or sour grapes; perhaps that's what I was thinking of." Then she leaned down and kissed my forehead, her warm smell of cooking blending with that of freshly mown grass coming through the screen. "Sleep tight now, Lucinda." And she drew the dampish sheet, the itchy grey blanket, up to my chin, lingering the way Ma had when I was small, very small, before Daddy started spending so much time at the freight shed.

"Sweet dreams, dear."

The moon was shining through the screen when something woke me, a rustling sound. I thought first it was mice, raccoons maybe, rooting under the porch. I pulled the covers over my head and listened. But when I peeked out, there was Uncle Leonard leaning in the doorway in his undershirt; in the moonlight it gleamed white as the lilies he and Ruby sold at Easter.

"Let me tell you a story, Lindy," he whispered, holding his finger to his lips. I shook myself awake, the cot's metal feet bumping the floor. Taking a sharp breath, I grabbed onto the sides.

"Don't be scared," he said. "Uncle'd never hurt you."

There was something odd about his face, even in the dimness: a pained expression; and he was breathing funny. I thought maybe he was sick, had come down with the asthma that hit a girl I knew at school.

"Is it an attack?" I sat up, uttering loudly that word that sounded grown-up, so Ruby might hear and come save him. Fuzzy with sleep, I wasn't about to get up, not yet anyway, not that fast.

He came closer, and I could see then he had his trousers open. One hand moved up and down inside them. Still, I stayed put, scared to move or slide away lest I end up on the floor.

"I want to tell you a story," he said in a squeezed voice, "about a snake, Lindy, a one-eyed snake...." His breathing was raspy, as if any minute he'd choke.

I could smell the sweat from his undershirt.

"Look, honey, you can see him if you want...see? He don't bite, no, he don't bite.... Just a story, a...nice...little...stor——"

He reached out and pulled my hand towards him. The scream stuck in my throat as I jerked backwards, the cot knocking against the wainscot, the floor. My heart thumped out a prayer from school: *Our father, forgive us this day...lead us not...our daily bread...into tempta....*

He got this awful, scared look, as if someone had just come in with a shotgun, ordered him to empty the till. "Shhh, shhhh," he hissed, and all seemed so quiet I thought Ruby'd have to wake and hear my heart pounding; that any second she'd come and flip on the light and ask what in God's earth was going on.

In a fever, Uncle zipped his pants, then dug in his pockets. "Don't you tell your aunt nothing, you hear me? It's none of her business, see, honey? Just between me and you — you got that?" His hand shook as he slid something under my pillow.

A quarter, I discovered when the sun finally rose. Picking it up with a scrap of newspaper, I gave it away next day at recess — to Marnie Johnson, the asthmatic one.

After that, Uncle treated me with kid gloves, the most careful kindness you could imagine. And in the most peculiar way, I sensed I had things made in the shade, all the blackballs and gumdrops I could eat. Except that from then on in, I insisted I was old enough, could help myself to the goodies in those jars, thanks very much; all he had to do was hand over the little brown bags.

But I never told Ruby, no sir. Figured if she ever found out she'd kill me, want me out of there so quick heads would spin; and then where would I have been?

Uncle never bothered me again; if anything, he turned sweeter than ever. But then, in a few short months he was dead, killed in that single-car crash-up. I always liked to believe it was guilt made him lose control, just plain feeling bad that jerked his hand off the wheel. God only knows, of course; but so I like to think.

I was twelve and a half when I "became a woman", as they say. The reason I remember is because I got to go home early, on account of the cramps. Low down in my belly, they were, like something trying to claw its way out. Thought I had to *go*, you know; put my hand up to use the washroom, but when I got there nothing happened. So I sat for a while, this queer weight tugging on my insides and you-know-where. When I got up to wipe, there was blood — the water under me bright as a Tequila Sunrise. My head started to swirl, everything the colour of that grey metal cubicle, and my knees got weak, so I sat down again on the warm black seat. The shape of a girl's hair is what those seats resembled; Marnie and her friends used to joke that if you stared down long enough, the white bowl turned into a face.

I didn't feel like laughing, not that day. I wondered whether I was dying, and what I'd say if the teacher sent someone to check on me. What a sorry sight, me squatting there: mean little tears squeezing down my face, my chubby white thighs pressed together.

Once, I'd heard Ma and Aunt Ruby whispering about some girl in town who had a baby at the drugstore, right there in the bathroom at the back. The girl claimed she didn't know she was pregnant; Ma, slurring her words a little, sucked her teeth and said, What garbage, how could anyone *not* know? For a long time I carried this horrid picture in my head of the child's face, a little round puckered moon, underneath the rusty water. It would come to me at the strangest times. There was never any blood, though, nothing gory; no mess at all, in fact — just this tiny perfect baby, boy or girl depending on the mood I was in.

Locked in that cubicle, considering my options, it hit me like the noontime train: it must've been rather like this for that girl. Except — swear to God, cross my heart and hope to die — the same couldn't be happening to me, could it? I couldn't be having a baby!

Well, the upshot was, Miss Todd came and rapped on the door, the *rinky-tink* sound of her ring tapping metal, then went and called Aunt Ruby. Perhaps she tried to get Ma first, but no chance. I stuck a wad of toilet paper in my underpants and waddled up the road to the store. A man slowed down and gawked, maybe wondering why I was walking funny, as if there were a two-by-four inside my drawers.

Ruby was just locking up, coming for me; she was wearing her good black muskrat coat. I don't know why; maybe she had some other business in town. Whatever it was, she didn't look too thrilled, tapping one foot on the step and pushing back the heavy sleeves as she twisted the key. It was cold out; you could see your breath. Up close, I could smell her coat, a menthol smell like mothballs or toothpowder. The fur reminded me of a forest, kind of: millions of little spruce tops glistening with melted frost.

She gave me a weak smile, as though I'd disrupted her plans; but then, without moving from the step, she drew me to her, so tightly that for a second my face was buried in coolness, the fur's silky sheen. It was like the time I caught a rabbit, a neighbours' that had escaped its pen, and held it, one fast crazy moment — my cheek to its side, its frantic pulse. Except Ruby's coat was too thick for me to feel what beat beneath.

We went inside and she put on all the lights; gave me a box of pads off the shelf and sent me to the bathroom. "Look at it this way," she said, "at least you don't have to get up and shave every day, like men do." And she advised exercise, keeping busy; nothing stupider than lying around moaning about cramps, she said, and started me off straightening canned milk. When that was done, she had me sweep the aisles, then roll dimes. Before we knew it, it was closing time and she said I might as well stay and keep her company for supper. When I was finally leaving, she stuck the rest of the pads in a bag.

Ma wasn't home; she was scarcer than hen's teeth, those days. The house was in blackness, the key in its usual spot, a soup can under the stoop. I let myself in, hung my coat on the doorknob and got out the bread, a few stale slices of white, and spread them with jam. While I was eating I opened Ruby's bag. Inside, with the pads, was a fifty-cent piece and a special belt, and a little note in her hand: "This might help too. Love, your aunt."

When Ruby and I get back, I go right to work on the window. It's so chilly out, the new glass feels like a skim of ice off a pond, and the damn putty keeps hardening on me. Still, I end up doing an okay job. The whole time I'm out there, picking out the slivers and shards, kneading and tamping and pressing the new pane into place, I keep thinking about the King. I can't get the image of him out of my mind.

I go over and over what that fellow — Elvis or not — might've had in mind with all those clamps. I imagine the real Elvis. A table leg needing fixing at Graceland? Some other home repair? Heck, with his fortune of course he'd hire a handyman; but then again, look at the publicity, living proof of what the tabloids say: under the glitter, stars are just average folks like you and me. Sure — like Ma once said, "Everybody's the same underneath, Lindy, so much so it'd bore you silly. *Every*one goes to the pot." I take that back. "Picture them sitting on it," were her actual words.

"Ah!" I think to myself, packing up my tools. The window's finally fixed, that's what matters. Wilf hasn't phoned, but about an hour after I'm done my chore, he appears.

"You'll never guess who I saw in town," I tease, just having fun.

"What?"

"Black, slicked-back hair; ducktail, sidies...?"

"Hmmm?"

"*Fun in Acapulco*, 'Blue Christmas'?"

"Huh? You're pulling my leg, aren't you. Tell me you're pulling my leg." He looks at me, horrified.

"I'm serious. I would not lie. I saw him, Wilf, honest to God. It was him. In the flesh, at Beaver Lumber. I swear."

He looks disturbed, as if he can't quite grasp what he's hearing — not amused or anxious for details, but alarmed, then disgusted. Grossed out, as those rangy teenagers often say, passing by the frozen-food case.

"You been reading too many *Enquirer*s." He starts to chuckle, but nervously, like someone out on a Sunday drive and the road, all of sudden, turns unfamiliar.

"Well" — he clears his throat — "what I came to tell you is, we've hit a snag. Crew ran into some old mineshafts yesterday — just after I dropped you off, matter of fact — and already we got inspectors out sniffing around. So work's been halted, guys sent home, till some kind of review's done of the route. Guess that puts the kibosh on things, for a while, anyways. You know what the gov'ment's like."

"Well sure: works in mysterious ways," I say, rolling my eyes, only half-interested. See, I can't believe he's not pumped up about

"Elvis" — or, at the very least, amused at my observation. He could've asked what the King was buying. But no, it's as if he thinks I'm some kind of nut for bringing it up.

"It looked just like him," — I dig in my heels — "I saw the guy with my own two eyes. Ruby too; ask her if you don't believe me."

He goes and gets himself a pop, drinks it in deep, bobbing sips. I'm reminded — sounds silly, but it's true — of the drinking-bird ornament Uncle used to have on top of his radio, years ago.

"Well, Lindy" — he sets down the can and pats my wrist — "I always did like a woman with a sense of humour." But he pauses, as if to consider something, and gives me this look, stalwart but almost at a loss. I feel my toes curl.

"Nothing wrong with an imagination, neither, I guess. So, how 'bout you coming out to the trailer sometime? Hmmm? You and Ruby, we could fit her in. You should see my digs. It'd give me a chance, too, to show you how I cook. Whaddya think?"

"That'd be nice," I say slowly, noncommittal. "What else have you got in mind to persuade me?"

When Wilf leaves, I realize it's been an hour or more since I checked on Ruby. Heck, it's been so quiet back there, God knows what she's been up to. Napping, maybe; reading, most likely — or setting the place afire, for all I know. I hid the matches, first thing I did after her doctor appointment. 'Course, where there's a will there's a way, and there are always Bic lighters. Childproof, they're supposed to be, but that means nothing if you're determined. I can just see her, awful thought, tracing the drapes with the little blue flame, moving to the arms of the couch. But the Bics are all in place, five of them, untouched, right beside the licorice pipes. I should throw those candies out, I guess; they look like old tires. Tomorrow, maybe.

Well, I don't smell smoke; that's something. Don't hear the TV, either — kind of odd, this time of day. Figure she must be snoozing, so I tiptoe out to the kitchen, real quiet, so as not to wake her. Maybe this is what it's like to have a baby — what I gather, anyways, from those tired young mothers that come in sometimes for cigarettes.

I go to pour myself a cup of coffee, mulling over Wilf's invitation, when I hear something, a snipping sound, coming from the parlour. Snip snip snip. Well, if that doesn't beat all, I think, she's back at her needlepoint, that kit I gave her; she hasn't touched it in weeks. Snip, snip, *scritttch* — that must be the scissors sticking; I've been meaning to oil the screw. Lord knows how long that old pair's been around. Scritch, scritch, *hee-haaaw, hee-haaaw*: the blades sound like a donkey, coming unstuck. God love her, you have to give her points for trying....

Then, before I've made it to the doorway, there's the sharp, ragged sound of cloth ripping. Good Christ! I go cold. *Don't tell me:* the drapes? the sofa cushions? God forbid — her good blue dress? For one crazy second I freeze in my tracks, scared to look in.

Next, there's a mousy snort; a sigh, the same smug sound a body would make helping herself to the last piece of a chocolate cake.

"Ruby?" Steeling myself, I work up the nerve to peek around the corner. "Ruby — *what* are you doing?"

It takes a minute to sink in — the damage, I mean. Oh, straight off I see it. But what I can't get a fix on is the why or wherefore.

There she is in her favourite chair, the shades drawn, the room dark as a cave. Even in the dimness I see the smile slide off her face, right off her chin sunk down on her stained, droopy bosom. The picture in my head of the King flicks and fades faster than a shuffled ace. All I see is Ruby hunched over Gran's quilt, what's left of it: her eyes full of dread, a confused kind of dread like a bird's caught in the teeth of a tom. Over her lap, the quilt lies — chopped to ribbons, gashed and hacked where the scissors wheezed through like a snaggy zipper.

She brings a scrap of rusty fabric up to her nose — the better to see or smell her handiwork? Oh God. The quilt's ruined beyond fixing — hacked-up velvet all over the rug, like tufts of dog hair; the baked-fish smell of rotting cloth. I choke back a sneeze. Ruby looks at the scissors in her hand — big rusty dressmaker's shears — and moans, a long, heart-rending sound more like a sob. Then she sets them, careful as you please, on the doilied table, the points turned away as if warding off the devil himself.

Those first few minutes I'm struck dumb, the words bagged up inside me.

"Why?" When I can finally speak, it comes out like a snort. She stares back, a long, haughty glare.

"Jesus!" I say, reaching for a shredded patch of gold and purple; smelly old batting comes apart in my fingers.

And I can't help myself, it comes gushing out like runoff from a storm sewer, before I can stop it: "My sweet Christ Ruby what in heaven's name — whatever would get into you, make you do such a crazy lunatic thing? Your mama's quilt, Ruby — don't you know what you did, what awful crazy thing — you've got no idea, do you? For the love of Christ, you're off the deep end now — Lord, the bloody *deep* end — Ruby, admit it, you're right off your rocker — you must be — and if it doesn't stop soon, you're gonna take me with you — oh God, *God!* What am I gonna do with you, huh? What in the name of Christ am I gonna do?"

Once it's all spilled out, the words hang like a nasty, nasty stink. I'm sobbing, tasting tears and snot, all the beautifying goop on my face dissolved in one salty mudslide.

Nothing for it, then, but to fall on my knees, start picking the furry, fibrous mess off the rug.

But when I look up, goddammit, would you believe she's smirking? Smirking, those bleeding scissors waving in one hand, her devil hand. Chop chop chop, goes the air. And she's gazing straight ahead as though she'd sooner that air were me.

Out in the store the bell dingles, and I get up, real shaky, my eyes on her hand as I back away and grab a Kleenex. Blowing my nose, I cobble myself together.

"Yup?" I yell out to whoever, in a quaky, waterlogged croak.

XXIV

Profits

It's that kid, that goddamn kid. When I see him, I step back, a big ball of Kleenex in my fist. Give my nose an extra wipe, dab the black stuff from my eyes. Do up my top button, stepping out to the cash.

He's slouching, draped over the counter like a sloth on a tree limb, watching my every move. Those watery eyes of his slide along the wall behind me, zigzag back and forth along the cigarettes, then wash up and down the length of me.

His eyelids are puffy, droopy for a kid that age; make him look dozy, half asleep. Through one eyebrow there's a silver ring, this is new, the skin around it crusty and red. In his left earlobe the same gold hoop, but higher up something else, a tiny silver barbell. In the right, a tag like the kind for marking pigeons.

"Whaddya want?" I say, too loud. The sound bounces off the Coke bottles to the side. I'm still shaking over the quilt, the mess in the other room.

"Export, plain," he slurs, his thin upper lip curled back in a leer. His jacket sags open, a Just Do It shirt underneath. Without taking my eyes off him I reach behind me — could put my hand on the fags blindfolded — and slap the pack on the counter, with a lightning *smack*.

To quell the shaking, I lean forward, palms down, fingers splayed like starfish. His pupils seem to funnel, so wide open you can barely see the weak blue rims of his irises. Suppose he's on devil weed, or what? Sure, it's more than tobacco kids crave these days. When I was young....

He looks at me with cool, sneering hate. Or maybe hate's too strong a word; more like I don't equal a pinch of squirrel shit in his eyes — that's how it feels. As though he'd tromp over your face in a second with those clumpy big boots of his, and never look back. That's not hate, but worse — I don't know the word for it. How a kid turns that way, Christ only could say.

But I won't stand for it. I press down the balls of my feet. You want to stare, kid? I can stare back twice as long. I can stare and stare until you say uncle. I've got forty-odd years on you, I want to say; what's to scare me? Especially after the disaster in the next room.... All this runs through my head, though at first I don't speak. Can't. I'm too busy training my eyes, thinking of ways to twist the knife.

My fingers arch and side-scuttle, snap up the pack of Exports still lying on the counter. A cough rags up from my throat.

"You nineteen?" I grill him. "You old enough to smoke?"

He looks at me like a dog caught pissing on some flowers.

"You got *i*-dentification?" my voice rakes and peels, like he's an orange and I'm the grater.

"You heard me — you got ID?"

A hacking sound starts somewhere behind me, back there in the flat. A hacking; a stiff, wheezy sound, like a car chugging up-hill in first. An old woman's sobs.

"Well?"

"I'm countin' to five, no ID and you're outta here. You hear me?"

The crying gets louder, and he pricks to it. I waver a bit; oh yes, he spies the crack in my armour, as Gran used to say: a tiny crack, his window of opportunity.

"Bitch," he drawls. "Friggin' douchebag."

And before I can stop him, he grabs the pack of smokes out of my hand and runs outside. Faster than a .22, more nerve than gunfire.

"You little son of a whore," I gasp, jangled as a bag of loose coin.

The crying's coming from the kitchen now, closer. Turning, peering back there, I see her. Hunched at the table, her scrawny shoulders racked. Her hands knotted tight together as if in prayer. *This is the church, this is the steeple....*

Like so much spilt milk, I think, what's the goddamn use? I go and lock up, and when I come into the kitchen her hand makes a lunge for mine.

"Six feet under" — she gapes at me — "I wish I were; dead." And she sounds like a child, a tiny child, apologizing for something it's done, something it knows is bad, though it hasn't a clue why.

"Oh for the love of Pete, Ruby, stop your nonsense." I blink and harden myself, then feel my hand go limp in hers. Gently I pull it away to rub her back, the flesh like paper under her dress. Her eyes are closed, you can see all the veins in the thin purple lids. She lays her pale, sagging cheek on the tabletop, its smudged, ringed surface almost the same yellowish shade as her face. Her scalp looks like pie crust through the tangled white hair. Her mouth slack, her lips dragging a little with each stroke of my hand on her shoulders. All of a piece, the knit of muscles beneath the slackened skin. All of a piece, but the centre of her locked, lost, someplace inside.

And then the tears creak out, one at a time, flecks of dew between those worn-out lids the same bruised purple as faded Johnny-jump-ups. They glitter, her tears, the split second before rolling down, as if the round, chrome fixture overhead catching them is the sun — almost.

"Shhh, now, shhh, dear," I whisper, my palm tracing widening circles over her shoulderblades, thin and sharp as a turkey's; circles weaving wide, then faint as a propeller's, but slow, steady, till she starts to snore, a deep-throated purr. I stop and rest my hand on her spine, the hard little knob at the base of her neck. Something inside me wants to rub and probe each frail, descending bump, to count them; but the flesh feels so thin — such poor, weak protection

— I'm scared to death of hurting her. Scared I'll rub the bones to dust.

And rising, oh God, slow and careful as if barefoot, treading slivered glass, I tiptoe out and empty the till. Wrap a big, thick elastic band around the bills; lump the coin together in the used envelope from Ruby's old-age cheque. Dimes and nickels shine through the crinkly little window; the dull gleam of a loonie. And to the tune of Ruby's breathing, that soft, grating snore, I open the safe, remembering just in time my hidden booby-trap, and oh hell, stuff the lot inside. The day's take, a grand total: thirty-two dollars and sixty-six cents, less five bucks for cigarettes.

You better call somebody, a little voice nags. The Mounties, sure; lounging around that new detachment, a neat brick bungalow, cedars out front, middle of nowhere. Call them.

But there's no way. "A pack of *cigarettes?*" they'd say. I can hear the dispatcher, his guffaw. "You're calling about a pack of cigarettes? Well good luck, lady. Call when you got something real to report."

Good luck yourself.

I'm halfway out to the phone, the old phone by the cash, and suddenly I'm that mad — ripping like a cyclone churned from a puff of wind; fit to be tied. The anger swarms up the back of my neck, it does, grabs ahold of me like some virus, some vicious bug.

Then I spy Ruby snoozing at the table, bent as a gnarled-up apple tree, wisps of quilt batt like dandelion seed leading to the parlour. Like the breadcrumb trail left by Hansel, it strikes me — am I crazy or what? But I can't help thinking, so where's the gilded bird, huh? Not on our roof.

Tomorrow, yes. Hell or high water, tomorrow I'm getting her in to see buddy — that doctor, what's his name? I'm in such a stew his name escapes me. Even if I have to tie her up to get her there; after the last visit she said she'd sooner get laid out alive at Pyke's than be *insulted* like that again.

Meantime there's that mess to pick up in the parlour, the quilt, what's left of it. Like the aftermath of a catfight, or a lawnful of caterpillars, the fuzzy kind, mowed down with a John Deere.

Till now, part of me hoped it could be mended, put back together. Like Humpty Dumpty. But it's done like dinner, the filthy old rag. If Gran could see! If not for the bloody waste of it, the awfulness of Ruby's "accomplishment", I might be able to laugh. If the queasiness weren't there in my gut — if I didn't feel, somehow, that it's my fault, what she's done — I'd sit myself down, yes, laugh and laugh till I cried. Or vice versa.

I should've packed it away, I meant to. Should've just blocked out Ruby's voice, washed and packed it like I was going to months ago, when her spells started. But she would've gone ballistic on me. "Lucinda? What have you done with Mum's quilt? I know you've done something with it, haven't you? Have you lost it? Admit it. No, you've thrown it out, haven't you? I see by the look in your eyes, I just know it. Lucinda, you have no right...when will you learn, dear, to keep your hands off things not yours?"

She wouldn't part with it long enough to let me run it through the rinse cycle. I should've gone ahead and washed it anyway, and put it away — but for what? For posterity? My posterior, more like. For the benefit of my fanny; something to warm it years from now, winter nights, after Ruby's gone.

The thought, the very possibility — Ruby *gone*; laid out four-square as her poster bed. A tightness creeps up my throat, into my ears. As if thinking such a thing will bring it to roost, like willing swallows to nest in a barn.

The quilt's remains fill two garbage bags, all that mouldy old cloth. Likely wouldn't've washed up, anyways, without the velvet's nubblies coming off, and all those tiny flowers and cobwebs, stitches to make you go blind. A miracle Gran didn't, though by the end of her days her eyes were shot. Poor old bat, nearsighted as a June bug, four-eyed as this couple who used to come in for little bottles of 7-Up every now and then. "Smash out the bottoms and use 'em for lenses," you'd feel like saying, the pair of them eyeballing merchandise up so close you wondered, you did, how they made out in bed, finding the right spots and all. Well, poor old Gran was like that, I remember, holding labels right up to her face to read 'em.

Oh, after Grampa died, Ruby'd take me upstairs to see her. Once I had on a dress, a big thick wool one, plaid, and didn't Gran ask why I was wearing a blanket, and later, why didn't I take off my coat? Another time, she made it all the way downstairs, surprising us both, Ruby and me. I was on a stool by the flour bin, measuring out five-pound bags, when she asked what I was painting.

You could've got away with murder right under that woman's nose, if you'd wanted to. Or so I used to think, though other times, in a blink, she'd catch you pinching a nickel or a DUBBLE BUBBLE gum. But the fact is, I was never around Gran all that much. She got to be like a ghost, creeping around upstairs — oh, sometimes you'd hear her, but like as not it was only the wind. And by the time she died — I was about twelve — I was wise to her. I figured it was her age, this business of not seeing — or of seeing only what she wanted to. Like mother, like daughter, maybe; as with Ruby's hearing, it seemed selective.

I'm knotting up the first garbage bag when Ruby creeps up behind me; there's her smell of tinned soup and bedclothes covered over with rose talc, the Avon I got for after her baths. She pauses in the doorway. I feel her watching over my shoulder as I stuff the last tufts of quilt into the second bag.

A wheezy, cantankerous sigh whistles through her teeth.

"Well, I declare, Dora. I never did see what you wanted that old blanket for, anyway. As if we didn't have enough old stuff around here already. You should fill up some boxes for the Sally Ann, or have someone haul everything off to the dump! Dusty old stuff, not healthy at all, dear. Bad for the lungs, it is, all this dirty old *crap*."

I don't turn around. I don't so much as bat an eye or let on she's there, but just keep filling the bag, till finally she hobbles off to her room. Her rosy scent trails behind, lingering; and something else, a sour odour, the same ancient, mildewed smell that's on my hands; or maybe she needs another bath.

I knot the second bag and drag both outside, stow them under the porch for garbage day. When I'm sure Ruby's fast asleep again, I put in a call to that doctor's office.

It's after hours, of course; a machine announces, "Leave a message after the beep." I clear my throat, spell out Ruby's name, then cough and tell the machine we'll be coming in next morning. This last part I repeat, so there's no mistake.

❖❖❖

They won't let us in, at first. "Appointments only, I'm sorry," the receptionist says in a rushed, syrupy voice. She turns and starts poking at a keyboard. "Tell him we'll wait," I say, not budging. And when she sees we're not going anywhere, she shrugs, pecking at keys, and tells us to have a seat.

The waiting room shifts and eddies like a game of musical chairs. When an opening finally comes, the doctor smiles, harried but pleasant as a summer's day.

"What can I do for you?" he wants to know, checking his watch.

"I'm not leaving," I say, "till I get some satisfaction."

"What's the problem, Miss Hammond?" he says, in a voice like Quincy's.

"It's like I told you last time, doc." I move right in, not mincing words. "But worse, a hundred times worse." It doesn't matter that Ruby's standing there wringing a knot in the front of her coat, staring me down like a bomber on D-Day. Quincy runs his hand over his hair, looking like the sufferer in a Preparation H ad — pained, but open to suggestions. Go for it, I tell myself, quit beating around the bush.

"Truth is, doc, I got about a foot left till the end of my rope!"

His fingers lace together, do little push-ups off each other. He nods, nonplussed, and asks Ruby to have a seat. His fingers unlace, motion me to sit too. Reluctantly I do, on a hard extra chair, its upholstery like outdoor carpet; I pinch my lips together as he starts asking questions, most the same as last time.

"Caregiving takes the patience of a saint, Miss Hammond. As I suspect you know." He smiles at me, kindly this time, leaning forward a little on his elbows.

He asks Ruby to draw a clock again, an infernal clock.

"Well if that don't beat all," I say. You could slice meat with my tongue, it's that sharp. If I were shopping, you can bet I'd take my business elsewhere — so fast his ergonomic chair would spin. This sits on the tip of my tongue, but I manage to keep from saying it.

And next thing I know, he's got his arm around Ruby's shoulder, shushing, comforting her, cosy as if he were a grandson, yes, a grandson.

"I can't stress how important it is for caregivers to maintain calm, Miss Hammond, to avoid subjecting the patient to stressful situations, anything that causes agitation."

He opens her file and scribbles notes. Without looking up he asks what arrangements I have in mind.

"Arrangements?"

"Plans," he says, "for long-term care. You realize, of course, that waiting lists are lengthy."

"A home, you mean?" It's not as though the thought hasn't crossed my mind — but a picture grips me of Ruby wearing a paper hat, singing *bok-bok-bok* from a wheelchair, making chicken wings to "The Bird Dance", her stare as vacant as those of spryer folk square-dancing past her.

"I just can't see it, doctor. Anything, but not a home. It'd kill her." My voice lowers to a whisper. "I mean, she is ninety. So my question, I guess, is, how long could this go on? I mean——"

"You'd be surprised." He shrugs, gives me a wan smile. "What kind of support have you in place? Friends, relatives, community support groups——?" His question trails off gently. I'm not sure what it is about him that's hateful. But it's like hammering on a door when you know there's somebody home and they refuse to answer. He senses my feelings, he must, turning his gaze on me, all steady-eyed sympathy and concern.

"Nothing specific, not really." I eye him squarely.

"You must consider what's best for your aunt," he says, the smile worn off.

"Tell me something I don't know," I snort, groping for a bit of humour. He looks at me as if I've got two heads; his expression is a mix of pity and surprise struck with coolness. That does it.

"I've been with Mrs. Clarke the better part of my life, *sir*, so I don't need anybody telling me what ought to be done."

Out on the street, my hands shake so badly I can barely take Ruby's arm to guide her back to the truck. Through this whole episode she's been surprisingly mute — not at all her usual self. I could kick something, I'm that wrought up; the nearest thing, one of those chalkboards outside a restaurant, listing the day's specials. Shepherd's pie is one, and a piece of advice enters my head: "Never eat shepherd's pie in a restaurant, it's made of all the leftovers off everybody's plates, all mashed up together." It was Wilf who offered this; I guess he'd found a cigarette butt in his dinner one time.

All the same, my stomach growls and I think how nice it would be if Ruby and I could just go in and sit and order up lunch.

No chance, not now. She's tugging on me like a horse against its traces. No choice but to take her lead, bump and skedaddle with her along the next block. We get as far as the beauty parlour, where she stops for a breather, still not talking. For some reason I glance in through the plate-glass window and, lo and behold, who's right up near the front of the shop but Edna, leafing through a magazine, her head stuck under a dryer. Holding tight to Ruby's coat sleeve, I stop and watch; something about Edna's pose draws me, or should I say her lack of a pose? Under the bright salon lights, her face looks stripped without her usual orangey-pink lipstick, her moss-coloured eyeshadow. She looks softer, older — like a plain beige purse. Her lips move slightly as she pauses to read something, again as she lays the magazine over her lap to blow on her fresh-painted nails. They're bright coral, her normal shade, but through the window her hands have a greenish cast, a stubby workaday look despite the care; and what comes to mind is "lobster claws" in dish detergent ads. Ruby reined in beside me, I watch, fascinated, till something — I don't know what — makes me tap on the glass.

The stylist, a girl in a pink miniskirt, glances over, almost sneering; then Edna herself, plucked eyebrows lifted, her face blank at first, wrinkling in recognition. An odd, sudden shame runs over me like a paint-roller, from the top of my head down. My hand grips Ruby's too tightly. And Edna does something funny, not exactly what I was expecting — who knows what I expected? A smile cracks her face and she waves, fingers spread wide, her eyes lighting as she mouths, "Hang on, I'll be out of here in a sec!" She wiggles her rump in the blue plastic chair as if to show she won't be long. Ruby begins to tug again, grumbling, and I realize with an almost itchy feeling that Edna wants me to wait. Before I can pull her back, Ruby's cupped her hands round her eyes like goggles; she presses them to the glass, scowling.

I don't know why, but it reminds me of one time I was in Halifax; I had to go on business, chasing down a chocolate-bar salesman Ruby wanted to cut a deal with. I saw some Russian sailors — poor critters right off the trawlers, you could tell — gawking through the window of a lingerie shop. All agog, ogling bra and underpant sets — not racy ones, though, nothing black or lacy, but white and sturdy as your Kenmore washer/dryer duo.

"Ruby, come away from there!" I give her arm a good, subtle yank, but even through the window Edna sees; I can tell by her expression, puzzled, amused. She slips out from under the big bulky dryer, which looks like something from the *Starship Enterprise*; you half expect to see Captain Kirk's helper, the glamorous dark-skinned girl, emerging from it.

Edna's got a fancy new do. With this hair she looks completely different; you'd hardly recognize her. Her brownish curls are streaked and patchy as guinea pig chips; still damp, they poke from her scalp like hard, fat wires. I don't know how much longer I can stand here, an armlock on Ruby. But Edna stops and pats her head all over with the heel of her hand, applying little pressure — God, you wouldn't want to flatten it! The girl in the miniskirt grabs a mirror and turns it this way and that for Edna to observe. Finally Edna nods and slips the girl a bill. I see her pat the girl's arm, mouthing, "Keep the change," her lips pale. Hard to believe, but she must've forgotten her lipstick. Even from that distance her lips have a parched, bloodless look, coral-red long bled and dried into the cracks.

Sometimes, I've noticed — when she's really dolled up, going all out for a dance or special jackpot bingo — she outlines her lips with a darker shade, painting the top one like a camelback couch, one hump with barely a dent in the middle. And I wonder, boy, how she can look in the mirror and not see how fake it looks.

But there's no chance now for speculation. The next thing I know, Edna's on the sidewalk with us, blinking in the sunshine, both hands gripping her purse like a St. Bernard holding a keg. In all respects ready, pert and perky as can be — ready for what, I ask myself, still gripping Ruby for dear life, and forcing my own wrinkled mug into a grin.

"What a lovely su'prise!" Edna beams at both of us, laying her palm on Ruby's pilled sleeve. Up close her nails appear plastic, so shiny and fresh they emphasize the scrubbed, worn look of her face.

"I'll say, Edna. Fancy meeting you, of all funny things."

She gives me this coy yet curt look, as though she doesn't quite read me, then swings her eyes to my top. Notices everything, Edna; doesn't miss a trick. But maybe that's not such a bad thing in towns like this, where folks would as soon run you over as smile or speak.

"Blouse looks good, Lindy. Suits you. I knew it would; said so myself, the day I brought it over, remember? Why, the first time I saw Dorilda in it, I thought, 'There you go, that's a tog for a full figure, not the stick she fancies herself.' Oh yeah, fit's important. So I thought of you, Lindy, right off."

"You didn't," I say in a deadpan voice, dropping my eyes in respect for her mournful look. I wait for Ruby to pipe up with some crazy remark — some raw question or rumour about the sister-in-law — and embarrass me right there on Prince Street, downtown Caledonia. Go on, I think, spit it out now, Ruby, if you're going to; get it over with; make us both look like stunned, sorry fools.

But instead Ruby keeps mute, studying Edna as if she's some foreign script. With the open-mouthed, blunt curiosity of a kid — like me, the one and only time I went to church with Grampa, his church full of holy rollers.

Ruby doesn't blink, taking everything in.

"Mrs. Clarke?" Edna keeps beaming, hardly bats an eye. "Well what a *gas* running into people from home," she gushes, as if we're tourists — from Australia, "and mid-week, too. I thought you two'd be hard at work. I'm here all the time, of course; my hub says they could pave ten ball fields with the tracks I lay, comin' and goin'. But you two...well, seeing as you've got the day off, don't be strange, now — what say we grab a bite? I'd say this calls for sugar, wouldn't you? Some kind of treat."

XXV

Paint Chips

She's like a runaway bus, Edna; a washtub full of suds bubbling over. Makes you wonder what drug she's on. Then I think she must be play-acting, but no — it dawns on me, with a kind of awe, maybe this is her nature. Genuine as vinyl, her chumminess.

The treat she has in mind is tea and pie at the luncheonette across the street. I follow with Ruby as Edna holds her hand up to traffic, plunging ahead. For an instant the sun takes hold of the fresh gold streaks in her hair, and I feel like a dowdy old rodent tailing the Pied Piper. It'd be different, maybe, if we were friends.

Inside the little restaurant, she's sweet as the dessert she wants us to have. Ruby wrings her hands and I decline, saying tea is fine, and for a split second Edna looks miffed — thrown by a slipped mat, though, not your full-fledged carpet. Sitting side by side in the yellow booth, Ruby and I watch her nibble a piece of cherry pie, the filling like globbed red beads. Blood-clot pie, Daddy used to call it, though secretly cherry always was my favourite.

I pour out tea for Ruby and myself from the two little teapots, peel back the lids from the tiny tubs of milk, real careful not to spray Edna smiling across from me.

"Watching our weight, are we?" she giggles wickedly, blobs of pie moving around in her mouth as she mulls over the taste. The filling stains her lips a purplish red. Her eyes, ringed with crow's feet, dance from mine to Ruby's. If you didn't know Edna's age, she could pass for a lot younger, especially with that new hair — her eyes are vivacious, lively as a thirty-year-old's; pretty, almost.

She sees me looking, sizing her up; stares back at my blouse, winks. An approving smile. Check.

"I wish you'd join me, you two. I feel like a pig here, having all the fun." Then her voice turns serious. "You're not into that nonsense, are you, that high-fat low-fat business? Why, just the other day I was reading...and then, swear to God, didn't we get this woman. Well, normally I wouldn't discuss our clients. But oh Lindy, you would not believe——! Legs like a peashooter, honest to Pete, I would not lie. Pipe-cleaner arms."

"An *eat*ing disorder, the official cause of death, they told my husband. Well I don't know where they get their notions from, these gals — off of TV no doubt. D'you s'pose that's where they get their ideas, Mrs. Clarke?" Edna shouts, turning to Ruby. "Thinking they gotta be so thin? Well I don't know about your late husband, dear, but I know mine likes a little meat on his bones."

Ruby's tongue moves inside her cheek, her chin sagging in a frown. But her eyes just stare back, not offended or amused either.

"So how's business, ladies?" Edna shifts gears instantly; say what you want, she's a quick study. "That Mercer kid and his friends giving you a hard time, hanging around? Give 'em a piece of my mind, I would."

Her lips open and close delicately, finishing up her pie. She licks her fork to pick up the last few flakes of pastry. Then she lowers her voice, choosing her words.

"You know, Lindy, far be it from me to butt in, but if there's ever anything you need...." Her voice goes shy, strange for Edna. "Don't you hesitate to call. Being a family outfit, we've always got someone around." She shoots me this knowing look, as Ruby stands up and starts brushing invisible crumbs off her coat.

"Don's right particular," Edna jokes, a bit too loud, "about leaving clients alone. He's always saying if it were our loved one, he'd want somebody in the house. Nothing sadder than a corpse,

Lindy, 'specially one all alone and lonesome. Now I really hope you'll excuse my being *on*professional."

She claps her hand over her mouth and her eyes light on Ruby's old engagement ring, the one she hasn't taken off in years; its row of tiny diamonds. Ruby put it away for a time while Uncle was still living, but once he was gone, do you know, she took to wearing it again.

"Oh my, oh my, Mrs. Clarke, that is a beauteeful ring," Edna coos and for the briefest flash, Ruby's eyes spark. A quick, tingling glint like the shimmer of scales underwater, or a spoon stirring tea. Then, in the gruffest voice, Ruby mutters:

"Whosoever hurts a child'll be cast to the bottom of the sea with a millstone round his neck — the bottom of the sea, Mum says."

Eyes glued to Ruby, Edna reaches out and pats my hand. On her face is a sad, knowing look. "Well, sure," she says, and leans towards me. "Now, like I said, Lindy, anything I can do, you just call. I mean it. Looks like you got your life cut out now, Lucinda Hammond — I know what that's like! Look, when Dorilda took sick, Dorilda, you know, my sister-in-law, the one that...." Edna's voice trails off as Ruby starts to move from our booth. Tottering a little, she bumps the table with her hip, clattering the teapots and Edna's plate. As she stumbles past the lunch counter I throw my hands up, whistling through my teeth.

"No denying it, Lindy. You're gonna need help. I don't guess I need to tell you." It's meant as a kindness, I know, but something about Edna's tone makes me want to slide under the table.

"Help?" I can't stop my high-horse tone. But Edna doesn't twig, and instantly I want to gulp it back.

"You've got a hard row to hoe — a perfect stranger could see. Doesn't take a rocket scientist to figure that out, Lindy. And like I said, I'm around if you get fed up or lonely. I'm not trying to be interfering or insult you or anything."

Turning, I watch Ruby shuffle past the cashier, a fat, pimply girl in a red uniform, perched behind the counter. She gives my aunt a fast, cold going over with her eyes, as if checking Ruby for missing cutlery.

"Oh well," I say, hopping up — Ruby says jump, I say how

high? — "what do I owe you for the tea?"

"Heck," goes Edna, "don't worry about it. Your turn next time."

"You're sure now?"

"No sweat," she says, suddenly abrupt — as if miffed again somehow, or disappointed. But as I make a lunge for Ruby, already halfway out the door, Edna perks up.

"I mean it," she shouts, as if we're the only souls in the place. "Call me, Lindy. Any time you want."

Ruby snoozes the whole ride home, her head thrown back, mouth sagging open. Her upper lip's furred and puckered with lines like the little rivers a hard rain cuts in a freshly graded roadbank. A face like the palm of a hand, Ruby's, carved with a lifetime's worth of lines. Lifelines. A face I've watched so many times I know it cold, barely need to look to see her expressions.

Still, a couple of times my attention drifts from the road and I find myself staring at her, that gaping mouth. Twice the truck dipsy-doodles over the centre line, thank the good Christ nothing's coming. A tractor-trailer appears, swaying towards us over the crest ahead, eating up the other lane. From someplace in her throat, Ruby's breath breezes in and out, ragged as the clouds overhead, and God Almighty, in the thirty seconds before that rig roars past something crazy grips me, cold as fingers down my shirt, and I think, just one jerk to the left, that's all it would take.

The eighteen-wheeler blasts by, rocking us right down to the shocks. One second, that would've been all. How your life can change in a second, they say. One measly second. But as I watch the rig climb the hill in the rearview, a fat rattling caterpillar scaling the asphalt ribbon, this muzzy warmth overcomes me, lazy as rays of sun on a sultry day. It starts in my shoulders and works its way up to a thick buzzing in my ears.

In my brain Wilf's face lights up like a bulb; then, like a blown fuse or somebody yanking the chain, snaps out. And next I'm hearing Edna's laugh, of all things. Edna Pyke, who'd've ever thought — and to my surprise, when I catch myself in the mirror, I'm grinning. Who'd've ever — and such a damned busybody, too. A noseminder, Ruby would've said, when she was sharper. But a good head, Edna — the thought hits the spot like a strong cup of coffee.

A good head indeed, no matter what you say about her. We've all got our faults. It occurs to me how, despite hers, Edna's what some might consider special — no saint, mind you, but if not Mother Teresa, at the very least charity-minded, an earthly sort of guardian angel: a helper — a busy one, granted. A picture fills my head of Edna in a white robe, dialling for dollars, being extra careful not to ding her nails. I want to laugh out loud, yet there's something about her you have to like, something cosy. All the same, my mind's made up. It'll be one cold day in hell before I give Edna Pyke a dingle, especially to ask for help like she expects.

The closer we get to Arcadia, though, the more I keep thinking of her laugh. There's something about it a tad too jolly. Not nervous, God no, Edna's too full of herself for that; but full of knowing. You have to wonder about her husband — must be totally grey by now, about ready to hand over the business to someone. Their son? If I recall he's out west, living near their daughter; funny Edna's never mentioned them. But that, I guess, is her business, family matters; the funeral end being *his*. Such a peculiar line for a livewire like Edna to be mixed up with; maybe not.

You'd get the scoop all right, being in her position; always be the first to get the dirt on people, the juiciest, goriest details. Sure; you'd know things the folks themselves didn't live to find out.

If Edna'd been around when Ma died, she would've known the full poop. But it would've been her hubby's father running Pyke's back then; he would've been the undertaker.

I'd been with Ruby full-time four or five months when it happened. The body was still inside when I got there; that's what the firemen were telling my aunt, huddled by the lilac bush at the side of the house, the side that still looked okay. On the one facing the tracks, the first thing you saw coming down the hill, the shingles above the kitchen window were charred black. Aside from this, the place looked normal — well, as normal as it could've with Ma back in it, alone as she was.

Things had gone sour for her in Toronto, where she'd been

living, I suppose, with that man she'd followed from Caledonia. Mr. Bellefontaine, his name was; Ma had asked me once to call him Clint. She reappeared one day, fresh off the train; said she didn't like the idea of leaving the house empty all winter, in case of vandals or the pipes freezing. Ruby asked when she'd decided to become such a homebody.

Ma had only been back a couple of weeks, though she'd already been over a few times wondering when I was coming home, and why Ruby didn't give her my job while she put her name in at other places, till something else came up. Something that paid better and might afford us the chance to be "family" again, her and me, as she seemed to think we ought. Ruby said it was as if someone in Toronto had handed her a crystal ball — one with scenes from another planet that had nothing to do with ours.

"You're crowding her, Ruby! You got no call to do that, you hear? She's my girl. I say you better let her dance to her own drum!"

Oh, I heard the row they had, pleas and insults pinging back and forth like a badminton bird.

"Excuse me?"

Ruby wouldn't give her the time of day. After a while, whenever Ma dropped by, Ruby'd put on her coat and slip out for some fresh air, leaving me to fend for myself even if it was busy. As my confidence behind the cash grew, more and more Ruby'd leave me to it, taking off for the odd little stroll or tea break in the kitchen.

She must've been out walking that afternoon, a mild, greyish one in November. Though there'd been no sign of Ma; she hadn't yet been in for her usual IOU of cigarettes and the canned soup I swear she lived on. Ruby must've been one of the first to get there. Someone had smelled smoke and called the fire department — I guess there were fears at first it was the old, closed-up freight shed. I didn't know a thing about it till a customer — Sam Kaulback — came in and said it was our old place on fire, lucky there was no one home. It was vacant, he thought, because he hadn't seen Ma. To most of the town perhaps she'd grown invisible, as people do who go away and come back to nothing.

A fat fire, we were told. The investigators said the whole kitchen must've flared like a matchstick, judging by the path of the flames. But she should have had time to escape, they said; an able-bodied person would've, unless she'd fallen asleep. Which was unlikely, given the hour and the signs she'd been in the midst of cooking: the remains of a big tin pot, and a half-singed burlap potato bag on the floor, spared as the blaze raced through the cupboards.

Maybe she was making french fries the way Daddy used to like them — to entice me to supper? I've never been able to get rid of the image: Ma humming some tune like the one from *High Noon*; Ma a tipsy Grace Kelly with some of Marilyn Monroe's swagger; the lard melting on the stove. Maybe it caught while she turned to cut a potato; or while she had her eyes closed, dreaming of getting her house in order, Mr. Bellefontaine, Daddy and their doings all behind her. Maybe she just stepped back to freshen her drink.

I have this picture in my head of Ma dancing a twirling tango around the burning kitchen, a flaming halo around her head, her cheap print dress on fire.

They told us she was unrecognizable. But there was little doubt it was her; she would've been the only one in the house.

Back in the luncheonette, I'd had trouble not gawking at Edna; she must've noticed. Whenever our eyes met, mine would slither to her pie plate, her hands and arms with the sleeves of her pink sweater pushed back: permanently tanned skin, freckled, a bit on the leathery side.

I kept picturing those arms around the undertaker's waist, white and doughy now, likely, though heaven knows he wasn't hard to look at the time Ruby and I went to see him about preplanning. Handsome devil in his younger days — as was his father, I seem to recall — though it gives me the willies to think of such hands on my body. But if it's ever bothered Edna, she shows no signs. Nope; by the looks of her, she drives, smokes and paints herself on the profits. I wonder how many caskets' worth of Revlon she buys in a year?

But there you go; you almost have to admire Edna, not a squeamish bone in her body. A fair amount of gristle, never mind that big ingratiating smile she's always flashing, which makes you wonder what's behind it, what sorts of things she's bumped up against in the dark over the years.

One thing I've noticed, though: she hardly talks about *him*, her husband, and as I said before, never mentions her kids. I can't help being curious about them — curious too, piqued actually (and here it is, like the pit inside a peach), why someone like Edna would be interested in us. A mover and a shaker, she is, in some people's lingo. Except for her cough and that laugh of hers, kind of horsy and uncomfortable, which makes you think, here's a woman knows twice what she lets on.

Maybe that's why she makes me edgy. Earlier, in the restaurant, as I studied her ring, something about her laugh brought back the past, memories I thought I'd locked away and pitched the key to. Strange, I declare, how things bubble up out of nowhere, like the Fuller Brush man landing unannounced at your back door.

The fellow's name, if I must say it, was Earl Salpetrio. Heck, I can still hear his laugh: cagey, a little like Edna's actually, saying, "Name like that, how can you forget?" He travelled selling paint for a company in Saint John, which I guess is where he lived. He was married. I was all of twenty-five, just turned. Meeting him, he said, was my birthday present.

He was staying down in Spenceport, on his normal route from Caledonia to Apple River and on up to Springhill. Our store was out of his way, a detour he "lucked into" — so far off the beaten track, he told Ruby, that he'd left most of his sample cards back in his hotel room. Pity, too, as his company had just come out with some "swell" new colours, seafoam and tangerine, sure to boost business with home decorators.

It was 1959 — oh, Ruby and I still stocked paint and fabric, but just your basic broadcloth, and colours like yellow and blue.

Earl Salpetrio drove a brand new Valiant, a shiny pinkish red. During our drive down to view his samples, he turned up the radio to an ear-splitting level whenever a Richie Valens song came on. Once he yelled across to ask what my mother thought of loud music.

"My mother? Oh," I said, "that's not my mother, that's my aunt."

"Sorry I asked," he said, slapping his forehead, "don't mind me. It's just that you — look so young."

At this point I told him I'd just had a birthday and wasn't so young at all.

"Right," he said. "'Member, the name's Earl — rhymes with purl."

And I said, "Good enough."

Earl Salpetrio wasn't what you'd call handsome, not by any stretch. He was short, with fingers clubbed from years of nail-biting. But he was a snappy dresser, and he had these wide-open, serious eyes with pupils that swelled and shrank like algae dunked, then pulled from the river. They were dark, dark as a raccoon's. His hair was greyish blond, cropped; the bristles on his nape glistened like freshly dried silverware. He had a pencil-thin moustache and he had nice wrists — not too thick but not too thin either, no fear of him being a pansy despite his taste for natty clothes.

I don't know what possessed Ruby to let me go with him that day. Oh, she'd dealt with him plenty of times on the phone; his company had done business with us for a cow's age. But neither of us knew Earl from Adam the morning he stopped by. Ruby nudged me when the strange car pulled in, when he came and introduced himself and explained his predicament, a bit embarrassed, scratching the side of his neck. "Darn shame about those samples, ma'am," he kept saying. "I could kick myself." Perhaps he was only out for a drive, who knows. But didn't Aunt Ruby pipe right up, "Don't apologize. Lucinda here, I'm sure she wouldn't mind a break — that is, if you don't mind taking her down for a look. You'd have to bring her back, of course, but then maybe we could discuss an order."

He must've known Ruby's idea of "an order" was five or six gallons of white or, if she was feeling adventurous, green, enough to do someone's porch. We'd been planning to get out of the hardware end. But even in those days Ruby could be unpredictable. Or maybe she was just tossing me the ball, as she sometimes did, to see how I'd react. She was all the time saying, "When you're in charge, Lucinda. When the day comes. When I'm no longer able."

So I went with Mr. Salpetrio to see his paint chips. All the way to Spenceport, all along the River Road, the radio blaring, he'd honk each time he spotted a Volkswagen (twice), but it wasn't so much being friendly as giving the drivers a fist-shake. "Damn those Nazimobiles," he'd say, and I thought he was just being funny. But by the time we got to his hotel I could see he wasn't the joking type, no, not one bit, but straight-as-a-nail. I should've known, I guess, from the steadiness of his eyes on me every time they left the road.

Questioning, his gaze was — at first. Though there wasn't a lick of doubt in it as the Valiant shimmied around the final curve, the last sharp one before Spenceport and his hotel.

I didn't think much of the place where he was staying, a run-down old inn with an iron fire escape up one side and a flickery neon sign offering "Rooms". Might've been nice when it was new; you could tell this place had seen better days. The letters on the sign were a faded pink, half shy in that shameless, all-out sun — unlike me, giddy with glee to be out and about during store hours, and on such a fine day to boot. Maybe it was the freedom, the odd, simple luxury, that made me do things with Earl I mightn't have done ordinarily; freedom, which went to my head like a belt of rum.

I didn't even think to ask why he'd taken a room there and not farther up the road, at the new motel in Apple River.

Inside there wasn't a soul around, even at the desk. Earl's room was one floor up. The carpet was worn and stained. Cigarette burns on the dresser, I noticed straight off as he showed me in. He threw his jacket over the one chair. I wanted to sit but thought it might seem a bit fresh of me to take the only seat, especially with his jacket on it.

"About those colours," I prompted, glancing about the room. There wasn't a sign of a paint chip or sample card — unless he was hiding them under the bed.

"Right," he said, kind of startled. For the first time he looked a bit distracted, even impatient. He *plumfffed* down on the mattress, patting the spot beside him.

"Oh come on, there's no big hurry, is there? Where's the fire anyway? Lie down, Lucy, I want to talk to you. Oh hell, I didn't mean it — who *said* that? Heck, you know I'm only horsing around. It's all the damn driving, you can see that, can't you? Just gimme a minute to catch my breath...."

Maybe I should've been scared — sure, the hair was pricked up on the back of my neck. But instead of chickening out, I returned his beady, sombre stare. The same look as when you corner a wasp, can either flatten it with the dishrag or swish it outside.

I settled next to him, our thighs just touching.

"However long you need — I'm in no rush," I said, half stunned at my brazenness. But I've got to be honest — there was something about his skin, the fresh-scrubbed shine of his forehead, made me want to touch it. Something that spiked my curiosity, like he wasn't quite real, this guy and his stuffy little room, the limp dirty curtain twitching in the breeze. Its smell, that's what I remember most: the carpet, the wallpaper. The stale, yeasty smell.

He grinned at me and lifted my skirt an inch or two, high enough to slide his hand over my kneecap anyways, and tickle the inside of my thigh. A warmth spread through me, then a heaviness, almost like cramps. All the time he kept his eyes on my face, on my mouth, as if waiting for me to say "stop". It was then I noticed how homely he was — yeah, homely; the redness of his nose, a tad bulbous; the weakness of his jaw. But I didn't care. These things didn't matter, not a whit. Not even when I imagined Aunt Ruby's voice someplace in the back of my head, talking inventory. And instead of being scared or shamed or revolted or even concerned about playing at least a short hand of hard-to-get, I lay back, unbuttoned my blouse and let Earl Salpetrio do whatever.

His fingers were rough and downright nosy, finding spots I hadn't known were there. His breath whistled through the hairs in his nose, which matched his eyelashes: short, gold and stubby. Like his hands, I thought, when I opened my eyes wide and watched his face.

His size startled me, I have to say, bumpy and ridged as a piece of bamboo. Thank God I didn't look. Maybe I winced, I don't know. I was trying so hard to be cool and calm and knowledgeable, as if I'd done this a hundred dozen times before.

I lay back and tried pretending I was someone else, some other girl, one of those glamour girls in a Sweet Caps ad. With blonde bouffant hair, in a red two-piece swimsuit with lips and nails to match. Even though Earl didn't seem to mind or notice that I wasn't.

But when it was over, I had to wonder what the fuss was about. Like some padlocked jewellery box someone might brag about owning but never actually opened. A letdown from the get-go, that pleasant warmth that washed through my belly when his fingers first did their walking. That feeling replaced by a cold, squishy ache, a swollen sogginess I can only compare to the feel of tinned clams, ones swimming in the can too long.

And afterwards, when Earl fumbled for his clothes, his gaze was no longer direct or intense but wishy-washy, dim as a puddle. His hands were clumsy helping me back into my things; chapped-looking too, I noticed, and smelling faintly of turpentine.

"About those paint chips," he said, patting his front pocket for fags, then making a dive for his briefcase.

The samples had been in there all along, it turned out. Nothing but a ruse, far as I could see.

After slapping his satchel on the bed and rooting through it a while, he handed me a whole raft of cards. He was cool as cantaloupe, as though there was not one thing the slightest bit fishy about it.

"I thought you said——" I piped up, poking him with my elbow. "Why, you could've saved yourself the trouble." My voice was a lot more playful than I felt.

He dug through his case some more and pulled out a picture. It was a snapshot of his family, a wife and three kids. Not bad-looking, any of them, if you like frogs: three snub-nosed boys the spitting image of their dad; the wife short like him, and pretty, if slightly bug-eyed.

He blushed, his shoulders sloped, eyes kind of hot and fevered-looking as he tucked the photo back inside, under a stack of brochures. His expression a lot like Ruby's the time a *Carry On* movie came on and I was slow switching to another channel.

"That Mona, I gotta say, she's the devil in a dress. She's one tornado, that woman. Know what I'm saying?" He sucked his teeth, kept shuffling through his case, arranging the papers in tidy piles.

What's your point? I wanted to cut in. I felt like shouting and growling at once: Watch, I'll huff and I'll puff and you *see* what happens. As he snapped the bag shut, I felt like seizing it and giving it a good shake. For the satisfaction of having those forms and samples of his fly every which way.

But he kept yammering. "I got to hand it to you, Lu——"

"*Lindy*."

"You're just like I thought you'd be, honest, from the first time we spoke." I had to shrug; except for earlier that day, I could not for the life of me recall the occasion. "Only you're ten times nicer."

I couldn't help rolling my eyes. "Whatever."

"It's a fact."

Then came an ugly silence, but for the sound of us breathing, me itching to be out of there.

"Trouble is——"

"Like you were saying?"

"About those new shades——"

"S'pose we let Ruby decide; she's the one does the ordering."

But it was as if I hadn't spoken.

"This doesn't mean I'd ever hurt you. Not intentionally, anyways."

Meanwhile, that clammy feeling had crept back into my pants and all I wanted was a bath, and no way was I using the tub down the hall. Moreover, this soul-baring of his was making me about crazy to hit the road. If I'd been curious earlier, my feelings now were flatter than a squashed fly.

I know it may sound sick, even disgusting, but all I wanted was to get home, get washed, get *something*, without Ruby catching on to what I'd been doing.

INTERCESSION
Memento Mori

Dora-Lucinda-not-Mum takes me to see that man again. I don't know who he is. He has grackle eyes; he crackles a sheet of white from a little book, asks me to draw. Something round, something not a face. A clock, maybe. Round as. The earth is. Round.

He and the woman-not-Mum whisper things. The woman — my sister? my niece? or *is* she my mother? — has a stupid smile.

"Forgetful...."

"Spatial difficulties...."

"Trouble remembering...."

"The *simplest* things...."

"Sorry," he says, "I can't be more specific."

Spe-cif-fuck.

"Forms of...."

"Dementia."

De-men-sha.

No sign...

No means of...

A firm di-ag-no-sis.

Means. That other word.

Alzheimer's?

Oldtimer's.

The paper crackles — burning grass?

I sniff.

Smoke?

No.

The man hands me a yellow stick. Again he says:

Draw me a clock, Mrs. Clarke.

Mrs. Misses?

Make the hands say two o'clock, he says.

No smoke. No fire.

My hand traces a flat ball.

What time is it, Mrs. Clarke?

No time. No chance....

We escaped with the clothes on our back, I tell them both.

The man puts his arm around me.

Don't touch me.

What arrangements—? The man looks at the woman not Dora-not Lucinda-not Mum. They talk in little voices.

Liar. I slap down the yellow stick.

Liar, I look them both in the eye.

Liar, liar, pants on fire, a child sings in my head, *Can't get off the telephone wire....*

If you holler, let him go — out goes Y-O-U!

Web, I tell them, wed. Tangled, tangoed. Whispers, whiskers. Whisky, whisk. Sweep, broom. Breath, sleep.

Thoughts chug like an engine through snow. Words flap, rags on a line: a clothesline, in drizzle. Inside me, the same grey. Of rain, maybe. Or sleet.

Out on the street. In a small smelly place with booths. Another woman the woman with me calls Edna.

Who are you? I want to ask but the tea is too hot and I want to sleep.

Even this Edna seems to know me.

Mrs. Clarke, she says over and over. Mrs. Clarke this, Mrs. Clarke that.

Shut up.

I stand and leave.

Dora-not Dora follows. Her face is shiny. She *looks* like my sister coming in from the rain.

Behind the wheel she talks, talks, talks. Points out things, keeps talking. When she talks she sounds like Dora.

Until the road turns off her voice.

XXVI

Peanuts

We got into the Valiant, Earl and I, a healthy spread of seat between us, and he drove me back up to the store. Ruby was holding
court as usual at the register, helping a farmer order feed. She paid
hardly any attention to us, except to remark, "So, you didn't tell
Mr. Salpetrio what we needed — well, I'm not surprised. Ten gallons of white, another ten of shutter green and, oh, you could
throw in some grey too, while you're at it."

She gave us both a perfunctory smile — who knows but she
could smell something off us, what we'd been doing. Though in
Earl's case I'd say any odours, any clues to that sort of wayward-
ness, were well concealed by chemical spirits.

Outside, as he was getting into his car, he kissed the side of my
head — I turned and he missed my face — and said, all ajitter, "I'll
be calling, Lindy."

Which he did, a few times actually. (I'll give him this; he was
true to his word.) But he always spoke with a hoarse, breathy tone,
as if doing his best to whisper and still sound normal.

"I've got to see you," he said each time. The pleading in his
voice was enough to make you cringe. Each time I told him, sorry,

I was awful busy.

"I can't get you off my mind," he said, the last call.

"How may I help you?" I answered, in exactly the tone Ruby had me use on customers, because she was right there and I knew she was listening.

"I'm afraid we don't carry those," I said. "You'll have to try elsewhere."

And I guess that did the trick, because he quit calling after that. What a load off my mind, no longer having to lug around the image of his frog-faced wife and kids.

And that was about the size of it, my fling with Earl. Except for a few months later, when Ruby came out with one of her comments, a real humdinger.

"It's like the taste for peanuts," she said, right out of the blue. "Once you develop the taste, that's it, you have to have it. A craving almost, dear; yes, just like the taste for salty foods. You never quit wanting it."

I still don't know how she knew — unless Salpetrio had gone whining to her. After I told him to try someplace else, he kept his dealings strictly with Ruby. Though I doubt, somehow, he would've had the nerve to mention our afternoon.

But sometimes the phone would ring and, if I answered, the line would go dead. Once or twice, in the split second between my picking it up and that little click, I half expected a woman's voice, a croakier version of his, perhaps. But no. The caller never spoke. And who can say if he ever told his wife about us?

As far as I remember, Ruby kept getting paint from the same supplier, the year or two longer we stocked it.

But that's a long, long time ago, and I've got other worries now — bigger fish to fry, as they say. As we pull into the yard I give the poor old gal a nudge to rouse her from her nap.

Ruby's eyes snap open, and in the same instant her mouth claps shut. She smacks her lips as though she's been dreaming about food.

Inside, I hear the phone ringing, that nervy sound that makes you feel like your limbs are rubber and you'll never reach it in time; part of you thinking: Oh go to hell, it's likely someone bumming money or flogging something. Then I think, Heck, what if it's Edna, somebody like that? They don't find you home and, first thing, word's out that you've had some accident or skipped town. The wilder the story, the better.

After the tenth ring I grab it, out of breath.

"*Hell*-o!"

Ruby's still out on the porch, for godsake. Make it quick, I think, wondering if she'll take off; how far she'd get, the twenty seconds my back's turned. Lord, you need a videocam in the back of your head!

"Lindy?" Wilf's voice crackles; I detect a funny catch to it even though he sounds miles and miles away. "You take off or something? I've been trying all day to get you. Jeez, I was starting to wonder if your phone's on the blink, or what."

Maybe it's my imagination, but there's something in his voice sounds a little ticked off. But like I say, it's probably just me.

In the background a roaring starts up, nearly drowns him out. I realize he's calling from the truck phone. The crew must be back at it, going full tilt to make up for the delay.

"Where are you?" I yell.

"Don't mind the noise," he yells back, "that's just the grader."

He says something else, garbled words that seem to go right over my head; he might as well be talking to the sky. Meanwhile I've got the line stretched like a bungee, listening for Ruby out on the stoop.

"Hang on a sec," I shout, an urgency in my belly as if I need the bathroom. "I've just gotta check Ruby."

But this goes over him and his voice keeps crackling at me.

"Just a minute," I cut in, and there's a sigh.

"So, Lindy, how does six tomorrow sound?"

"Six what?" I'm almost dancing, I'm so keyed up. It's all I can do not to let the cord snap back on itself.

"Huh? Six o'clock! My place, the trailer — how 'bout it? I'll surprise you. Got a pen? I'll tell you how to get there. Come on now, grab a pen."

"Mind if we have company?" I can't help sounding leery.

"Ten miles north of Caledonia," he goes.

"The boonies, you mean," I start to say, as the back door snaps shut and there's a rustling: Ruby getting out of her coat.

"Yeah, the boonies all right — you're a fine one to talk, holed up where you are." He laughs. "Listen, you sound kind of ...busy. You on the moon or what? Pull yourself out of it. Let me cook for you; I'd like to. Give you a little break." He pauses as the grinding behind him grows fainter.

"What about Ruby?" I prod.

A humph, another pause.

"Well, the more the merrier, I always say. Though I'm not too used to entertaining more'n one woman at a time."

"What do we bring?"

He breathes in, considering. I picture his shrug.

"Oh — jeez. Just yourselves."

"Wilf?" I pause. "We can still have a good time." I sound like a broker — worse, as if I'm apologizing — but something in his tone makes me think he could take back his invitation.

"That's right," he finally laughs, with a good-natured snort. I hear the window whirring down. "So, is six good?" he asks, his voice the tiniest bit testy.

"Oh yeah."

"You got some paper handy?"

I grab the closest thing, a dogfood coupon, and take down directions on the back. "Ten miles north, right at the Irving, left at a church," I reel off.

"I'm looking forward to this, Lindy," he says, suddenly gruff, remote. Maybe somebody else has gotten into the truck, or he's hungry — that's it, I think: he hasn't eaten in a while.

"So what's cooking?" I pipe up, as he says goodbye. He doesn't catch it; there's just the click, a bit of static, as the line goes dead.

When I turn around, Ruby's in the kitchen with her slippers on, drinking the dregs of an old cup of tea left from the morning.

"Jesus!" I grab it from her, then think, what the heck, if it makes her happy, what's the difference? But I go and turn on the tube and, while she's watching, brew her a fresh cup — though, Lord knows, she'll say that's too hot.

Throwing together supper, I mull over Wilf's invitation. I should be excited, should be thinking about what I'll wear. But my main worry is what to do if Ruby goes mulish on me and refuses to come. I can't leave her alone, wouldn't dare, now. What I need is a babysitter — a bit late in life, I'd say.

A carrot in one hand, peeler in the other, I go in to broach the subject.

"Can I warm up your cup?" I start, then see it's untouched. Her tea's stone cold, the way perhaps I should be serving it.

"How'd you like to go out for supper tomorrow, Aunt Ruby?" I slide the cup out from under her curled fingers; a little tea slops onto the doily.

"What's that?"

"Supper. You remember Wilf?"

"Wolf?"

"Wilf, you know — m-my friend, that fella we had over once — remember him? Mr. Jewkes, the man working on the new road."

She gazes at me, sucking in her bottom lip.

In that moment, her eyes look like drops of green soap gone hard: the smelly old stuff Gran used to bleach flour-bags. She had this idea for making quilts out of them — not that she ever had to, mind. God knows she had the pick of the goods in the store.

But she got funny when she got old, Gran did; full of funny notions. "Waste not, want not," she used to tell me, though from what I could see, she'd never wanted for anything in her life, her married life anyways. To my knowledge, the only quilt she ever sewed was the one that's in the landfill now. Lord knows what she did with those flour-bags after they were washed and split. If she made quilts, they must've gone to charity, because we never saw them. Not me, Aunt Ruby nor Ma — though when Gran started saving flour-bags, the last thing on my mother's mind was quilts. Well, besides the weight of one on her bed — more likely the weight of Mr. Bellefontaine, or some other man.

Later, in my bed, I dream about Wilf: some vague, messy business. He's talking to me through a phone, except I can see him. We're in the same room, but he's on the other side of a sheet of glass, bulletproof like the kind in courtroom dramas, those TV programs showing prisoners speaking with lawyers. I'm sitting at a bare wooden table, listening, nodding; smiling encouragingly through the glass. I'm not sure which of us is the prisoner, which the lawyer. But something about Wilf's gaze gives me the creeps; it doesn't match his joking voice. His eyes are cold and steady through the glass, which looks licked and smudged, and smeared with lipstick; they're not Wilf's eyes at all. He has a brush cut. His body is tightened and shrunk to the size of someone half his age: youthful, svelte — heck, a bit on the short side, but...desirable. He's wearing grey cuffed trousers, not his usual jeans.

The walls of the room are concrete blocks freshly painted pale yellow, like the interior of a school or hospital; institutional.

"Somebody open a window," I shout — the paint fumes are that strong, they're making me woozy — but there's nobody but Wilf to hear.

He puts down the phone and moves closer. In the same instant I get up from the table and, standing tiptoe, pressing myself to the glass, I close my eyes and pucker up, waiting for his kiss — well, the sticky warmth from his breath. When I feel it, my heart drops like a dumbwaiter.

"Okay — so it's you," I sigh. "I guess this is it, Earl."

But when I open my eyes, it isn't Earl and it isn't Wilf staring at me through the glass, but Uncle. A tree-root dangling from his fly, an ugly purple tube like on a horse — the ancient stallion that pastured near the slagheap when I was small.

The rest of the dream I can't recall.

Like a craving for salt — sure; Ruby was right about the flavour. But she was wrong too; I've learned the hard way there are more pressing, if less tempting, things in life than chips and nuts. That doesn't mean I've lost the taste.

When I snap out of the dream — lying there in the dark, my sheets clammy as a root cellar — my mind creeps back to Wilf. The thump of my heart pitches to a sharper tempo.

Imagining one button opening after another, I try picturing the flesh under those sturdy, roughneck clothes. If he'd been born thirty years later, I imagine he'd be like those young fellows you see sometimes passing through in shiny new Jeeps, en route to some outdoor adventure, skiing perhaps, or fly fishing. In another life, sure, I can see him wearing a suede ballcap, sunglasses, maybe one of those khaki vests with all the pockets, zippers and flaps, like anglers wear. The only difference being that a lot of those young fellows must be vegetarians, they look so pale and gaunt through the tinted glass, and Wilf has colour.

Yes, he does; in my mind I've got his shirt off, one of my hands working down over the wiry grey hairs on his chest, the big hard mound of his belly — his belly, which I'd rather not see naked. So I skip that part, go lower. Imagine my fist around something like a dinner roll, kneading....

I imagine him moving against me, touching a spot, a certain spot.

Before long, Wilf's face and body disappear, leaving just that feeling, a swollen liquid wave that is honey-roasted cashews, dark chocolate, sugar salt and spice rolled into one.

A taste, all right. A craving.

Who knows but Ruby gets the same, in that bed of hers all these years without Uncle...?

We have a bugger of a time finding the trailer, Ruby and me. On the dirt road north of Caledonia we take a left, then a right, just as Wilf instructed. But instead of an Irving station there's an Esso, and by the time we get turned around and on the right track it's practically dusk, and Ruby's jumpy as a cricket.

The dark makes her worse, I've noticed, and even though it's finally spring, darkness comes on too fast, draping everything like the black cloth those old-time photographers used to flip over their cameras.

"Dammit," I mutter under my breath. It's got to be after seven. I have this sinking feeling, picturing Wilf and a tableful of shrivelled-up food. But just as I start to panic, we come upon what must be his driveway, set off from the woods and the ditch by two white wagon wheels flashing reflector tape.

"This must be it," I tell Ruby, who has taken to humming — half to herself, half to God knows whom, her poor old mother for all I know.

The lane to the trailer is long and straight, as level and wide as the side road itself. My heart stirs with...heck, what would you call it? Anticipation? After the struggle to find the place, after the grand entrance, I'm expecting some kind of estate. Not the yellow-sided mobile home we find perched in a clearing, a solid wall of spruce backing it. Out front is a floodlit patch of grass, two lopsided flowerbeds ringed with painted rocks.

The trailer itself is lit up like a Christmas tree. Wilf appears at the door; peering out into the yard, his face fills the window. From the truck it's hard to make out his expression, impatient or worried — about us getting lost, or dinner being burnt?

The white rocks glow in the darkness soft with the smells of woodsmoke and spruce gum. He wasn't kidding when he said it was the middle of nowhere — I mean, this is the sticks! A little shudder goes through me as I help Ruby to the ground. For some reason she's brought her purse — another thing for me to keep track of. Gently I pry it from her and lock it inside the truck. She doesn't seem to mind, though all the way to the porch she keeps tapping her wrist, as if feeling for a watch or bracelet.

"Who is that man?" she demands as Wilf, cracking a grin ear to ear, opens the door.

His smile lights the long, skinny room as he takes my jacket and Ruby's coat and goes to hang them in a narrow closet. When he opens the door, things tumble out — a mop, an orange vest and a camouflage hat, a jaunty rainbow-coloured feather stuck in the band. One hand on the small of my back, he shoves the stuff back in, and shows us into the kitchen. The smell of food wraps itself around me like a warm, delicious mist.

It could be Betty Crocker's kitchen, swear to God. Everything's neat as a pin: spotless harvest-gold appliances, pots on the stove with their lids just so. A lovely big roast with a bone-handled carving set stabbed into its centre. Frilly yellow curtains at the window above the sink, a hand-crocheted dishrag dangling from a ring. I don't mean to be rude, but it's all I can do not to gawk as if taking notes.

Wilf waltzes us into the living room, long and dark as inside a freight car, a tunnel. Everything is deep maroon: the flocked wallpaper, the chairs, the low velour couch. It makes me think of a bordello — not that I have first-hand knowledge — but for the ailing spider plant dangling from a white, beaded hanger, and the wide-screen TV filling one wall. Then I remember the big black dish as we drove up, like a huge, netted bowl or bug-trap outside.

Ruby goes straight to a La-Z-Boy (it looks like real leather, oxblood, with little controls on the side) and pushes back till her scrawny toes point to the ceiling. They look knobbed and yellow through her pale nylons; she must've slipped her shoes off at the door, which I realize I've forgotten to do.

His hand never straying from my back, Wilf seems not to notice or mind. He leads me to the sofa, which lets out a puffy sigh as I sit and arrange my knees around the low, smoked-glass table. Stacked neatly on it are some magazines, mostly *Popular Mechanics*; I glance past the covers at the mottled red carpet beneath.

"Drink, girls?" he asks, and for the first time I notice the slick of sweat on his brow. Ruby gawps at the blank TV screen. I say, "Whatever you've got," and follow him out to the kitchen.

"We can eat any time," he says, pouring Coke into thick-bottomed tumblers. He gets the ice from a special dispenser in the fridge, tops up two of the glasses with rum. His hand shakes taking the one with plain cola in to Ruby. I lean against the sink and take a sip; the drink's strong enough to make my chin wag. In the other room I hear their voices, Ruby's far-off and faint, Wilf's boisterous, friendly; the TV being switched on.

I feel like I'm all feet and toes watching him bustle around the kitchen. He ties on a barbecue apron to carve the roast, which is still bloody inside, the same shade as the furniture. I know right away Ruby won't touch it. I keep sipping my drink while he mashes potatoes, then help carry in plates.

The dining room is small and dim, like a square cubbyhole somebody thought to tack on. The places are already set.

"Okay, Ruby!" he yells to the blaring TV. After a minute or two I put down my drink and go get her.

Wilf sits at the head of the table, which is a bit too long and too wide for the room. He's forgotten to take off his apron; the strings strain against his belly.

Three times Ruby asks his name. Each time he answers, "Wilf Jewkes," as if it's the first. She devours the food around the edge of her plate, skirting anything touching the meat. Then she burps, of all things, and there's this stubborn silence.

But the food's awfully tasty and I help myself to a second slice of beef. Nobody talks; Wilf just keeps giving me these loaded, hopeful glances, till Ruby starts banging her knife against her plate, and Wilf gets up and pours her another Coke.

Ruby accuses him of trying to make her drink ink, India ink.

At the end of the meal Wilf remembers the salad — chunks of hard, pale tomato, lettuce and cuke, which he plunks down on the table with a new jar of Miracle Whip.

I say I'm stuffed and lean back.

"My sister behaves like a slut," Ruby mutters, out of nowhere, and Wilf gets up to fetch the rum. "You'll just have to excuse her."

"Lips that touch liquor shall never touch mine," she caws after him.

When he comes back, his face looks hot. As he goes to refill my glass, I slap my hand over the top — "Whoa!" — and rum splashes everywhere, a sticky burning wet.

Ruby, meanwhile, has gotten up. She wanders towards the living room, Wilf trailing her. I hear him putting the TV back on, telling her how to use the remote.

"Come and talk to me while I wash up," he says, peeking in at me, so I go and stand in the kitchen watching him work. I feel kind of awkward, wondering what the heck he wants to talk *about,* now that dinner's devoured and there's nothing to speak of left on our plates. Besides, he's in a sweat now, obviously; the apron strings are cutting into his neck, little dark blotches showing through his dark green shirt as he scrapes fat into the garbage.

"She's a card, that aunt of yours," he says to the dishwasher. "Bet she was one corker in her younger days." We listen to Ruby in the next room, zapping from show to show, the vicious white noise between channels.

"She is that," I say, grabbing that fancy dishrag off its hook and wiping down the sink — never mind that it's already clean.

When I turn around he's reaching for something on top of the fridge. It's a little blue box, kind of furry-looking, soft. He plops it into my hand.

"What's this?" I step back, dizzy, I guess, from the rum.

The room swims. Wilf's face lengthens and stretches as though it's under water.

"Go on, open it, Lindy. Let's see it on you."

The box snaps open like a set of dentures.

I start to slide, to lose my footing on his shiny cushion floor. The room must be a hundred degrees; my face feels like hot pudding. I feel instantly sick, all that Coke and rum and beef, my head like a dust cloud over my stomach.

The ring twinkles from its blue velvet nest.

"Sweet shit!" I cover my mouth but too late, it comes out anyway: a high-pitched choking giggle, a gurgling brook full of giggles, a river, a torrent. My hands are all thumbs; they shake so badly I can barely pick the thing up.

"Go on." He coughs, his face like a Canada Day balloon. "I hope it fits." His hands are shaking too; they feel soggy as hot bread in a plastic bag as he helps me slide it on. My liver's doing loop-the-loops. It takes the two of us to get the ring over my knuckle.

"This is *not* real," I gasp, then, "Oh my frig," when I see that, yes, it is. "Wilf — Wilf Jewkes, what the hell?" The tiny solitaire glitters on my spotted, veiny hand. "G'way with you, Wilf. You can't be serious. Tell me you're not serious — are you?"

The look in those eyes tells me he is, yes ma'am, bet your sweet bippy, as they used to say on that foolish show, *Laugh-In*. Dead serious. It makes me want to run, run fast, to the bathroom, to the truck, anywhere.

"Holy good shit, Wilf."

His face goes flat as pavement. "You don't like it?"

"Well sure I like it, but...it's just that—"

"I'm not in no hurry, if that's what you're scared of. I — we — got plenty of time...."

"—I ain't used to surprises," I say, in the hillbilliest voice I can muster offhand, the sweat jumping out under my arms. I feel instantly stupid. And he's not thrown, not for one minute.

"You think about it, now, hear? Like I say, there's no rush, we got our lives in front of us. But you think about it, then give me an answer."

What exactly's the question? I think, but for once have the

presence of mind not to ask.

"Fair enough." I nod, and he wraps his big, heavy arms around me. When he kisses me, his lips are hot and slick and sweet with cola.

Fear, shame and excitement break out like a rash of impetigo; I feel it all over my face.

"Oh my, oh my," I manage to bleat, squirming from his hug, needing to be someplace alone, someplace where he can't see me — any place — just to get a gander at my hand. It's like the first time Ruby paid me, only a million times more complicated; yet I feel like I'm twelve: the shame and wonder of that crisp cash-money, me looking at it, counting it and not wanting to spend a dime.

And it's all I can do then to go collect Ruby, tear her away from her show and get us out of there. I barely remember to thank him for supper; I don't even kiss him goodbye.

"Oh my, oh my, oh my," I marvel all the way home, and I probably shouldn't be driving but I'm doing it anyway. And Lord, Lord, as we bounce down the side road and onto the highway, I pray that out there somewhere is a guardian angel. Not just one, but two — oh hell, make that three: one for each of us.

XXVII

Break and Enter

How things can change — if not in a second, then in an evening.
And how I wish we could pass on this fact — like turning down a
helping of meat — the moment we pull in.

I know right away something's wrong, even though it's late
and it's dark and I'm still dumbstruck by the twinkle on my finger.
I know right off there's been trouble. What kind and how bad, it
takes a while to register. But soon as I see the door jimmied off the
hinges, I know. Three or four steps and I know, and I fairly shove
Ruby back into the truck and lock her in.

Sweet jumping Christ, I can barely credit it: we've been robbed.

I know what they tell you to do in situations like this: sneak off
quietly and call the cops. But I'm not thinking straight, marching
up and peering in. The door's a black hole, like the entrance to a
cave, and all the mess, shattered glass and tins and wood, dark
lumpy rubble in a place with no light. No light whatsoever, except
what falls from the moon and a streetlight, a pale round pool of it on
the gravel outside.

It's all I can do to train my eyes and keep my heart from jumping out my throat. It's the kind of scene you dream about: a bad, bad dream, a fever dream, the kind you get with mumps or measles, a nightmare where later you pinch yourself, the pale tender part inside your arm, and squeeze real hard to remind yourself what you're seeing is real, you are awake.

Oh I'm awake all right, but God, how I wish I weren't.

Venturing in, I about break my neck slipping on a loose can. Every blessed shelf and freezer is turned upside down and torn apart, toppled jars and tins everywhere; what isn't rolling, smashed and spattered every which way. Spread in the slew of smashed glass and plastic is a black puddle that in the moonlight looks like blood, except it's gummy-thick and sugary, sweet when I squat and touch it and smell it off my finger. A sickly mix of jam and ketchup, floor polish and soda pop, and God knows what all else.

But worse is the silence, the dead-weight silence, nothing but the hum of the upended freezer, the echo of that rolling tin; and outside, a faint scratchy sound coming from the truck, Ruby scrabbling like an animal. For a second, frozen, I think I hear breathing — till I realize it's mine: high, shallow sniffs, my lungs pulled tight as the top of a Crown Royal bag.

On my hands and knees, dodging glass, I crawl up the aisle — crazily I think of those nuts who walk on beds of nails and feel nothing. On all fours, I creep like a baby to the counter...Christ knows what's going through my head, something I got off *Dragnet*? Keep your head down and they won't shoot. These words loop around and around my brain as I pull myself up to the counter.

Right away I see the phone ripped from the wall, the cord hacked up like so many licorice Nibs, and on the countertop a big pink rock like the one that sailed through the window that day.... And as you'd expect, the bejeezus has been banged out of the register, the till hanging empty and loose as an old tongue, no spring left to it at all.

I cannot fathom the mess, the evil that'd wreak such mayhem.

And just when I think I've taken in the magnitude of it, I see our new red pop cooler slammed face-down on the floor. The pale stretch of wall behind it looms like a blank picture window, a sickly yellow-grey in what little light seeps in. Splayed everywhere is jigsaw-puzzled plastic, a shiny dark river of pop leaking out underneath.

At that moment I guess I cry out, losing all caution. If the burglars were anyplace near, by now they'd have leapt out and slit my throat!

I start to weep, loud sobs racked straight from my chest. Outside there's a keening coming from the truck, shrill but muffled and far-off as if from the hills. Shut up oh God shut the fuck up, I pray and cry and curse all at once — to myself? to Ruby? — as I pick my way to the cooler. It takes me ten minutes to reach it — maybe ten seconds? — moving with the same dead-slow motion as if trudging through deep snow or a dream.

Except in a dream it mightn't seem so peculiar, what I find when I get closer. Poking out from behind the cooler, jammed between its metal footings and the wall, mired in dust and sticky grime, is Ruby's ledger. That old black ledger I've seen her reading, oh God, how many times, and when? The pages are glued together in a Lime Rickey slime, raspberry fingerprints all over the cover — what I can make out in the dark.

Takes me a minute or two to realize they're mine, the fingerprints, even longer to struggle to my feet and straighten up, the filthy old book half stuck to my bosom. But in that minute it seems the only thing worth saving, Ruby's ledger, the only thing meant to survive.

About as useful as the phone lying on the floor, I think in a brazen, shell-shocked way, stumbling and staggering outside. I can't even think about going back to check the safe. The stupidity of what I've done — going in alone — strikes like the slap of cold air on my face.

But the feeling of risk — my having walked blind into what could've been the eye of danger — doesn't quite hit till I make for the truck. Run, run for God's sake, a voice unhinges and screams in my brain, even as I pause, like some bleeding idiot, to inspect the door and think of a way to at least prop it over the hole.

Ruby's face like pale rubber stretched and pasted to the window, the awful scritch of her nails on the glass, drags me to my senses. It's only then my feet do what they're told, and I dash, head down, as if fleeing a barn aflame.

The ledger's still in my arms; I clutch it like a life-preserver, an oxygen tank, while bashing at the door handle. It doesn't want to open, then I remember it's locked. Ruby's face streams through the glass in one long white wail, her hands fluttering like doves around her head. Her voice is reed-thin, a shrieking fit to raise the dead, to wake the neighbours clean to Ferrona — if there were any.

"I've got to find a phone," I scream through the window. "Listen to me! Shut up shut up shut *up*, Ruby, don't you know we've been robbed? Can't you see we've got to find help? Help. Somebody, someplace. Help...."

But her hands just keep shaking and twittering in this crazy hell-bent dance, till finally I put my hand on the keys deep in my slacks pocket. Something snags it the way a wart would, and I remember Wilf's ring like a bitty piece of glass on my finger. I almost have to stop and ask myself how it got there.

"Shove over," I scream, jumping in — it cuts me in two to yell at her, but she's sprawled across the seat, those hands flying at me. If there was one spare rag of time, I'd haul off and grab them, and hold her in my arms, that tight, until she stopped. However long it took. Hug her till every ounce of craziness got squeezed out, whatever the hell it is that's been sneaking in and snatching her away. Bit by bit, a little more each day: the craziness, as if she's on a boat slipping farther and farther out, and I'm on the shore watching, and all I can do is stand there waving.

"Stop it stop it stop it!" I catch her hands, grip them till it feels as though the bones might snap, her wiry, brittle bones. And in the midst of her flailing, her shrieking — this poor crazy woman who is not Ruby, not anybody any more — it's as if the craziness fills me too. Infectious as a whirlwind ripping through the truck. And I must be going nuts, truly, because what I think of next is a chicken, a bony headless carcass. Which part of me could let go and devour, bones and greasy shredded meat and all — as if that bird were the craziness itself being cooked down for soup. Oh yes. I'd swallow it whole, screeching like a banshee till there were the two of us, Ruby and me, crazy as coots. And like a fox I'd feast on that soup till nothing was left but the grease on my chin, a bone or two beside me on the seat. I'd lick my lips and there would be

Ruby as she used to be, tut-tutting at me to use a napkin. Sober-eyed, sharp as a tack and strong; the way she was.

"Calm yourself," I finally utter, letting go of her, weary as Moses parting the sea. "Just stop and calm yourself right now." And with no warning Ruby pulls herself into a huddled shuddering ball, whimpering, and there's a smell and — God God God Lindy, it's your fault, you stupid bitch — I realize she's fouled herself.

But what I do is turn the key and start up the truck, spin out onto the road in the direction of Ferrona, so reckless that Ruby's old book clunks off my lap onto the floor. Ruby uncurls herself, gaping down at it. And her eyes go like haystacks in a high, high wind, the sight in them spinning, lifting, scattering.

I roar right past the Mounties' detachment, their squat brick place with the shrubs out front, cruiser parked alongside. I go right by without even thinking to slow down for the speed-limit sign. All I listen for is the fast *tick-tick-tick* of the engine, and Ruby's worn-out, long-drawn gasps.

She told me to call, Edna did. Any time. Day or night. And streaking down that pitch-black winding road, laying rubber on the curves, Betsy's old tires screeching fit to raise bears, maybe I don't even know it myself yet, where the heck I'm headed, but Edna's is precisely where we end up.

There are lights on at Pyke's, as I hope, the yellow brick-fronted building like a school or warehouse. Turning into the big paved lot, I catch a glimpse of the foyer, the soft golden glow of lights inside.

The heavy glass doors — sturdy as a supermarket's — are locked; instantly I'm reminded of the time, years ago now, when Mr. Pyke held those doors for Ruby and me, shook our hands and said, "Nice meeting you," after an appointment we had with him. Good God, a churlish laugh almost trots out of me despite the fix we're in. But it just goes to show, you never can tell. Where a body ends up, heaven only knows.

I stop long enough to press my face to the window, my breath fogging the glass. From the gold corridor inside, cosy baseboard lights wink red and yellow. Above them the dim walls arch like goldenrod, goldenrod half fuzzy, gone to seed; those small guiding footlights festive as Christmas ones, comforting as children's plug-in night-lights. For whom, you have to wonder.

But I'm reassured. I have my arm around Ruby now, pulling her with me like a Siamese twin, a spare limb. Through her coat I can feel her nerves twitching, her frail old heart pounding.

For the first time in ages, I'm almost glad of her presence. Part of me could almost stop and bury itself in her shoulder, in the musty, scratchy warmth of her coat.

"God help us," I mutter, tugging her along, my voice gently cracking. She moves with me so easily now that she could be a bit of grey goosedown, a feather like the ones that used to poke out of her and Uncle's pillows....

My feet, it seems, barely touch the walkway, concrete slabs lit with domed plastic Moonrays. The ground glows white beneath the luminous sign: D.S. Pyke and Son, Funeral Services. Twined round the words are spindly black lilies sprouting from a silhouette urn.

Ruby doesn't twig. Could it be she's sleepwalking? It's like escorting a ghost, an empty shell; towing a car that's lost its transmission. Docile as a lamb, she is — lamb already shrink-wrapped for quick sale.

Making sure we step over all the cracks, I lead her — a tipsy, feathery dead-weight — around the side facing the parking lot. The Pykes must have a private entrance someplace. Speeding up, I head for some garage doors that gleam in the moonlight like buckteeth.

It must be two in the morning.

Always someone home. I think of Edna, her soothing talk-show tone.

Halfway to the garage, the brick façade gives way to white siding; the warehouse roof dips to accommodate a bungalow pitched like a tent between the building's front and rear. Neat black shutters frame the windows, and between them is a door painted pink or purple, it's hard to tell in this light. There's a straw hat hanging on it like a wreath, gussied up with dried flowers. To the side is a little sign saying "Private" in peel-back, stick-on letters slanted black against gold; and right underneath, a doorbell which glows in the dark.

Holding my breath, I push it, counting one, two, three. In my head the numbers blend with a mishmash of prayer: Our Father who now I lay me art in heaven hallowed be thy sleeeeep. As the noise chimes out through the dead-still house, I half expect alarms to go off, or the skin-prickling howl of a large, vicious dog.

God only knows what time it really is.

Always someone home. Counting, praying, anticipating Edna's voice, I glance at Ruby gripping my hand, obedient as a shrivelled schoolgirl now, her face so white. Her eyes wide and vacant as the moon above, with only the faintest flickering of cloud across it. Please, pleeease, I plead, half silently, half aloud. The sweat is like tomato juice under my arms, that thick and clammy. The ungodly cheerful chiming burns my ears.

Just as I'm about to turn away, an outdoor light flashes on and the door shimmies open, jiggling the hat doodad, and Edna appears, an angel of mercy in her shiny pink robe.

"Jesus Murphy!" she gasps when she sees who it is. "Why, what in God's name is going on — this time of night — Lordy! You two better be glad I was still up reading, otherwise I'd've never heard the door. Takes me a while to go down, but — sleep of the dead, I'm telling you, once I'm under; I'd sleep through World War Three!"

A sweaty wave sweeps down my back as she stands gawking at us, one hand tightening around the neck of her robe. It's as if she's tracking UFOs, two of 'em, her eyes big and round — not so much disturbed or alarmed as baffled. As though she can't quite nail down who we are, though of course she recognizes us. And Lord knows what she's thinking. I have a wicked time myself, scraping my eyes off her face. Stripped of paint, even plainer than it looked in the luncheonette, it has the hard, blanched appearance of a drought-baked field. Good God, sprouting from her chin are two tiny bent hairs like corn stubble.

The imitation coachlight overhead doesn't help, washing us in its fishy hue, the same greenish shade as water in a goldfish bowl; and I remember with a sick jolt where we are and why we've come. But in the moment or two before she asks us in, Edna goes on fixing me with her pinched, myopic stare. Until at last she seems to snap alert, grumbling, "Don't mind me, I just took out my contacts." She's downright grumpy, deserves to be. Who can speak my relief as she comes unstuck, loosening up, and pokes her hand out, finally, closing it around my wrist? She hauls us in like stowaways off a wrecked ship.

"I hate to do this to you — just barge right in," I gush in the warmth of her hallway, inhaling the strange, flowery smells of food and perfume and something medicinal, antiseptic — Dustbane? I cut straight to the heart of the matter.

"There's been some trouble, Edna, up the store. I...I didn't know where else to turn, frankly. This time of night."

Meantime, somebody else has gotten up. I hear them bumping around in another room.

Jowly, bearish with sleep, Edna's husband shambles out in wrinkled green pyjamas. "Ed, honey, what's going on?"

In the pure white light of their hallway I remember Ruby cowering beside me, poor poor Ruby, and that odour only partly covered by the smells in Edna's house. Gently I shake off her grip. Both her hands fly up to her face, and it's then I see the blood crusted under her nails.

The husband comes up behind Edna, scratching under his waistband.

"Who do you want me to call?" Edna seems to spring into action, with hubby gawping over her shoulder.

"How do you do?" I mumble, awkward as all get-out given the hour, but oddly calm too. "Our place's been robbed," I say, and shrug apologetically, scrutinizing him in spite of myself and the situation.

He looks a good deal older than I recall the last time we met, the only time, I should say. He's pudgier, for sure, and greyer, and in those wrinkled pyjamas appears anything but slick. There's not a hint of ghoulishness — though I can't help eyeballing the hand on Edna's shoulder, pasty and ordinary as white sauce, I'd have to say, the skin a bit puffy around his wedding band.

A womanly hand, almost, maybe because of the ring. A hand you could picture scraping batter or stuffing a turkey. Not — well, you know.

"We've been broken into." I shrug again. "I s'pose the first thing would be call the Mounties."

Don Pyke gapes as if I've got four heads, then shifts his stare to Ruby. I know I should be shoving past to use the phone, like they do on *911*. But something stalls me, slows me as if I'm walking on the moon: zero time, zero gravity. Nothing any longer matters.

"I think they should know," goes Edna's husband, shaking his head. He's gruff but polite, officious — never mind the pyjamas. Here's a man, I think, who knows how to handle the throes of disaster.

"It's not that urgent now," I offer, as if to reassure or console *him*. I don't bother mentioning how I drove right past the detachment. Nor does it seem all that important, now, to say the phone line was cut. It doesn't seem worth it, going into detail with Ruby present — as if she weren't already upset. We've got something more pressing.

"Your bathroom——?" I whisper to Edna, ignoring hubby.

"First door to your left," she says, calm and knowing as if calling a round of bingo — as if this is old hat, folks coming in at all hours to use the washroom.

She rushes ahead and snaps on the light. There's the rattly roar of a fan.

"He'p yourselves to towels and warshcloths; they're all clean. Don't scrimp now; don't worry about it," she says, closing the door behind her.

Ruby's eyes thrash around the gleaming room — the flesh-coloured facilities and matching tile. Halfway up the walls, the tiles meet wallpaper flecked with silver, black and peach; it reminds me of canned salmon. The room smells of Irish Spring and, sure enough, there's a fresh bar on the vanity. At little intervals hang perfectly folded towels, all the same mauve, that look like they've never been used, the creases in them fresh as the day they landed in Zellers' Martha Stewart aisle.

I'm so busy taking all this in, I barely notice Ruby watching herself in the fancy mirror; around the edges are gilded cracks to make it look old, I suppose, antique — Roman, maybe, or Greek. I don't have time to ponder which, wondering how I'll get her out of her clothes and cleaned up, and what on earth I'll put her in when I do.

There's a gentle knock, and Edna's hand pokes in — like a magician's, honest to God, offering bunnies. A pair of nylon briefs appear, white Hannas, size large; a bit long in the tooth but clean. Some queen-size pantihose, taupe, still in the package. Outside the door there's a pause, the flick of a lighter.

"Dorilda's," Edna wheezes. "Those clothes I gave you, Lindy? Plenty more where they came from — I was gonna throw 'em out, but look, you never know who might be able to use them. I was plannin' to take a couple more bagfuls up to the Legion, for the box, you know; then I figured it might seem kinda funny — icky — handing down old undies. There's some would be insulted, you know. But in the case of emergency...." she's quick to add. Despite the fan, I believe I hear her exhale, the smoke breezing through her teeth.

"I'm obliged to you, Edna — really. Dorilda too," I throw in; it seems only proper.

When I turn from the door, there's a hunted, horrified look in Ruby's eyes gazing at me from the mirror, like the expression of a shoplifter caught in the act. She raises one limp hand, playing "Simon says" with her reflection. Dodging it, she steps aside, wobbling a little, lunging sideways as if to catch out whoever it is staring back at her.

"Dora?" Her voice is a whimper amid the roar. "Why are you here? Why do you keep wanting to steal from me?"

Forcing my mind to Edna's towels, the tiles, the swoopy gold faucets, I grip Ruby's hands, gently let them fall to her sides as I wrench her skirt up, then squat, closing my eyes as I work at her underthings. One by one I undo her garters, the cracked rubber like yellowish old skin, the nylons puddling around her ankles. She's surprisingly meek as I work down her girdle — like a pillow with the stuffing pulled out, she's that limp and unresisting.

Concentrating on Edna's Irish Spring, I manage to get her drawers off without too much mess, one hand around each bare shin as I ease her feet through, one at a time. I swish them out in the gleaming, icy bowl, tuning out the shock to my hands, and the water's colour — dark, dark blue, from some kind of freshener or germ-killer, I suppose, which looks almost black against that salmon porcelain.

335

My hands numb, I run hot water and wet a facecloth — the only used-looking one in a little mauve basket by the tub — and hand it to Ruby. I study the gold swirls on the light switchplate while she drags it between her legs, then I take it and give it a cold swish too.

As I'm straightening up, our eyes meet in the mirror, hers mortified, confused. Mine burn; our reflections ripple before me. There's that tinny taste of blood — from inside my cheek, I realize.

Edna hovers outside again. "Anything else I can getcha?" she says, in a hoarse whisper barely audible against that grating fan.

"A Sobey's bag'd be great," I whisper back loudly, "if you've got one handy." Seconds later she slides one in. I wring out the sopping things and stuff them inside; knot the bag tightly and shove it deep inside my jacket pocket. I give my hands a good long scrub with Edna's soap.

Ruby puts on the fresh underpants without a fuss, leaning into me with her knees. The pantihose is a different matter; I have to make her sit on the edge of the tub to get them on.

When she's shipshape, I breathe in one last whiff of that soap, its scent as deep as the redness of my hands, and take her arm as we slip out into the hallway. Edna's waiting; I tell her I've forgotten something in the truck, and while she settles Ruby in the living room, I dash out and lob the bag into the back.

Inside again, I let Edna lead me to a flowered wing chair; let her plump the cushions around me. In the background I hear her husband on the phone.

"Don't worry your head," I want to call out, shutting my eyes. "It's not worth the bother now." But I figure a man like that — even when it's a little late — is best left doing what he's good at, whatever makes him happy.

Edna flutters around Ruby, tucking her up on the matching sofa, sliding a rosy chintz hassock under her feet. She wraps an afghan around her, and a creamy Hudson's Bay blanket with stripes that in these cosy pink surroundings remind me of candy. Lifesavers or cough drops, the kind of sweets you like to suck on and make last.

"I owe you, Edna," I work up the steam to tell her. "I appreciate all this, I do." She glances up from her ministrations, a proper Florence Nightingale in that glossy robe that shows the outline of her rump. When she straightens, it gapes and reveals a patch of bony, freckled chest.

"Think nothing of it, Lindy — I'm glad to do it. What else are friends for but to he'p?"

Her tone sounds weary and cheerful as a Waylon Jennings song. It greases my heart with guilt.

"Look, I'm sorry about this, Edna; I truly am. Fact is, the whole evening's been like getting hit by lightning, you know what I'm saying? I mean, *normally*.... But I've got no call coming to you like this, getting you up in the dead of night." My eyes wander over the dusty-rose shag rug as I speak.

But Edna just pulls her robe tighter, and in that soft pinkish light, even without a stitch of makeup, her face is kind, appealing. Yes, even as she hobbles off to the kitchen, her bare feet yellow as a gannet's, her toenails a garish purply-red, I realize how kind. Beautiful, in a surprising way.

I glance at Ruby; her eyes are closed and there's an odd smoothness to her face. Then I take a good look around the room, so much rosy pink it's like a Mary Kay convention. On an end table are some pictures, a silver-framed photo of a smiling girl in a stewardess cap, another of a young man and his family, a chubby wife and a herd of kids dressed more or less the same in blue tartan vests and pants and jumpers. The man has dark-shadowed eyes like Edna's husband's. The stewardess, if you squint, looks a smidge like Edna herself.

"What do you take in your tea, again?" she hollers in presently. I hear the click as hubby hangs up.

"Whatever you're having, Edna," I mumble back. "Don't fuss on our account."

Her husband pokes his head in. "The Mounties'll be down shortly for a statement. I explained to 'em how you ladies are, well, in shock."

His smile looks sincere, but the way he says "ladies" makes me blush as dusky a shade as Edna's carpet. I look over at Ruby, out like a light now in her nest of blankets, her mouth wide open as a trap door, a mineshaft.

How life changes indeed, I think; give it an hour or two.

Like passing through the belly of a whale or a submarine — a trailer, for Pete's sake, if trailers had hatches. Going step over step from one chamber to another, each with no bearing on the last sealed shut behind you — and barely time to cool your heels.

It must be three in the morning.

It's while we're drinking tea at the dining-room table, waiting for the Mounties, that Edna notices Wilf's ring.

"What diamond?" I fairly start from the chair, clattering my cup. "Oh. *That.*" I realize I'm trembling again — the jolt of caffeine, the lack of sleep? Or perhaps I've been dozing, who can tell? But suddenly the scope of things comes closing in. A bright white panic grips me by the neck.

"What am I gonna tell the officer, Edna? What'll I say? They'll think I'm half cracked for going in there like I did!"

Edna shakes her head, for the first time looking a bit fed up, weariness starting to show like light through shims. Her eyes look woozy, as though she's longing for bed.

Which must be where her husband's escaped to; I bet he's one of those lucky dogs who can sleep or wake at will. The nature of his work, I suppose, never knowing when his services will be required. Being on permanent call, worse than a doctor. I wonder how this sits with Edna; not badly, judging from her looks.

She seems to know I'm thinking about her; despite the wooziness, she smiles suddenly, her eyes green and direct as a cat's above the rim of her cup.

"You just tell 'em what you feel like, Lindy; tell 'em the break-in shook you up so bad you had to calm yourself first, that's why you took a while reporting it."

"They're gonna think I'm nuts, driving all this way. When the buggers might've been right under our noses."

Edna goes to peek in on Ruby, sound asleep in there on the sofa. While she's up she pours more tea, the two of us hunkering over our cups at her brass-legged, glass-topped table. Those green eyes of hers soak up everything.

"Hang the store anyways, Lindy." Twisting her cup round and round in the saucer, this is what she comes out with. That gaze fixed on my face like a net.

"Nothing but a drag on you, in my opinion. I mean, I wouldn't go telling the RCMP that, but...." Serious, straight as a pin but rolling her eyes, she drags out the "RC". This cracks me up, suddenly, madly, my laughter breaking out like a chick from an egg.

Must be the hour, the sheer stunned craziness of everything catching up with me, and having Edna looking on. Slowly she joins in. I laugh and laugh till my head spins, aching-dizzy in the spiky shadows from her chandelier.

The two of us cackle like fools, like a pair of goddamn roosters. Till Edna sobers up enough to jump back to square one: "So. The ring, Lindy. Wouldn't be from that fella of yours, would it?"

I choke and splutter, wipe the back of my hand over my mouth. "As a mattera fact——"

But just as I scoop up the wits to tell her, I'm saved. First by the slam of car doors outside, next by that fancy door chime. It's like the bell-ringing of angels, unearthly; a whole bloody carillon pealing at dawn.

Edna offers to keep Ruby while I go off with the police; she promises to watch her like a hawk — even give her a bath. Never look a gift horse — I tell myself. At the door she gives me a clumsy hug, the officers looking on, brusque, impatient. "Anything of hers you think she'll need, out in the truck?" she thinks to ask, as if we'd had the time, Ruby and I, or the inclination to pack. "Oh, forget it — she'll be fine. Don't worry about a thing, I'll bring 'er up in the morning."

Don't you worry either, I want to holler to the Mounties as I'm climbing into my vehicle. No rush now; not like it's an emergency.

It's not till I'm halfway to Arcadia — the cruiser lights faint as the flash of a deer's arse ahead — that I remember Ruby's treasure, the sticky old book half wedged under the seat. At a crossroad I pull over and reach for it, set it beside me on her half of the seat. The image of Ruby sleeping on Edna's couch slithers through me, leaving a chill like water in a metal vase.

Stepping on it, catching sight again of the slow red flash lighting the distant trees, I bump my hand over the cover. It has the feel of old skin rinsed in Kool-Aid.

Fingerprints — the notion settles in my gut heavy as a plate of greasy fries. First thing they'll want is fingerprints; what they get will be mine over everything like a dirty shirt.

A voice inside me giggles, giddy, drunk on the lack of sleep. Who gives an owl-shit? It's all too late. Whoever ransacked the place is likely as far as Moncton by now. Farther, I think, watching the speedometer skip, then dive, marking a speed about as fast as a pervert making his way to a church supper. If I went much slower, dogs could piss on the wheels.

But it doesn't matter. "Nothing matters," I say out loud, one hand flat on Ruby's book. It offers a queer kind of comfort, there beside me on the seat. And later, when I'm showing the Mounties into the kitchen, and what's lodged in the doorway but Grampa's safe — as if marooned by a flash flood! It's scuffed on one side, where the scumbags must've yanked and dragged it out from beside the stove. Apart from this, like everything else in the room, it appears untouched — thank God for small mercies. It takes some doing to crack the combination, but when I finally succeed, there's the bag of money inside, exactly as I left it, a trace of pink plastic sticking out. "No need to count," I assure the officers, and one shakes his head. "I can tell just by looking it's all there."

Once they're through their questions and poking around, I get them to help me move the safe back — no mean feat, enough to bring a heart attack on some. On the way out, one of them looks fit to expire.

Then I'm alone, brooding over the mess, the old ledger on the table. Barricading myself in the kitchen, I bolt the door leading into the store. Sitting with my back against it — albeit both hands on the frying pan and the biggest knife in the drawer — I greet the day with Ruby's tome spread before me.

Dawn's pale, angled light streaks the pages, spilling across Gran's odd script like grapefruit cocktail, something pink and sweet-looking but sour. Sour enough to curl my tongue, make me suck in both cheeks and feel — hot damn! — as if I've been raised on vinegar. Nursed on the stuff. Lordy, and chucked beneath the wheels of a train.

XXVIII

Snake Oil

Here Practise and Invention may be free,
And as a *Squirrel* skips from tree to tree,
So maids may (from their Mistresse, or their Mother)
Learne to leave one worke, and to learne another,
For here they may make choice of which is which,
And skip from worke to worke, from stitch to stitch,
Until in time, delightfull practice shall
(With profit) make them perfect in them all.
Thus hoping that these workes may have this guide,
To serve for ornament, and not for pride.

Bert said he had word from our pa, Fan. At first I barely recognized him, that brisk autumn day; I had to stop and ponder who on earth it was standing at the door. His hair was grey, the colour of sleet, and he'd grown heavier since I'd seen him last — sweet Dinah, how many lifetimes past? — drinking beer that night so long ago in our kitchen. Oh, but he was still handsome, in a burly, sloe-eyed way.

"Bert? Bert Putnam? Heavens to Betsy—" I fumbled, stunned when I put a finger on who he was. I pictured Silas's mother just inside, in the parlour, her ears pricking like a terrier's.

For an instant he looked put out, his slow, hopeful grin sliding into a grimace as he backed a step or two away.

"Wait" — I reached out and caught his sleeve — "it's just, well, I never figured on...."

His eyes fixed on mine and he smiled again, bolder. The wind snapped the paper in his hand, and I glimpsed Pa's strange spiky handwriting.

"I figured you might take some pleasure hearing your father's news, Effie. Guess it's been a while since you wrote one another, eh? I kinda thought...."

Memories rose of me slamming through the gate with my school books, Bert's stroppy voice calling after me. The sight of him and Pa at the table, Bert's long brown fingers around his mug of beer. It had been a decade or more since I'd even considered his name.

"You gonna ask me in, Effie, or what? Kinda chilly, I'd say, to be standing out here reading. Or, you like, I can come some other time."

I could hear Tryphena inside, her skirt rustling like newspaper.

"Euphemia? Dear? Didn't know you were expecting comp'ny," she whimpered when I brought him into the hall. His gaze was like a gull's in the mirror, as he nipped off his cap and slouched past the sitting room. I believe their eyes met for the briefest second, Tryphena's pale and squinting as she dropped her needle-point. Her parched face fell blank as he nodded to her. Then he followed me to the kitchen.

"What is it, dear? What does he want? Deliveries to the back door, Euphemia — how often must I remind you? Good heavens, think where his boots might've been," she cajoled from the parlour, as if addressing thin air. How often, indeed. I braced myself for her to come out and investigate.

"I see you've done some good for yourself." Bert gave me that grin of his — a flash of gold, and slanted, I realized, because a couple of his teeth were chipped.

"Some good," I repeated, pulling out a chair, blushing. Rolling my eyes in spite of myself. I prayed my mother-in-law would resume her needlepoint. I willed her to do so, thinking hard of her clutching it in her usual fashion, ridiculously close to her face; Tryphena poised as if listening for God's voice with each whisk of the needle. If anything, her weakening sight of late, and any other frailty, had honed her hearing.

"I shouldn't've happened in on you suchlike," Bert muttered awkwardly, half rising as I flew about making tea, jiggling cups and saucers.

"Don't be foolish," I said, seizing him by the wrist — in jest, though not entirely — to force him back to sitting. I was that hungry for company, Fan; it seemed an eternity since I'd been with people; people, I mean, other than my husband, his mother, her church ladies.

In hindsight, perhaps I shouldn't have appeared so eager. But I was overwhelmed by the reason for his visit. It had been years — good Lord, I'd practically lost count: eleven? twelve? — since I'd heard from any of our family.

When I grabbed Bert's arm, something in him seemed to retreat. "So what does Pa say?" I prodded. I hadn't had time yet to feel jealous or slighted that he'd chosen to write Bert and not me.

Bert's big hands thrummed the table while I poured tea and took the letter from him, handling it like a pressed flower.

"Go ahead," he urged, when I hesitated, fearing bad news.

But there was nothing to cause particular alarm or worry; instead Pa's words summoned an icy sense of relinquishment. He and two of the children, the last two, had moved on to Pennsylvania, where Pa was working in a new steel mill. Mary and Peter were still with him, he said, our littlest sister "doing a fine job keeping house." The others — Will, Zeke, Sarah and Joseph — had long "gone off into the world," the world being the States: Will to the Midwest, the rest scattered wide. There was no mention of where, or what exactly they were doing, Fan; and not a single query about me. And that was the extent of Pa's news, interspersed with boasting about the wonders of ingots and new machinery, the wealth of opportunity for a smart young chap "like himself" — Bert — to make money.

It was an invitation, Bert's look told me, as he read my

disappointment, my bitterness, that Pa hadn't so much as enquired after me.

"Your old man never was one to go in much for homely details," he said. "Too bad there isn't a bit more. But you know what folks say, Effie, no news is generally good news. I thought you'd appreciate hearing this an' that — that's all. Christ, wish there *was* more — like how much they pay down there, for starters." He gave me a little nudge, same as when we were kids in school. Then he looked at his cup, pink and fragile as an egg in his stained hand. "Oh Effie, buck up — I only meant to let you know things are well with him, as well as you'd expect."

There was more rustling from out on the sofa.

Bert threaded his fingers together, bracing his hands under his chin as he watched me. Then, quietly, he unlaced them, sliding one out and laying its palm upon my wrist. A long purple scar branched like a twig between his thumb and forefinger. "I'm that sorry," he said, "about your mam. And your little one, too. I heard, Effie, see; feel bad for not saying something before — but I'm sorry for you."

I shrugged, craning towards the window so he wouldn't see my eyes' hard glitter. When I turned again, he was scouring the kitchen with that gaze of his: the fancy glassed-in cupboards, the polished faucets. He caught me looking and smiled, a wan, crooked smile that spoke of earlier times: the yeasty smells of coal dust and homebrew; chipped glass and clamouring kids.

"When I heard, I wanted to come see you."

"Water under the bridge," I said, so falsely; sweetly. He blinked and took my hand; spread my pale fingers between his and squeezed. Forward, he was. Fresh.

I should've pulled my hand away, but I didn't. There was something comforting, invigorating, about his grip, the strength of his knuckles pressing my ring into my finger. I had to remind myself that this was Bert, Bert Putnam, who once upon a time would've reached up next and yanked the hair from my head, and tortured me with names. Southpaw Ma, when he used to see me minding Mam's brood, tagging along with us towards home. Heffie Henglish, after my recitations in class: "I wandered lonely as a cloud...."

Sticks and stones may break my bones....

There was a rustle in the hall and Tryphena appeared, tapping the jamb with the walking stick she'd taken to using. A bit of yarn trailed from one shoe. "Eupheeemia? Are you here? I'm feeling a mite faint, dear. Would you be a pet and fetch my salts?"

Our hands flew apart. Tryphena's fist knotted around her stick. Bert's chair grated the floor as he rose, poised to make a hasty exit.

"Won't you introduce us?" she asked, in a brittle, quavery tone, the old-woman voice she'd acquired after her husband's decease.

"An old family friend," Bert spoke up, collecting his cap; "you could say that's who I am, Miz Lewis."

Something inside me wanted to cry, Don't go, not yet. Stay for one more cup.

"I'll be on my way now, Effie — ma'am. I've got a decision to make. I was just after asking Effie for some advice. Her educated opinion."

A scowl creased Tryphena's face: bafflement.

At the front door he eyed me slyly, pulling on his cap. "It's true — oh, never mind what you thought when we were kids, Effie, remember, when I used to tease the tar out of you. To me you've always been, well, refined. Honest. Someone with a head on her shoulders — whatever — opinions, I mean."

Maybe I imagined it, but as he spoke there seemed a kind of want in his eyes, Fan, a wistfulness.

"I want to hear what you think, is what I'm saying — so, should I go find work down there with your old man, or what?"

"Heaven's sake," I said, embarrassed, "how would I know? As if I'd have the gall to say what you should do."

I could hear Tryphena in the kitchen, sniffing about like a hound; likely wrinkling her nose at the tea leaves in the drain.

"'Get out now, while the going's good,' that's your pa's advice. The company here's on the skids."

He gave me one last, patient, thoughtful look, but made no move to take my hand or touch me.

"It was good seeing you, Effie. Mustn't let it go so long next time. I've missed you — sure, that sounds half cracked, doesn't it? But ever since I heard about them bad turns you've had — your troubles — Missus Cox, the baby...."

Thirteen years now, I thought again, sucking in my stomach, not speaking.

"So I'm kinda late. You'll be thinking, What's that fella up to anyways, deserves no better than a boot in the rear. But look, sweet Christ, when I got that letter——"

Tryphena came shuffling from the kitchen, her arms folded, her face like skinned-over milk.

Ignoring her, he tipped his cap to me — "Grand to see you again, Effie" — and then he was gone, that quick. Part of me wanted to run out after him and call him back for a proper visit, never mind the old woman; to sit and chew the fat, get caught up. Instead, I rapped on the glass and waved, and as he turned down the street he glanced back once and touched his brim. And I thought again with the oddest tingle how appealing he was, though his shoulders were now a little stooped. Underneath everything he was the same — the Bert who might've kissed me, once, had there been room for it in all that childish tormenting.

And there I was, a stodgy married lady at thirty-two; Silas and I having passed our fourteenth anniversary. The years of marriage — my being kept like a budgerigar — hadn't done much for the figure, I'll admit. But my face was still pretty, Fan, my skin still young.

It was hard to believe, following with my eyes till he was out of sight, that Bert was only a year or two older.

There'd been little chance to enquire about him, I thought as he disappeared: where he had been all these years, whether he'd stayed in Arcadia or moved about for work; whether he had children, a wife. I assumed so. What a prig I must've seemed, not to ask. But I had no opportunity — on that occasion.

Later that fall, there were rumblings of trouble at the Arcadia Iron Company — not that Lewis interests were directly affected. Not at first, anyhow. But rumours arose of the company shutting down its furnaces come spring, threatening hundreds of jobs. Silas, more out of panic than out of his usual caution, began working even longer hours, hoping, I suppose, to bolster business — to diversify, as he said, to expand. Why exactly, I'm not sure, since all the merchandise in the world wouldn't sustain us if customers left town. Crazy logic, it struck me; but it wasn't my place to object.

One wet November afternoon, Bert called again. Tryphena was napping, warding off a chill. I held my finger to my lips, pointing upstairs, laughing as if to make light of it, and led him straight to the kitchen. But he didn't seem in the mood for levity; didn't so much as ask after the old lady's health.

This time he had a photograph Pa had sent from Pittsburgh.

"Looks pretty good, doesn't it?" he said, sweeping his hand across the picture, a greyish scene of massive buildings and belching stacks. He gave his tea a rough stir. He seemed pensive, restless; less earnest this time. I couldn't help wondering why he'd bothered coming to see me again, what it was he wanted. "Your pa says there's no future a-tall for fellas here, and you know, talk is, Arcadia's as good as cooked; the company done like a dinner."

There was a bitterness to his voice which I didn't appreciate. As if it were my fault things weren't ideal at the works.

"Well," I sighed, pushing the picture away, "I suppose like everyone you must go where the jobs are." Good Lord, it sounded as glib as something Silas — or his mother — would say. The moment it popped out, I imagined the complications likely involved. "Your family — of course, one doesn't like to uproot them," I pussyfooted, affecting pity I didn't quite feel.

"Family?" he muttered, giving me a look.

It was then he grabbed my hand, Fan. Not gently and consoling as before, but urgently. Uncouth, to be sure — to some manners of thinking. But it was as if he were begging advice. Advice! When all we'd ever been was acquaintances; schoolmates but scarcely chums.

"I've got nobody else to worry about, Effie. No nice sheilagh home fixing my bread, if that's what you're getting at. No ma'am, I'm on my own, always have been. So it's not some other woman, nor a yowly mess of kids, holding me back. It's — the place, that's all. A fella hates to leave a place he's always been."

Some *other* woman?

The kitchen was chilly despite the fire; there was a draft, thick raindrops pelting the windows. But I felt sweaty suddenly, almost feverish, and wondered if I'd come down with Tryphena's bug.

"Do you mind?" I said, as he kept hold of my hand, gripping it so tightly I felt squeamish. "Do tell, then — what exactly it is you want?" The rub of Tryphena's tone from my mouth scared even me.

Bert dropped my hand, rocking back in his chair till I worried the rungs would snap. He shook his head, and I saw how his steely hair needed washing; and he looked at me, his eyes stark as the starlings on the clothesline beyond the window, and said, "I don't know."

I got up and shut the damper on the stove.

"I'm not feeling so well; perhaps I've caught whatever's ailing Mother. I think maybe you should——"

I watched him roll up the photo, shove it inside his coat.

"Good luck, then," I said feebly, as he stood wringing his cap. "You'll let me know if you decide to go? If there's more from Pa?"

His gaze shifted, and I felt Tryphena's presence. Looking like death, she lingered at the doorway, wiping her nose.

"Missus." He nodded, avoiding her stare. "So long, Effie," he said, and gave me this sly but hunted look, in fun yet not without sympathy. "I'll be in touch — what say I'm the go-between for you and your father? Keep you both up to date. Sorry to trouble you," he said, and winked. "Don't worry yourself, I'll find my way out."

As the door shut behind him, its tiny leaded panes shuddering ever so delicately, Tryphena turned to me, squinting, her lips pursed, chin cocked. And then she started praying.

"The Lord is my shepherd; I shall not want.... He leadeth me beside the still waters...in the paths of righteousness...thy rod and thy staff they comfort me. Thou preparest a table before me in the presence of mine enemies: thou anointest my head...my cup runneth...."

How much longer, I thought, fleeing to empty the teapot. Save me.

Christmas came and went, and for two months I heard nothing further from Bert. At New Year's, a front-page story in *The Arc-Light* declared that the Arcadia Iron Company had been purchased by financiers from Montreal, allaying fears that the works would close. Still, the town never got over its jitters; the rest of that winter

Silas complained how slowly stock was moving. You couldn't help wondering how or where, once planted, the seeds of uncertainty would sprout — even in the lives of the Lewises. No one felt immune. That's how deeply rooted was this fear that prosperity could come and go, like a thief in the night.

It was a harsh winter that year, 1907; especially hard on old people. In the second week of January Tryphena took to her bed, and she did not get up from it again. But the season didn't just haggle with the elderly; I have to wonder now if it didn't infect me too, with an urge I mightn't've succumbed to otherwise.

His mother's death in early February dealt Silas a heavy blow. For weeks afterwards he moped about, red-eyed, insomniac; he took to lying in her old room so as not to disturb me. Five whole days he suspended business, questioning the use of carrying on if, as he put it, the end of all earthly transaction was the grave.

He was inconsolable. Who knows, had I been a better wife he might have rebounded more ably. But there seemed so little I could do, beyond offering myself. A fat lot of good that did, too — my turning to him, my going to him in that cold, narrow bed.

In all our connubial life, I'd assumed Silas's reluctance, his eventual avoidance of me, was his mother's fault. Her presence, if not bodily, between us in the sheets, was manifest in his attitude, and during the most intimate moments. After I lost Adam, suffice to say I lost interest, and Silas's fear of hurting me became almost obsessive. Oh, in the early years I fantasized about trying for another child, but my heart wasn't in it. I was too afraid. And always present was that voice — "the ways of the flesh, the wages of sin" — apportioning blame.

Who knows, it might have offered him a measure of solace, the act. But to put it crudely, my dear, innocent sister, where Silas excelled at erecting commerce, he failed miserably in the connubial fashion. I suppose in the end it was this that pushed us apart. This and the cold that winter — the chill of my bare feet on the moon-streaked floor, the stillness of that strange little room in the dead of night. My lips touching skin that might as well have been wax. It was as though a lake had frozen between us, its surface slick and black yet not solid enough to risk crossing.

All this finally drove me to the arms of another. This and the simple need for warmth: to rub body and soul together like sticks, like two open palms.

He had such surprising hands, rough but gentle; hands that summoned feelings like wings, wings that lifted me out of myself. And arms. Arms that hugged like an octopus, those arms I was driven to.

I'm ashamed to say whose; perhaps I don't even need to. But he re-entered my life knowing me in ways my husband never could've. It was Providence, I figured; fate.

Or is this an excuse, a weak justification for my behaviour — when none, it would seem, is sufficient?

One day in late February — slightly more than a fortnight after we committed Tryphena to the ground — Bert came to the house. No, he said, there was nothing much new with Pa. But he had arrived at a decision, it seemed; and that was to go to Pittsburgh. My father had promised to put in a good word for him. He would head south at the first signs of spring, once the local travelling improved.

It was a brilliant, bitter afternoon. We sat in the parlour, a fire blazing, doors shut tight to trap the heat, and still the house creaked with cold. I served us each a nip of strawberry cordial with our tea, hoping that would chase the frost from our veins. As he started in about his plans, I swear my teeth were chattering.

He'd brought a pamphlet this time, a glowing report from the company in America, chock full of statistics about tonnage and yield. All Greek to me, I protested over our refreshments. "Come on, now Effie; don't be modest — you with your mercantile sense," he kept coaxing, insisting that I read it, certain I would more readily understand it than he.

Though the pamphlet was thin, its contents were dense. Even with my gift for arithmetic I was lost, could make neither head nor tail of it.

"It's been ages since I did much in the way of figuring." I finally swept it aside, reaching for the little bottle of cordial. "Another drink, Bert, a tiny bit before you go?"

Because of my ineptitude, my inability to help, I expected him to decline and take this as signalling the end of our visit. He rose, pausing to admire my quilt draped over the back of his chair. Without warning, he gathered it up and brought it to the sofa; wrapped it ever so carefully around my shoulders. A funny thing for Bert to do, an odd thing; not something you'd have ever imagined him doing.

Perhaps he's tired, I thought, as he eased himself down beside me. He'd been working late-night shifts, which was why, as he put it, he had the pleasure of this afternoon.

I was still wondering why he felt so compelled to confide in me, to keep me abreast, as they say, of his situation, when he did something even more peculiar and unexpected. He moved closer, so that his leg touched my skirt. And before I could slide away or object, he reached his palm to my face and held it there, his thumb along the curve below my ear, and he kissed me, Fan.

Who'd have ever thought? Bert, Bert Putnam.

His mouth tasted of strawberries, and of something metallic. His skin smelled of shaving soap, and I couldn't help picturing cold grey washwater, I was that stunned.

And when he finally spoke, he told me softly that he did not want to go to Pittsburgh; no, he did not look forward to going a-tall, he said. And he kissed me again.

"What are you doing?" I tried to squirm from him, my voice fanning off like wingbeats up a chimney, drowned out by the hiss of the fire. "It's not right," I whispered, clamping my eyes shut. But in my head all I saw were his arms around me: those forearms tinged with black hair. And then I felt his tongue, the warmth of his mouth; his taste again, like something salty: blood. Under us I heard the jounce of springs, felt the shifting lumpiness of the sofa. My body yielding. A feeling like the wind, Lord, that old lost feeling. That feeling like the wind shuddering in, swelling my chest; a crystal glitter in my veins.

He broke from me, sitting back, the look on his face like a cat hearing a sound — wary. The look in his eyes like a house in want of tenants.

"I shouldn't ever have — I'm sorry, Effie."

Those eyes of his: my undoing.

"Well, I'm not." I arched back against the cushions. "Being

sorry is for nincompoops." It was the first foolish thing that entered my head, Fan.

But my words hung there as if the world had stopped, everything suspended in that upright, chilly room: the spurting flames, the clock's whirring upon the mantel. A quarter of five, it said; Silas would be home in an hour.

But for me time had stopped.

There was only this person, this other body with such solid, graven arms; his faint smell of sweat mixing with the musky scent of the fire. This fellow I'd known but never really regarded all those days of my life — until that bitter afternoon, in the soft reddish light from the windows, the dancing blues of the fireplace.

There was a singing inside my skull, beneath my heart, filling my limbs. A longing. An urgency. Like the rush of sparrows seeking a nest.

He slid to his feet.

"No," I cried, and he sank to his knees beside me, enfolding me in the quilt. That greedy, careless song in my bones now blotting out all sense, all remorse.

"Life is too much regret," I said, my voice brittle, half breaking. This startled him; he rocked back on his heels, hands on his thighs, regarding me.

"Ah yes, regrets...."

And I saw the fineness of the room in his eyes, all its appointments; the fire's glow; and the clock's ticking, our time flying past now. Soon Silas would be at the door, hanging up his coat and wanting supper.

"My prayer," I blurted, knowing that if I let this moment pass, it would go the way of all others.

And he started laughing, Fan — a deep, low chuckling — and I do believe his face went red.

"Oh, Jay-sus — you're not gonna start praying on me, are you?" Back to the old Bert, that rankling urge to nettle.

But I clapped my hand over his mouth and rolled to the edge of the sofa, the old springs groaning, fit to spill me onto the rug.

"No regrets — you understand? If we're discreet——"

He turned my hand over, held the back of it to his lips, tracing the veins with his breath.

"Tomorrow, Effie? The day after? It's up to you, my girl. You have to say...."

And I named an afternoon, straightening my dress, tidying the pins that had shaken loose from my hair. I gave him a time, Fan, and then I saw him to the door, shook his hand as he was leaving. A silly gesture, but sealing a pact.

Which, you see, it was — of sorts; and so much better than saying, Don't leave. Promise me.... For if I had doubted we would get this appointed time together, my heart might well have turned to lead — there, in the doorway — brittle and cold as what threaded the windowpanes; and my feelings become glass.

If you deny me.

My chance to join the living.

For how else to describe it — the pulse that lingered after he'd gone — but as bloodsong?

XXIX

The Needle's Eye

Two Methods for Removing Printing from Flour Bags:

I.   1)   Wet bag in warm water.
     2)   Spread out flat and soap lettering well
          with laundry soap.
     3)   Put into solution composed of
          2 quarts warm water
          1 cup bleach (Javel or Javex).
          Let soak one hour.

II. First soak in cold water, rub lettering with green
     face soap, roll up, let stand overnight. Next day
     rinse in cold water, again soap any lettering, put
     into a vessel, cover with hot or cold water and boil
     for about 10 minutes. Result, beautiful white
     cotton.

—from *Five Roses Cookbook*,
Lake of the Woods Milling Company

Adultress, fornicator, whore of Babylon. Tryphena, had she

lived as long as Noah, wouldn't've found a Bible's worth of epi-
thets enough to condemn me — nor all the prayers in the world
sufficient in seeking retribution for my behaviour. She would not
have uttered words evil enough to describe it.

But in my eyes, Providence winked — not once but twice,
many more times besides — by sparing her the trouble.

I am guilty as sin, the words writ large on my forehead, tat-
tooed, it would seem to me; yet somehow illegible to my husband.
He has never so much as guessed.

I was wicked, yes; but God is merciful. Righteous. And soon
enough, in the oddest way, I received his blessing. The evidence of
his grace.

And surely it would've been a sin to turn Bert away the afternoon he came to me, the day we'd agreed upon. A sin, an abomina-
tion, to spurn such pleasure; to be ungrateful.

It was a Thursday. I was waiting, you see; more than a little
anxiously, in case he reneged on his end of the deal. At a quarter
past one he knocked; I let him in. We wasted no time on niceties:
refreshments or chat.

I'd dispensed with a corset, content all the morning to wait in
my chemise, *sans* stays, under my clothes. I led him into the parlour, held his hand as I reclined upon the sofa. My cheeks were
blazing, I could feel them; but I shut my eyes, and in the roaring
quiet between my ears I waited for his touch.

He kept wanting to kiss, Fan, as though I were to be tasted
first, some endless supper without dessert. As if we had forever,
not just our appointed hour. *On your marks, gentlemen; get set.* —
I kept thinking, turning my head away, willing his hands to
travel...and travel. Half wishing we could be like people in the
store, he a customer making a purchase and I the clerk tapping the
counter, anxious to receive his money. The clock a-ticking....

The sofa springs complained as he kept shifting about, that
blood surge filling me, its warmth meeting his mouth. Till finally I
sat bolt upright and unbuttoned myself, and shut my eyes again,
straining from his lips, his gaze: that awful look of trust. And I
became Effie, Mam's young helper, as if unbuttoning the boys'
pants to hasten bedtime (*C'mon, you little sods, I haven't got all
day!*) And he was in my hands, the length of him, with one quick

breath of protest — "Do you think it's all right, girl, right here in midday on the davenport?" — when really, like me, he was beyond worrying. The two of us, Bert and Effie: bodies, faceless. Limbs and flesh and skin only, our blood singing....

His size surprised me; so did how quickly it was over — not to criticize either; the contrary. Such melting sweetness.

"Oh Effie," he said quietly, dressing afterwards, quickly, furtively; shyly. Turning towards the fire to do up his pants. The sweet squirming wetness between my legs fastened me to the scratchy sofa. I stretched like a cat.

"Could've at least taken a minute to fetch a blanket to lay on." He shook his head, blushing, waiting for me to laugh. But when I did, he looked away, perplexed. "Good Christ, girl," he joked, not knowing, perhaps, how to take my pleasure.

The hands on the clock stuttered forward.

"You're something, Effie. I've never seen the likes...I.... How many times in my life you figure I imagined——? Sweet Jesus, never thought I'd live to see this, you know. I've...got such a feeling for you, I honestly do, always have had, and don't tell me you didn't get a drift of it before; sure, I never told you, but I guess.... Would it be foolish to say I could go out now and God take me, strike me dead, and you know, I'd die a happy man?"

And he was Bert again, of course, with all of Bert's scents; his faint perfume of sweat, the swampy smell of his socks. But his eyes were different: sober, steadier.

"Good comes to them that wait, I've heard it said. Guess it's true, i'n' it, Effie?"

I reached for the quilt from the chair, wound it round my thighs. Our gazes locked.

"Next week, then?" I said, light as air. "Thursday?"

But as he kissed me and let himself out, even as the door clicked shut, I was wanting him again; already I was counting the hours.

Sweet, so sweet, the deed — the five or six other afternoons we passed together upstairs upon the "guest" bed, Tryphena's small, saggy four-poster. "The wild thing", he called our activity, whilst licking my ear. Teasing me onto the pillows. Sometimes I could barely credit that such pleasure and the connubial act — shared so infrequently with Silas — were even related.

And yet there was an earnestness, an odd propriety, in what we did; even in Bert's desire, as though he never quite believed what we'd stumbled into.

I always made sure he carried his shoes upstairs, in case something brought Silas home early. I was careful, scrupulously careful, that all appear tidy, squeaky-clean as a fresh-scrubbed floor. Nothing amiss, not one stray speck of dust to arouse suspicion. Yet I felt sure Silas must see it: my misdemeanour bold as a strawberry stain on my face! How could he not? But he had no inkling, and this to me was marvellous.

Still, it couldn't have lasted; nor would I have wanted it to.

After one of our trysts, didn't Bert bring out that pamphlet again? We were lying together, not talking, simply taking in one another's warmth, my cheek against his barrel chest, his armpit. Suddenly he got up and rummaged through his things on the chair. When he slid back in beside me, he had the pamphlet. I kissed the hollow under his earlobe, darted my tongue over his nipple. He folded over one dog-eared page and started studying some figures, waiting for me to snuggle close and add my two cents' worth.

Well, I wouldn't; the very prospect bored me. Worse, between those columns of numbers all I could imagine were roaring flames, Pa stoking a furnace. His diffident pride, his silence. The way he'd shaved me from his life like a curl of wood.

Bert's oblivion irritated me. There was an ingenuousness about it — a kind of heaviness about him — that chafed at me.

And where, at first, I found the weight of his body, his breath, his smells, all his essences invigorating, in combination they started to put me off. As though beneath these lay a dullness, a coarseness which, not much later, I would look back upon and find repellent.

"It don't get better than this, does it, Effie?" he remarked one day. No sooner were his words out than I glimpsed him wiping himself on one of my good towels, linen imported from Ireland. And it was then, yes, exactly then, that a certain shame sprouted inside me, dormant all those weeks but unstoppable once germinated.

After our last encounter, immediately after, I suggested —

gently, the way I'd once suggested to Tryphena that tea might work wonders for her ailments, instead of all those potions — that it might be best if we ended our appointments. That our trysts, though pleasant, were not worth the gamble of Silas finding out. I wasn't prepared for Bert's response.

"I love you, Effie," he said, swinging himself out of the bed. I felt the tears jump behind my eyes, my limbs, caught in the sheets, stiffen. When he stood staring down at me, there was a thickness about his expression, like smoke; his eyes looked stung. He reached down and lifted my chin, his knuckle grazing the hollow above my voicebox. Why else, he demanded, would he put off leaving for new work? Why else would a fella keep clinging to a sinking ship?

He sat down heavily, folded me in his arms — those big burly arms pinching my bones together — and asked me to leave Silas. Leave my home and Arcadia Mines and everything, for a new life with him in the States. He held all this out to me like money on a collection plate. And he asked, almost desperately, "What's to lose?" I tried squirming from him so he wouldn't see my fears, my guilt, my *smallness*, in the wetness on my cheeks.

With a choking laugh, I said he must be cracked; who did he think he was, expecting the moon of me? The moon and the Big Dipper! And he accused me of being hard, of having a heart like an ingot under my soft, loose good nature. All the time he spoke, he clutched my hand, more and more tightly as if he'd never let go. Then he called me sanctimonious, a sanctimonious something I would rather not repeat.

I told him he was foolish and deluded and thinking with a part of his body not his brain. To expect me to give up my life! What did he take me for? And at that point his mouth fell open and I could see inside: the pink of his tongue, the gums pulling away from his teeth.

And he said, "I took you for a lady, Effie, one with class. My mistake, eh? Well, I'll be pissed — turns out you're no better than Ada Skoke, you hear me? Just like Ada, up at the Waverley selling herself; no, worse, giving it away, the cow before the milk.... You're cheap, Effie; I'd never have guessed. Oh, you fooled me all right. At least, with Ada, a fella gets his jug filled right up front at the table, no arsing around."

Even as he ranted, my shock at what he'd just said was scalded into contempt; and he rocked away from me, looking shamed, wounded. Cocooned in a blanket, I shrank towards the wall, pressed my face to it. Closing my eyes, my voice stalling at first, I said wearily that it was over, that our "love" could never have been. And if, in his anger, he'd given me a way out, any tenderness I felt for him hardened like a knob of sap. For in my mind's eye I imagined myself eighteen again, on the river with Silas in his father's boat, our wet toes almost touching. The rowdy, tinkling laughter of a girl coming through the willows, the flash of pale flesh. The body on top just as white as hers, naked as a newborn.

As Bert threw on his clothes, I turned once and smiled foolishly, cruelly; the kind of smile that creeps over your face when everything behind it struggles to remain quite sober. Then I pulled the sheets above my head and counted his footsteps as he left, the muffled gunfire of his boots upon the stairs.

The Lord works in mysterious ways; despite her fanaticism, there always was an ounce of truth to Tryphena's maxims. I'd have said so even before detecting the difference in my body, the subtle change.

Everything happens for a reason.

"The wind bloweth where it listeth, and thou hearest the sound thereof, but canst not tell whence it cometh, and whither it goeth: so is every one that is born of the Spirit."

Perhaps I should've been more canny and realized that nothing we do has no effect, that daily living is like boarding an express. Once you embark, you can't just jump off — at least, not where or whenever it suits you.

I have grown wiser.

Though when at last this wisdom dawned, it was a trifle late — as was my monthly visitor. By mid-March I started to suspect what I'd thought was impossible — a miracle, really. In desperation, one raw dawn when the world outside was an icy glare, spring light cracking the sky like an egg, I went to Silas — to confess? Heavens, no. Seeking camouflage, I turned to him in the manner we'd abandoned for so long.

I was never unfaithful again.

In early April we attended a concert at the Waverley. The furnishings in the reception room were pushed aside to accommodate the audience; Silas and I had front-row seats. The pianist was a sombre young man from Boston or New York — it wasn't clear which, on the bill posting his performance.

He played as if not a soul were there, his fingers a blur against the keys, rippling like the moonlight on the river outside.

A chill wind scoured the valley, but inside we were warm, packed into the gaslit room decked with flowers for the occasion. As we shifted in our straight-backed chairs, the pianist rippled through Brahms, a piece by Ravel. *Jeux d'eau*, it was called; notes breaking like ice, cascading, then rippling higher, higher, in a way that curled the tiny hairs upon my back.

A jardinière spilling paperwhites sat on a small table near our seats, their sour perfume growing stronger by the minute as that wild music crashed and tinkled. Beside me, Silas listened with his eyes shut, his arms folded over his chest — I wondered if perhaps he was dozing. Such a hush fell over the audience, except for the odd timid whisper, some barking into hankies.

My mouth pooled with saliva — my Dinah, the scent of those flowers, the stinky proximity of so many squeezed into that room! I couldn't help it; in the middle of the next piece I had to escape to the powder room for a splash of cold water on my face, a deep breath of different air.

As I made my way back to my seat, I glimpsed Bert, good God, standing to the rear of the room, a rapt yet bitter set to his face as he listened to the music. I could tell he'd seen me.

Silas opened his eyes and smiled when I sat down, patted the top of my hand. "Aren't you well, dearie?" he said, any concern quickly dispelled by the lustrous occasion. He had no idea, at that point, of the cause of my queasiness, centred under the maroon silk of my sash.

It was a colour that brought out my paleness, I knew. The stiff collar of my dress caused my chin to double — oh! — owing to the slight puffiness of my face. I kept my head canted towards Silas's, my eyes upon the musician. Even so, from the back of the room I felt Bert's eyes burning a hole in my lovely black-feathered hat, through to my scalp.

At the end of the concert, the pianist opened his eyes, a faint smile on his lips, and took a deep bow. As the audience surged forward, hands outstretched, aflutter, I jumped up and, pulling Silas, scrambled through the crowd.

There was no sign of Bert; perhaps he'd beat it next door to the saloon.

Walking home under the cast-iron heavens pierced with stars, I told Silas we were expecting. "A child?" He could not fathom it. "Queerer things have happened," I said, and I do believe that, right there on Broadway, the shaky boardwalk creaking under our feet, Silas cried. Tears of amazement — bright, hard specks that glittered in the gaslight, not unlike the pinpricks in the sky.

Not a week later, a mishap struck the town, what people call a freak accident. A fellow got pinned beneath a dipper of molten steel, causing an explosion. Two more were maimed. They recovered, but the first man died instantly. The unfortunate fellow was Bert.

The company blamed it on carelessness, which, I'll tell you, raised the town's hackles. As some of Silas's customers said, it was a good thing Putnam left no wife or kids, for the company offered little compensation. In death Bert turned into a celebrity of sorts — as much as can any man who works with his brawn. The Putnams' old place, up the other side of Foundry Hill, became a kind of a shrine the two days and nights they waked him.

Business dipped as patrons of every stripe went off to pay their respects; Silas himself spoke about closing up the day of the funeral, as a way of siding with the customers. He talked about the two of us going up to offer regrets to the family — a couple of brothers, a wayward uncle and old Mrs. Putnam, Bert's mother. A woman so tight with her money she squeaked, Bert used to say when we were teenagers. His mother, nonetheless.

Well, I put the kibosh on Silas's idea. It wasn't our place, I said. Truth was, I don't know what I would've done, walking into that hard-scrubbed parlour — holier than church, I imagined, with the smells of carbolic soap and candle-wax. The coffin propped on kitchen chairs, no doubt. I could see it in my mind, Fan. Could imagine the stone flesh under the burying clothes — a spare suit of the father's, perhaps? Saved after the old fellow himself died, to be worn by others on certain occasions? Weddings, funerals.

"We'll go to the service," I directed Silas. "That's more fitting, and that way you won't necessarily lose the whole morning."

The mourning: I hadn't considered that, or the mud.

The rain, either; a needling, persistent drizzle. The two of us standing well back of the gravesite, me gripping Silas's arm like a stick to beat off my nausea.

Bert's workmates had erected a fence — white pickets, with a latching gate — around the plot. It was easy to stay in the background, my husband and I blending into the crowd. Poor Mrs. Putnam was bent like a crow under her big black bonnet, her widow's weeds shiny-black with wet.

I should tell her, I thought, picturing the seed swelling inside me. I imagined it as a sunflower seed, grey-striped as the rain, splitting; a tiny lime-green shoot unfurling: a foot.

I should tell Silas, confess like the Catholics do — these thoughts swam through my brain as my eyes fixed on the faded, crumpled plume of that bonnet ahead.

Oh God, make things right, I prayed, watching from a long, lofty distance the rough pine casket being trundled, jerked and lowered down, down, out of sight.

And I wept, yes, consoled by convincing myself the tears were drizzle. By picturing Bert's hands, his other parts, washed clean. Silas braced my arm, gave me a look fit to melt my heart: as if to say, "Mustn't take things so hard, my dear. A lady in your delicate condition." He whispered, "Are you quite fine? I should've known, you're usually right. Of course. You should've been more insistent, Phemie: it isn't our place to be here."

Our place, indeed.

A thick, freezing rain started as we left the cemetery on foot, descending the hill quickly to outdistance Bert's raggle-taggle family. We overtook a woman stumbling along by herself, stooped against the wind — her drenched black skirt a tad short, its hem frayed, entangling her calves. Looked as though she'd been through the Boer War, or worse, Silas's raised eyebrow told me. His grip tightened on my arm as we passed and she glanced up at us, her face distraught and bitter; it had the same bleached look as tree-roots washed up by the river.

"Jezebel," Silas muttered, once we were out of earshot, pulling me closer to him, keeping his eyes to the ground.

Ada Skoke. Like the cool sweep of satin over bare shoulders, recognition danced over me. It was perhaps the first time I'd seen her face that close; any earlier encounters hardly mattered.

Where the Lord plants a seed, I thought, only the wind can know. Believing thus, I let Silas hurry me along.

And so my secret rests.

And months later, the following November, when my legs opened and the child's head pushed and tore its way out, even with the gush of blood and life my lips stayed sealed.

The night before Ruby's birth I dreamed of a garden, the small plot beside the store filled with sweet rocket, alyssum, lily of the valley, pansies. Even as the wind howled around the eaves, a raw wind promising early snow, I woke and lay on my side listening, not the least bit sleepy, a sudden energy ticking inside me. Energy and dread, of course, fear like a mongrel, attending even as I listened to Silas's slow, peaceful breathing.

They say you forget the agony of childbirth, but oh, I remembered. The poor weak infant, drawn, inhuman as a dressed chicken: that sad first birth. To drive memory away I fixed on the notion of flowers, the varied dry textures of seed pods; made mental lists of the ones I would order come spring (!) while weaving in and out of a profusion of blossoms: purple, yellow, fuchsia.

By dawn I was ready. I felt the baby loll and press my bladder, its feet drum my ribs. Felt my belly tighten, yes, the signal, way down low in those deepest parts, then easing, like tight-laced stays of whalebone loosening off. A pleasantness, at first. The wind outside howling. In spirit I might've risen then, dressed and run out to the street to be danced away, finally, like the last dry leaves piled round the roots of trees, pillars, porches.

But I stayed put and when Silas woke, as usual, at five to six, I told him to call the doctor.

My jewel, my tiny gem. Who would've thought a child could

be so sweet? The warmth of a tiny sucking mouth: that firm, hard tug, enough to make you wince in pain at first. My body and soul transfused. Silas over the moon in love. The sleep of an infant, Lord, like the petals of a rose, Fan, that short-lived. Who could credit the sweetness, the exhaustion? That velvet love that sweeps you in, enfolds and imprisons you, as if in a room with walls of glass? The love of one's child like the sky: limitless, smooth, black, transparent. Invisible, potentially crushing.

Her tiny brows were like goosedown; the feather-soft scalp, a peach. My love like a wolf hunkered ready any moment to spring, tear preying flesh if need be. The wide blue infant eyes bathing my face: seeing all, seeing nothing.

What can prepare you for this?

The wonder.

The lack of sleep. The baby's soul-tugging hunger, those early days; my arse-dragging weariness — as her daddy, so uncouth, would've called it.

And it wasn't as if she were a demanding baby. Others called her placid; they cooed over her, marvelled at her lack of fretfulness, of colicky crying.

The trouble was, I loved too much, a love that swells fit to crack your ribs and make your soul quiver. When she overslept sometimes I panicked, held a mirror to her rosebud mouth, the little sterling hand-mirror Silas had given me on our wedding day. And once she started smiling — her pink, baby grin, mouth like an empty oyster shell — you know whose face I'd see.

Which helps explain, perhaps, why I began writing to you, though for thirteen years I resisted; it took that long to succumb, to get up the "nerve". But without you I might've gotten lost; without your presence, who knows where I'd have vanished to?

By the time Ruby was four months old, I took to spending time in the store again, the one thing I'd let go of all those years before. Something about being in the house all day, alone with my love — like burying one's face in a warm, fat feather pillow. Pale blue milk arcing from the nipple at her slightest cry, and nappies — the smell of piddle and milk gone sour — and all that cooing attention!

Ruby slept in her cradle behind the counter while I dusted and tended the cash, and Silas tallied accounts out back. Slowly my days quit being soft, shapeless clouds, and I perceived them as gifts instead, boxed and sorted. My love thinned and spread out a little — like porridge, Fan, when Mam would run short and stretch it with water.

Ruby was still feeding every few hours when I started back at the store. I thought at first my life would end this way, day in, day out: nursing, dusting, making change. But bit by bit Ruby outgrew soakers, gowns, bloomers; smiling the same sweet gummy smile at everyone who came in, ministers' wives, roughnecks; the next day making strange. And the next, crawling shotgun around the floor, sticking anything not nailed down into her mouth. Lord! A going concern. And do you know, it never got easier, not really. I came to understand the wisdom of God's ways: why the love of my life was an only child.

Presume nothing, though, for six years later the utterly impossible happened. Silas's own miracle.

Ruby had just started school when Dora arrived, a hellion from the get-go. The spitting image of her father, with her fiery red hair. But that's where the resemblance ended; and so, for a while, did my work in the store. At five days of age, Dora developed colic. Ruby would get herself up, fed, dressed and off to school to escape the crying. Silas would scoot past the crib as though it held the Beast itself, I swear; yet other times, he'd rock, kiss and croon to her, smitten, truly, as if his heart had been torn, all sense had absconded.

Later came the tantrums; the devil's own defiance.

He'd wanted Dora christened after his mother. But I wouldn't have it. Perhaps I should've backed down, because after her birth he was never the same towards me; never paid quite the same attention, affection beyond courtesy.

The Lord works in funny ways, indeed; I won't speculate on men. But in Silas's distraction there's been a silver lining. It has granted me a little more room.

One blustery day — in earliest spring, the streets still a slew of mud and melting snow — I found this ledger, started remembering things. Things you might've liked to know, I figured — or mightn't have, depending. The writing's been in fits and starts, whenever I've had a breath between chores, when customers and the girls have been scarce, and Silas scarcer.

Dora is seven now, and Ruby thirteen — the age, I suppose, when a woman's life begins. Folly to say youth is wasted on the young; but oh Fan, if I had only known....

Euphemia's List

Things to look forward to in my next life:

1) No feeding. No roasts, absolutely no pies. No cracked hands from peeling potatoes.
2) No washing. No dishes, no soap scum or wet cuffs.
3) No clothes to hang out.
4) No clothes to bring in.
5) No ironing.
6) No sewing, no mending. No holes.
7) No sweeping, dusting, scrubbing or polishing.
8) No picking up.
9) No counting.
10) No connubial duty.
11) No night sweats.
12) No beds to make.
13) No crying.
14) No regrets.

May 29th, 1920

XXX

Powder-Puff Mechanics

After the robbery, there's nothing for it but to go driving. So that's exactly what we do, Ruby and me, first thing every morning, soon as the breakfast dishes are done. We go out in the truck and drive, drive, drive — all day sometimes, through hell's acre and back. Some days we don't get home till *Oprah*'s almost over, the credits rolling up over her chubby brown face, that big wide smile of hers, pretty as Bambi's. Sometimes the phone'll be ringing off the hook, as though the person on the other end's been trying all day to get through.

I can pretty well guess who it is. The sound of that ringing makes me queasy enough to go back out and wait in the truck till it stops.

See, I simply do not know what to say, if it is Wilf on the line. Chances are he'll be wanting some kind of answer to that business he raised that night in his kitchen. So far I've been saved by the robbery, that much I'll say for it; saved from making any decision.

Not that he's been breathing down my neck.

Still, when the phone rings like that, my belly knots. It's like choosing between picking up a live grenade and leaving it sit. But the look Ruby gives me when I don't answer the phone: as if I'm right off my stick! A couple of times she's made a lunge for it. Saved again; both times it's been Edna saying she's been trying to get me all afternoon, or all through the show, to tell me there's somebody on I ought to watch.

Once she said I had her worried we'd gone off the road somewheres and landed in a ditch; next we'd be showing up on slabs in hubby's workshop, the two of us blue and stiff as slate. When I didn't answer right away she butted in, "You can't run from your troubles forever." At that point I clammed up tight — which I regretted afterwards, seeing how some, like Edna, take silence the wrong way: like a sticky drawer jammed shut on their thumb.

I couldn't've put her off too badly, though, because the very next day she was back on the blower — all out of breath, so I knew right away, when I forgot and answered the phone, that it must be something big. "Haven't you heard?" she yelped. "The cops've nabbed some fellas, two young thugs they figure were the ones did it! You better call, Lindy, find out what's what."

"Uhm-hm." I torqued up my voice a notch or two to sound halfways interested. As I did so, my stomach growled with a funny emptiness. "Got something on the stove just now" — I gave her that excuse. "I've got to run."

"You will give 'em a call?" she persisted. "You'll keep me appraised?" I suppose that was hubby's lingo — apprised or appraised — a word that made me think, all of a sudden, of braised beef.

"Sure will," I said, then thought of something. "Edna, would you do me a favour? When you're phoning, would you let 'er ring twice, then hang up and call? That way I know it's not some old crank."

"I see." She sounded suspicious at first, then cosy. "Well I guess — I s'pose I could do that."

Hanging up, I felt rather smug and pleased with myself — till I glanced at Ruby and the door to the store, the piece of two-by-four I'd nailed across it once the man from the insurance had finished his business.

Let sleeping dogs lie, was the first thought that entered my head when he came to tally our losses; or light a match, the second one. Now the notion of opening that door was about as appealing as cutting into a can of night crawlers.

The cheque came surprisingly quick — the cheque from the insurance, compensating us for damage and loss of business. It was a decent amount; after I'd picked through the mess, it seemed the only things stolen were cigarettes. Even once I'd paid a couple of fellows to clean up and cart the damaged stuff to the dump, there was a tidy sum left over; 'course, I had to fork out a bit for the new phone, a cordless model on sale at Canadian Tire.

All the same, at first it felt like a windfall — hitting the jackpot, winning the lottery or a pass to Club Med; Easy Street — till I sat and matched the numbers to the actual hours, years, spent.

Down the pipes, if I didn't re-open. But what would've been the point?

So I couldn't help seeing this as God's way of doing a favour. Albeit a backhanded one, and damned peculiar, when I thought of my life — fifty years, if you added them up, passed like pennies over the same dusty counter.

They say when he closes a door he opens a window; how you reckon in a jimmied door, I'm not too sure.

See, that night driving back from Edna's, the cruiser like a firefly up ahead, it was as if part of me had passed on the double line, beaten the cops to the store and walked through again, up the aisle, behind the cash, and then kept going — through the kitchen, out to the yard, past the river and south past Ferrona, Hopewell, heck, clean beyond Spenceport....

But if in my travels, my drives with Ruby, there's been a window opened (a "window of opportunity", as the insurance man kept saying, snapping pictures, speculating on motives) — a breeze blowing through, strong enough to twitch a curtain — I'd have to say I haven't found it. Not yet.

Ruby likes the truck, once she calms down to watch the scenery zipping past. More and more the movement puts her to sleep, like a baby in a cradle; never mind the potholes.

After weeks and weeks, there's hardly a speck of gravel we've left unturned, swear to God. Miles and miles of country roads, and we haven't left the county yet.

Once Ruby's drifted off, I often crank up the radio, Wilf-style. Sure, and I'll even hum along if there's an oldie I like, a Merle Travis song, or one by Charley Pride. Jouncing up and down — poor old Betsy, every rusty bolt and spring taking its lumps — at times I almost feel the worry melt away, that's right, slide off my back like one of Edna's sister-in-law's slinky blouses. For a moment or two, anyways. Then we'll hit a rut and Ruby's poor old eyes will fly open, vacant as an empty henhouse, and so much for that little bit of peace.

Except when you have it, you've got to make the most of it. So I tell myself two or three minutes are better than none; like that saying, "Make hay while the sun lasts."

And with the days warming up, spring sliding into summer, there's more of that, at least. When we started these jaunts, I'd watch the ditches — so much litter that time of year: April, early May. The smell of dog doo, everything thawing and breaking up, making way for new roots. To be honest, our first few drives after the robbery, something about the earth itself left me cold: the rawness, all that soupy green. It was like rubbing salt on a wound. Throwing fertilizer on weeds.

But in some crazy way I feel better now the maples are in bud, dotted red like so many fuzzy caterpillars. The warmth beaming through the windshield makes Ruby nap longer; soothing, perhaps, as a mother's hand on a child's brow. It does the trick. And it makes it easier to get up in the morning and fix the "vittles", a word that makes me think of Granny Clampett. Sheesh. At times I think a rocker on the back of Betsy would be just the ticket: strap Ruby in and let her rock to Glory. Except I'm too busy with the here and now, making sure we eat.

We've been running down the stock, using up whatever wasn't smashed or spoiled in the big to-do — the B&E, as Edna calls it, a term that sounds like an abbreviation for sex. Cheez Whiz, flaked ham, 7-Up; not quite fast food, but close enough. I don't have the heart for cooking any more, perhaps I never did. Now even the thought of frying up bologna makes me jumpy — lounging that long over the stove — yes, as if standing around with a firecracker under one's feet. That's how it feels, being within a pole's length of the store.

One morning, Lordy, the sun's like spit from a lemon lozenge: everything awash, that yellow. I get Ruby up, dressed and fed by eight, a parcel of tuna sandwiches slapped together, wrapped in the last of the wax paper; a Thermos of caffeine brewed. Ruby is meek, so very pale, absent. I button her coat the way you'd sneak up on a sound in a bush, expecting, maybe, to see a thrush; finding that the rustling was just the wind, a Popsicle wrapper trapped in the branches.

When she yawns, her teeth are still beautiful. It's her expression that hits me like a slap: empty as a mouth without dentures. The sun makes her blink, her frail, bluish lids slow as the old green blinds we keep drawn all the time now in the store. Looks like a war zone inside, like something out of Lebanon. Closing the blinds is like zipping your jacket to your chin, knowing you haven't a stitch on underneath. The shame of having anybody — townsfolk or strangers — peek inside like having the zipper whipped down and being made to parade buck naked from here to Ferrona and back.

But on this particular June morning I forget about blinds, the need for covering up. Song sparrows pipe us to the truck, their sweet, brazen back-and-forth full of hope. I glance at Ruby's face for some kind of glimmer but she looks tired, bone-tired, just from travelling out to the yard. Or from some journey in her head; some long, tricky path staked out over bumps and boulders — who can know? She grips my sweater sleeve with white-knuckled strength and mutters, "Dora, Dora." My hair's still wet from the shower, and for a second her eyes widen. She shakes a trembling finger at me and croaks, "Get in out of the rain, girl. The rain, rain, rainnnn...."

In jig time, though, once those wheels start rolling, she's asleep, slumped and slouched into herself. I turn on the radio and a song leaps to life — some new country tune, bouncy and joyful though the words, when you make them out, are mournfully sad. It's nothing you can sing to, and when the deejay's voice cuts in, I switch the thing off and tool along in the delicious, rattling quiet. I keep my eyes on the horizon till the yellowish haze above the mountains stiffens to blue.

When we reach a crossroads, without thinking I make a right, following the scenic route to Caledonia, the road they plan to close once the new one's finished. Then I head north, up towards the vicinity of Wilf's place — though it's not intentional or even clear to me where I'm headed, honest, till the Esso comes in view. The sign startles me the way I imagine it would startle a cosmonaut seeing a golfball on the moon. Before I fully realize where we are, the Irving station appears, white as a new pair of briefs on the line. Oh my. Then, as though it's Betsy herself commandeering the wheel, next thing I know I've turned off down the dusty dirt haul towards the trailer. Five hundred feet in and I feel like James Bond — if you can imagine a spy in a rusty Ford pickup, a sick old lady riding shotgun beside her.

His driveway looks different in daylight; the twin cartwheels marking it from the spruce look less white. In fact, they're a little tilted, missing spokes. Propped beside them are metal rods with bike reflectors round as bug eyes. I pull in quick to let another truck pass.

He's probably working, I figure. I heard on the news one night that they want the new road paved in time for tourists. And the last time Ruby and I toured through Westchester, sure enough, there were construction crews in the woods.

I put 'er in neutral and sit there, as if I'm waiting for a string of traffic to pass — never mind that we and that one other truck are it. Listening for the engine's pinking, I reach for my purse on the seat between Ruby and me. An awful ugly purse, it occurs to me: white vinyl, the strap just about chewed off. I feel around for something in the secret pocket — the only reason I remember now for having bought such a cheesy-looking bag. Small and hard as budgie grit, the ring is still there, where it's been since that crazy night at Edna's.

Ruby's head snaps forward, her chin sagging to her chest; her mouth furrows, showing the faint pink of her tongue like a cat's, asleep. A little string of drool beads her coat. I jerk the truck into gear and creep forward, so slowly you can hear each pebble crunching in the drive, till the trailer comes in sight. Then I jackrabbit the brakes — no, it's not Wilf's truck I see parked in the yard, but a silver Chevette; and there's a woman wearing garden gloves, kneeling in the dirt. She looks up in surprise, half-heartedly waving the trowel in her hand. She's got grey permed hair, a pleasant enough face; she's wearing sneakers and a red blouse and dark pressed jeans just a bit wide in the hips. My first thought: I've got the wrong place. My second: OhmyGod.

She lays down her trowel and I see what she's been planting: a plot of pansies, neat and tight as your arse, in the flowerbed out front. It's a rough little circle ringed with white painted rocks, a touch I found homey and rather sweet that one time Ruby and I visited — what I saw of it, pulling up in the dark. Then, I'd pictured Wilf outside having a beer, taking a brush to those stones, taking the time, too, to put in flowers. Not something a man would normally do, I figured; not a bachelor, anyways.

At the sight of those pansies, my heart does a loop-the-loop and nose-dives — that's the only way of putting it. And in the instant the woman gets up and starts coming towards the truck, I slug 'er into reverse trembling, and hightail it out of there so fast, honest to Pete, the gravel flies fit to sandblast the paint off those foolish white cartwheels.

The lurching and skidding shakes Ruby awake. "Got to pee," she says, her voice thick with spit, and I step on it till we hit the Irving. After our trip to the ladies', still shaky, I park by the air pump and unwrap lunch; I barely touch mine, but Ruby sits wolfing down her sandwich till a girl in a big sedan full of kids pulls in and makes us move.

All the way back to Arcadia, Ruby sniffles and moans, shaking her head, complaining about the weather, how it won't stop raining. By now, of course, the sun is blazing overhead, slanting down strong and hot. Birds chirp from every bush and tree, the leaves unfurling their tender quirky green; there are dandelions bursting everywhere. It's ladyslipper weather, as Ruby used to say — though frankly, I always found it hard to get excited about those flowers; they looked to me like babies' scrotums, or how I imagine babies' scrotums would look: small, reddish-pink, with that smell of diapers.

Warm grey road-dirt dusts the windshield. I don't bother answering Ruby's complaints; I'm too busy wondering about that woman, imagining her inside the trailer, scrubbing dirt from under her nails. But there's more to my silence; I don't respond because there is nothing to say. I'm like a kid scrounging inside a marble pouch and coming up empty-handed, without so much as a peewee to trade.

I'm like a bus out of gas.

"Rain rain rain," she goes on and on and on, till the word slurs into itself, one long endless errrrrr: something sputtering, stalled.

When we finally get home, I settle Ruby in front of *Another World*, take the phone into the bathroom and bolt the door. With the tap running, gushing, I make the call — the call I've been avoiding all my life, it would seem.

The woman's voice on the other end is rushed; kind but matter-of-fact in a way I don't quite trust. Hanging up, I feel like Judas with the bloody rope burns on his neck.

That night the phone rings a few times: long, loud bursts separated by silence. I know it's not Edna.

Once I get Ruby to bed, I go into my room, the door open, one ear cocked, always cocked, for sounds of her getting up in the dark. Weary, I slip Wilf's ring from my purse and hold it just so, till the little gemstone catches the light, its hard, bright edges sparkling like tinfoil. I push the ring over my knuckle, hold out my hand like Jesus raising the dead, and admire it. I feel a pinch inside, a sharp twist like a wrench tightening a nut.

Snapping off the light, I lie there a while in the dark, turning the ring round and round on my finger. I even fancy falling asleep with it on, except I'm not much for jewellery; even as a girl I couldn't hack the feel of things on me, just knowing they were there: bracelets, chains, earrings — rings of any kind. Even the ring Ma gave me once, that was her mother's. It had a dull, dark stone, jet till you held it to the sun, and then it looked red as a fresh, deep cut. I lost that ring one day wading in the river; I must've been seven or eight, it happened before Daddy left. I was too scared to tell Ma. She never asked where the ring went; never noticed, maybe, that I'd quit wearing it. But ever since, I've thought rings looked best on somebody else — the type like Edna, who wears rubber gloves doing housework and planting things.

Next day the weather turns — chilly and raw at first, but by the time I buckle Ruby in and start the truck, it's beginning to warm up, the clouds riven with blue.

I drive with a strange resolve for once, a destination. The appointment is for ten o'clock. No slow scenic routes. We take the highway past Caledonia, through a district on the outskirts. It looks like a subdivision: new, sided bungalows; flat, scuffed lawns; and low, sprawling buildings, schools or warehouses, bordering woods. The one I'm interested in appears wedged into the forest, a big brick complex. There's no playground outside, no swings or monkey bars. It's fronted by grass and a curved flowerbed, and the sign says "Resthaven". A delivery van swerves past us towards an underground loading bay. I pull into a spot by a round bed of tulips, the buds just opened. In front of the truck, a robin pulls a worm; there's a whole flock in the branches overhead. If not for the roar of the building's ventilation system, the birdsong would be out of this world.

Ruby's face goes lank.

"Nope," she declares whimsically. "Nope."

"C'mon, girl-dear," I fairly chirp at her, hating myself. "Let's just have a boo. Won't take long."

Her face pulls and twitches in bewilderment. Panic.

"No rain," she says, the shaking of her head like a tremor. "No rain today, no."

Her jaw clamps shut, sets like concrete.

A soft damp breeze blows through the truck. It flattens her hair to her scalp like splinters silver as smelt shooting upstream — each sharp as a dressmaker's pin sticking into my bosom. She gapes straight ahead at the windshield — absorbing what, God only knows. I can't see her eyes, but I have an inkling of how they must mirror the muddied, greeny-blue glass. Slowly her mouth sags open in protest; a little girl's voice comes out, that meek.

"No Dora no rain not today, no, no."

She hunkers down, her shoulders oddly squared, defying me. Defying the breeze, the sticky sunshine warming her face; the clouds. And saucy as the Road Runner, you know what she does? Lifts a quaking pointer and, fox-sly, like Quick Draw McGraw, pushes down the lock button; one fast move. "NO rrrrrain!"

"Ho-kay." I give in. Moving too fast to sigh or reconsider, I jump out, locking my side too. For one awful second I fear I've left the keys inside; but no, there they are in my pocket.

The glass door slides open when I reach it, just like at Beaver Lumber, admitting me into the bright, cheery lobby. I feel as if I've been vacuumed, sucked up like a piece of lint. No dirt or dustballs in this place, though; none that jump out, anyway; not in the reception area. The smell of Endust and floor polish greets me, and something else, soupy, warm — overcooked meat? But they're not bad smells; not sharp or medicinal, like you'd expect.

Soon enough the director appears, the lady I spoke to on the phone. She looks nothing like her voice, which sounded pert, efficient, young — the voice of a lively brunette? This gal's heavy, pear-shaped; grey but attractive, her salt-and-pepper hair cut in a wedge — the Viyella type that spends a fortune on clothes. (Right down to foundations, I'd wager; Lord, no ripped Hannas for them.) Mrs. Hart, her name is. She slips a white smock over her dress before we embark on our tour — *tore*, she says, like something being ripped.

"Ms. Hammond," she's careful to call me. "Your aunt," she says, pronouncing it like "ant", the kind at picnics, the kind that eat wood — carpenters — like the one I noticed earlier on the kitchen floor, migrating from the store.

Her fingers pushing buttons, heedless of her long, pink-pearl nails, Mrs. Hart leads me through a series of doors that buzz shut behind us, just like in *Get Smart*. We turn down a mauve corridor, the walls papered with posied borders, big rosy bouquets like the ones brides throw at weddings. The smells change, the scent of floor polish laced with something sweet, pineapple juice maybe; cold tea; and something else, alkaline, sour.

On either side, doors dot the hallway, opening into rooms. Hospital rooms with hospital beds, except that, from what I can glimpse sweeping past, the walls are crammed with quirky things: knick-knacks, posters, Phentex hangings; photographs. Large family groupings; smiling combos of couples, kids, babies.

Farther down, the hallway bulges like a weak spot in a vein, accommodating a circle of old people, faded, slumped, arranged in chairs. All kinds of chairs — it's the furniture I notice, not the occupants; I don't mean to sound heartless. God, the chairs; a dog's breakfast, really: rockers, gliders, wheelchairs, straight chairs, easy boys — everything from a pink velour wing chair like one of Edna's, to this high-tech black sling that looks more like an instrument of torture than something to park your fanny on.

Strapped into it, rowing back and forth like sixty, back and forth, is a lady who looks younger than me, her neat brown hair cut in a bob. Where's the fire? you feel like asking, there's such a snake-cold look of purpose in her eyes. Steering me past, Mrs. Hart remarks how that chair's a godsend, affording Miss So-and-so harmless, constant motion while ensuring the others' safety. "Before that," says Mrs. Hart, with the faintest hint of a grin, "she kept trying to run them down with her wheelchair."

In the pink wing chair sits a handsome white-haired gent, dapper as Ronald Reagan, immaculate in a white shirt and navy vest. Mrs. Hart introduces us and for one blessed minute the fellow smiles up at me, slack-jawed, a watery glimmer to his eyes like a new moon through fog. When he tries to speak, I notice the ground-down nubs of his sparse bottom teeth. And I see he's strapped in with the kind of belted contraption mothers use to tie up youngsters for car rides.

"Residents can free-range on this floor — they are allowed to move around," Mrs. Hart says pleasantly, moving to a tiny, shrunken lady whose skin looks transparent, her face flat as a map. Smiling, the big woman swoops down, her paisley skirt sweeping the floor, and with those pink eagle claws unsnaps the doohickey at the lady's waist. "Judy here can come and go," says Mrs. Hart, but the woman's expression doesn't change; it stays sweet and foolish, imbecile. A neat white floss of hair fine as spider silk is piled on her head — she was a looker once, you can tell. "Say hello, Judy," Mrs. Hart coaxes, beaming. Nothing; if the lights are on, there's nobody home. Still smiling, Mrs. Hart ushers me on. Enough already, I want to whisper, but I can't bear to seem crude. Considering I'm surrounded, all these wizened white faces watching, staring like Buddha into space. I feel like Dorothy, I do, parachuted into Oz; or Sally Saucer stranded in the circle. *Turn to the East, Sally, turn to the West, turn to the very one that you love best....*

There's a poster on the wall advertising Loonie Bingo, a Saturday-night hymn-sing, a TV night of World Wrestling.

A lady in a wheelchair looks anxious to greet me; she sticks out her hand and, dizzy, I reach down to shake it. Too late, I realize she's knitting — with invisible needles. "In three years, Patsy's done all of five rows." Mrs. Hart winks, and I guess the poor thing must be deaf. But no; suddenly she pipes right up.

"In 1928" — she fixes her sharp black eyes on mine, dead serious — "in 1928 I went there to have my hair done, yup. The barber...." There's a pause, her toothless gums chewing the words over. "The barber was a big dark fella, a nice big man. Nice dark man yup big and handsome yup I'd've liked to fuck him yup — I would've — liked to — fuck him."

"Fuck him fuck him fuck him," the old geezer in the navy vest mimics, talking to the ceiling, his voice cranking over like an old-fashioned phonograph — like the RCA Victor that Daddy used to have in the front room, the one with a picture of a dog listening to his master's voice.

Sweet, holy Moses. The pineapple smell has turned plain sickly, and the sourness underneath it can only be one thing — the odour of piss — cut with something else, like the smell of used dental floss or spoiled meat.

"Your tour's been quite...enlightening," I start to tell my guide, when another old goat ("ambulatory", as she notes) comes barrelling towards us full steam, repeating in a singsong moan, "I got to get to Springhill Spring-hill Sprrrrring-hill, got to get there in twenty minutes, see, I got to get to work, see, twenty minutes I got to get to work, Springhill Springhill Springhi...." There's an ugly-looking stain on the seat of his trousers. A pretty little nurse slips out and takes him gently by the elbow, stalking off arm in arm with him like the kitten in a May-December romance. "Your ride's a-coming," I hear her consoling him, all the way down the hall and out of sight. "Should be here any minute."

The floor gleams.

"Would you like to see a room?" Mrs. Director checks her watch and leads me out of the circle, away from the chairs towards an open door. She doesn't knock, but something makes me tiptoe. "I wouldn't normally do this, of course — but you see, we're full up at the moment; unfortunately, there is a waiting list. But Pearl won't mind us peeking in; she's just having a little rest — aren't you, Pearl? Can you hear me, Pearl? No, I guess she can't. Never mind" — she smiles at me — "we'll be quick."

Curled on her side in the hospital bed is a driftwood doll, swear to God, that's how small and thin and white she is, this sleeping woman lying with her knees drawn up. She looks like a hammock, her body under the sheets — a worn, empty hammock becalmed on a porch, no wind to stir it. Against the pillow, her face is craggy as a witch's, the skin translucent, the flesh sucked and drawn tight around her cheekbones like mottled, wrinkled parchment: lampshade paper. Threads of yellowed hair wisp from her scalp. Her eyes are screwed shut, the crow's feet spoked like a wheel. I can hear her breathing, a hoarse, shallow whistling. Her hands are bent into fists, the fingers warped and twisted in upon themselves; the nails are blue. Mrs. Hart reaches down and briefly, tenderly, strokes one of her wrists. Then, perfunctory as a cop, she tucks the hand gently under the sheet.

Not for a minute is she unkind or bossy. But I guess I'm waiting for something further — the flicker of a tear? It doesn't come. When she glances at me, I'd bet the last of my insurance money that she can see the knot in my throat. Her look is that knowing; what Oprah would call "professional". I suppose if you watched over death every day, maybe it would be like seeing blood, you'd just get used to it. Like counting teapots in the cafeteria, or running the Loonie Bingo: somebody's got to do it. I'm not in a position to judge how.

"Well," says Mrs. Hart, breezing back out into the corridor. "That about concludes our little *tore* — unless you'd like to see the garden. Our ambulatory residents get all the fresh air they desire; we find it gives them a real boost, you know, especially the older ones. Does Aunt enjoy the out-of-doors?"

"Not much," I mutter. Ruby's idea of nature was the flowerbed the town used to plant on a hillside, marigolds and petunias in the shape of an ore cart and pickaxe; "Welcome to Arcadia" spelled out in white gravel.

We take an elevator to the basement level, buzz our way out to a fenced enclosure, not a garden so much as a big shady pen with benches, a picnic table set on cement slabs — a patio with a collection of worn-looking chairs under the roof's overhang. Scattered here and there are wooden flowerboxes with the stubs of last year's plants sticking up. What I notice most are the huge, mossy hemlocks just beyond the chain-link fence, their bark like elephant skin, their feathery boughs swooping down.

The yard's deserted but for a tiny gentleman in a jaunty hat and all-weather coat, resting on a bench beneath the branches. His head's tipped back, the fedora at a crazy angle. He's either asleep or watching something in the trees: a bird, or the sunshine shifting through the needles?

Mrs. Hart touches my arm. In this light you can see the line where her liquid foundation tapers off, her orangey-beige chin against the white of her throat. "If you like, we'll return to the office; I've got some forms you'll need to fill out. Be prepared for as long as a six-week wait. Of course, that can change. But you'd be wise to start the wheels in motion."

XXXI

Steaks

Like Morse code, the phone rings: two long dashes split by dots of silence — just long enough, I figure, for Edna to light a smoke. Sure enough, it's her; Lordy, her voice like the response to an SOS, it's that breathy.

"You'll never guess," she starts, then pauses; there's a deep *whoooosh* as she exhales. "The Mounties let them two suspects go, Lindy! Insufficient evidence, I heard at the g'rage, while I was gassing up Hub's van." She takes another puff, allowing me to digest this. Mostly what I think of, though, is Edna at the wheel of Pyke's windowless van — a black one with chrome gewgaws on the sides like the handles of a casket, only about as functional as hood ornaments.

"Sheesh," she says, "business is crazy these days — people dropping like flies, seems like. Hub says January's the busiest month, but I dunno, I'd say his memory's short. Nothing like the warm weather to bring on death — y'ever notice? Me now, if it were up to me I'd wait till fall, late fall, maybe Christmas, to croak. Can't see it myself, this time of year, can you? The leaves bursting out, fish jumping as they say, everything so nice——"

"What about those suspects?" I cut in. "Never did get who they were. What else did you hear down at Bubba's?" The name lobs off my tongue as if I go there all the time, though I don't and wouldn't; Ruby and Uncle always said Carmen's garage watered their gas.

My question gives Edna something to work on, a scent to a hound, and I settle back for a chit-chat, half wishing for a cigarette myself, what with the faint *pop* of her lips taking a drag. I picture her in her kitchen, all made up, dressed to the nines — or on her cellphone, at the wheel of the funeral van.

I'm just getting comfy when I hear someone pulling in outside and, before I know it, pounding on the screen door. "Can't they see we're closed?" I growl. Ruby, thankfully, is in watching TV — "watching" a polite way of putting it. The noise acts like a lullaby, maybe; the same way — who knows? — as those nature tapes you see advertised: waves crashing on rocks, gulls squawking.

"Hang on a minute," I have to interrupt. "Got someone at the door."

"Tell 'em you don't want any," Edna jokes, "unless they're giving it away — or the guy's six foot tall and on that new impotence pill. You hear about that, Lindy? My soul, what'll they come up with next!"

Well, golly. He catches me off guard, sneaky as those Mormons who seem to come out of the woods in their suits, just to land on your porch.

"Shiza!" I'm flabbergasted at the sight of his face through the screen, shady and smiling as a newspaper shot. "Gosh, I mean, what the — well, hell's bells, come on in." Then I spy the gal in the truck; the one who was outside his trailer that day, puttering in his yard.

Before I say boo, he's stepping out of his shoes. "No need to," I want to say, "unless you've stepped in something." Beat-up tennis shoes on a man you can no more see serving a ball than hiking up Everest.

"I'm gonna have to call you back," I grab up the phone and tell Edna. It's doubtful she's even come up for air; God, still talking as I hang up.

My heart's pounding fit to bring on a stroke; I feel the blood rush to my face. And I realize it's been weeks since I saw him last — must be, 'cause his hair's longer and his face is tanned, well, the same ruddy shade as a russet apple blushing.

"We've got to talk," he says, sober as a judge, looking at me. His being in sock feet puts us about eye level. "I thought we had some kind of understanding, Lindy."

He stands there like that big pushy rooster on *Bugs Bunny*, honest to God, hands in his back pockets, his burly forearms thrust out — they're a deep brown, what you can see below the sleeves of his red knit polo. Yet he's fidgety too, in a way I haven't seen before; shrugging his neck like a pigeon, he keeps glancing out at his truck.

"Who is she?" I finally say, trying to sound casual, you know, like a TV voice: Oprah or Phil asking someone what brand soap they use.

"Huh?" He seems almost stunned. "Bernadette? You mean my sister?" His face goes redder — red as his shirt — and I see he's sweating. He pulls out a Kleenex and dabs his forehead. "Look, Lindy, if you think you're getting the runaround——" He shakes his head, collecting himself. We both stare at his socks, clean and white as if they just came from Zellers. "She's down from New Brunswick, been down all month. I've been trying and trying to get a hold of you and introduce you two — she's only here till tomorrow. Wanted to give you a chance to get acquainted, anyways; see what you think of each other." He eyes me, looking hopeful yet disappointed too. "I'm taking her out tonight — she doesn't get down too often. Figured we'd try that new surf'n'turf place in town. Wondered if you'd join us — you and Ruby, o' course. I've told Bern all about you, and she's dying to — well, you know, all this time and I figured I'd better quit talking and show her the goods — or else she's gonna think I've been yapping through my hat, see. Making it all up."

Harharharhar-heeee, goes the bottled laughter on TV; otherwise there's not a peep from the next room.

Wilf's eyes skim over me like a washcloth, then come to rest on my left hand. His grin see-saws when he sees it bare.

"No dogs pissing on your back wheels, I gather," he says,

bucking up. "Christ, I thought you must've moved away, the times I've stopped by and nobody home."

He smiles again, but something about his look reminds me of an empty jam jar stuck back in the fridge.

"A'right, I'll come," I say, trying to look him in the eye. But my gaze keeps shifting towards the truck. His sister catches me looking, grimaces and waves.

"Well, good — nice one," he says, giving my arm a fake little punch. Then he steps closer, clapping both hands on my shoulders, studying my face. He looks pleased, shy, hangdog, all at once.

"Unless there's someplace you'd like better — Italian? Chinese?" He shrugs, still gripping my shoulders. Under my shirt I feel a twinge, feel my bosom move.

"Long as it's not fancy," I say, still trying to get a gander at the sister. She looks like a nun, it occurs to me. At least, she does from this distance: the same no-nonsense plainness. Watching from the window, I imagine her in a habit, built like a plug; why I didn't see it earlier, heaven only knows.

On impulse, heck, while she's looking, I rub up against him, yes, as though there's been not a minute's break between us, not one little interruption in our cosy back-and-forth; and I kiss him. Right on the mouth. No two ways about it. And that Bernadette out there gawking, as though somebody'd turned over a rock and, Lordy, who could guess what just crawled out?

"Till tonight?" He pulls back far enough to whisper, his lips slippery-warm as marge left out overnight.

The second he leaves I'm dialling Edna. And in return for a few major details — my voice pleased as punch, self-important; that's how it sounds, anyway, bouncing back to me off the kitchen cupboards — I ask a favour of her, something I wouldn't have dreamed of doing before.

"Listen, Edna — can you watch Ruby? I'll pay you."

I can practically hear the spit hit the phone, with the long, drawn-out *sheeesh* through her teeth. I listen for the wheels turning — Edna working up some excuse?

"Don't be a stunned arse, Lindy — 'course I can. Well, I mean, prob'ly. What time?"

I tell her.

"And Lindy?" she goes. "As for money — don't insult me, woman."

For the date I put on control-top hose and a skirt, if you can imagine. Halfway out the door, I rip off the stockings and go bare-legged, my feet in sandals, some old Dr. Scholl's I used to wear in the store. If the freckles on my shins spread closer together, I'd have a tan, I think, hesitating just a moment.

Edna plugs in the kettle to make Ruby's tea. While her back's turned I slip on Wilf's ring — just to get used to the feel, so I won't fuss and fidget on our evening out. By the time I climb into Betsy, it feels like a wart, a part of my finger at least.

Then halfway to Caledonia I have a panic attack, thinking I should've worn stockings. Don't want that sister of his getting ideas. I should've pumped him with questions first: "What if I look like a gold-digger? What if that's what she thinks?"

Lord knows *what* she imagines, after seeing the store, the windows like ones in a bomb shelter.

The rest of the way to the restaurant, I lambaste him in my mind for inviting me, for dragging his sister to Arcadia in the first place.

But when I pull into the lot and spy Wilf's truck, the backs of their heads like bookends up front, I forget all this. I even forget Ruby, back there with Edna doing God knows what. For a minute I forget everything but the smell of Wilf's hair, that clean oily smell like the soap-on-a-rope in his shower — the one I sniffed, Lord help me, when I snuck to the bathroom after dinner that night, while Wilf was trying to teach Ruby to use the remote.

I get out and walk over, tap on his window. His face cracks into a grin. "That a gun in your pocket, or you just glad to see me?" a movie-star voice, Mae West, croons in my head — nerves, I guess, nothing to do with Wilf's behaviour. He cranks down the window and pats my hand. His sister winces a smile, eyeballing me. "Hello, Lindy," she says, friendly enough.

"You forgot something." He looks at me funny, and I see he means Ruby.

Inside, we take a booth, the two of them side by side, facing me like a jury. I slide to a spot in the middle of my bench, squeaking left and right — my legs sticking — depending on who's talking, brother or sis. I can't help longing for those pantihose curled up at home in the porch.

The sister orders a rum and Coke, Wilf asks for beer. I start with a virgin Caesar — it seems the thing to have — when the waitress finally appears. The drink stings my lips and I realize I've been licking them over and over, like a heifer tonguing a blue salt block.

While we wait for the food, I escape to the ladies' and smear on lipstick, wishing it were Vaseline. Back at the table, Bernadette's on her second drink. Wilf has switched to Clamato, celery growing from his glass like a tree. He winks at me. His sister's talking about her pension plan, some screw-up with the cheques. But even after a drink and a half, she speaks properly, carefully; Ruby, in the good old days, would've approved.

In the middle of our garden salads, Wilf reaches out and takes my hand, rubbing his thumb over the little diamond. Our eyes lock, his beaming — sweating — gratitude. His sister keeps talking; he doesn't need to say anything. Mostly we just listen. The steaks arrive, thick T-bones served on breadboards; Wilf has also ordered a shrimp platter to share. Once everything's in front of us, he orders wine, a whole carafe of sparkling Duck, which the sister says gives her headaches.

"The more for us," he says, topping me up. "I'm in the party mood, Bern." There's so much food on the table, we push the plates around like bumper cars, his sister with her fork and knife poised, impatient, you can tell, to tuck in. For once I have no appetite. Neither, apparently, does Wilf, because the two of us sit there gawping into one another's eyes — me stuck firmly now to the spot across from him.

The wine, though, is cool and sweet as evening air laced with lilacs, lilies and.... Good God, the next thing you know, our food's gone cold and our elbows are almost in our plates and we're kissing. Kissing right there at the table, the sister taking extra care with her steak, eyes on the knife as if she's performing surgery.

"Of all the shameful behaviour," she mutters, to no one in particular. Then, still staring at her utensils: "Wilf Jewkes, you oughta be ashamed."

Without taking his eyes off me, he says, "That meat done enough, Bern?" And without blinking: "Isn't she something? I told you she was something, Bern. Never mind, eat your steak."

After that she doesn't say boo, just polishes off her meal and goes out and sits in the truck.

"You better get her in for coffee and dessert," I say, but by then the bill has arrived, the Duck is gone, our dinners like a spurned doggy's breakfast. "All that money, and we hardly ate," I whisper on the way out, sobered by the night sky. A zillion twinkling, giddy stars — like my little rock, multiplied. Wilf just grins and shakes his head.

I think right then I've died and gone to heaven. But walking me to my truck, he tugs on my arm, pulling me back, landing me square on my Dr. Scholl's.

"I'm not trying to rush you, or rope you in, Lindy. But there's something I've got to know. You told me you'd do some thinking on it; well, it's been over a month now. I'd like to know: you got an answer for me yet, or what?"

I gulp, keep looking way up at all those stars, seeking out the Big Dipper.

"Okay," he says. "But I'd like an answer by the end of summer. See, once the road's done, I'm thinking I'll retire. And I got this hankering to go to Florida for the win——"

Just then somebody leans on a horn, a godawful siren blast. It's got to be Bernadette.

The call comes out of the blue, about as expected as a candy man flogging black and orange 'jubes at Christmas. It's a sticky afternoon, sweltering in the house. I've got us parked outside, Ruby's plastic chair in a patch of shade; I'm trying to read to her for a change — the newest *Enquirer*, the latest scuttlebutt on some actress-child offed by her parents. There's an article, too, about freeze-drying people's heads — yes, their heads, to be reattached later to bodies cured in the meantime of cancer and AIDS — *much* later, I'd suspect. Gosh, some place in California will freeze-dry you whole, the story goes; talk about being put on hold, in case a hundred years from now they find a cure for ageing!

I've been reading aloud to Ruby, but two paragraphs in she shows no interest, so I give up and start reading to myself. I'm eating the stuff up when the phone rings. Slouched down in her new white chair, a blue-striped umbrella clamped to the arm, Ruby watches a horsefly as if it's making the sound, the jangly noise coming through the screen. (Though the phone's portable, I can't seem to break the habit of leaving it in the kitchen.) I'm so engrossed in the *Enquirer,* to tell the truth I don't exactly leap up to get it. In fact, I take my time, making sure Ruby's tied in first with the old plaid scarf I've been using on her.

By the time I growl, "Hullo?", I'm in a sweat, crotchety as a tree. A lump jumps to my throat as I realize it could be Wilf. But it's a woman, a businesslike voice vaguely familiar but not exactly chummy; not someone selling things or bumming money.

"Ms. Hammond? We have a spot," she says, rushing on when I pause. "This is Resthaven calling, Juanita Hart.... A private room, as you requested...short notice, I know. Sometimes that's the way it works...."

It's as though the ceiling's tilted, falling, showering rubble. The only thing I see is the back of Ruby's head beyond the screen, nodding underneath that foolish gay umbrella. And with this comes instant panic — good God, what was I thinking, leaving her alone out there? What if she tips her chair, squirming to get free?

"Can't talk right now," I blubber, "I've got to go."

"Ms. Hammond?" The voice is piqued, same as when you tell those telemarketing folks, look, you're just not interested.

"I understand that it's difficult. But we need to know — you *did* ask for private, did you not? If I'm not mistaken? There are dozens waiting on our list, as I'm sure you appreciate. I could put you down for semi-private, if that's what you'd prefer — oh, I know cost's a factor. But frankly, heaven knows how long it could be before another spot comes up."

Jesus. *Jesus.*

The back of Ruby's neck looks greyish, sinewy, through the screen. The faintest wisp of breeze tugs her hair.

Around my chest, my neck, there is a rope — how else to explain that dry, parched tightening, as though my very lights are being squeezed up and out?

"All right," I finally tell the woman. "But you'll have to give me time to get things squared away."

It's the worst that could happen, honestly. Like having the deciding move foisted on you in a game of checkers, even when you've been itching to quit or go to the bathroom. If you like to play. And there's not a blessed thing to cheer for, winning or losing, once the game's in the bag.

Worse; it's like burying someone still warm.

I can't help myself, I think of execution: those vans pictured in the news from Texas, transporting bodies zapped by lethal injection. The famous last meals cons ask for, their final night on death row. The *Enquirer* printed a list once: serial killer, beans and wieners; axe murderer, french fries, tinned stew.

I forget, did Judas hang around after blowing the whistle? I think he was there boozing at Christ's last supper; probably burped wine stringing his noose to the tree.

The ugliest sin, I'd have to say, is forcing somebody's hand. A close second, going behind their back.

"Aunt Ruby?" I whisper in a little-girl voice, same as if I were twelve again. Tiptoeing up behind the lawn chair, I train my eyes on her neck. She's so still, perhaps she's asleep. Lordy, I pray that she could be — in that wakeless world, sleeping that deepest of slumbers. Slumber, sweet Dinah; doesn't the sound conjure up novelties? Pyjama bags, the zippered Humpty-Dumpty we carried one Christmas; not one blessed unit sold.

Up close, I catch a whiff of the faint sour smell of her skin, spotted as the tissue we used packing those bags back off to the distributor. It was no good for gift-wrapping gloves or hose, this being when we offered such a service.

So long in the same body, Ruby. It's enough, almost, to let me think mine's still supple, not like a balloon out of air.

I bend and, reckless, foolhardy as the prince nuzzling Snow White, kiss the nape of her neck.

If she feels it, I can't tell.

For supper that evening I fix tuna salad served on lettuce leaves, lemonade from scratch. Ruby always liked the taste of lemons. Now her mouth opens and closes around the drink like a puckered valve — trying to decipher sweet from sour? In the end she spills it and I mop up, thankful at least for the breeze tickling us through the screen, promising a cooler night.

Wilf phones and offers to drive us. "Nope," I say, "it's something I've got to do by myself."

"Anything you need, Lindy, gimme a shout — okay?"

Ruby lies on her bed, staring at the walls, while I dig out her old striped suitcase. She'll need nightclothes, I figure; underpants, a bedjacket. Rooting through her dresser, I go crazy and throw in dresses, jewellery, knick-knacks too — all the stuff you imagine a body would need on a long, long trip.

At the bottom of her undies drawer is Gran's book, where I stashed it after going through it. I didn't know what else to do with it. Like a serving of something odd and not to your taste at a dinner out somewhere — what do you do? Sneak it off your plate and into your serviette at the first opportunity? Ruby glances over, no recognition, as I hold the book in my hands for a bit, then slide it into the suitcase, underneath her slippers.

To close the lid I have to lay the bag on the floor, get down on all fours and park my bum on top. Ruby looks down. A tiny belch erupts from her lips — a guffaw.

"First thing in the morning, dear, we're gonna take a little spin."

It's the only warning I give. Then I crawl in beside her, yes, in that high, creaky bed, the overhead light blazing down on us bunked up together. And I lean into her, her frail, sagging body, and put my arms around her. My arms make a circle, holding on for all I'm worth. Till my face is buried in the bony crook of her arm, its fusty smell in my nose, and I'm weeping like an ugly old baby. Wondering who's holding who.

That night I dream about Ruby sitting on a bench in the nursing-home garden, except the big trees are gone. The sun is blazing down; the only shade is from the blue-striped umbrella clamped to her wrist like a watch.

In the morning I do the chores as always. Seems as though there should be some sense of occasion — I should be dressing in black and Ruby in her good navy dress, a string of pearls at her throat; our hair should be washed. There isn't time. In the end I put Ruby in a dress we bought one summer, one she's never worn, baby blue overlaid with leaves like palm fronds against the sky at dawn — a tropical sky, a Florida sky? — the way they might look if you lay on your back, cool sand for a pillow, and gazed upwards.

To distract myself while buttoning her up, I picture Wilf in a little trailer down in Orlando, maybe, or Palm Beach — one of those places snowbirds go.

Outside, her dress shimmers like Saran Wrap; it's the polyester in it.

"We're going for a drive now," I tell her, with the nonchalance of a hit man. A villain on *Miami Vice*.

I fling her suitcase into the back.

For a second, buckling her up, I imagine there's a glint of pleasure in her eyes — our little daily ritual recalled? I want to haul her back inside, dump the suitcase on her bed. "Just foolin'," I want to say, as if everything has been a drama — a really bad one on TV, the off-knob kaput.

Quick as it appears, the glimmer vanishes. The purse on her lap sits like a lunch box; her elbow on the armrest, her palm on the door handle, are limp, relaxed: *We're going for a ride.* There's a certain ladylike poise to that bent hand, a hand you could still picture in a white glove, the kind of glove in a Pledge ad.

For one long minute I pray the truck won't start, but she does, choking, sputtering to life. I pick the scenic route. Not a peep from Ruby, sitting straight as though riding up front on a chuckwagon. There's a slash of pink lipstick on her mouth — my idea — smudged now, half gummed off, her mouth a muzzy bloom in the middle of that pale, shrunken face.

We pass hillsides dotted with livestock, brown workhorses grazing and cows marked like dominoes against the dandelion-specked green.

"Leonard?" she says — at least, that's what it sounds like; urgent, hopeful. "Leonard. Loves. Car."

It's a voice that would have me bite the ditch and turn around. "Leonard? Yes," I answer, chewing tears. "Uncle."

But then her look clouds back to the same dogged *nothing*. Like wind blitzing through an empty mansion, fanning dust through cobwebbed rooms.

Passing brick-and-siding bungalows, I feel myself shaking, my foot jiggling on the accelerator.

When the home comes into sight, I have this urge to keep going, and almost do — I miss the big curved driveway, pull a U-ie in front of a school to go back.

In the lot, she won't get out. Of course I expected this, the need to coax and cajole. To lie.

"We're just going for a little visit." I get a hold of her arm, try gently prying her from the seat. Confusion flits over her face, then a look of feverish despair. "Mum-ma? Mum-maaaa?" One hand closes around her purse strap as if I'm out to rob her; the other's gripping the dash.

"Just a quickie, Ruby, just a little vis...."

As gentle as you can be using the strength of a Doberman's jaw, I commence peeling each of her fingers from the dash. An awful, desperate whine comes from her throat; almost like a far-off memory of something, I taste blood, realize it's my lip. I'm about to give up, I am, when someone appears. A nurse in a turquoise pantsuit, gently patting me aside; reaching out strong arms. I don't see her accomplice at first, a gangly young fellow in a bright white smock.

"It's hardest on the family," the gal says in a firm, soothing voice. "Waaay worse for the ones who know what's going on."

I lurch backwards, tug at the suitcase stowed beside the wheelwell. The young fellow's long arms reach in and take over.

As if from someplace far away, I hear other kind, cheery voices. "You'd be surprised how quickly our clients adjust. You mustn't worry. She's in the best of hands. We'll take good care of her."

"We know what she needs."

"It's the best thing."

Someone, perhaps it's Mrs. Hart, escorts me to an office where I sign something, then takes me up to the room. And I sit there alone with the door closed, waiting while Ruby is "processed" —

a notion that, never mind the state I'm in, makes me think of cheese.

I wait and wait, distracting myself by scrutinizing the room, the nicely draped windows; inspecting baseboards, sills, for signs of dirt, the bare yellow walls for hooks, nails or scraps of tape. The bareness finally gets to me and I lose all nerve, knowing that if I don't get out now I'll need a room myself.

Haven't I read somewhere that it's best sometimes to disappear? To let what can't be controlled sort itself out?

"The hardest part is leaving. You may not believe it, but nine times out of ten, clients are fine once the loved ones go; once they settle in."

I always hoped I'd have the gumption — like running the last few steps of some awful marathon, or sitting out the end of a just-for-fun, prizeless dud of a bingo game — the gumption to stay around long enough to kiss Ruby goodbye.

But what I do is unsnap her suitcase, line up the toiletries on top of the smooth blond bureau. Slip a roll of five-flavour Life Savers under the strange, cold pillow. Then I beat it out of there, sneaking down the fire exit, three chilly flights of stairs.

"We'll call and tell you how she's doing. We'll keep you updated. Apprised." A voice like Mrs. Hart's seems to bounce from my eardrums, echoing with each giddy footfall, off every painted metal step.

I'm crazy now to be outside breathing buggy, unconditioned air. Climbing into the truck, I pant like a collie, have to sit for a minute figuring what to do next, how to turn the key in the ignition.

Then I lay rubber, hightailing it out of there faster than any thief. One wild stew of thoughts swirls through my brain, only half on the road. I find myself thinking of my first day of school: the teacher prying my arms off Ma's waist, telling her to run for it. Which Ma did, that pretty red hair flying out like a banner, all I could see of her getting tinier and tinier, sprinting across the bridge. I never took my eyes off her, not till she was out of sight. I cried and cried, but not once did she look back.

I know a little now of what she must've felt.

XXXII

The Wind

On her way home from doing errands, Edna picks me up in her little blue Sunbird. The plan is to go down to her place and play cards with her and a couple of gals from the Legion, Edna's friends from the ladies' social committee.

"They got the Smirnoff's on sale at the commission in town," she says when I get in. The back seat's full of groceries. "That's how come I'm a tad late. You don't mind, do you; I knew you wouldn't. Say, Lindy — you okay? Sheesh, looks like you could use a drink yourself, girl."

I'd had a call a bit earlier from Mrs. Hart saying Ruby was settling in "nicely", not eating a lot but getting plenty of rest. Getting ready for Edna's bridge party — a little touch-up with the curling iron — I concentrated on that word "nicely". Pulling a monkey face in the mirror, I mouthed it: *nicely, nicely*. Putting up fences in my head around places I could but would not go.

I figured I was doing pretty good.

"The girls are coming over at seven. But Hub can handle 'em if we're a bit late. Imagine, would you, Hub in a roomful of women — ones that talk! Oh, save me." Edna cracks up, slapping the

394

steering wheel, and I wonder if maybe she's been tippling a little on the sly. "Believe me, it'd do the man a worrrllld of good. You ever notice with men, they don't laugh? I mean, they never just let 'er rip and have a good, bust-your-guts laugh. What's wrong with 'em, you figure?"

"Could be their work, now, Edna."

"Well, I s'pose." She keeps laughing — practically gives us both whiplash, backing up, then pulling out onto the pavement.

Instead of heading left to Ferrona, she makes a right down the hill towards the river, squealing her tires on the turn.

"Best not keep 'em waiting too long," I remark, discombobulated not so much by the direction she's taken as by being in the passenger seat. Just shy of the bridge Edna lights a cigarette, eyeing my foot pumping invisible brakes.

"I don't even know these gals," I start rambling, "and actually I'm not much for cards. You prob'ly should've picked somebody else, Edna. Someone more — skilled, maybe."

She slows, then speeds over the bridge, swooping past a honking truck to pull left onto the dirt track beside the river — the spot where, it's said, parked teens watch the eel races.

"My Dinah, who taught her to drive?" I'm asking myself as she puts the Sunbird in park, cranks down her window. She starts to talk — a rapid fire string of words aimed as if at something outside. It takes a second to realize she's lecturing me.

"Don't be so goddamn pig-headed stunned-arse foolish," she mutters, suddenly turning, waving her smoke at me. Something, I don't know what, makes me reach for the Player's on the seat, grapple for one of my own. "Don't be so foolish!" Without stopping for air she throws me her lighter. "What you need, Mizz Lindy, is some kind of life. What I mean is — take my advice — you got to get *out*. Get your mind off Ruby, off of all this *stuff* you can do dick-all about."

Like taking the best advice off the Women's Television Network, I try and swallow it. Coughing and choking on smoke, tears a-springing.

"Well, I don't doubt you'd know everything," I sneer, then could kick myself. But it's as if she hasn't heard, anyway.

"Men," she frets, twisting around to rummage for something,

packages of cheese singles, sardines and crackers spilling out on the seat. "D'you suppose Don'll remember their names? The girls," she calls them again, her cigarette delicately glued to her lipstick.

"Listen to me, Lindy Hammond. I think what you need is a drink, right now. While I lay some sense into you. Jackie and Madonna, they've been looking forward to meeting you; I've told them all about you. Told 'em what you been going through, you know — people understand, Lindy, they *do*. That saying, what's it again? That peckerhead Bill Clinton's wife? 'Takes a village to raise a kid,' something to that effect? Well, the same's true for us all. Nobody's perfect — you hear what I'm saying? And no goddamn one's an islant."

An islan*t*, she says, and Lordy, I think of Ruby's old penchant for speech.

"See that bag there — you reach that bottle? Sure, it's in there. Now did I remember to buy mixer...? Those girls won't mind waiting; they're used to it. Don'll warm 'em up — *not!* But seriously," she keeps talking, fishing out a sleeve of plastic cups like the ones you'd serve juice in at a picnic.

"Ooops, no ice," she jokes, wielding the torpedo-shaped bottle of pop like a club, pouring with one hand, smoking with the other, two cups balanced on the dash. Even crammed into a bucket seat, behaving like an adolescent — acting more cracked than a sidewalk — Edna looks like a million dollars. A million dollars waiting to be spent.

"You did the right thing by Ruby," she says. "Feeling like some guilty old jailbird won't do neither of you any good. You've got to take the plunge. Got to get out in the world. I'm not trying to be some noseminder know-it-all; I'm telling you this for your own darn good. You got to mingle, girl."

She cranks down her window some more, tips most of her drink out on the ground.

"There's Wilf," I butt in, defending myself. But Edna's eyes narrow.

"Oh yeah, he's a good head; a sweetheart — now. You wait till he has you warshing his jockeys!"

I take a gulp of vodka and lemon-lime — sweet and piney, what I can taste under the nicotine.

"You're a case, you are." She shakes her head, pouting into the rearview to freshen her lipstick. "But I'm rooting for ya, whatever you decide."

"He's talking about going to Florida," I throw in, stubbing out my cigarette, laying the half-smoked nail in the pullout ash-tray.

"Ah." She nods, blinking as if there's mascara in her eye. "Well. Better think about what you want, all's I can say. You're a case and a half, Lindy. But I like you, yeah. You got a wicked sense of hu-mour; aren't too many with that. Hub, for instance. Heck, even them girls from social; they can laugh a'right, but they can't take a joke. My own kids, for godsake. Beautiful kids, don't get me wrong, 'specially seeing what some end up with."

She pulls on her eyelid, her lips dragging down, and I notice a little glitter like my diamond on her cheek.

"Yeah, they turned out good, though Don would've liked Gary to stay and take up the business. And Glenda, well, I'm always at her to settle down, start thinking of kids. Oh, but she's good. Smart. Though God only knows I worry — all those strange warshrooms in all those hotels, not to mention the ones on planes; you know what I mean. Once a mom, always a mom — even, I s'pose, when the little buggers are pushing retirement."

She blinks again, trying to laugh; there's a tiny streak down her cheek, shiny and pale as parts of the river.

"My own kids don't have your sense of humour. Crack a joke and it's 'Mothhherrr'. Looks like a model, Glenda, yup; but, do you know, on the inside at times she's pug-ugly.

"I dunno...." She stops long enough to light another smoke. "I guess what I'm saying is, well, good friends are pretty hard to find." She takes a long drag, holding in the smoke, watching the water. A slight breeze has come up, shirring the surface. It ripples and glistens like scales, the current uncoiling, swinging out wide and green.

"From what I hear, so are good fellas," I say after a minute or two, to break the silence.

"No, no, you got that wrong," she cuts in, still not looking at me but waving her cigarette, primping the kiss-curls around her ear. "Don't you know?" She turns, and it's the devil himself snorting. "The saying goes: it's not the good ones that're hard to find, but the hard ones that're good."

Well, I blush about as red as the seat. But it strikes me funny, too, and one after another we start to howl, the two of us shaking in those bucket seats till folks driving by must wonder why the car's rocking.

I have this feeling that things'll be okay. Never mind my worries about having saddle-bag thighs — and the possibility that sooner or later I might have to bare them. Or my fears, right now, of ending up with a handful of spades tonight at Edna's.

Rolling up the window, she backs out onto the pavement — with care this time, though the smoke's so thick inside, honest to Christ, I wonder how she sees the road. But we get to her place, no problem. And even the card game goes all right, though Edna's husband hangs around overly long, asking how come the vodka's opened. Yes, the evening goes just fine — considering Edna's friends spend half of it swapping recipes, and I'm a plain lousy player, about as good at strategy as a lawn ornament.

One of the women, Jackie, drives me home. That night I dream of Ruby in her nursing-home bed — maybe it's the vodka I've had, or the Nanaimo bars the other gal brought.

I dream that Ruby's curled on her side, curled like a sea monkey, a fetus; her wasted, tiny, sawtooth face a bony shadow against the bedclothes. It's hurricane season in the dream, that time of year when gales come up from down south, causing all kinds of damage; in the States, houses blow away; here, sewers overflow.

Ruby's in that hospital-style bed with the rails up. Her hands are spotted fists, her knees pulled up; she hasn't eaten in days and days. She's asleep, resting. Waiting.

Somebody's opened the plate-glass window, forgotten to shut it. The wind is flattening the pines and hemlocks outside. The needles glint like money, the same shiny rush as a roll of dimes cracked into a till.

Ruby's breath comes hoarsely, ragged and shallow, as if she's snoring.

The wind bends the treetops to snapping. Coming through

the window, it ruffles the drapes, thick beige ones drawn against the woods, the clouds racing like cars across the sky.

It ruffles the drapes and stirs some pictures thumbtacked to the wall. A black and white snap of Ruby's Leonard leaning against a forties Ford, perhaps, curved and shiny as a June beetle. A faded brittle photograph, her parents in front of the store: Grampa bug-eyed, stern; Gran a pale flower, not all there, her jaw set with forbearance, her eyes elsewhere.

And there's one of me. Lordy. A studio portrait, colour, done when I was maybe forty. I'm not smiling; wouldn't, because the fellow snapping the picture was so silly, kept telling me to say "sex" to show all my teeth.

The warm rush of air billows the drapes and rustles the blankets, filling the room with the piney scent of tree gum, of evergreens.

When I glance back at the bed, Ruby's gone. There's nothing but the outline of her body, wrinkles in the sheet, the faintest warmth from where she slept.

On Labour Day, Wilf takes me to see her. It's a spur-of-the-moment visit; we've been tooling around together, trying the new road — checking the grade, Wilf says; have just lunched at the Big Stop on the highway out his way. It's been a week or more since I've been in; my last visit, they had Ruby up, looking real pretty, the centre of attention in that circle by the nursing station. There was music playing, "Rock of Ages", from a tape player at the desk, a couple of old dolls dragging their palms together, clapping time. Ruby was dressed in that slippery blue dress, her hair freshly waved.

An old gent in an argyll vest was telling her all about his work, some business he'd run. Ruby was sitting straight as a plank in a dark green wing chair, this whimsical little smile on her face, listening. Well, she appeared to be listening. But a few steps off the elevator, it was obvious to me — heck, any fool could see — that what he was saying poured in one ear and right out the other, like water through a rusted-out bucket. Still, when I went over she squeezed my hand, even cocked her cheek for me to kiss. She gave the queerest little shudder of faded delight.

"Oh! It's you, Dooor-a."

But this day, when we arrive after lunch, Wilf holding a big bunch of glads we got at a roadside stand, she's not sitting in the circle. A perky little nurse, one I haven't seen before, tells me she's in her room, "resting comfortably".

Lord God A'mighty. The sight of Ruby in that high, hard bed, a shiny chrome crib, snatches my breath away. Lying there, a wisp of a thing, weak-looking as skim milk against her mint-green nightie, she's staring upwards; could be counting the dots in the ceiling tiles for all I know, her eyes are that wide.

"We brought you something," I announce, reaching down to grab one hand, expecting, at the very least, a grip back. "Gotcha some glads, Ruby, see? Nice big coral-pink ones, kind you don't see too often...." I nod towards Wilf shuffling in the doorway, flowers like a bouquet of spears in his arms.

"Ruby?" I prompt, speaking a little louder, peering down, hoping to break her gaze. It's blank as the stare on Raggedy Andy, the new-looking rag doll in bed there beside her.

When she finally turns, just enough to eyeball me, all I see is suspicion, like the fleeting, tempted scowl of a ten-year-old offered a Tootsie Roll by a stranger. Her hand shrinks back, the scowl replaced by a toddler's look of making strange, recoiling in godawful fear as if I'm some stalker jumping out from behind a tree. Then, just as fast, her eyes wash blank, blank as a tissue yanked straight from the box.

She doesn't know me.

I trip and teeter ever so slightly, one of my Dr. Scholl's catching on something. There's a banging clatter: glasses knocking, rattling ice-cubes, sloshing apple juice; a bunch of bendable straws spills onto the bed. Wilf grabs my elbow, steers me backwards. The smell of glads is overpowering; it's like the smell at Pyke's underneath the pleasanter ones of Edna's Pledge, Pine-Sol and potpourri.

Pot-porry, Edna calls it. A fancy name for dried-up rose petals and crushed cinnamon stick....

"Where d'you figure I could find a vase?" From somewhere I hear Wilf asking the nurse, the strange, cheery one in pink. She speed-walks past us, a flash of brown, bouncy hair; fluffs the pillow, straightens the bedside table. As she draws the sheet, Ruby's frail old hand flies up and grasps her tanned, bangled wrist. Ruby's eyelids bat, her lips flutter — for one split second, like a girlish flirt, it's as if she's dancing towards something. Searching.

"What, Ruby?" I strain forward, Wilf's arm like a bridle.

I fumble for the straws — pick-up sticks — in their pink-striped paper wrappers.

"This is Wilf, you remember Wilf? Mr. Jewkes, my buddy, who'd come see me in the store?"

The only sound is the air conditioner's hum.

The chill would raise goosebumps in your armpits.

I shove the handful of straws into the nightstand drawer. As I go to close it, I see something scuffed and black. Inside, underneath some cotton swabs, is Gran's old ledger.

"Ruby?" I try once more, my hand closing around the spine, lifting the book out. Ruby's eyes are shut now; Wilf is nowhere in sight, having nipped out — one last little chore — to get water for the vase.

There's a Sobey's bag in the wastebasket. I pull it out, used Kleenexes and all, and tuck the book inside. Then, Lord help me, don't I spin on my wooden heels and click out, escaping, bag in hand, to one of those seats in the hall. It's a soft velour one; the comfort I take, scudding my wrists over the armrests — such a silly comfort, like burying your face in a sick cat's fur.

When Wilf comes back, the glads in water, he skulks past the others in chairs. Reaching down to pat my arm, he starts to speak. "It's okay," I croak, holding a finger to my lips, shaking my head. Raising his eyebrows, oh, till they look like a pair of awnings too high to shade the windows, his cheeks puffed out in a sigh, he totters back into the room with the flowers.

"I have to get out of here," I breathe as he slips out again — my voice less a whisper, perhaps, than a squeal. That ring of blanched faces turns towards mine, their mouths like the dots in a page of question marks.

Wilf never asks me what's in the bag.

Later, after he's dropped me off, in the cool of evening I go out back and build a fire, using crumpled-up pages from an ancient *News* and odds and ends, pieces of board and wrecked shelving I've forgotten to have carted away. I pile everything into the rain barrel, a rusty drum used once upon a time for storing gas. Dribbling the works with the fluid from a cracked-open Bic, I strike a match and toss it in.

The flames shoot into the dark, an orange fireball for a moment or two lighting the night. From the ditches and fields comes the chirr of crickets, that live-wire hum, *backtoschool, backtoschool,* that once conjured up smells of erasers and schoolbags and the thick brown paper sacks we used to put them in. The sound mixes, then fizzles under the fire's *crackle-pop.*

When the flames die down a bit, I reach for the bag on the ground. I almost fling it in, but stop myself; already there's the smell of scorching paint and something else, like burning rubber. So I slide out the contents, the ledger, the soiled tissues too, and toss them in one by one. The Kleenexes flare and bloom like roses igniting the cover; briefly there's a stink like burning skin, then the same fusty odour as rotten wallpaper ablaze.

For a minute or two I stand watching the pages peel back, one by one, and shrivel, aglow — words curling in on themselves — till the heat gets too strong on my face and I have to move back. Pulling up a plastic chair, I sit shivering a little in the damp, smoky dark, waiting for the fire to burn itself out.

While I'm sitting — the last red cinders flying up towards the stars — the phone rings inside: a muffled burst chased by silence. Seconds later it rings again, but I'm slow getting up, creaky, and by the time I reach the kitchen it's quit.

The clock on the stove says almost midnight — too late to call her back, though, knowing Edna, it probably isn't.

Only then do I realize how weary I am, and ready for bed.

"Come for supper, Lindy." Oh my, that Wilf — if Edna loves to talk, he lives to eat. "We'll make a night of it, huh? All this running around we do, girl. Feels like we live our whole life in the truck. Come on over, I'll barbecue; we can watch the ball game, listen to some music. That show's on later, the one you like, on CHEX, the one plays all the oldies you like? Heck — we'll crack a beer or two, see what gives. Eh?"

Yes, he's got the gift of gab, too. The longer I know him, the more I think sometimes he could beat Edna on that front — almost. But when he talks, I listen. Cradle the phone like a big white seashell and listen, listen for the click of spit on his tongue, each kindly pause — never mind his tendency to run on.

"You with me?" He stops to check. "Jeez, sometimes it feels like it's the Road Runner I got the hots for, the bird of my dreams. Don't sit your arse down in one spot long enough to warm it — you and that Pyke woman, the two of you, no grass growing under your feet."

I guess I can see his point — not to say I understand it. It's true, though, I'm always on the go. The weeks fly by like crows raiding a nest, that fast. One night the four of us — me, Wilf, Edna and Don — have a whale of a time dancing at the Legion's Harvest Moon benefit. And before I know it, Edna's got me signed up for bake sales, bingos and fundraising card parties.

"There's other things could use raising, you know, besides money," Wilf quips from time to time.

"Don't get me wrong now — last thing I'd want's a couch potato, some old nesting hen. But wouldn't you think we could spend a night together — a whole night, I mean — without you having to jump each time Edna or that morgue-faced man of hers says 'bingo'? Sure, I like bingo and dances and two-for-one steak entrées as much as the next fella. But next you know, that Edna'll have you baking date squares and tending bar.

"All I'm saying is, it'd be nice to get some time alone together, not gallivanting here and there with the Pykes. Nice enough folks, but Jesus, not like you'd want 'em in the bed with you!

"I mean, didn't you just see that woman?"

I have to say it, I don't like all that cajoling any better than the next gal would — but mixed in with his friendly coaxing is a dollop of pride. I can hear it, same as when anglers used to come in years ago, boasting about prize trout caught thanks to fancy flies they bought here.

Come to think of it, maybe in a funny way that's what Wilf feels like, one of those flies being cast out, then reeled in — at my leisure, depending how the current pulls.

I still owe him an answer. And since he and his crew finished the road — a couple of months late, otherwise on schedule — he's had more time to steam and stew.

"Supper, eh? Depends what's cooking." I pause just that little second longer to leave him dangling. "A'right" — another pause, and I guess for an oldster I must have something going, because this time I can almost feel his grin through the phone — "long as you let me make the salad."

"Pack a bag," he cuts in. "Pack your whole kit-bag of Avon, whatever. Run away with me, Lindy — just tonight!" He says it as though he's joking, and I laugh along. It's a lark, all right, one that's bound to nose-dive and crash any minute. I'm wondering what the heck I'll do after dessert, after the World Series, once the sporty cheering stops and the credits roll.

Make damn sure it's dark in the room, that's what — good and dark, I think. Swallow all my pride, every last stitch of nerve unravelling like greased yarn. Shut my eyes, hope for the best. Let his fingers do the walking and the talking.

Heck, it mightn't be too bad, once I got warmed up. Fun, even, if I could relax. The same pleasure as a bite of chocolate: sweet, salt and bitter rolled into one, that shudder of pleasure. If I could feel that urge, to suck in my cheeks and savour it. For as long as it lasted: a minute? Five seconds?

Maybe longer now there are pills, those little blue ones for men that Edna jokes about.

Addictive as peanuts?

I could try — so long as he didn't ask questions. I guess I could give it a whirl.

"Besides" — his voice brings me back to earth — "there's something I want to show you."

It's still light when I arrive, one of those perfect Indian summer nights, the cusp of fall. Pulling into the yard, my toothbrush, a spare pair of panties tucked into the secret compartment of my purse, I can see the amber buzz of moths flitting in the spruce. I wouldn't mind sitting a minute to watch them. But Wilf's out on his porch, waving, and I have this queer thought that I should've brought a nightgown — heck, a robe, a pyjama bag — laid my cards straight out on the table, so to speak, rather than go half-hog, waiting to see what happens.

Playing it by "air", as Uncle Leonard used to say.

Wilf has a pair of TV trays, two webbed lawn chairs set up outside. That stoop of his is the size of a stamp, but never mind. His big gas barbecue's fired up, two thick sirloins sizzling, the smoke chasing the bugs away.

As dusk falls there's a woodsy bite to the air, shadows stretching across the patchy clearing studded with tree-roots and the leggy remains of his sister's marigolds. Wilf turns on the pink and yellow lanterns strung from the trailer's soffits, and we sit there listening to crickets. It's funny but we don't talk much, wrapped in the cosy, humming quiet, sipping drinks — fancy concoctions he's whipped up in the blender, frothy as milkshakes, topped with swords and lemon wedges. After a while he checks the grill, then drags his chair a little closer to mine, draping his arm around my shoulders, the two of us relishing the snap of fat against the flames.

He rubs the top of my arm. Goose-fleshed, I lean forward to pull on my sweater. Then he hugs me close, reaching over to kiss the side of my head. It's that sweet, respectful kind of kiss Uncle used to give me when I was small, before he turned bad. My first thought's horror: my hair must smell awful, not to mention feel like dried corn syrup, with all the gel I've used to glue it in place. But then I don't care, and neither, I guess, does he, the two of us lulled by cricket-song, the hiss of fat, till all of a sudden there's a burnt smell, and Wilf rushes inside to fetch plates.

I remember too late about the salad, the bag of greens going limp in the truck. Wilf says, "What the hell, stay put," and whacks off chunks of cuke and tomatoes rescued from the bottom of his fridge. The skin on both resembles turkey wattle — a turkey's gobbler — but we make do, glopping Miracle Whip straight from the jar. The meat's cooked like shoe leather, the potatoes burnt — but never did food taste better, fruit flies and cinders from the grill thrown in for extra flavour.

"Everything always tastes best outside," Wilf remarks, and it's true. We practically lick our plates clean, bits of black crumbs stuck in our teeth, slicks of grease on our chins — only come up to wipe it away with our napkins. They're souvenir ones his sister's sent from New Brunswick, pictures of the Magnetic Hill on them.

"Now there's something worth seeing," he razzes, shaking his head, then easing back in his seat to pat his belly. "'Nother margarita, Lindy?"

When he comes back outside with two fresh drinks, he's got something tucked under one arm. In the dim pink light I can't make out what it is right away, not till he sets down the glasses and starts unfolding it. He takes his time, smoothing out the creases.

It's a map, a map of the eastern seaboard from Calais, Maine, to Miami. There's one long route traced with pink Magic Marker; meandering south, it ends at a little black star in the middle of Florida, some place called Haines City.

"I got this time-share, see? Nice little mobile, fenced yard, a view. An orange grove right outside the front door!" There's a pause before he starts again.

"I've been thinking of selling, Lindy; buying down, guess you'd call it. Trading this place in for something smaller, a Prowler or a Viking, something towable anyways. The truck's got two-fifty horse — you can pull a pretty decent rig with that. You know, I like the idea of my own place. But then this time thing came up."

"Edna says they've got good shrimp down there. You know, she and Don've——"

"Raw bahs, that's what they call those fishy places, oyster bars and such, right on the quay. Raw bah, you know, that Yankee accent? 'Y'all come back now, ya he-ah.' 'Y'all sa-ell frayups?' Frappes — you know, Lindy, milkshakes."

He's rambling now, his grin trailing away as he gazes off at something in the woods, what you can see in the darkness; a raccoon, maybe a porcupine. A moth flits in the pink glow overhead, then lights on the map. Swat goes Wilf's big hand, but the thing wobbles and scuds away just in time, leaving a powdery smudge on the state of Georgia.

"You could come when you're ready," he says, watching the blur of wings, fuzzy and soft-looking as the burrs by the step, hovering once more by the light. His eyes are fixed there; gazing up, I notice a crack in the pebbled plastic. You have to wonder how long his lanterns have been outside, like those Christmas lights people forget and leave strung up year-round. I think how pretty they'd look, festive and fairy-like as Disney's castle, in the middle of a blizzard. Shutting my eyes, I try to picture the glow from the road.

"Figure if I leave next week I'll miss Josephine — the hurricane," he's going on. "Don't want to be driving into the eye of a big one."

I'm still thinking about snow, and here's the crazy thing: how I'd miss it. That wet mushy feel, like a damp, woolly blanket thrown over the world, all those smells of woodsmoke and road salt hemmed in — like a bad case of wind trapped under a goosedown duvet.

"You don't say," I murmur, looking down at the map again, squinting now on account of the dark. Wilf scrapes his chair back, its metal legs buckling in a way that makes me almost gasp, picturing him falling backwards, maybe slipping a disc. But he jumps up, spry for someone so heavy, grabbing a slurp of margarita on his way inside to fetch a flashlight.

It's gotten chilly. When he comes back out he says the Red Sox are winning, and the living room's more comfy.

Funny, but it's as if we can't quite bring ourselves to fold up the chairs and go in — not on a night like this. Not with the stars coming out one by one, hardly a cloud in the way. It's cool; God forbid, in that breeze there's a hint of Hallowe'en. But we cosy up, two full-bellied old crows side by side, the pair of us sharing the scratchy grey camp blanket scrounged from the truck. Wrapped up together, we peruse the map, that blue-ticked, hairnet-tatted mess of roads under the round torch beam, all those green, pink and yellow states — choosing the route I don't doubt I'll take.

Acknowledgements

I wish to thank Pamela Donoghue for her ready ear and wicked wit; Sheree Fitch for always calling at the right moment; my publisher Jan Geddes and George Elliott Clarke for their encouragement; and the late Margaret Cann for her example. Margaret, your light shines now and always. I'm thankful for the patience and support of many others — Bruce Erskine and our sons; Elizabeth Williams, to whom this book is dedicated; Mary Holmes Dague; Mary Evelyn Ternan; Cindy Lynds-Handren; Susan Reid; Jane and Steve Roberts.

As well, I am grateful for the assistance of geriatric nurse Heather Smith, RN, and the administration at Armview Estates; the Queen Elizabeth II Health Sciences Centre and Dr. Daniel Carver for his lecture, "Disease of the Century"; the Alzheimer Society of Nova Scotia for the video, *Dancing Inside*; the Public Archives of Nova Scotia; Trueman Matheson for *A History of Londonderry, N.S.* (Hantsport, Nova Scotia: Lancelot Press, 1989). And finally, thanks to my editor, Gena K. Gorrell, for her unfailing eye, and to Jane Buss for her boundless energy and expertise.

The Bible passages that appear in the novel are from the King James version. The epigraphs to those chapters making up Euphemia's epistle are from "The Prayse of the Needle", by John Taylor, the Thames "Water Poet" (1580-1653). The poem was first published in 1640 in James Boler's *The Needle's Excellency*, and later appeared in Miss Lambert's *Handbook of Needlework*. Excerpts used in the novel are from the version reprinted in Pamela Clabburn's *The Needleworker's Dictionary* (London: Macmillan, 1976).